RUN, LILY, RUN

Also by Martha Long

Ma, He Sold Me For a Few Cigarettes
Ma, I'm Getting Meself a New Mammy
Ma, It's a Cold Aul Night an I'm Lookin for a Bed
Ma, Now I'm Goin Up in the World
Ma, I've Got Meself Locked Up in the Mad House
Ma, I've Reached for the Moon an I'm Hittin the Stars
Ma, Jackser's Dyin Alone

RUN, LILY, RUN

Martha Long

TRANSWORLD IRELAND

TRANSWORLD IRELAND
an imprint of The Random House Group Limited
20 Vauxhall Bridge Road, London SW1V 2SA
www.transworldbooks.co.uk

First published in 2014 by Transworld Ireland
a division of Transworld Publishers

A CIP catalogue record for this book
is available from the British Library.

ISBN 9781848272095

Addresses for Random House Group Ltd companies outside the UK
can be found at: www.randomhouse.co.uk
The Random House Group Ltd Reg. No. 954009

The Random House Group Limited supports the Forest Stewardship Council® (FSC®),
the leading international forest-certification organisation. Our books carrying the
FSC label are printed on FSC®-certified paper. FSC is the only forest-certification scheme
supported by the leading environmental organisations, including Greenpeace. Our
paper procurement policy can be found at www.randomhouse.co.uk/environment

Typeset in 11.5/14.5pt New Baskerville by
Falcon Oast Graphic Art Ltd.
Printed and bound in Great Britain by
CPI Group (UK) Ltd, Croydon, CR0 4YY

2 4 6 8 10 9 7 5 3 1

To my ma – thanks, Ma, for bringing me into the world,
I know it cost you dearly.

Acknowledgements

I utter a humble thank you to Transworld Publishers, who put trust in me without a manuscript or even the idea for a book of fiction.

Yes, they gave me a contract, they even gave me my beloved Ailsa Bathgate, editor from my old publishers Mainstream – they now gone to sleep and lie among the great and the mighty. Their names Bill Campbell and Peter Mackenzie stand now forever on the roll call of great Scottish publishers.

Yes, but we talk here about Ailsa Bathgate, the editor. She who has suffered me and agonized over every word and every page of my long and sometimes rambling wanderings through the world of words. I am indebted, Transworld, thank you.

Also, the lovely Brenda Kimber, quietly speaking, 'Keep the head while all around are losing theirs!'

Who but me, and everyone I have touched with my flappings! She is a calm port in a storm! Thank you, Brenda!

Ah, I saved the best for last, Claire Ward, the genius who designs the book jackets and draws you the reader in!

1

'POOR YOU, CEILY! Ye're only twelve an you have te be all growed up but wasn't it lucky ye got yer birthday yesterday? Or maybe now ye wouldn't be a really big girl. An now I'm big too! I got me birthday as well the other day, I'm now seven!' I hiccupped, smilin now instead a cryin. It was comin wit me havin tha great thought.

'Lily, if you don't shrrup I'll give you a kick up yer skinny arse! I can't listen to any more of ye – if you're not cryin ye're whingin, now you're ramblin an talkin mad an I'm goin te go outa me mind. SO SHRRUP! SHRRUP, SHRRUP!' Ceily screamed, tearin at her hair.

I started te cry again, the deep sobs tearin up from me lungs, an huge snots started bubblin down me nose an pourin straight inta me mouth. I stuck me tongue out fer me te lick an taste it, then I swallowed. Now I can still feel the wet heat of it slidin down me neck an disappearin inta me belly as I turned an stared around the darkenin room then looked up te Ceily again, wantin her te make the fear an the pain in me an all me loss go away.

She stared at me wit her eyes red-rimmed an swollen-lookin like she was in shock, but I could see her mind flyin. She was waitin fer the answer te come, then she would take charge. There was no one else.

A few days ago, I came back from school te be told me mammy was in the hospidal. It was only tha night when Ceily arrived in from work, the neighbours, they were waitin te tell her the true, real bad news. They heard the screamin comin from our front room, Mammy had tried te open the street door but collapsed before she could get out. Be the time they got her te hospidal she was dead. Her bowel had burst, poisonin her they said. It ran right through her so fast, there was nothin they or anyone else could do fer her.

I remember when we came back from the hospidal an everyone had finally left, all the friends and neighbours wavin an smilin wantin te get out an home, away from the sorry sad sight of the pair of us – tha's wha Ceily called it. Then she said it was me standin wit the bony knees rattlin, grippin a tight hold of Molly me dolly, an then herself, Ceily, she bein left te get on wit it in the empty little house now suddenly cold an terribly bare without Mammy. They promised te look in on the pair of us an we were not te be afraid te ask, if we wanted or needed anythin. Then they were gone, rushin out the front door bangin it shut behind them, leavin us wit the emptiness.

We didn't have a father neither, I often heard me mammy talkin about him. It would be at night when she was sittin around the fire wit Delia Mullins, she was her very best, bestest friend since they were childre goin te school together.

We were supposed te be up in bed sleepin, but not me. I would be out on the landin earwiggin. I would be dyin te know wha they're talkin about, because childre are not never allowed te hear their business.

So I heard them talkin, whisperin in a low voice, but I still heard anyway, wha they were sayin about me father an tha he was no good. He cleared off, but not before satisfyin a glint in his eye, leavin me mammy te carry me an I less than the size of a green pea. I was the scrapins of the pot, she said, three born dead before me, an in between she lost four childre. She had no relatives, her ma had scarpered off leavin her wit the granny te drag up – tha meanin she havin te rear herself.

I knew all tha from years a listenin, earwiggin Mammy calls . . . called it.

Now we're just back from buryin Mammy in her grave. But she's not really dead. Tha was not my mammy they lowered down tha dark hole then turned an walked away. Sure she'd be freezin wit the cold an left all on her own. I shook me head thinkin about it. No! She's not dead, an the cheek a people fer sayin tha!

'Look at the state a them shoes!' Ceily suddenly screamed.

I stopped roarin, goin inta sudden silence as the pair of us gaped down at the extra inches now plastered te the soles of me one good pair a Sunday shoes. I only wore them fer Mass on Sundays, but got te keep them on if we were then goin out somewhere fancy, like up fer a walk te the Phoenix Park, then down onto O'Connell Street te look in the shop windas. Then the best bit! Into Caffolla's fer our chips-an-egg tea.

'Come on, let's get movin. We better get this fire started te warm the house up, then get you sorted fer school tomorrow, I need te get you a clean frock an socks, an I better polish them shoes,' she said, lookin down at the caked mud smotherin me lovely brown-leather strapped shoes.

We had stood, sinkin so far down inta the mud I thought we were goin te be buried along wit the coffin as we watched them lower it down, all the way into a deep hole wit our dead mammy inside they said. Terrible it was – it had rained hard non-stop fer three whole days solid, without a let-up.

'I'm goin te have to cut the toes out a them shoes when you grow out a them. It's tha or nothin! We don't have money any more fer luxuries,' Ceily sniffed, liftin her button nose an throwin back a curly head of coppery bangles, one got in her eye an she whipped it back just as another thought hit her.

'Wha are we goin te do fer money?' she suddenly whispered, lettin it out on a breath as the fear hit her, makin her eyes stare out of her head wit the shock. 'We won't have Mammy's money any more! She earned more than twice wha I'm gettin. Not te mention the food tha she brought home.'

I got the picture of Mammy bringin in the cooked food wrapped up in wax paper left over from the mad people's dinners when she was finished her work. She had a good job – workin wit two others she was cookin an servin the breakfast, the dinners and teas fer all the mad people in the Grangegorman Lunatic Asylum.

'Does tha mean we're goin te starve, Ceily?'

'No don't be stupid! We'll manage,' she snorted, lettin out a roar at me. 'We'll have te get you a little job, ye can work after school an over the weekends, I'll see if there's anythin part-time goin fer meself at night, an I'll work the weekends too. Don't you worry yerself, little Lily! Between the pair of us, we'll get by!' she promised, grittin her teeth then fixin her eyes on the now dark room seein her way te the days ahead. Then she muttered, 'We have te be careful, tell no one nothin. If anyone asks,' she said slowly, droppin her head an starin right in at my face, holdin me eyes pinned te her.

I listened knowin somethin bad was comin.

'Say we're doin grand,' she warned, narrowin her eyes te put a fear in me. 'Otherwise the authorities will be down on us like a ton of bricks wantin te whip us away into a convent! We'll be ended locked up!' Ceily snorted, takin in a deep breath lettin her face turn sour an her eyes narrow.

'Why? Wha did we do?' I said, lettin me mouth drop open an feelin me chest tighten wit a terrible fear – maybe they thought one of us had killed our mammy!

'Because, you little eegit!' Ceily roared, losin the rag. 'You're too young an I'm not old enough to be mindin you! I'm not even supposed te be mindin meself never mind left school an now workin since last year,' she snapped, lettin tha thought hit her, makin her even more annoyed an afraid. Then she shook her head whisperin. 'As sure as night follows day they'll come after us!' she muttered, starin inta the distance an talkin te herself wit the eyes gettin tha picture. Then she clamped her mouth shut before openin it again, sayin, 'Mammy had took a chance an got away wit not sendin me back te school. We needed the money. But now? Oh Jesus, we need to light a penny candle an say a prayer we'll make it through without gettin caught an comin te harm, Lily!' she moaned, cryin at me wit her voice keenin an her face pained.

I stared waitin te see if any tears came. But they didn't, she wouldn't let them.

2

I CAME RUSHIN BACK from school wantin te change out of me good school clothes, leave me schoolbag an get goin fast over te old Mister Mullins who owned the corner shop. I didn't want te lose me new job, this was only me second day an I certainly didn't want te be late or he might sack me. Ceily had begged an tormented the life outa old Mullins te give me tha job, he didn't want me, because he thought I wouldn't be able te carry the heavy bag. An even worser! I wouldn't be able te manage the big black 'High Nelly' bicycle tha went wit the job.

But Ceily wouldn't take no fer an answer, she knew he was stuck since she heard the whisper Frankie O'Reilly had turned fourteen an left school. He couldn't do the paper round any more because he was gone off now an got himself a job in the sausage factory – well his da did! An tha was only because he worked there himself. Now Frankie was doin his apprenticeship, startin first wit sweepin an cleanin up all the blood, guts an bones left over from the pigs.

Ceily was over like a bullet, wantin me in quick. 'Get the job fast before word spreads tha there's a handy number goin,' she muttered, lashin herself out the door, headin fer Mister Mullins.

He melted down under the strain of Ceily's torments. 'Right,' he said, but I was only on trial! One false move an I was gone, out the door, no excuses. He had a business te run, an it wasn't a charity for the Saint Vincent de Paul neither.

The first thing tha hit me as I rounded the corner onta our street was the little black motor car sittin right outside our front door. I stopped dead in me tracks, peelin the eyes up an down the empty street – nobody has a motor car around here, or even knows anyone who owns one. Yeah, it's definitely smack-bang sittin right outside our door, so it must be fer us!

Me breath caught, the air started comin up fast through me nose an I clamped me gapin mouth shut. 'Wha's happenin? Who's after us? Oh Mammy!'

I could feel me heart hammerin in me chest as I started te run, I wanted te fly in the other direction but I needed te know. Ceily will be in trouble but there's a pair of us in it, I can't leave her by herself.

Me hand was shakin as I tried te get the key in the door, then I heard the voices. I stopped tryin te open the door an put me ear close tryin te hear wha was bein said. I could hear shoutin, tha was Ceily all right, so she is here! She's not at work. Then there were other voices, all arguin an shoutin over each other.

Somethin very bad is happenin. It's just over a week now since Mammy died, Ceily said te me last night. She said as well she was expectin trouble, tha I was te keep me eyes open an be ready te act! She didn't say wha tha meant an I didn't ask, because she's worse than Mammy now fer tellin me te stop moiderin her wit me questions.

Before I knew where I was I had turned the key in the lock then found meself standin just inside the sittin room, still holdin onta the doorknob. Me eyes shot te the scullery takin in the crowds a people all millin around packed tight te squashed they were, wit them all thrown together. I could see elbows diggin out wantin a bit of space te make a move. Half the street must be here, along wit the parish priest an even a few strangers.

Me eyes landed on the priest – he was wearin a long black soutane hangin down under a heavy overcoat, an a big wide-rimmed hat shook like mad on his head wit the state he was in.

'How dare you?!' he screamed, stampin his shiny laced-up boot an bangin his walkin stick. He was slammin it up an down tha hard, an wit me head followin him I could see he was puttin a dent in our oilcloth wit the rage on him.

'How DARE you speak to me in that tone of voice and even DARE to answer me back?!' he roared, throwin the head, makin his face go all purple then gaspin, lettin out huge wheezes tryin te get more breath.

'YE'RE ONLY THE PARISH PRIEST NOT GOD ALMIGHTY HIMSELF!' screamed old Granny Kelly from next door, pushin in te face him.

'ONLY TOO RIGHT! LET ME IN! I'LL TELL HIM!' shouted Foxy Flynn, throwin back her heavy mass of flamin-red-roarin hair, then diggin her big man's arms out clearin a way fer herself.

Suddenly he waved the stick, pushin it out through the crowd, makin a lunge fer Ceily. The crowd heaved back, lettin their arse bulge inta the sittin room, then heaved out again as someone grabbed hold a the stick. He slapped hands an got it free, then Ceily screamed as he grabbed a hold of her jumper.

'NO! Lemme go! Go te hell! You're not takin me anywhere!' she roared, twistin his free hand an draggin him wit her inta the sittin room an the crowd heaved wit her, but he wouldn't let go. She dug her fist in hammerin his hand loose.

'YOU WILL ALL BE CURSED!' he shouted, wavin the walkin stick an throwin the head around makin his eyes bulge an his hat wobble givin everyone the evil eye. Then he flew the hand an stick back at Ceily, tryin te grab hold again. She was red in the face darin him, breathin hard an shoutin back inta his face along wit all the neighbours, but the loudest was Nelly Tucks who lived on our other side. She was wearin her grey-an-white-flowered apron wrapped around her, it was still lovely an clean because it was only Tuesday, an she washes it on a Monday. But it looked like she got no time te wrap a scarf around her head an hide the curlers, never mind get them out first thing this mornin. So instead of a lovely mass of curly hair, she was now a holy show wit the pipe cleaners stuck up in the air.

'Get yourself back outa this house here wit your black-guardin, an don't be comin where ye're not wanted!' she roared, movin closer te Ceily an takin her, then pullin her tight wrappin her arms around her just in case he might grab hold again.

I stood stuck te the floor gapin wit me mouth open not takin a breath. I could feel me chest an stomach painin me, it had gone tha hard. It was all this holdin meself tight, now I was stiff like a plaster statue, I was holdin meself tha still. An wha's even worser, I was forgettin te take in air. I shook me head feelin it swimmin an bulged me eyes out tryin te see better, but they won't work right, I can't see. An now I can't make it better. I can't help meself – it's all this shock.

I turned me head slowly from one happenin te the next still gapin wit me mouth open, then flyin it when I heard the roars then easin it back again, tryin te take it all in. All the bodies were in the sittin room now pushin an shovin. Father Flitters was tryin te get his hands on Ceily an the rest were tryin te get their hands on him. But there were too many hands in the way an people were gettin themselves clattered, then I heard an agony as someone got hurt.

'Mind me corns! Youse dirty-lookin eegits, will ye's not take it easy after breakin me toe?' screamed Granny Kelly, givin an awful moan then collapsin on top of Biddy Mongrel.

'Oh Jesus! Get an ambulance! This woman's on death's door! Lookit the state a the colour she's turned! She's all colours!' screamed Biddy, givin Granny Kelly a push wit her wantin te get a better look, but instead, pushin her too hard an gettin her sent flyin wit the arms wide open head-first inta the chest of Father Flitters! His arms flapped inta the air savin himself an blindin Nelly Tucks as she got a belt of the flyin stick. The roars were unmerciful an me heart stopped, thinkin now we were all goin te be arrested!

'MURDER!' Nelly shouted, lashin back at him wit a dig in the mouth knockin out his false teeth. I watched them flyin through the air then land in the open mouth of Granny Kelly as she toppled wit him, screamin her lungs out. They all ended up in a heap wit Granny Kelly now sittin in his lap. It looked like somethin that ye think should be funny but somehow I couldn't get a laugh, because it was then me eye caught sight of two people moochin around in our kitchen scullery.

It was a man an a woman – she was wearin a dark-green hairy wool coat wit a big Tara brooch holdin together the top of the wraparound collar. I watched as she shoved her head wearin an aul black-felt battered hat wit a nobby pin planted on top inta our two presses on the wall. She was makin sure te poke the head well in, gettin a good look fer herself. Then she bent down leavin her arse stuck in the air an pulled back the curtain hidin the tin bucket underneath the kitchen sink. It was half full now catchin water drippin down from the leakin pipe. Well, it dripped away because we had no one te fix it.

I stared watchin the coat an frock rise, then seein the legs of a big pair of pink knickers suddenly appear. I wanted te see more, but she quickly stood up whippin down the coat an straightenin herself. Then pointed back down wit her finger, sayin somethin te the aul fella. He was standin there wit a big black notebook an a pencil at the ready, holdin it in the air, waitin te hear wha she said.

I watched as he nodded suckin on his gums, then lifted his bottom teeth givin them a rattle an sucked them back down again, then started writin. She fixed the pancake battered felt hat on her head then whipped around the scullery lettin her eyes take everythin in. Then I saw she was lookin in different directions. She's cross-eyed! I thought, wonderin can she see all a the room at the same time.

Now they slid around narrowin gettin a hungry look, wantin te find somethin else to fault. I could see the left eye comin in my direction, but before I could ease meself back out the door, the right eye lit on me!

'Ah! The child!' she shouted, lightin up at the sight of me. 'Come! Come here, child,' she ordered, wavin the finger at me.

Wit tha the long skinny aul fella swung his head around – he was wearin a black suit wit narrow trousers turned-up at the end, an even wore black laced-up boots like Father Flitters.

'That's the other one!' he roared, gettin all excited mashin down on his gums an leanin over fer a better look at me as he fixed the little pair of eyeglasses sittin on the end of his beaked nose. 'Are we done here?' he said, whippin himself around te look at the aul one.

'That's it! I think we have covered everything,' she said, throwin her head around the scullery an out te me, givin one last look makin sure she hadn't missed anythin. Then she plastered the hat hard down on her head, ran her hands over her huge chest an down her coat, makin sure everythin was ordered an sittin the right way on her.

'Right! Time to leave,' he said, whippin off the glasses an noddin te the woman.

She was already on her way, makin a fast move inta the sittin room lookin fer the priest. He was buried somewhere, still lost in among the crowd.

I knew I should move, but I couldn't get me legs goin, they were shakin like mad an I didn't want te leave Ceily.

I watched as the pair of them swam inta the crowd, shoutin, 'Make way, please! We are from the NSPCC! The National Society for the Prevention of Cruelty to Children.'

All heads turned te take this in.

'We know who tha is! Ye's don't have te spell it out fer us!' shouted Granny Kelly, diggin her elbow inta Father Flitters, wit him tryin te work his way outa the heap. 'Youse will take them two childre over my dead body!' she warned, lookin around an bendin down findin her missin slipper, then wavin it at them makin them duck back.

'Call the Guards!' they shouted.

'This is anarchy!' shouted Father Flitters. 'A mob riot! HEATHENS! The lot of you! PAGANS!' he roared, throwin his head back all red-faced, then shovin his way out usin his elbows. He was after losin his hat lettin his baldy moonshine head be seen, an he not a blade a hair left, but fer the two bits left hangin around his ears.

'Enough of this nonsense!' he suddenly barked. 'Take that girl! Get the other one!' he shouted, wavin the stick an pointin it over at me.

Ceily screamed as he an the woman then grabbed a hold of her. I could see the other aul fella hurryin, makin his way in my direction. I started te shake watchin as she went mad screamin an fightin, she was shakin her head wit her hair flyin around her face an people were now grabbin hold of her tryin te wrestle her outa the priest an cruelty woman's grip.

Then me eyes peeled on the man – he was nearly on top a me ready te grab out an take hold a me.

'Wha'll I do?' I shivered, moanin te meself an lookin over at

Ceily again. She was screamin an cursin cryin her eyes out now! 'Oh Mammy,' I keened, rubbin me hands an hoppin me feet then bitin an suckin me fingers wantin te make me think.

Suddenly Ceily lifted her head an let a roar over at me. 'RUN, LILY! GET OUTA HERE FAST! HIDE!'

I stood still starin, not able te move.

'MOVE! GET YERSELF GOIN! HURRY!'

Wit tha I turned me head just as the aul fella reached out fer me. 'Outa me way!' I screamed, seein a crowd a people all blockin the door. I dug me head in through the crowd usin me arms as batterin rams an kicked back gettin yer man in the leg just as he grabbed hold a me jumper.

'OWW!' he screamed, lettin go a me after gettin a kick outa me wellington boot.

Hands pushed me outa harm's way then people moved in te block him.

'POLICE! Guards! Someone call the Gardai!' he screeched.

I looked back seein him watchin me gettin away runnin fer me life, he was stuck in the doorway wit everyone heavin an pushin. They were all tryin te get inta the house te see wha's happenin an he was gettin lifted offa his feet an sailed back inta the room.

I dropped me head fer extra speed an ran like the wind. I turned the corner seein the road ahead a me, then heaved in a breath makin te run like me arse was on fire.

3

I WAS WHEEZIN PAST the shop an got a blur of old Mister Mullins sittin in the winda lookin out at the world passin by, then it hit me. Where am I goin to? Where can I hide like Ceily told me te do? An more! I was supposed te be workin!

Without thinkin I whipped meself around an started flyin back. 'HELP ME, MISTER MULLINS! MISTER MULLINS, THEY'RE AFTER ME!' I screamed, tearin inta the shop an sendin the door flyin, runnin straight fer Mister Mullins. 'DON'T LET THEM GET THEIR HANDS ON ME! THEY'RE TAKIN ME AWAY!' I roared, shakin the arm offa him nearly pushin him offa his stool.

'What ails ye? Who's after you? Calm down, child! Take it easy,' he puffed, wanderin his eye to the door te see who's on me tail, then spinnin back te me, tryin te take in wha's happenin.

Me chest was heavin up an down wit the fright, an the panic eruptin in me was makin me lose me senses. All I could do was stare at him, wit only the noise a the sobs comin outa me mouth.

'You're in a state. What's wrong with you?'

'It's . . . it's . . .' I hiccupped, the sobs slammin me chest out, but I couldn't get anythin else te come.

I stared at him lookin straight inta his eyes wit me chest

heavin up an down, he stared back wit us waitin fer me te stop suffomacatin meself an the words te come.

'The cruelty people,' I staggered, lettin it all puff out in a sob.

'Who?'

'They're after us!' I croaked. 'An so is Father Flitters – me an Ceily! They got her. I ran. Don't let them catch me!'

He nodded his head up an down slowly, helpin me te get the words out, now I shivered an sniffed, waitin te hear wha he thought about tha.

'Cruelty people,' he said slowly an quietly, repeatin te himself. 'Do ye mean the NSPCC?'

'Yeah! Them ones! Tha's the ones,' I said, noddin me head like mad, happy he knew straight away.

'Ahh, now I get the picture,' he said slowly, noddin his head an clampin his lips, lettin his face smile but it wasn't a happy smile. Then he narrowed his eyes, sayin, 'Are they up there now?'

I nodded like mad givin a hiccup. 'Yeah! An they're tryin te tear Ceily outa the house, but she won't let them,' I said, hopin they didn't get her.

He took in a deep breath thinkin then looked around an leaned over te grab up a jar loaded wit sweets. 'Right! Sit up there,' he said, liftin me up onta the wooden counter plantin me sittin next te the jars a sweets all lined up beside me. Then he screwed open one a the jars. 'Here, have that. It's good for shock. Ye need a bit of glucose, so suck on that,' he said, shovin a sugar barley inta me mouth.

I was suckin an suckin, nearly enjoyin me sugar barley wit only little sniffs comin outa me now, when suddenly the door pushed in makin the bell ring an I nearly wet me knickers wit the fright.

'What's goin on here?' roared Delia Mullins, standin wit her raincoat drippin puddles around the floor an the scarf stuck te her head wit bits of soppin hair stickin out. She looked over at me sittin on the counter lookin like I was enjoyin meself suckin on one a her sugar barleys. 'Where did you get to, ye little monkey? Do you know I have had te traipse up and down half this town delivering your bloody newspapers, doing the job you were supposed to be doing!' she roared, lettin the eyes stare outa her head lookin like she wanted te kill me. 'An what do I find at the end of it? You sitting in here all nice an cosy while me da feeds you the profits out of the bloody shop!'

I stopped suckin an went dead still wit me tongue hangin out an the sugar barley halfway te me mouth starin back at her. I wanted te start cryin again because I was afraid a me life. Delia had a terrible temper when she was crossed, an she always lets everyone know not te ask the da fer credit because the answer is NO! An ye's better not come inta the place askin, because she's the real boss. But we all know tha's not true. Her da owns the shop an when she's not around he'll give it te you, she's only lookin after the shop an mindin him an tha's her only job. People say no wonder no man would go next or near her, she's so mean she thinks she owes herself money. An anyway, she's too fat an she has a hairy chin. But she does do wha her da tells her when he growls at her.

'Leave easy, Delia. There's trouble afoot,' he said, throwin the eye at me, then noddin the head when she stared at him. 'I need you to come wit me, we better lock up an make tracks fast around to—' then he threw his head at me again, an nodded over te Delia.

She stared back at him readin his eyes without sayin nothin.

'I'll get me hat an coat,' he said standin himself up, then made fer the back headin inta the livin quarters.

Delia looked down at her soppin-wet clothes then lifted her head slowly, lettin her eyes rest on nothin givin a big weary sigh, then made easy te drag herself around the counter an collapse onta her da's stool.

'Jesus, what a life I have for meself,' she muttered, talkin te herself under her breath. Then she lifted her big leg pullin down the zip on the brown-suede boot an dragged it off. It was soppin wit the wet an black wit the dirt after lettin in the rain an walkin through all the dirty filthy puddles. I watched as she lifted her toes wrigglin them in front a the smelly paraffin fire te warm them up an dry out her nylons.

'Come on! Are you ready?' Mister Mullins said, after appearin back in wearin his top coat wit the trilby hat sittin on his head.

'What are ye doing with that stick?' she said, throwin her head at his brown wooden walkin stick wit the rubber stopper at the end. 'You never use that!' she said. 'Are ye planning on hitting someone with it?'

'Come on, don't be asking so many questions, ye have me hair turned grey before me time,' he said, lookin sour then makin fer the door.

Wha about me? I wanted te say, followin him around wit me head. I gave a quick look down at the floor seein I would break me neck if I jump.

'What do ye mean, "Come on"?' Delia snorted, lookin shocked at tha idea. 'I'm going nowhere, look at the state I'm in! Soaked to the skin, freezing with the cold an starved with the hunger!' she roared.

'Don't question me, Delia. You take the child down off the counter an follow me fast. I have a job for you to do. Hurry! I'll talk to you on the way there,' he said.

'What about the shop?' she said, lettin a roar outa her.

'Never mind that, we'll close up. Sure half me bloody customers are right this minute probably up around there!' He flew at her, swingin the arm lookin fed up. 'Busybodies! All wanting to see the scandal,' he said, losin the rag himself now because he had te keep givin her excuses why she should get movin.

I wanted her te get a hurry on too, but first let me down offa this counter. Then I wondered where me sugar barley got to I worried, givin a quick look around the counter. It's gone! But I don't remember eatin it.

'Good news travels fast, and bad news even faster,' he said, snortin an lookin away in disgust, while Delia muttered an cursed shovin her boot back on.

We finally got goin an Mister Mullins pulled the shop door shut after him, lockin it, then we were on the move. I rushed ahead wantin te get there fast, then stopped te look back seein how far behind they were. Mister Mullins was walkin fast wavin his walkin stick, but not too fast wit a great hurry on him. He was more like takin the night air wit a bit of exercise, an Delia along fer the company, keepin in step.

Me nerves was gone. I rushed on ahead wishin they would hurry more. Ceily could be gone by now, an tha means I may never set eyes on her again, then they would come back lookin fer me!

Then a thought hit me. Where would I hide? I have te live somewhere, wit someone te mind me! The thought hit me so fast I took te me legs an started flyin them. 'Ceily! I want Ceily!' I started te roar, cryin me heart out again wit the sudden fright.

'COME BACK! Don't go up there on your own!' Mister Mullins shouted, rushin te catch up wit me.

'LILY CARNEY! GET BACK HERE THIS MINUTE!' roared Delia.

I stopped dead in me tracks an turned around gettin even more of a fright wit Delia.

'Do what you're told, you, and stay here with us, otherwise

you'll be landing yourself and everyone else in a heap of trouble!' she snorted, grabbin me hand an givin it a shake. 'Now stop your whining, this'll be sorted out,' she said, lettin her voice drop, noddin at me.

We rounded the corner, lookin up te see our footpath was black wit people. They were all millin around, stretchin back down the road an across te the other side. The ones outside my house were all shovin te get in, an some were pushin te get out. We could see a police squad motor car outside, sittin just up in front of the cruelty people's black one.

'Oh holy Jesus!' Delia moaned, lettin it out in a prayer whisper.

'Curse a them bastards!' Mister Mullins muttered, suckin in his mouth an snortin out through his nose. 'Worse, look at the fucking circus!' he muttered, cursin an lookin at Delia before throwin his head up at the crowds.

'Come on! At least the young one must still be there! Maybe they couldn't move her out with this lot,' she said, startin te rush now really hurryin.

I started te keen, hearin a nervous tune comin up outa me chest. I knew any minute it could break out into a scream. I had me mouth shut tight an I was breathin heavy breaths out through me nose. 'Don't let them take me Ceily,' I sang but it was really a keenin moan – I didn't want Delia te hear tha in case she roared again.

We got te the crowd an Mister Mullins pushed his way in. Delia let me hand go, sayin, 'You stay right there against that wall an don't move. Now stay well away from that crowd an tell no one nothing. Don't answer any questions! Do ye hear me talking to you?' she roared, pointin her finger at me knowin I wanted te rush in after Mister Mullins.

I turned me head back to her givin it a little shake. 'Yeah, OK, Delia,' I went, sayin an givin a big lie.

'Right!' she said, not lookin too sure but havin te believe me. 'Listen, Lily, if you go into that house you'll get yourself trampled, not just that, but you'll walk yourself back into a trap. They're only waiting in there to take you away. Do you realize that?' she said, lookin very worried at me.

I nodded, not worryin about tha, I wanted te get back in te Ceily.

We stared at each other wit her wantin te make a move an me wantin her te get on wit it.

'DON'T MOVE FROM THAT SPOT!' she shouted, then turned an rushed inta the crowd pushin an shovin her way in, roarin at people te let her past.

I didn't move, I waited me patience watchin her go, rockin on me feet shiftin from one foot te the other just waitin till she disappeared.

Then I was off, flyin in after her wit me head down an me elbows shoved out, squeezin, diggin an knockin wit me fists, then outa nowhere I got lifted in a big heave an landed packed tight te suffomacation. I grabbed me breath suckin in an out fast, then let it go in a big puff an gave a blink te see where I landed.

Where am I? I can't see nothin because I'm now buried in people's bellies, I can only hear the shoutin, it's comin from all sides.

I lifted me neck stretchin it, gettin a look at our stairs just in front a me. They're thick black wit the people, not just tha, but the ceilin's hoppin wit a whole lot more a them all millin around up there.

Who told them they can do tha? Who they think they are? Tha's our very own bedroom! An we have our bestest good candlewick bedspread up there, it's still coverin Mammy's bed. Ceily said we're not takin it off, because tha's wha Mammy was laid out on fer her wake. Then, after when the men carried

Mammy out in the coffin te bury her, Ceily shut the door behind them mutterin. 'We won't be settin foot in there again, not fer many a long day te come. Tha room will stay just as it is,' she whispered, lettin her eyes turn te me wit them lookin very sad. They looked like she wanted te cry, but she was too annoyed te let tha happen.

Yeah, Ceily an me always sleep in the one bed together, tha's in the other little bedroom. Mammy always had her own bed fer herself, but sometimes when I was little or when I do be sick she brings me . . . she brought me in wit her.

'Them people's not supposed te be steppin foot in Mammy's room, the cheek a them!' I roared te meself, givin a lash out wit me fist at the fat arse of an aul one sendin her heavin on top of a lot fightin an roarin. They were at tha because they were all mashed an mangled, gettin squashed on the stairs.

'OH, MERCY!' she screamed, flyin head first on top a Biddy Tanner sendin her lyin plastered, smotherin Mitchie Mulligan gettin him buried under the heap.

'Get me outa here, youse animals!' he roared, ragin wit the sudden fright.

'Feckin never mind shaggin you! Get yer head outa me stomach!' Biddy shouted.

'AHHH! Oh my Jesus, I'm kilt!' someone cried, tumblin down the stairs an gettin tangled in the bodies.

'WATCH OUT! YOUSE COWS BASTARDS ARE GOIN—' the voice roared, just before the rumble as people started topplin. Over an over they rolled wit the mountain now hittin us, an we all got flung back, buried an mashed te nothin. But lucky me! I ended on top of a pile sittin wit me feet danglin an the rest a me see-sawin. I could see hands start flyin an hear skin gettin slapped, now I could hear muffled threats an even feel under me the killin annihilations.

'HIT ME, WOULD YE?' roared Dinah Nagle.

'TRY THA!' Slap! 'POLICE!' screamed Tessie Small.

'MAMMY!' I screamed.

Voices from everywhere roared in me skull.

'MIND YERSELF, BLIND EYE!' shouted Hoppy Dolan, the aul spinster from around the corner.

'WHOSE A BLIND EYE?' an arse roared, tryin te lift itself outa the heap.

'Let me up! Let me go! Save me!' I panicked.

'Is it me, you dried-up aul cow, ye're talkin to?' asked an awful-lookin head suddenly appearin up outa the lumps a bodies.

I stared seein the state of it! 'Gawd, tha must a gor an awful shock,' I said wit me gapin mouth movin me lips. I watched the head lookin around starin through a pair a mad bulgin eyes an a matchin red face wantin te see who it was fightin wit. Then it lit on Hoppy seein her starin back.

'YES, YOU, YE BLIND-EYED AUL HAG!' Hoppy croaked, suffomacatin herself wit rage on a lump a spit.

'Wha?! Me blind eye? An when's the last time you, ye hoppy fucker, took a look at yerself in the mirror, you dyin-lookin aul gannet,' roared the head wit the neck thrown back all stretched now, wantin te commit murder.

'Dyin is it I am? Look who's talkin! I'll give you dyin! I'll show you who's dyin fast enough, ye dirty aul toerag! Let me at yaaaaaaa!'

The head ducked seein the claws comin an they ended on the wrong one. Suddenly a scarf came flyin, an someone squealed wit the noise goin right through me ear.

'Me scarf, me head! HELP! She's pullin the hair outa me!'

'STOP THEM!' a voice erupted.

'BRING THE POLICE!!'

'NEVER MIND THE POLICE! WE'RE HAVIN A RUGGY-UP!' shouted a young fella roarin from the back.

'Oh no! Get me out! I'm caught in the middle a the ruggy,' I keened, shiverin an now startin te breathe in an out fast wit me losin me wind. I spun me head lookin fer someone te help me or te find a way out fer meself.

'MURDER! HURRY! THERE'LL BE KILLINS!' an aul one roared, openin her mouth right over me face blastin the ears offa me. Then a wrinkled old hand wit skin hangin flew out, an tha sent me wavin back against the door jamb.

Wit tha the crowd from behind pushed in liftin me feet offa the floor.

'Mammy!' I screamed, flyin out me hands wit shock. I managed te haul meself up fer air on the back a two aul fellas. I grabbed a hold the neck of their shirts an held on wit me knees bent an me neck stretched, lookin like an injun hangin on his horse.

The crowd shot forward rollin the eyes in the back a me head makin me dizzy an givin me a jaunt I didn't want. 'Oh Mammy! Help! I'm dead!' I shivered in meself. 'An wha's more worser! Delia will kill me, makin me stone dead tha's fer definite, when she sees I wasn't listenin.'

Then the heave stopped to a standstill at the stairs again. I slid down feelin me legs like jelly wantin te make me way fast out from the stairs an away from the slaughter. I was now headed in the direction a Father Flitters. I could hear his voice roarin, it sounded hoarse an was comin somewhere te the left behind the stairs. Tha's where they might be all a con-gramagated holdin onta our Ceily. 'I have to get te her, she'll know wha te do now we have Mister Mullins. An Delia's my mammy's friend,' I puffed, talkin te meself as I crawled between the legs of a man, he was bendin down an makin room te haul up Biddy Tanner, she was lyin stretched out on top a Nelly Dempsey.

'Delia even made me a dolly,' I told meself, crawlin up an

under people when I saw a way past. I got her fer me birthday, I thought, feelin the steam run down me face. 'She's called Molly,' I muttered as I kept goin. 'She's made a duck feathers an her head an legs is made a straw.'

'Yeah,' I whispered, keepin meself movin, takin no notice a the killins goin on all around me. 'This must a been wha it was like in the war, when the Black an Tans tormented an even kilt the people in their very own beds! Mister Mullins told me all about tha. He knows everythin, because he was one a the men, the Rebels, tha thrun them outa the country! Yeah, he was a fightin man, an everyone looks up te him because the women nod their heads outa respect, an even the men touch their caps when they pass him. An wha's more! They do even like him better than Father Flitters. Well, maybe they don't actually like *him*, even though he's the holy priest. They do run when they see him, tha's because they're afraid a him. Yeah, now the war? I definitely bet tha war must a been somethin like this, runnin fer yer life,' I sniffed, feelin me nose goin watery an me eyes get hot. I'm sweatin but I can't stop because I'll only get mashed.

'Right, keep thinkin about Molly, because I got te save her as well! She has real jet-black hair – it's horse's hair – an she has lovely navy-blue eyes made a buttons. An her mouth is stitched wit red thread. Yeah, I got te find them,' I told meself, but Delia says I better watch out fer not te walk into a trap! 'Tha's wha Mammy warns me as well. "You walked yerself into a trap when ye opened your mouth," Mammy shouts. She says tha when she sees someone moochin fer somethin they shouldn't, or when they're about te hang themself tellin a pack a lies. I do tha all the time, then forget wha I said. Ceily says I should give up lyin, because I'm too stupid an I'm not very good at it.'

4

WHEN I LIFTED me head again I was lookin straight up at Father Flitters, he was plastered against the wall wit people movin in close wavin their finger an everyone shoutin, they were all tryin te let him know wha they thought about him, but nobody would listen because they all wanted their own say. He stood starin inta the back wall wit roars comin outa his mouth lookin like he was gone mad. His hat was nowhere te be seen an I could see the stick was missin as well, not just tha but I saw a fella standin beside me wearin his lovely black woolly scarf – he had it wrapped around his neck. Then the missin hat suddenly appeared, it was floatin itself along the air wit no one wearin it! Me mouth dropped an I stared, it was movin further back now headin fer the door.

Suddenly an aul fella roared, 'MIND ME BUNIONS!' An the hat came flyin back in my direction. I watched as it lifted, then I saw wha happened. It had been sittin rattlin on the neck of a scruffy-lookin young fella wit the hat ten times too big fer his head. Then I saw the face appear as it turned around an saw me starin. I watched as his eyes lit up an he pushed the hat outa his way te stare back, then he had the cheek te give me a big wink lettin his mankey scruffy face crease into a smile.

I put the evil eye on him wit me mouth goin pointy lettin heavy breaths come down me nose. He didn't care! He was too busy lookin very happy wit himself, just like he owned the joint. An the dirt a him, the smelly ornament! His face is mouldy black wit the dirt an I could see white streaks comin from his dried snots.

I know him. Tha's Sooty! He's one a the Hamberleys! He's black as the ace a spades because his da's a chimney sweep an sometimes he has te help him. Tha's when the da shoves him up the chimney te see what's blockin his brushes. He told us one time his da lit a fire under his arse when he got stuck, he did tha te get him back down.

'An did ye get back then in a hurry?' we asked him.

'Yeah I did an all! Like greased bleedin lightnin,' he said, showin his white teeth an the white in his eyes – the only thing te be seen in his pot-black face.

Now look a him, the cheek of him! Who does he think he is comin inta my house? He thinks he's big but he's not! He's only a scut wit his nine years old! I'll catch up on tha in another while. He's not gettin away wit this!

I dropped me fists te me sides an leaned me head on me shoulder givin him a stare, lettin him know I was goin te give him a fight. He just shook his head lettin the hat rattle, tormentin me. An I can't get at him! Him an me have te keep pushin our way te stare each other out!

There's sixteen a them Hamberleys an they're a crowd a moochers, always lookin fer trouble. Tha's why me mammy says I'm te keep away from the lot a them tenement childre an not even look in their direction, certainly not never play wit them.

The school inspector does be kilt tryin te catch them Hamberleys, but they all have him runnin in different directions an he ends up banjacksed. All he can do then is pedal off on his bicycle, but he waves his fist back te warn them! 'Don't you worry, me boyos! I'll be back! I'll stand yet on

Kingsbridge Station an wave you all off as you head down to the four corners of the country! I'll make it my business to ensure you'll get sent to the most godforsaken, barren, remotest reformatory this country has to offer. Oh by Jesus see if I don't! Them Christian Brothers will make men of you, oh by God yes they will! They will make or break you!' I heard him once warn wit a shake of his head grittin his teeth, then lean over an spit te the ground.

We had all been watchin the goins on, laughin an runnin te see if any a one a them got caught! But tha voice had made me shiver then, an I suddenly gave another shiver now, thinkin about it. Yeah, warnin wit his fist an his eyes starin, slowly sayin he'll get them yet, one by one he'll pick them off. Just like now wha they're tryin te do te me an Ceily – get their hands on us an lock us up.

But it doesn't worry them Hamberleys. Look at one a them now – him! 'Nor a bother on him!' I snarled, givin him a dirty look then turnin away wit me disgust, then I turned an looked back at him again. Tha eegit thinks he's gorgeous wit Father Flitter's hat shiverin on his chicken neck, but he's not! 'He's goin te roast in hell fer robbin a holy priest,' I snorted, starin back at him wit me chin stuck out an me eyes squintin.

Then the real thought hit me an me breath caught in me neck wit the suddenness of it. They robbed the holy priest! Tha's really a terrible shockin sin, I thought, not able te get over it. 'You can't rob a priest, because he's a God anointed! Done by only God himself,' I puffed, pushin me breath out hard. 'Tha fella's goin te be struck down dead any minute!'

I whipped me head back te see if he was struck. No, he's not dead yet, he was still there lookin bigger now, wit the hat stickin up in the air. He saw me lookin at him again, an lifted his chest te give me a bigger grin. I was ragin an stuck me tongue out at him, then he leaned forward lettin the hat fall over his eye an stuck out his own tongue back. The crucification cheek a him! He's not gettin the better a me!

I was just about te cross me eyes an flap me ears at him, because he has cauliflower ears from all the boxin they get, when suddenly he lifted his hand an waved Father Flitters' stick at me! Me mouth shut tight then dropped open again.

'You're goin straight te hell,' I muttered, leanin me neck out an openin me mouth wide, lettin him see me tongue makin out the words. Then I drew in me breath an looked away feelin satisfied, yeah, an now Father Flitters will kill him! He'll go straight te the school an drag him out be the neck! I'd love te be there, but I'd hate te be in his shoes! ''Cept he doesn't have any!' I sniffed, lookin back an liftin me eyebrows wit a dirty smell in me nose, then settled meself te look up now at the priest. Then I blinked an stared up hard at him wit me tryin te think.

He looks different somehow, he doesn't look himself, I thought, starin him up an down tryin te figure it out. I studied his purple face wit the pair a bulgin eyes, they were starin an blinkin in time te the words comin outa his mouth along wit spits. No, he doesn't look important now, he looks like someone tha's well scrubbed an fed, mebbe a mad relative of someone well te do. But then, instead a gettin him locked up, they just let him wander off te go mad on his own. An now he's causin trouble by bein a danger te himself an a nuisance te the people. Tha's wha the big people always say, just before they get someone carted away an locked up in Grangegorman, the mad house. Tha's the place tha sits waitin for them.

I moved in closer shovin me way. I wanted te really study him now, because I didn't know holy priests went mad.

'I am taking down names! I have you all well marked!' he said, pointin at his empty hand. It looked like he lost his notebook as well. 'Make no mistake about that,' he croaked, losin his voice because it was gone to a hoarse whisper.

Then someone shouted, 'Go ahead! Do we look worried?' laughed Babby Kelly – our local lunatic everyone calls him! 'An furthermore!' Babby snorted, wavin the finger, 'I'll get me dog te bite the arse offa your dog, Henry, when I next see him! Tha vicious Highland terrier bit the arse offa me, so he did! An you stood an let him, so ye did!'

'Tut tut! That's terrible language te be lettin outa yer mouth an he the man anointed!' someone moaned, clickin their teeth soundin shocked.

I mooched closer te see all the shockin Babby Kelly was doin. He was movin himself in then back, grabbin a hold a his shirt tails lettin the priest get a full blast a shocks. They were comin wit all the insults roarin outa him. Right inta his face they went splatterin spits an all. Then he looked around feelin very important because everyone was laughin. I looked down seein he'd nothin else on but the bare feet an a pair a trousers. He must a ran out after Granny Kelly. He was her growed-up son, but she wouldn't let him outa the house in tha state, I thought, shakin me head wit the sorrow. He's an old man, but she still has te mind him because he's an 'unfortunate', me mammy calls him. Tha's because he's not all there in the head.

The priest carried on like no one was talkin. 'You will all be excommunicated,' he shouted, givin a keenin moan. 'I will read your names from the pulpit,' he warned, shakin his finger an snappin it under people's noses makin their heads follow an their eyes cross.

Then he let a roar whippin his hand at them makin them all duck. 'Each and every one of you will be named!' he choked, throwin the head back an takin a fit a coughin.

We all stared up leavin our mouths open, waitin te see if he was goin te make it an get a breath back, or mebbe even suffomacate. But suddenly he got goin again wit a strangumalated gasp.

'The Bishop will be notified about this!' he whispered, now shakin the head tryin te get the wind inta him.

Somehow I felt a bit disappointed – I never saw anyone drop down dead before, an I wondered wha it would be like.

'YEAH! TOO RIGHT! AN WE'LL BE THE FIRST TE DO IT!' someone shouted from the back. It sounded like Fitzer Mangle the coalman, he hates Father Flitters because they had a big row. It was when the priest came bangin on his door wantin te know why his wife was out an about after gettin her new babby. An she not even 'Churched'! Tha's a mortal sin, because when a mammy has a new babby she's not allowed te even cut a slice a bread until she goes straight te the church to get the priest's blessin, because she's a sinner. She didn't do tha because Fitzer put his foot down an told the priest to fuck off an take him an his sins wit him! We all heard the row. I was about five at the time, an Millie Maypole came rushin te bang on our door an everyone else's – we were te come quick an see the row, she roared, all excited wit herself.

Father Flitters stopped talkin fer a minute te take him in, then he sniffed an lifted his head openin his mouth an carried on. 'The Holy Father himself, THE POPE, will hear about this and be utterly scandalized.' Then he lowered his voice. 'You have brought the Irish Catholic nation into terrible and shameful disrepute! You have dared to lay your hands on one of God's holy anointed!' he barked, wavin his finger in the air givin them a sorry warnin, thinkin now it was the Sunday Mass an he up on the altar tellin us all we were goin te burn in hell because we were terrible sinners, because tha's the way he talks then.

But where's Ceily? It suddenly hit me! I whipped me head around feelin a scream wantin te roar outa me – it was comin wit a terrible thought. Mebbe they took her? An where's Mister Mullins an Delia? I couldn't see a thing wit all the bodies, an the heat an the smell comin outa them was makin me suffomacate, I'm goin te get sick!

'LET ME OUT! I WANT TE MOVE!' I roared, throwin me hands out pushin an aul one in a hairy black smelly coat tha was squashin her arse inta me face.

Suddenly there was a roar an we were all milled against the wall.

'CLEAR THE DOOR! Give this woman safe passage!'

I ducked me head out between two aul ones pullin the coats offa them, sayin, 'Excuse me, missus!' But I still couldn't see past the back of an aul fella, so I kept me head goin, usin it te batter him an gettin him te budge.

'Stop pushin!' he roared, lookin around at the two aul ones, then I was down on me hands an knees crawlin through his open legs. 'HOLY JAYSUS!' he roared, gettin staggered back inta the chests of the aul ones.

'MIND YERSELF, YE DRUNKEN AUL EEGIT!' one a them roared, givin him a clout.

When I squeezed up fer air I could see now it was the cruelty woman – she was collapsed all red-faced wit the eyes half closed an the pancake hat swimmin on the back of her head, it was hangin caught by the nobby pin. She was gettin dragged along half carried out on the arms a two big meaty policemen, she looked bad because she was holdin her chest moanin. The skinny man was trailin behind gettin helped out by another policeman, he was leanin inta him all collapsed an moanin te himself.

Gawd, Mammy! The pair a them are in threadbare order! I thought, starin wit me mouth open. Tha's the all a them, but where's my Ceily? An Mister Mullins an Delia?

I got a dig in the chin from an elbow as an aul one pushed in flattenin her arse against me face an makin me snort in a lungful of pissy frock.

'There ye are, Aggie! Wha brings you?' she said, slappin the shoulder of Aggie Flynn who knows everyone's business.

Aggie squinted at her, then put the headscarf behind her ears te hear better. 'I could ask you the same thing, Nelly Porter.'

'Well!' Nelly said. 'I was just about te ask you is there any news. What's happenin here?'

'I'm sayin nothin,' Aggie said, givin her gums a quick chew, then turnin her head away wit a sour look.

'Ah go on, tell us!' Nelly said, givin her a dig wit the elbow.

Aggie looked back an chewed on her gums starin, dyin te tell.

'I'm listenin, go on! I won't say a word,' Nelly said, liftin the eyebrows an noddin the head te get her goin.

I opened me mouth leanin in wit Nelly, wantin te hear everythin.

Aggie snorted in a big breath then whispered it out, sayin, 'As I said, Nelly, I'm sayin nothin, ye didn't hear this from me!' Then she looked up at Nelly, waitin.

'Oh God no! Sure who would I tell?'

Satisfied, they leaned in closer pressin their heads an I moved wit them leanin me head inta the middle.

'Did you not hear? The big push is on, this place is up fer grabs an they're shiftin the young ones out today,' said Aggie, then she eased in a big breath holdin it wit her nose pinched, an they stared at each other lookin very shocked but satisfied, because they had terrible news te talk about. Then she shook herself wrappin her arms under her big chest fer comfort, before sayin, 'As we speak they're in there now tryin te peel tha young one out, she's hidin in the lavatory, the tilet!'

'Go way!' breathed Nelly, puffin in the breath an pullin back fer a better look.

'Oh indeed! Barricaded herself inside, she has. An that's not all! I heard she knocked the skull offa some poor unfortunate who tried te crawl in under the half door! Only tryin te help he was, missus! Destroyed he is! They have him laid out now in the saturated-wet, freezin-cold backyard waitin fer the ambulance! Catch his death a cold he will,' complained Aggie, liftin her chest thinkin about it wit a very sour look.

'Tut tut! Shockin! I never heard the like of it,' keened Nelly.

'Sure wha do ye expect? Bein dragged up an no man about te put manners on them!' snorted Aggie.

'Oh indeed! An tha little one is no better! Sure do ye know wha I just heard?' moaned Nelly, gettin more shocked by the minute.

'No, wha?' Aggie gasped, even more shocked.

'Well! See if you can beat this one! I heard tha holy little terror up an landed her foot on the—'

She looked around te see who was listenin an didn't lower her eyes te spot me, then moved in closer te whisper. I moved in too, the more fer a better listen.

Aggie pulled her scarf back holdin out her ear te Nelly's mouth wantin te miss nothin. Then we all dropped our mouths open an stopped breathin.

'PRIVATES!' Nelly screamed in a whisper, then took in an awful long breath holdin it in her nose gettin a terrible bad smell.

'You mean between the legs?' Aggie keened in a long moan droppin her eyes the length a Nelly, then shakin the head up an down te see if she was right.

Nelly slowly nodded back lookin crucified, sayin, 'Poor man, only tryin te do his job he was. Sure did ye not see him get stretchered out be the police?'

'Who? Do ye mean tha long skinny aul fella wearin the suit an the baldy head?'

'The very same! Tha was the cruelty man, sure the only

cruelty done was te him! Tha little divil knocked the bejaysus outa him!'

'Go way did she? An the size of her, missus! Sure she's tha little, one puff an ye'd blow her away! Sure, she can't be no more than six year old!'

'I'M NOT SIX! ME BIRTHDAY CAME! I'M SEVEN NOW!' I roared, whippin me head from one te the other hittin me finger on me chest pointin at meself. 'Did youse not know tha?' I snorted, pointin at them now.

'WHA? TALK A THE DEVIL! HAVE YOU BEEN STANDIN THERE LISTENIN TE OUR BUSINESS ALL A THIS TIME?' Nelly screamed, grabbin a hold a me arm.

'TALKIN A BUSINESS! But excuse me, missus, wha did I just hear the pair a you say?'

'Who? You talkin te me?' Nelly said, whippin herself around lettin go a me.

'Yes, you!' a big woman wit a red face an a huge chest said, foldin her arms, holdin them up, then stretchin her back chewin on the jaws. 'The pair a ye's! Wha did ye mean be sayin this house is up fer grabs? I'll have you know it is no such thing! Because as we speak this minute my Delarosa's name is goin down on the tenancy for this place! We slept all night out on the footpath waitin fer tha corporation te open its doors an we was the first in! So youse can put tha in yer bleedin pipe an smoke it!'

'Here! Don't be draggin me inta yer rows! I had nothin te do wit this! I only came in te see if anyone was in trouble!' shouted Aggie, pushin her way out headin fer the door after gettin an awful fright.

'Is tha right now? Well, for your information I had me name down as soon as Mary Carney was stretchered outa this place!' snorted Nelly.

'Well, youse are ALL wrong! Because I have it now on good

authority my Annie Regina is gettin this place. We're more entitled because we live in the neighbourhood,' a squinty grey-haired aul one said, fixin a big brown overcoat wrappin it around her because it was too big an the buttons was missin.

'Who are you?' snorted Nelly. 'An wha neighbourhood would tha be, may I ask?'

'Four blocks as the crow flies I live!' the grey aul one snorted, openin her mouth wide sayin it slowly.

Nelly opened her own mouth slowly, leavin it hangin an flared her nostrils like she gor a bad smell, then moaned out through her nose. '"As the crow flies," she says. Bejaysus ye're right there, missus, ye'd need wings te get where you are! Stuck out right in the arsehole a the country! Did ye get a lift here in the hay lorry?'

I stared then followed, turnin me head slowly, waitin fer the grey aul one.

'As I said, neighbours!' she sniffed, turnin the eye away gettin an even bigger smell herself.

'Bejaysus! Ye're not gettin my Delarosa's house, talk like tha will get youse kilt! I'll swing fer the pair a ye's!' the big woman suddenly exploded, grabbin Nelly's hair in one hand an the grey aul one's in the other, bangin their heads together.

The place erupted, I gor a mouthful of arse nearly knockin me teeth out an Nelly got pulled te the floor. People shouted, more hairs were pulled an fists flew wit feet sendin bodies flyin crowdin on top of the ones rollin around, an them tha wanted te scatter were bein pushed screamin an cryin like the Banshee. It didn't stop the women buried under the heap, they rolled an snorted lashin out hands makin mincemeat tearin lumps tryin te kill each other.

Me world shattered. I danced up an down wit fright not knowin wha way te move, I gor a dig in the head an me mind went.

'MAMMYEEE! CEILY!' I wet me knickers an lost me rubber wellington boot as I got throwed on top an people walked on me pushin me down farther into a gap wit the killins an then I couldn't breathe no more! No air, no air! Me hands is trapped, me legs is tight, I can't kick! Me chest is burst they're buryin me, I'm dyin. 'No, Ma, don't let them kill me!' I heard meself whisperin inside me head.

Then there was a rumble like a voice talkin te me an somethin tuggin at me. Suddenly I was shiftin up, pulled, dragged and torn, squeezed up against hair, the greasy smell of cloth in me nose, me hand scrapin against rough coat, me face knocked against the hard leather sole of a shoe. I smell wet fish an hard bone – it's someone's open mouth wit teeth an tongue draggin across me eyebrow. I taste the salty skin of a scaly leg – it's soft an hairy an smells like piss. I'm movin faster now, then suddenly lifted. I feel hot air on me face an up me nose, light is pushin through me closed shut-tight eyes! I feel meself stranglin on me coat an someone pullin at me. Then I hear it – the voice again only louder.

'COME ON! GET UP! GET OUT! GET MOVIN!'

I get tore up more, swung sideways dragged, then torn loose. All a me is movin now. I'm trailed over a heap of bodies, me eyes open but it's a blur. Now I'm stood on me feet wit me head flyin dizzy, then pulled an dragged lashed inta people an torn through gaps till I'm standin on the road wit only a faraway roar left shoutin behind me. My ears are wringin an me chest is screamin, but I can hear the sudden quiet an feel the cold air on me face an see the dark winter night wit the stars up above shinin down. I'm alive!

I bend meself in half an open me mouth wide, then start te take breaths in an out a me nose an mouth, I go fast an hard! I can't stop, I never will again get enough of this God's holy air! I want te breathe fer the rest of me life an never stop. It feels lovely.

I stayed stooped over feelin me heart hammerin now wantin te slow down. Me red-hot face soaks up the cold damp air like it was thirsty fer a drink. For a while back there I was drownin – no air could get inta me because I was smothered an buried under bodies!

'Come on! Keep goin, look! They're comin out te get you!'

Me senses started te come to me an I heard the voice roarin at me. I looked up te see Sooty hoppin up an down wearin his priest's hat an bangin his stick wantin us te get runnin. I followed his hand pointin at the door seein heads lookin an hands pointin, wit people makin te get to me. The door was jammed wit people fightin te get in an them tryin te get out, no one could shift. The footpath was crowded, jammed wit everyone shoutin over each other an lookin like they were havin great excitement. No one wanted te leave, to go an miss the best fight since the Black an Tans.

This all comes te me from an awful long distance. I can hear the roars but they're comin from far away like me head was under water when I get me wash in the tin bath an me ma ducks me head drownin me.

I stood in the middle of the road an looked through the dark night over at the house where I was born. It was wide open now an people were pressed against the windas, they were tearin down the curtains, smashin into all our things, laughin, cryin an fightin, an all packed tight inta the four corners an walls of our house, even Mammy's room. Tha's my home, my house, me an Ceily's, but now we have nothin no more. 'Oh Ma, Mammy! Where are you? Come back to us, don't stay wit God – he doesn't need you! We do! I'm waitin on ye, Ma, you can't be gone. You wouldn't go away an leave us on our own. I'm goin te find you! I'm goin—'

Where will I go? The graveyard te tell her she has te come back now. No! I'm goin te Holy God's house, the chapel, te tell God to help me find me mammy an bring her home. My mammy didn't die, she wouldn't let tha happen, she would even stand up to God! *Are you mad?* she would say te him. *Will ye go on outa tha, sure haven't I too much te do wit tryin te keep this pair together in body an soul, to wha? Be goin te heaven just to suit you?!*

Yeah! I shook me head slowly, thinkin about this, there's a mistake. Things happen tha childre don't understand. Big people are always complain about tha when we want te know somethin an they don't want te tell us. The body they sent from the hospidal only looks a bit like my ma, but it wasn't her. Anyway, she wasn't even sick the day I went te school an she never came home. Yeah, she's just missin tha's all, but I'm goin te find her. Then it hit me. The hospidal! Tha's where she is! But wha one? There's millions, an I don't know me way.

Me heart slid down me chest an broke, I can't get goin! Where are they? Which way will I go first? CEILY! She will know, an she'll be delighted when she hears me good news! I'm not as stupid as she thinks!

I whipped me head back te the door seein them all packed tight around my house wit even more runnin in this direction – it's everyone comin te make their way an mill inta my house. I can't get in te get her there.

I know, I'll fly around the back lane an get in the back door to the yard. Yeah an tha's where they said Ceily was. She's stuck out there hidin in the lavatory.

'WAKE UP, YE DOZY GOBSHITE!' Sooty roared, makin a sudden move, then crashin our heads together as the pair of us leapt te go at the same time.

'My head! Ye banged me,' I shouted, rubbin me forehead feelin a bump startin up.

'Owww! Me teeth, me jaw! Ye blind-lookin mental eegit!' he roared, rubbin an lookin te see was his teeth loose or any blood on his finger.

'I'm not! You're an eegit yerself an a robber! You robbed the priest's hat an walkin stick! The devil'll be after you!' I snorted, turnin away te run an find Ceily.

'Where you goin?' he shouted, standin still an starin after me.

'Mind yer own big business!' I roared back.

'So fuck off! An next time don't expect me te dig you outa yer bleedin hole!'

'Yeah, an fuck you too!' I shouted back, feelin annoyed wit him an ragin wit God, an to hell wit the devil! I'm goin te curse like mad, an none a them is goin te stop or worry me! The no-good lot robbed my ma an hid her away from me. Me an Ceily! I hate everyone now I does . . . I do. Because they're no good, they're only out te get you when ye're down! Me mammy often mutters tha to herself when she gets robbed by the coal- or milkman.

I slapped along in me one bare foot an wellington boot tryin not te slip on the shiny black cobblestones because they were wet from the cold night air, an as well, makin sure te stay in the middle a the road so nobody could grab me from outside the row a houses. I threw me eye over makin sure no one was lookin te get me, but they was all too busy lookin up the road watchin the fights goin on outside my house. I turned left at the end a the houses an rushed up the lane seein gate doors jumpin wit dogs barkin tryin te get out to take a bite outa me. Then I heard a thumpin noise wit slappin feet flyin up behind me. Me heart stopped an I came to a sudden standstill gettin ready te duck back an away from wha ever was after me.

5

'YOU! WHA DO you want followin me?' I roared, snortin back at Sooty comin to a sudden stop, then slide, to creep around me.

'Nothin! I'm not after you! Have me own business, goin te me own house,' he snorted, lookin like he was after me because he had nothin better te do.

'Fuck off!' I said, dyin te say tha word again an turnin te run on te me own gate at the end a the lane.

'Yeah, an fuck bleedin you too!' he shouted, ragin after me.

'Oh yeah, an fuck . . .' I couldn't think a somethin better, 'bleedin you too,' I snorted.

'An double fuck you, ye smelly shitty arsehole!' he roared.

'Oh ahh! Tha's shockin curses! The devil will roast him in hell! Fuck the devil!' I'm sayin tha because I don't worry about him no more, he can roast me too, because I lost me mammy an tha hurts more.

I got close now an I could hear the shoutin an people arguin, wit everyone havin a different mind. I slowed down te listen, hopin te hear Ceily, or know wha's happenin.

'Didn't I just tell ye tha?! You are repeatin me!'

'No, these are me own words! I said to you—' then it was lost as a scream came up.

'Get yer hands offa me, you big brave hero wit yer molestin women an childre!'

'Here, you! Don't be molestin tha old woman!'

'Who?! Me? Just wait a minute now, who are you callin old?'

'Out! Move! Shift! Will you all get out of here or I'll have the lot of you arrested!'

'On wha charge, guard? An where's yer army?'

'Ah, God bless yer innocence, son, you must be just up from the country an you not even shavin yet! Jaysus, I've seen more fluffy hair on a babby's arse than's on your shiny face. You're makin me laugh, guard! The state a you, against this lot? An here we have only the whole a Dublin now, found their way te nest in this place.'

I stood starin lookin up at the wall hearin the noise roarin over the top, then looked down at the brown doorknob an back up at the latch. Me belly sank. I can't reach the doorknob – it's too high up. An I forgot, Mammy keeps it well locked, you need a key te get in, an anyway, there's even a bolt across from the inside so ye can't get in at all. She only opens it fer the coalman, tha's te let him in an dump the bag a coal in the shed, we get tha every Friday when she gets paid. Yeah, the shed is just empty now, we got no more coal.

Then a picture flew inta me head, it was the last Friday when he came. It was rainy an dark outside, I was sittin on the floor by the roarin red-hot fire doin me schoolwork, but me belly was shoutin because it was waitin on me dinner. Then Mammy roared te me from the scullery te watch them sausages hoppin around in the fryin pan, then she came rushin in wearin her brown slippers wit the white fur around, an wiped her hands on her apron before reachin up te take down the toby jug wit the coalman's money sittin inside. She keeps tha up on the mantelpiece wit all her money in it, tha's te pay the rent te the corporation fer the house, an the money fer the milkman.

We could hear the coalman bangin on the back door, shoutin, 'COAL! You in there, Missus Carney? Open up!'

'Jaysus, he'll take the door down,' Mammy muttered, rushin back te get the key hangin on the wall behind the scullery door an then rushed out lettin in a big roarin cold wind splatterin rain on the oilcloth.

'Bang tha door shut behind me, Lily love, an watch them sausages. An don't touch any. I have them counted!' she warned.

I slammed the door shut behind her an rushed te turn the brown sausages swimmin in the drippin left from the roast meat before they burned an turned black. I could see she already had made a big plate a chips an half a dozen eggs was left sittin in a bowl waitin te be fried. The smell was killin me. I wanted te grab one a them but I didn't want te get caught. No, not when we're havin me all-time favourite. Mammy is very strict, if she says don't do somethin an ye do, then you end up wit only sausages an eggs. Tha's wha happened te me one time. I had te sit an watch Ceily stuff her gob wit my share!

I lowered me head as the picture started te leave me. Tha was the last Friday we had Mammy, I didn't know how happy we was, I was only happy normal, like it was the weekend an I had no school an we were goin te get our favourite dinner. Then next day we could go inta town an head down Moore Street te get the messages fer the Sunday dinner an the food fer the week. When we had tha done, Mammy would take us inta Woolworth's café, then, fer a plate a chips an eggs. After tha we would drag the shoppin home, wit Ceily givin out te me tha I wasn't holdin my side a the shoppin bag up, tha I was only draggin outa her! Mammy would get fed up listenin te us when we really started te roar. Then she would say, 'Would the pair a youse ever stop tha fightin, or tomorrow youse won't set foot outside the house. I'll take meself off for the day an enjoy it without you! Then you may kiss goodbye to your tea in Caffolla's. Now! Did you hear an get tha good an proper?' she would say, noddin her head. 'So let tha be the end to it!'

We would go quiet then, because we knew she meant it. She only says somethin when she means te do it.

Then the bad thought hit me – I remember again she's not here, she's gone! I went like jelly, I collapsed back against the wall lettin meself slide down on me arse hittin the ground wit the weight of it. I stretched out me legs without thinkin, then felt the cold wet soppin inta me, it's now makin me arse an legs go all freezin cold. Gawd, me coat an frock will be all dirty an destroyed, an now when Mammy does get back she's goin te kill me!

No, she won't, she's in her coffin! a thought whispered in me head.

'But I don't care about tha because tha's not true!' I muttered, stabbin me eyes at the ground.

But then wha happened te her? Where did she go? I want te cry me heart out, because the Monday came an I went off te school not knowin. Did I say, 'Goodbye, Mammy'? Did I look at her? Wha was she doin when I was openin the front door? Did I get a look at her? Why did I not run te her an wrap me arms around her? Oh, if only I could sit beside her now an stroke her soft wavy hair.

She didn't like her hair at all, she would often say tha when she was combin it, gettin herself ready fer work, or when she was goin somewhere. 'Oh would you look at the cut of me?! The hair is nearly gone from me head it's tha thin, an Jesus! Would ye look at the grey?! Oh dear God, wha happened to the years? Where did my life go to?' she would whisper, shakin her head slowly inta the mirror, then turn away sighin. 'I don't know. I wonder if I should have done somethin different.' Then she would shake her head again, lookin like she regretted wha she did, because she was after doin somethin wrong.

But I loved her hair because it was my mammy's, an I loved strokin her face an slidin me fingers inta the wrinkles around her skin an under her chin, she liked tha she did. She would close her eyes lettin her head drop back, sayin, 'Oh that's very nice. You have lovely soft hands, Lily love, God bless them.'

'Yeah, Mammy, I'm goin te be a hairdresser when I grow up!'

'Indeed you will, an a great one at tha,' she would tell me. Then I would twirl me fingers around her wavy hair gettin curls an playin wit it, tryin te make her a new hairstyle.

But wha she loved best was when I would stroke her face pullin up the skin hangin round her neck, then she would start te nod off te sleep mutterin. 'I'm gettin old before me time,' she would laugh, flickin her eyes open te look up at me sittin on her lap.

'How old are you, Mammy?' I asked her when me own birthday came, because she never got one.

'Thirty years older than you, chicken, today. We have our birthdays on the same day,' she laughed.

I had now got te be seven, an she was . . . Was tha much? I shook me head thinkin about it, no! Because Granny Kelly has a lot more wrinkles an her hair is snow-white wit the grey. So they're all liars! Mammies can't die when they still have childre! No she's only gone somewhere, somethin's goin on but they won't tell me!

'Wha you doin there? Are ye not gettin in?'

I looked up te see Sooty starin down at me like I had two heads.

I stared back sayin nothin.

'Are you cryin?' he said, lookin shocked.

'No,' I muttered, wipin me eyes then feelin the wet.

'You are so! Ye're cryin!'

'I AM NOT, YOU!' I roared, ragin because he caught me an I didn't even know I was.

'You are! Ye're a cry babby, girls are always cryin,' he snorted, lookin at me like he gor a bad smell.

'Mind yer own business!' I roared, not feelin in a humour te fight him.

'You're cryin because yer ma's dead!' he laughed, hoppin from one foot te the other, delighted he had somethin te torment me wit.

'YE'RE A LIAR!' I screamed, leppin te me feet.

'She is!' he said, leanin inta me wit his chin stuck out.

I grabbed a hold a his hair an swung fer all I was worth. I wanted te mill him te mash! 'Ye're a dirty, filthy, smelly, shitey liar!' I said, yankin the hair wit every word, pullin the head offa him.

'Lemme go! I'll flatten ye te meat,' he screamed, stampin his foot on me wellie an diggin his head inta me belly. He tore me around an I danced me feet gettin me balance an swingin him back the other way. Then I heard someone screamin wit the cryin, an let go hearin it was meself.

I stared at him fer a minute wit me mouth open not gettin a breath, then it came lettin a terrible roar a cryin outa me.

He stared back rubbin his head lookin at lumps a hair pulled out, sayin, 'You're a savage, Lily Carney.' He said it in a squeaky voice because he got hoarse from screamin.

I turned an ran te the corner, then dropped me head in me arms an cried me heart out wit me elbows restin in the corner a the wall. 'MAMMYEEEE! I want me mammy te come back!'

I couldn't help meself, I'll never stop cryin, I'm lost all by meself! Me shoulders leapt up an down wit the cryin an me belly hurt.

'I'll never be able te laugh or be happy again without you,

Mammy,' I told her, hearin me voice choke out the words because they kept catchin on me breath.

Suddenly I heard her, me mouth stayed open an I lifted me head starin inta the dark te listen.

Lily love, her voice breathed beside me – it's comin in me head, but outside me as well an all around me!

Don't be cryin, I'm not far away. I'm right here beside you, so stop bein afraid.

'Mammy! Where are you?' I whispered, turnin me head around tryin te see, but it was gotten very dark wit only the street lamps shinin down the lane.

I hear her! But where is she? I listened hearin the wind moan an held me breath waitin. But now all around me stayed empty. I couldn't see inta the dark corners – only shadows wit papers blowin in the wind. I closed me eyes an held me breath hard, tightenin me chest so I could hear.

Lily! I heard her breathe.

Me heart leapt an I wanted te scream wit the cry. 'Mammy!'

Shush, chicken, be a good girl listen! Mammy won't ever be far away, no harm will come to you, I won't let it! Now be easy, there's my grand girl.

I waited fer her to appear, te talk again, but nothin happened, yet somethin had changed, the air felt empty like she was gone. It was as if I had been somewhere else, not here, not in the dark lane wit the cold an the wind an the empty air. I stood very still, tryin te work out was it good or bad. Mammy was gone an I was here in the dark. But I was right, she's not gone far away, she just talked to me.

6

'COME ON! I'LL help ye!'

I heard a whisper feelin a hand on me shoulder. I lifted me head givin a big sniff seein Sooty wasn't wantin te fight me any more. We stared at each other fer a few minutes sayin nothin, then he clamped his lips together like he just had a good idea.

'You stand against the wall an put yer hands out an I'll shinny up an see wha's happenin. How about tha?' he said happily, hoppin around again wantin te get movin.

'OK!' I said thinkin tha was a great idea, then I could get back in an see Ceily!

'Stand back against the wall an bend yer knees.'

I did.

'No, not like tha! Stand straight, ye're only kneelin!'

I stood up straight waitin.

'OK. Put out yer hands an bend yer knees.'

I did, then me arse sank an I ended on the ground.

'Ah you're an eegit, girls are no good fer nothin!' he roared, turnin his head an walkin away.

I stood meself back up wonderin wha I was doin wrong.

'This is the last time,' he snorted, marchin over an pushin me against the wall.

I put me hands out hopin he would get goin. I wanted te see

my Ceily. 'Will ye get me up when ye're over?' I said, just as he leapt his foot onta me hands then the other, holdin tight te me shoulders.

Me knees collapsed just as he leapt onta me shoulders, an the pair of us went down givin me a kick in the back a the neck, he went head first sailin straight fer the ground.

'Ye dirty stupid-lookin eegit!' he roared, still tumblin as I lay flat seein stars an me ears ringin. 'I'm goin home! I gor enough a you,' he keened, soundin like he was cryin as he shoved his hands down an lifted himself up, rubbin his head.

Suddenly we heard shouts an people runnin, we looked up the lane seein gangs a fellas laughin an pushin, lookin like they were makin a getaway, runnin from somethin. Then we heard an unmerciful long piercin sound, it nearly took the ears offa me head, it was comin from my house, an it sounded like a police whistle.

'Animal gang!' Sooty shouted, lookin up wit his neck stretched leanin over te see better wit him hangin on one foot. 'Them's terrible trouble, hide, Lily! They beat you up!'

Wit tha we heard bells ringin as an ambulance flew past the lane like it was millin its way fer my house.

Then all of hell came as the side door to my house started bangin, people got pushed against it an voices roared an more screamed as a terrible fight broke out.

'I'M KNIFED! Help me, someone!'

'Watch out fer the knuckledusters! DUCK!'

'Don't let them head caps near!'

'I'M CUT! Ah sweet Jesus! Razor blades hidden sewn inta the hats – they're hidden inside the peaks a the caps!'

'MURDER! PEOPLE ARE GETTIN KILT!' a woman's voice screamed wit it tearin out of her heart like someone was cuttin it.

Me own heart hammered in me chest an I felt meself shake

an suddenly goin icy-cold as I looked from the house wit tha happenin, then back up the lane seein some a the animal gang. They were now come to a stop an lookin down, wantin te know wha was goin on here. Then we heard more noise as a big black van flew past, it was tearin along screamin on two wheels wit policemen hangin outa the sides swingin off the runnin boards.

'THE BLACK MARIA! They're bringin mobs a police!' shouted Sooty, gettin all excited wit his head jerked in tha direction. 'They only let tha out when there's a riot! It's te get the coppers here all at the same time, then it gets te carry away all the rowdy fightin people. Wha they do is, pack all the baddies in tha an get them te the cop shop quick an handy in a hurry, tha's without havin te pick them up by the feet an drag them all the way there. Because ye see, they need tha when there's too many rowdies,' he said explainin, lookin satisfied wit tha idea, then noddin back at me.

I stared at him, not knowin any more wha te think or do. Wha way te run wit nowhere te hide. We were backed inta the lane wit no way out. I could see Sooty was frightened outa his life too, his voice was shakin like mad an he was shiverin, but he was still tryin te make everythin come all right, by talkin about the policemen comin te help us.

So I nodded too, wantin te be like him an stand me ground. So I stood starin not wantin anythin else in my mind an just wondered about tha. 'Then how do the police get back them-self, Sooty?'

'Walk! Like they always do, or they give them the big High Nellies fer long journeys,' he said, knowin everythin.

'Oh yeah, because they only have the one motor car,' I said, happy now because I worked tha one out.

Then we spun our heads seein somethin happenin at the door.

'Get back! Get outa the way!' a man's voice shouted, then the door was gettin open an people pushin before it was even wide enough.

I stared wit me mouth open then screamed as me body jerked te life. 'CEILY! CEILY! WHERE ARE YOU? COME AN GET ME!'

Sooty shoved me outa the way jammin me up against the wall as people tumbled out, they was pushin an shovin steppin on people tha was hurt an lyin on the ground covered in blood. Them tha could were runnin an staggerin te get out, wit all a them wantin te escape.

'BLUEBOTTLES! SCATTER!' a load a rowdy fellas I never saw before shouted, laughin as they squeezed makin their way out the back door not carin who they hurt or knocked.

'Stay still. Teddy boys wit the animal gang after them!' Sooty whispered, movin me back into a dark corner not wantin us te be seen.

They fell down then pushed themself onta their feet, standin on people who got knocked over, then took off laughin, chargin up the lane wavin bicycle chains an crowbars.

I stood hidin meself behind Sooty, I was shiverin wit fright watchin them animal gangs.

'Everyone says they're very dangerous because they fight wit chains an meat hooks an anythin tha comes te hand, nobody is safe around them, no one is!' Sooty muttered, starin after them wit his eyes narrowed not likin the look a them.

The screams got worse an people went mad gettin tangled an stepped on inside the door. Then we looked up seein faces an hands appear on the wall, then climb over an lep for the ground.

'Mammy!' I screamed as a fella started te jump over me head just as Sooty yanked me by the neck an landed me standin in the other corner, but not outa harm's way. More an more were jumpin now, an some were staggerin inta me.

I grabbed hold buryin me head in Sooty's back. 'Save me!' I screamed, startin te shake like mad an me teeth knock wit the fright.

'Go easy!' he keened, losin his balance an staggerin then hoppin back onta his foot.

I looked at him, watchin his eyes te see wha we should do. He was busy rockin backwards an forwards seein wha way te run.

'We're goin te be kilt, we're goin te be dead, stone dead,' I keened, singin it in a song.

'Where's me da? He'll save us,' Sooty moaned, just as men turned an fought their way back down the lane wit the police chargin them lashin out wit baton sticks, then gettin sent back as men came at them wavin hatchets an knockin them down.

I turned an buried me head in the corner hidin behind me hands, then knelt down an covered me ears wit me head buried in me lap. 'Mammy, come an get me, save me, Mammy! Don't be gone.' I rocked, implorin me mammy te come fer me.

'She's here! Save us, Mister Mullins!'

Without warnin I was yanked te me feet wit Sooty draggin me. 'Lookit! We're here!' he shouted, grabbin hold a Mister Mullins starin at us wit his eyes lookin mad an his head drippin wit blood, then he whipped it around te check wha's happenin on all sides a him.

'Jesus Christ heaven on earth protect us,' he moaned. 'You, Neddy! Quick, son,' he said, grabbin hold a Sooty an throwin him onta his shoulders. 'Here, you'll be safer behind that wall, bang on the back door, they can see ye coming from their window. Tell them to open this back door an whip this child in!' he said, pointin at me but not takin his eyes offa Sooty. 'Up ye get, bend yer knees an don't jump, slide down. Go on you can do it!' he said, landin Sooty on the wall watchin him whip his legs around then slide down the other side.

'Hurry!' he shouted, hearin Sooty give a painin moan sayin he stepped on a rusty tin can. Then he put his hand coverin the side a his mouth, shoutin, 'Ceily! Help Delia, she's gone under! For fuck sake! Jesus help us!' he said, wantin te move but then lookin down at me hangin on te his coat wrappin meself inside the end of it.

I peeped me head around wantin te find Ceily, but I can't see nothin, the crowd is too thick.

The fightin got worse, an now the police was beatin everyone back as more an more a them turned up te scatter the crowd. They came runnin from all directions meetin at the top a the lane, an some even flew in on their High Nellies. They leapt off an dropped them against back doors an some were left where they fell, then they were on their feet runnin, chargin wit their baton sticks raised blowin their whistles. Down the lane they came, lines an lines a them, now marchin shoulder te shoulder as they got closer, leavin no room te escape. Then the police drew their batons tearin right inta the crowd and brought them down crackin skulls an grabbin hold a necks tryin te round up anyone an everyone. People who were hurt, young fellas tha were childre, old women an bad men, they were all the same, they were all bein cornered an rounded up.

Bricks started flyin an milk bottles hit the wall an smashed te smithereens beside us. I went mad an disappeared inside the back a Mister Mullins' coat, I'm just not wantin te see any more wha's goin te happen te us.

'Bastards! Bastards the lot of ye's,' spat Mister Mullins, pullin me around te bury me beside him inside the heavy overcoat. Then Sooty's voice shouted from behind us.

'Are you there?' said Mister Mullins, rushin te lean his ear against the door.

'She won't open the door, Mister Mullins! Missus Finnegan says it's too dangerous!'

'Mister Mullins! Are ye there? This is me, Annie. Listen te me! Put Lily over the wall, we'll catch her!' Annie Finnegan, the grown-up daughter, shouted.

Wit tha I was whipped inta his arms an went swingin fer the wall. Me breath caught.

'Come on! Up you get,' he said, sendin me neck first an pushin me arse heavin me onta the wall, then peelin me hands offa it as he swung me legs around leavin me danglin wit him grippin hold a me hands.

I don't like heights! I looked down at the terrible long way I was goin te fall. I knew fer sure I was goin te be kilt stone dead. It's like a mountain! Me head went dizzy wit the fright. 'Ah oh!' I keened, me breath heaved up me belly an came out in a puff of shock. Then I let rip wit a piercin scream. 'Nooooo!' Then me breath caught again an I choked. I could see stars, me head was flyin wit them, everythin was goin round an around an I never felt meself spinnin so fast wit the fright on me. They're gettin me kilt! Then I felt a hand pullin on me foot an the other one gripped tight te the leg of me boot an I was dragged down.

'Let her go, Mister Mullins! I have her!' shouted Annie Finnegan.

I let meself go dead waitin te see how much pain ye got just before you were kilt stone dead. Then I was bein turned an grabbed inta the hands a Missus Finnegan an mashed against her big chest, the softness was lovely, an the smell of onions off her made me think I was home.

I must have dozed, because when I opened me eyes Missus Finnegan looked down an rocked me inta her arms, sayin, 'Shush, go back to sleep, ye're all right now, child.'

Me eyes stayed open seein Annie restin herself on the kitchen windasill lookin out watchin the back wall. The room was dark an nobody was talkin, I could see her big childre Tommy an the rest a them, they were all sittin around the fire watchin the red-hot cinders an listenin te the shoutin an fightin an the murderin screams goin on. It sounded like it was all happenin beside the winda, but I knew it was all goin on outside in the laneway, an my Ceily was out there somewhere caught wit all them fightin, an so was our mammy's house. But I wasn't shiverin no more, an I was too tired te even let the fright worry me, tha was sittin somewhere in a place I wouldn't feel it. I was content now te sit on Missus Finnegan's lap, I can be safe an warm here an just wait fer it te be over. But she's not me mammy, so I can't cry or ask her any questions, an definitely not be bold, because I don't belong te her.

Then a thought hit me, I know wha I'll do! I can snap the head offa God, it's all his fault anyway. *God, if ye're listenin, you took me mammy away, so ye can't take me Ceily too. I want her te come back all in the one piece. So don't let anythin happen te her, God, or I really am goin te hate you, an ye can send me down te the devil to roast in hell, because I won't care.*

Yeah, I thought, suckin away like mad noddin me head. God loves us, so he's not allowed te do tha. I won't let him. Tha was very mean a him, no wonder I'm not talkin te him! Then I lifted me eyes offa the floor an looked at me thumb. Ah no! I'm gone back te tha again, I stopped doin tha when Mammy put vinegar on it, she said I wasn't a babby any more, I was five then an the other kids will be laughin at me. I stared at it lookin back at me, it was all white an shiny, then I stuck it back inta me mouth. Don't care, I want it, let them laugh at me, I'll just give them a box in the snot, tha's wha Ceily says.

7

ME EYES SHOT open an me head turned slowly around the strange room. Where's this? I could see a big brown wardrobe sittin over in the corner, it had a huge long mirror down the middle. Tha's not ours! Me eyes moved takin in the vanity dresser wit the stool in front an the drawers down the side. Then I looked over to a winda seein the heavy drops a rain pourin down. I could hear the clip-clop of a horse makin its way slowly, goin somewhere out on a road. Then further away the buzzin sound a traffic an people all goin about their business, an now a dog just barked somewhere close. He's probably roarin at the horse. Then I felt the soft warm mattress under me an gave a little bounce, feelin the springs. Ah, this is great.

I shifted meself more, feelin the springs bounce me up an down. Yeah, I really do like this bed, it's full a comfort, wonder where I am? There's no one here but meself, I thought, lookin at the white heavy door shut tight. Mammy always left her door open a bit, tha was so we could talk te each other, an she could hear wha was goin on.

Then me eyes lit on the chair beside the bed, them's my clothes! I looked at me frock an cardigan sittin there an me blue coat hangin on the back. The black rubber wellie was lyin underneath, an I looked te see was the other one here. No, it's on its own. Wonder where the other one got to? Suddenly a terrible thought hit me! Where's me dolly? Where did Molly get to? She always comes te bed wit me, then lies there waitin when I go off te school.

Then it all came back te me. The mad fightin people, everyone wantin te tear our house down, an Mammy's gone!

She's not back yet, I thought, lookin around the room again, hearin an seein nothin an no one. Now Ceily's gone missin too!

I leapt outa the bed wit the fright an yanked open the door seein another one beside this, then stairs in front an two more doors up on another landin.

'CEILY!' I screamed, slappin down the stairs an whippin open a door.

Two faces looked up at me sittin around a table.

'Ahhh! There ye are, love, ye're awake,' Ceily said, soundin like Mammy an lookin at me, seein me gettin a shock.

'And the dead appeared an arose to many!' said Mister Mullins, starin at me an smilin. He had a big white bandage wrapped around his head, an his mouth was all cut an swollen. It looked kinda crooked, twisted or somethin. I looked back at Ceily. Her face was snow-white an she had a big massive black an blue eye, an her eyebrow was all cut an swollen. She had a big lump of white cotton wool wit a plaster coverin it, but ye could still see the huge swellin underneath.

'Come te me,' she said, seein me standin tryin te take in wha's happenin.

I flew at her an climbed onta her lap, nearly knockin her offa the chair.

'Oh Jesus, go easy, Lily! I've had enough batterin in one day te last me a lifetime,' she said, cuddlin me in one arm an restin her face in the other, lookin really worn out.

'Come on, feeding time!' Mister Mullins said, gettin up an

goin over an turnin on the gas cooker, then strikin a match te light it up.

'Are you all right? I looked in on ye earlier, but you were out fer the count,' Ceily whispered slowly, soundin too tired te do more.

I nodded, wrappin me arms around her neck.

'No, Lily, not yet, chicken. Me neck's a bit sore,' she said, pullin me hands away.

I leaned me head in te get a look, keepin me hands te meself. Now I could see all the black an blue marks, it looked all swelled up.

'Come an get this,' Mister Mullins said, puttin a bowl a steamin porridge down at the chair next te Ceily. 'Go on, love, eat tha, it will bring yer strength back, you must be starved wit the hunger. Jesus, when was the last time you got fed?'

'It seems like yesterday went on for eternity,' said Ceily, soundin very old just like Mammy did when things got too much.

'Take it easy, Ceily girl, one thing at a time, we will get our way through this don't you worry,' he said, noddin an shakin his head at her, speakin quietly but lookin like he meant it. 'Eat up your porridge, Lily, an leave me an Ceily to get on wit a few things,' he said, sittin himself back down an openin a school copybook.

Ceily sat up an moved in her chair lookin te give him her attention.

'Now, here's where we are,' he said, lookin down at his writin. 'For the next few days, or at least as long as it takes, you keep Lily an your own head down. No work, no school, stay right here without showing your nose out the door. Let everything die down an I'll do the rest. OK, here's the plan. As I see it, the authorities can make you a ward of the court because you have no protection. No living relatives, or ones anyway that's made themself known,' he said, lookin disgusted at the idea. 'So you'll come under our protection.

'I'm going to tell them powers that be, Flitters and the like, the NSPCC, I'm your relation. Your great-grandmother an my grandmother were distant cousins, that way, if we go that far back they won't be able to trace us. So who's te know the difference? To all intents and purposes, we are related. So that's the end of that. No more argument. Now, as your relative I can get the tenancy of your home put into my name. That way, the Corporation won't be able te step in and take the home away from you. Now, when you come of age I will sign the tenancy back into your name. And just in case – we better cover ourselves for all eventualities – I will get a will drawn up makin sure there is a record of that. Anything happens to me, Delia will hold it in trust for you, just as I'm doing now. To all intents and purposes, that house is rightfully yours an little Lily's.

'So today I will set up a meeting with these shower a gob-shites. And if there's any trouble out a them, by Jaysus they will rue the day they ever heard a Frank Ronald Mullins! I didn't survive the Black and Tans and then the civil war fighting for our freedom by being a softie!' he said, givin a snap of his head an clampin his teeth together, hissin out air.

'The next stop then will be to round up all the neighbours and get the house fixed up, whatever it takes, whatever has to be done, will be done. Don't you worry about that, Ceily! You'll have your home back shipshape lookin like a new pin. OK, love? Never fear. We will put everything to rights.'

She nodded her head tryin te give a smile, but it slid off her face lookin like it pained her.

He stared at her lookin pained himself an annoyed she had that. Then he looked down at the red flowery tablecloth not seein it because he was busy thinkin. Then he said, lookin like he was talkin te himself, 'Whatever happened yesterday will never happen again. The British were arrogant bastards who ran this country for eight hundred years, but, give it to them, they had order. My own people, the Irish yesterday, they behaved like something inhuman. Wild an tribal, overrunning everything that makes us civilized, makes us separate from jungle savages. Scratch the surface of human beings and this is what you get, barbarians!' he said, turnin around te lash the fire sendin a flyin spit shockin it inta givin a big hiss, then turnin te look back at the room, lookin like he had tasted somethin rotten.

I looked down at me bowl seein it was empty, tha was lovely, but I'm only gettin started. Me belly is still hangin empty, it's missin all the food I didn't get since . . . ? Well not yesterday anyway, because I only got me breakfast then, an me sambidge an milk at school dinner time. I'm starved wit the hunger, I thought, lookin up an down the table te see wha's left.

Me eyes lit on the pot a jam an fresh loaf a bread an butter sittin wrapped up in waxed paper. We don't get jam. I love tha, but Mammy said it was too dear. I took in a deep breath wantin them te notice me, but not too much, just enough te keep feedin me, then forget an keep talkin, because nobody ever lets childre hear wha they're sayin. We're too young te understand an it's not our business, they roar, shovin us out the door.

I looked from one te the other, seein them starin at nothin. Mister Mullins was takin big sighs an Ceily was yawnin, then back te the starin.

No, I'm goin te starve, they're takin no notice a me, this is very bad altogether. I lifted me chest an gave a big cough, lettin me eyes stare at the jam.

'Finished! Did you enjoy that? Be God all you were short a doing was eating the bowl,' he laughed, lookin at how shiny I left it. 'I don't suppose you'd be wanting any bread an jam,' he said, shakin his head at me.

I was ready noddin me head then shook it, gettin confused. *OF COURSE I WANT THE BREAD AN JAM!* I roared in me head, lettin me face drop wit me heart scalded at the loss of it.

'Look at the face on it, mustard an mortal sin,' he laughed, reachin over te cut a huge chunk of fresh loaf, it sank then bounced up wit the freshness, an I could hear the crust groanin under the big knife as he sawed through it. Me mouth watered watchin him lather on the goldie-colour butter then lift the lid an heap on a big gollop a raspberry jam.

'Here ye go! Get that down you, we all need a bit of cheering up,' he said. 'Maybe tonight we'll have a big plate of fish an chips when we close up shop,' he said, rubbin his hands an smilin at Ceily, lookin very happy wit himself a tha great idea.

I was on me third chunk a bread an jam an I didn't want te lose time eatin it, so I stopped me chewin leavin half stickin outa me mouth, then pointed fer more.

'No! You've had enough!' Ceily suddenly exploded, takin the finger offa me wit the slap she gave me. 'You'll eat poor Mister Mullins outa house an home if ye keep tha up! Come on, Lily. Tha's not hunger, tha's just sheer greed,' she snorted, givin me a dirty look.

'Ah, leave her be. Childre will be childre,' he said, heavin himself up an openin an shuttin the door behind him leavin me wit Ceily in one a her ragings.

'Lily! Get some sense!' she said, roarin down at me in a whisper, breathin her snorts all over me. 'You have te be good fer me from now on, an don't be makin us out te be trouble. If we get too much fer these people they will get fed up wit us an leave us te the mercy of the world an his wife. Now you saw wha happened yesterday, people are only out fer wha they can get.

They don't care about you an me, they have their own troubles, an God helps them tha help themself. Tha's wha they were doin on the back of my dead mother. She was gone now, an we were easy prey te move in an take our home an house from under us, Lily! Mammy always warned us about tha! She would say, "Fight yer corner! People are without mercy when it comes to a struggle fightin for them an theirs."

'So don't you ever forget tha again, Lily! People will eat you alive if ye don't stand yer own ground. Now, the Mullinses is one in a million. Mister Mullins is a very good man, he looks out fer the poor, but he's nobody's fool. Very few would cross him, because there's very few tha could be his match. He's a very treacherous enemy, tha's why people stay on the right side a him, an because they respect the man he is. I know you understand nothin a wha I'm sayin now, but I want you te learn one thing. Whatever I say you listen, because I have put on years in these last ten days, especially wit this last twenty-four hours. I know now where we stand wit the world, an I'm goin te make it me business never te be at the mercy of it again.'

She was sayin it right. I didn't understand wha it was all about, but I knew somethin had changed in her, she sounded more like Mammy now than the old Ceily. She used te be more like me, well a little bit, because she knew an awful lot more. Now suddenly me sister is gone, she talks an sounds like an aul one. I wonder if tha's good or bad.

'Where's Delia?' I suddenly said, thinkin I knew there was somethin missin.

'Hospital,' Ceily said not botherin te look at me.

'Why?! Wha's wrong? Is she dead too, Ceily?' I whispered, seein now the red blood on the collar a her blouse, I didn't notice tha till now. Even her green-wool jumper is torn, there's a big hole in the neck an all the wool is left hangin. 'An wha happened te yer eye? It's all swollen an black an blue!'

'Ah, don't worry about it. Tha will go in time,' she said, givin a quick rub te the plaster over her eye.

'An wha happened te tha? Why's ye gor a plaster on it?'

'I had te get a few stitches,' she said, takin her hands away an leavin it alone.

'Did someone hit you?'

'Don't ask any more questions, Lily. Let's just take it easy, we're lucky te have got out alive,' she said, starin at me then puttin out her arms fer me te come.

I snuggled inta her lap an stared up at the cut. Her eyebrow was twice the size of the other one, an her eyeball was all bloody an she had a big lump under it.

'Ceily, ye look terrible,' I said, wantin te beat the snot outa them tha harmed me sister.

'Thanks, Lily, you do wonders fer me, but ye're no oil paintin yerself. Look a you sittin here in yer knickers an vest, the face is manky dirty an the hair looks mad like a wild thing, an that's not te mention the dirty black knees! Jaysus you need a bath, but we're far from tha, just gettin through these next few days is goin te take everythin we can throw at it.

'Which reminds me, where's your wellington boot? You only had one when Annie Finnegan helped te carry you here in the early hours a this mornin.'

'Don't know,' I said, leavin me thumb hangin outa me mouth while I thought about this. 'Must a got robbed by the robbers!' I said, not knowin any other reason. 'I asked ye, Ceily, why's Delia not back here?'

'Because she's in the hospital I just told you!' Ceily snapped, grabbin hold a her hair.

I climbed offa her lap makin me way back te me own chair an went very quiet. I stared down at the table not knowin where else te look, because all the bad things tha happened was comin back inta me head again. Ceily looks heartsick, she's not herself an everythin is gone wrong very bad since Mammy died.

No, maybe she will come back, it could be just a mistake. Then everythin will go back to the way it used te be. Ceily will be laughin an then sometimes shoutin because I robbed some a her stuff. Well she says tha, but I only do be tryin on her things when she's not there te see me. Then Mammy will shout at her then shout at me, then we will sit down an have our tea an talk all the day's happenins over by the fire. Except I don't get te hear about the good bits, Mammy puts me out an up te bed.

Yeah, I thought, liftin me eye te look over at her. She was cryin, her head was shakin in her hands an her shoulders were heavin up an down. Wha will I do? She doesn't want me te hear her. She's tryin te hide it. I looked over at the fire burnin down te nothin now, makin the kitchen go very cold, everythin seems very cold, like me world all around me is a very cold place. It's sorta dark here now, like everythin tha makes you laugh an feel happy is gone off somewhere, robbin the light an takin the heat. But when Mister Mullins was here it felt like everythin was goin te be all right again. But it's not. Ceily is sickenin an her heart is scalded, because we've gone an lost too much.

8

SUDDENLY THE DOOR opened an Mister Mullins appeared back.

'Here we are, take this an have that,' he said, comin te lift me up swingin me across the room, then land me sittin in the fireside chair. 'Now, let that keep your eyes peeled an your jaws busy,' he said, puttin a comic inta me lap then sayin, 'Open!' An shoved a gobstopper inta me mouth.

He stood starin, watchin me startin te suck an wrigglin meself fer ease, then fixin the comic on me lap, now feelin I was in the height of comfort.

'That's you satisfied,' he said noddin down at me, then turned his head lookin at the fire, sayin, 'Next, let's get this fire roaring back into life.' He smiled givin a look over te Ceily.

She lifted her head givin a quick smile, pretendin te laugh. But then she wiped her eyes fast wit the sleeve of her jumper an you could see she was ready te cry again, because her face lifted up like it wanted te break.

He lifted the coal bucket sittin by the fire an grabbed the shovel, but just then the shop bell went as the door pushed in. He hesitated then dropped the shovel an rushed out, sayin, 'Ceily, would you ever bank up that fire while I see to this.'

She didn't answer, an I looked over seein she had dropped her head in her arms restin them on the table. I stared seein her not stir, she's fast asleep.

I looked at the coal bucket then hopped up. I'll do this, Mammy never lets me near the fire, but I can do it here. I dropped down on me hunkers an grabbed up the shovel, then tried te lift the coal. It's too heavy. I dropped it an grabbed up lumps a coal wit me hand an started te decorate the fire. One bit here, another bit there. I kept goin till the bucket was empty.

The fire was now out black but it went nearly up te the chimney. Tha's tha, we'll have a lovely big fire when tha gets goin. Then I looked back in the bucket again, seein there was tons a black dust. I just had an idea, Mammy always uses tha te bank up the fire. She says it makes the coal burn slower, tha way we spare the coal. I know these things because I do watch her.

I lifted the bucket but it was too heavy, an I couldn't get it on the shovel. I know wha I'll do, I'll shake it on by throwin it at the fire. I stood back an aimed it, then gave the bucket an almighty swing seein black dust swarm an fly lookin like black smoke.

'Aw, fuck,' I muttered, goin dead still watchin it flyin inta the air smotherin everythin black. I looked down seein me white vest was now the colour a black, even me arms was covered an so was me legs. I stared down seein me feet now goin from white te black wit dust droppin. I'm twins wit Sooty! Wish he was here, he'd know wha te do.

'Ceily!' I muttered, lettin it come out in a little quiet squeak. She didn't hear me, I turned me head slowly seein she hadn't made a shift. I couldn't move, not knowin wha te do next. They're goin te kill me! Just then the door whipped open an I heard a roar.

'What in all that's good an holy have you gone and done?

What have you been up to?' Mister Mullins said, lowerin his voice now goin inta real shock.

I blinked because the dust was swimmin in me eyes. 'Eh . . . The dust . . . it blew outa the bucket!' I said slowly, lookin down starin at the bucket still swingin in me arms.

He couldn't move neither, he just stared watchin it still makin its way up te the ceilin an slowly across the room settlin anywhere an on anythin it could land.

'Put that bucket down an don't touch anything,' he said, grabbin it outa me black hands then haulin me up, sayin, 'Have you seen the state of yerself? Get a look there.' He held me under the arm wit one hand makin me dangle sideways, then wiped his hand across the mirror shiftin dust, then pushed me in fer a good look.

I stared at two white rings around me eyes sittin in a pot-black face, an sucked in me breath wit the shock.

'Ye're a bold girl!' he said, after seein I gor a good look, then rushed me inta the scullery an dumped me down on the drainin board, next te the wash trough.

'CEILY, look after Lily, she's been up to no good!' I heard him shout, while I sat danglin me feet over the big trough. I didn't want te get them wet, because the water was all cold.

Ceily came staggerin in wit the hair thrown over her face not knowin where she was. I took loads of air up me nose holdin it, waitin fer her te wake up.

'WHA DID YE DO? WHA DID YOU JUST GO AN DO NOW? An after everythin I just told you!' she screamed, whippin the mass a bangles outa her face an makin a run at me.

'IT WASN'T MY FAULT, HONEST, CEILY! IT WAS THE BUCKET! IT FLEW OUTA ME HAND.'

'Don't kill her! We'll just starve her, no more sweets for the next year!' Mister Mullins said, rushin over te put his head in the scullery.

'You have no boots now, no vest, an yer knickers will never dry in this weather!' she said, lookin down at me navy-blue knickers now sittin past me knees. They're very heavy, an Mammy only changes them once a week, because they need tha te dry properly.

'You'll have te go round in yer skin!' she roared, whippin the vest over me head sendin dust flyin te land on her. 'You can't keep yer hands to yerself,' she muttered, lettin the cold tap run an grabbin the dishcloth.

Me nerves was gone watchin her scrubbin the big bar a Sunlight soap inta the cloth, then it came fer me! Smack inta me face smotherin me, then it went fer me neck an ears, smackin its way down me chest an inta me belly.

I screamed wit the bubbles blowin outa me nose an freezin me skin.

'Stay still!' she roared, batterin me wit the cloth when I upped an reared, tryin te get loose.

'Easy, easy!' Mister Mullins shouted, rushin in te see wha's happenin.

'I'm tryin te wash this scruffy maggot,' she said, lettin her grip go a me.

I leapt inta the sink then cocked me leg over, tryin te slide down an escape.

'I'll leave you to it, but don't go too far an kill her, all we need now is to be up for murder!' he snorted, turnin away leavin me at the mercy a Ceily.

'You cursed little demon!' she screamed, grabbin hold a me be the leg an yankin me under the arm, landin me back on the drainin board an bangin the arse offa me. She scrubbed, rubbin the skin offa me an I screamed, beggin fer mercy. The water was blindin me eyes an the soap was blockin me nose, I'm goin te die! She's suffomacatin me! Then it was over an I sat drippin while she muttered lookin around fer a towel.

'I won't never te be doin this again, Ceily,' I gasped, makin me neck an chest jump up an down wit the hiccups.

'Bet yer sweet little life on tha,' Ceily muttered, smellin Mister Mullins' towel then decidin it would do me.

I was sittin back now in the fireside chair wearin me frock an a big pair a pink thermal knickers belongin te Delia, they didn't fit me, because they went all the way down te me ankles an back up again. But Ceily says I'm te wear them because I'll catch cold an these'll keep me warm. There was nothin te put on me feet because the boot's lost an there's a big hole come in me white sock, so now, as well as tha, I'm havin te wear Mister Mullins' big woolly socks te keep me feet warm. They're miles too big, an they're stickin out like two long poles, so I can't walk now, because I keep havin te pull up the knickers an lift me feet inta the air.

Mister Mullins is delighted, he said tha'll put a stop te me gallop fer a while, then he ran laughin holdin his hand over his mouth. I'm a holy show, an Ceily doesn't care.

She's out in the scullery washin me knickers an vest mutterin te herself. She's ragin wit me, specially since seein the mucky dirt dried inta the back a me coat. I thought she was goin te kill me!

'I'm goin te brain you!' she screamed, but I ran fer me life holdin up the knickers wit the socks flappin, tryin te make it down the stairs.

Mister Mullins had te save me. But then he complained he hasn't had the like a this carry-on since Delia tried te blow up the house he snorted, givin me an annoyed look. Then he said, 'She was only a young one at the time and that's not today nor yesterday! Now don't be wearing me out. I'm not getting any younger,' he warned, wavin the finger at me. I followed the finger not worried because he doesn't mean it, then looked up at him.

'Wha she do?' I asked, feelin shocked Delia was even more bold than they say I am meself.

'Don't ask,' he muttered, shakin his head wit the memory. 'She came down here early one morning and tried to make the porridge,' he said. 'By the time the match did catch the gas left runnin, well, we knew no more until we heard the blast an the roars coming up through the ceiling. She lost the hair on the head for a while, but lucky she didn't lose the face. Jaysus spare me,' he moaned, still shakin the head as he dumped me down on the chair. Then he went out laughin behind his hand.

Now I've nothin te do an I can't even go out te play. I sighed in me breath lookin down at the fire. It was still out cold just puffin out black smoke. The room is freezin, pity tha, because we could a had great comfort. Me comic! I have tha, I suddenly remembered, pity about the gobstopper, tha would a gone lovely wit the comic then I'd be in the height a ease, but Ceily grabbed hold a tha an flung it out the winda.

'You're gettin nothin!' she roared, tearin it outa me mouth.

If Mammy was here, she'd kill her!

I pulled the comic from under me an sat back fer comfort, then felt the huge knot in the back a me knickers. I leapt up pullin the frock te get at them, but the knot Ceily put in the waist te keep them up was too tight te open. I pulled them down an sat them on me lap tryin te open the knot wit me teeth.

'Wha are you up to in there, Lily Carney? I don't like the sound a you, ye're gone very quiet!'

Me head whipped up an I flung the knickers away hidin them. 'Nothin!' I said, whippin me head back te see them sittin on the coal fire. Owww! She'll kill me!

I leapt up grabbin hold a them, seein they were now manky black. 'Oh Mammy! When she sees these I'm meat te mince! Get them back on fast!'

I was too fast an bent down goin head over heels hittin the floor, gettin me foot caught in the leg a the knickers. Me heart pounded an the thump on me head made it spin. I couldn't see them I was tha blind.

'Mammy!' I squealed, tryin te untangle meself. I got back up on me feet feelin me face hot an me head swim, it's all the shock I'm gettin.

'I'm ready,' I puffed, fixin the knickers on meself then sat back an closed me eyes lettin meself rest without botherin about the knot pokin the back a me.

I'm gettin worn down, I thought, holdin me hand over me head like Mammy does when she gets a shock. I'm gettin old before me time! Too many shocks can't be tha good fer ye. Ceily's right, I am cursed. But then so is she!

9

'I BETTER HEAD OFF,' Mister Mullins said, standin himself up an lookin over at the mantel clock. 'They'll be openin the doors soon to let in the visitors. Let's hope there's good news,' he said, lookin down worried.

'Yeah,' Ceily said, standin up an collectin the dinner plates. 'Tell her I was askin fer her, won't you, Mister Mullins? Pity I can't come up an see her meself.'

'No, best you stay put, Ceily. The less you show your face the better, we need to let things die down. Right, now on the way back I'll call into that Father Flitters and get the ball rolling, the sooner we get this sorted the quicker you'll get back to normal,' he said, movin te take his hat an coat hangin on the back a the door.

'I better shut up shop for a couple of hours, more's the pity,' he said, lookin like he was thinkin. 'But you don't know who's going to walk through that door, they have the authorities behind them, Ceily, an God nor man won't stop them this time. They'll be out to really get you now. Ye see you beat them yesterday and they don't like that, it got their backs up. Further, it gave bad bastards like the animal gangs an excuse to hit back at them. That lot will brag they were only trying to protect their own against heavy-handed authorities, stop them coming in where they're not wanted. Protect? Me arse!

Wasteless moochers some of them, wouldn't work in a good fit, looking to rise trouble more like, then they ended bringing the roof down on our heads.

'Now as it is them powers-that-be will want to come down on you, hard and fast, show you can't step out of line an buck the system. They'll be out in full strength to hammer you down, put people back in their place an keep them there. I know how it works, Ceily, no, it's not about you two any more,' he said, shakin his head lookin very worried gettin down in himself. 'You are only a pawn in a power game now, and by Jesus, everyone in this has their own axe to grind.

'So watch out, they'll be prepared this time,' he said, givin the head a shake an clampin his mouth shut. 'God knows, we can't have a repeat of more madness, it wouldn't take much to start people off again. Them animal gangs get their enjoyment fighting each other, there must a been a quare few of them swarmed up here last night when they got the first sniff of trouble. Liberty gangs, come to take on the ones here. Jesus, the word spread so fast they were like flies landing on hot shit! Then the others. God almighty, the sight of that greed yesterday, all wanting to plunder a dead mother's grave and she not yet even cold in it. Oh! And to hell with her helpless childre. Swines, if they can't take what you have, then they'll make sure you can't have it either. For some, that's what yesterday was all about,' he said, droppin his voice an shakin his head thinkin about it.

'Oh this is a whore of a city, rotten with savage slums,' he slowly growled, lookin like he was talkin te himself. 'The stinking hovel tenements, they're a cankerous sore left to fester in a cesspool of weeping pus. The city back streets, a no-man's-land to dump and bury alive the unfortunate poverty-stricken people, oh yes, so thick are they tightly packed, the sun won't get in and a fresh breeze couldn't squeeze between them. Worse, it's all hidden under the skirts of a beauty, a grand and Georgian Dublin, that's where only the respectable walk,' he smiled, snappin his hand in salute but not lookin happy.

'Jaysus they'll even eat their young!' he muttered, wrappin his arms an turnin himself te drop against the wall wit the head bent an the ankles crossed. 'And that is what I fought for? Bring back the fucking English!' Then he turned an spat inta the fire again, only this time it sat shiny an wet, there was no hot coal te make it bubble an burn. Then he turned te look look hard at Ceily, wantin her te know somethin.

'Yes,' he said, givin his head a quick shake. 'Let me tell you what they were after. With up to twenty people living in a room no bigger than a toilet for some, your place was a palace, a walk through the gates of heaven for them that can get their hands on it. What more could ye want? An artisan little house, corporation owned and comes with its own life tenancy. A cheap rent tied in and no more rack-renting private landlords. Them that suck the very marrow from the bones of the poor, and all for the privilege of letting you perish to death in a vermin-infested, disease-ridden hellhole. You're up against it, childre, turn your back against no one, Ceily. When you're down and out, it's a dog-eat-dog world.

'But listen!' he suddenly warned, grindin his teeth. 'It will happen that some brave soul will harm a hair on the head of you two young innocent childre, but that will only be when the last breath leaves my body! Do you know why?'

I looked te Ceily, wonderin wha's goin te happen te us now. Wha has got him in a state so sudden? An seein her starin up wit the mouth hangin an the eyes bulgin, an she slowly shakin her head. I turned me head back an looked up doin the same, shakin me head slowly, hopin he wouldn't turn his sudden torment on me or Ceily!

'In a word, simple! I owe a deep debt of gratitude to your great-grandmother. But first let me tell you about her daughter, your grandmother, Ellen Foley! She was my first girl-friend, we were walking out for years, years we were! Right from the first day our mammies walked us down together and we started school,' he laughed. 'Four year old we were!' Then he shook his head lookin away from us, goin very quiet. We said nothin an just stared up at him waitin, watchin, while he stared inta the distance thinkin. He was now lookin very sad.

'Our mammies thought we would get married,' he smiled, shiftin his eyes te look down at us. They look like he wanted te cry, cos they were gone all huge an watery.

'But fate had other ideas. I married at seventeen young Marie Beauchamp. Jesus, she was a beauty! Sky-blue eyes that lit up a room and warmed the cockles a yer heart when she gave you a smile! No more than my other little beauty, Ellen Foley! Her with the velvet blue eyes and the brown burnished coppery bangles that caught the light from a candle and lit up her head like she was wearing a halo! That making her into a saint or better still, a pagan goddess! I was a spoilt young fella for choice! The long and the short of it was she married Georgie Powers so I never got to marry the pagan goddess! But poor Ellen was unfortunate. Georgie Powers, with no work to be had in Dublin he signed up for the merchant navy and took off to sail the world. That was the last anyone ever heard tell a him again.

'A few months later, Ellen was left with a new babby. She now had no man, no money and no way to survive. She handed the babby over to her mother, that was your great-grandmother, and that babby was your very own mother Mary, who grew up and married your father Jembo Carney. Then Ellen took off for unknown parts. It was believed she ended her days in America. But nobody knows, that was just hearsay. It was said old Ma

Kelly received a letter from her, but who knows? From that day to this, no one ever heard tell or set eye on her again. As I said, who knows if she's even dead or alive?

'Meanwhile, I had married and me and Marie were blessed with a new little babby born the same time as your mother Mary. That was my little Delia! So they grew up together, your mother and my Delia! My Marie practically reared your mother, she spent more time around in this house than she did in her own home. It was so much so, one day your great-grandmother complained a strange young one calling herself Mary Carney turned up at her door demanding to be let in saying they were related! Then it all turned on its head. Ye know, childre, you never know the hour or the day when shocking bad luck and misfortune is going to turn around and strike you down,' he said, lowerin his voice an leanin down whisperin te us. 'It happened te me an I wasn't even here!

'I had gone inta hiding from the Black and Tans. Nineteen twenty it was, the Black and Tans were all over this place looking for the rebels that blew up them an their barracks. We used to drop grenades from the top of buildings and outa windas, catching them as they flew past in their open lorries! Bejaysus! They didn't do that for long!

'Anyway, I was now a wanted man, I had a price on me head and there were plenty of takers. Informers were shot, but it didn't stop people. If poverty didn't get you first, people would risk their neck for a penny ha'penny! Never mind the hundred quid to be paid for the capture of my skin! My Marie was a fierce and protective woman. She would slit your throat as quick as look at you if you dared threaten, or put in fear them that she kept wrapped around and close to her heart. For all else, she was gentle as a lamb. Every night this house was raided, every morning Marie would wake up early and start the day putting back the home to rights, trying to salvage what she could out of the broken furniture and smashed dishes. Then the whole thing would start again that night when the Black and Tans would smash down the door and tear into the house ransacking and destroying, turning to smithereens everything they laid hand on.

'One night they went too far. A young brute of a fella grabbed hold of my Delia crying in the bed after being shocked outa her sleep. The poor child didn't know where she was. The next thing she knew, she was flying through the air an knocked senseless against a heavy wardrobe leaving her lying half dead. Marie picked up the poker from the fire grate in the bedroom and downed your man, knocking him inta the next week. The last thing she ever knew . . . was when another cowardly bastard pointed a gun and shot her stone cold dead. In the back a the head she got it! That was it! From that night on, Delia Mullins was moved in with the Foleys. Emmeline Foley your great-grandmother reared her and your mother, Mary, together. And the sad coincidence is, Delia was only the same age you are now, Lily! Seven year old! So! Life has a terrible way of repeating itself. Delia is now going to step into Mary's shoes and take over.'

'She is? Wha, become our mammy?' whispered Ceily, lookin like she can hardly get a breath wit the shock at hearin all this.

'Yes, she's going to move into your house and look after youse! So, as I said, there's no need for you two te be worrying yerselves unnecessarily. We can't bring your mother back, but by God! We can do everything else in our power to take good care of you, as if you were one of our own, but sure ye might as well be.'

Then he stared inta nothin an sighed in a deep breath, sayin, 'OK, I better move, but you can keep an ear out for the paper deliveries. They'll be dropped at the side door, when that happens, open it quickly and drag them in. Then you can sort them out and leave them on the counter, other than that, keep your head down.'

Ceily nodded watchin an listenin, takin in every word he was sayin. She looked serious an very worried like she was really afraid, but then tightened her jaw because you're not wanted te see it.

'Try not to worry yourself,' he said, seein her worry but he havin te get a move on. 'Bye, see ye later,' he said, lookin te Ceily an givin me a wave. Then he was gone.

I watched the empty space, hearin the door shut wit a bang, makin an awful breeze. Wit tha, the sudden draught blew a puff of black smoke straight inta the room leavin soot, then up me nostrils it went an down me neck poisonin me. 'EH HUH,' I coughed, givin a big bark wit me tongue hangin out, tryin te get rid of it.

'CUT THA OUT!' Ceily roared, whippin her head around the scullery door te me, lookin the image of a lunatic. Her eyes was all red an black an her brown bangles was all matted standin around her head.

Gawd, she looks like one a them monsters ye see at the fillums! I hope she doesn't go mad an kill me! You never know, me mammy used te say all sorts a people was locked up, an not all a them mad neither. I moved outa harm's way, an sat meself over by the smoky fire an picked up me comic. But then thought better an put it back down again, not wantin te turn me back on Ceily. Tha one can be very vicious when she gets goin. Mammy used te say if she didn't control tha temper a hers, she could find herself locked up! I would a been safer wit Mister Mullins, pity he didn't take me wit him.

Yeah, I would a lovin tha, maybe even school would a been better than this, an I hate school I do. I hate tha aul Sister Mary Agony, because she hates me she does. Ever since she caught me eatin the apple in the chapel when we were waitin te go inta the confession box te practise fer our first Holy Communion. I got thrun out before I could even get near the box! I missed it all I did! The unfairness, I'm still ragin thinkin about it. The rest were all braggin about how they got te tell their sins te the priest an now they was all big! Because you can only do tha when ye're on your way te bein a big young one. I was ragin, an Mammy gave me another wallop when I got home an told her nothin had happened. 'I didn't get te do me confession, an tha's not all of it! No, Mammy, wait till ye hear!' I told her. The apple tha she gave me was robbed be the nun, an I only gor a few bites took of it!

I thought she'd be ragin. She was, but not wit the nun! 'I gor another wallop fer tha one!' I sniffed, thinkin back an gettin the memory of it.

10

I WOKE UP WIT an awful shock, wonderin wha was happenin, where was I? I looked around the strange room tryin te remember where this is. I knew it wasn't me own house, everythin was different, even the smell. The room was lovely an warm an the fire was roarin red, wit the red-hot coals an the flames lickin up the chimney. The lamp wasn't lit yet, so it was dark in all the corners, yet the room was come te life wit shadows dancin up an down the wallpaper all thrown out by the light from the fire.

Oh now I know where this is! Then I remembered it all. I'm wit Mister Mullins in his house, an Ceily is too! I must a fallen asleep, but it's dark out, I thought, lookin over te the winda wit the backyard, seein it pitch black. Where's everyone? Where's my Ceily?

I looked across, seein the chair on the other side of the fireplace empty. The table was bare since the dinner hour, so no one is gettin the tea ready. I'm starvin wit the hunger!

I got up an opened the door out te the shop, seein it was pitch black, it had only the street lamps shinin a bit of light inta the front a the shop winda. I stared, hopin somethin would happen, someone would appear. No, nothin, nobody here! Wha am I goin te do? Why have they left me all on me own?

I shut the door an rushed te open the other one leadin te

the hall an side door. I stared there too, lookin inta the pitch-black hall wit only a slice of light comin in through the skylight over the door. I could barely make out the stairs goin up te the bedrooms, but I'm not goin up there! The bogey man is sure te be there waitin te get his hands on me! Tha's wha everyone tells me, even Mammy! Because I'm always very bold, they say.

I shut the door fast, lookin te see if there was a key in the hole so I could lock him out. No! I'm at the mercy of all the monsters waitin out there in the dark, if they know I'm here on me own they're goin te come in an get me!

Then I heard somethin, a rattle in the hall. I sucked in me breath an held it listenin, the lock squeaked an the door pushed open. Me heart jumped wit delight! They're back!

I went te rush, then stopped, just in case it's not them. I stood starin, waitin fer the parlour door te open then watched as Mister Mullins came slowly in lookin like a very old man wit a bad stoop in his back. I stared, wit me mouth open seein him makin his way inta the room, then stagger over te hold onta the windasill an look out at the backyard. I looked around te see where Ceily was, but nobody came through the open door an it was now very quiet wit the hall door shut.

Wha's happenin? Why's he like this? He didn't take his hat or coat off an he now home in the house, an his skin was gone grey it was turned tha white, an the rest of it turned purple around his mouth.

I went out te look in the hall anyway, but it was still pitch-black an now still no sign a Ceily. Then it hit me. She's asleep up in the bed! I need a candle te go up there. There's no oil lamp lit.

'Ceily!' I whispered, hopin she'd hear me an the monsters wouldn't.

I moved further out te the dark hall an stopped. 'Ceily!' I shouted gettin a bit annoyed.

I listened, hearin nothin. I made me way back inta Mister

Mullins but he was still leanin on the sill an starin out at nothin, it was too dark te see anythin. Tut! Wha's wrong wit him? Where's tha Ceily one? I was nearly cryin now wit the rage comin on me!

Tha's it! I marched out an felt me way along the wall then up the stairs holdin onta the banisters not carin about no monsters.

'Ceily!' I shouted tryin te hurry meself. Still no answer! She's here, I know she is, I'm goin te ate the head offa her! The cheek a her takin her ease all this day long leavin me te look out fer meself. 'Mammy would kill her fer doin this!' I snorted, slappin me way to the bedroom ready te roar the head offa her.

I made fer the bed I'd slept in an looked an felt me way all round – no sign!

'Where are you, Ceily?' I keened, wantin te scream now wit the fright. She can't be gone. Tha's stupid. Maybe she's somewhere in another room.

I rushed out an hurried up the the rest a the stairs holdin onta the wall makin me way blind then opened a door on the landin an felt me way in. Light was comin from the street lamp at the front a the house an I could see the big bed was empty – no one here.

I looked around seein the brown wardrobe, the dressin table an the chair by the bed wit women's clothes folded on the back, the room smelled a mothballs an lavender, this must be Delia's room. No Ceily here. No Mammy. An I got no one te mind me. Should I be annoyed – ragin or cryin?

I thought about this, yeah, this is very annoyin. Wha's everybody up to? Ah, here's another door, she must be in there!

I rushed out an turned the doorknob hurryin in. Empty! This was a man's room. I could see the trousers, shirt an vest lyin on the chair beside the bed, an still no Ceily. This is Mister Mullins' room.

She's gone! Ceily left me! I turned an hurried back down the stairs hangin onta the banisters tryin not te plunge meself down onta the dark hall. I hurried back inta the sittin room seein Mister Mullins look around at me an stare, like he was tryin te work out wha I was doin here.

I stopped dead an stared back, afraid te open me mouth.

'Are ye all right, child?' he said, then forgot all about me an turned te stare at the fire beginnin te go low now wit the coal nearly all burned out.

I stayed without movin fer a long time, feelin me legs get pained, an it got darker an quieter but nothin happened an nobody moved. The clock ticked away the time hour after hour an still we stood. Finally I shifted, I moved over te the table an stood there hopin somethin would happen. Mister Mullins didn't move, he just kept starin an I knew it was now the middle a the night. I'm cold an tired now, I feel stiff, an the hunger is draggin me belly down. But I'm afraid te move an afraid te talk. Somethin very bad has happened an I know Ceily is not comin back. Tha's why I don't want te know, an I don't care about the cold an the hunger pain in me belly, because I don't want te eat no more.

11

I LEAPT UP GIVIN a scream. 'Help! Save me!' Then looked seein I was standin in the middle a the room. Wha happened? Me heart pounded, but nothin was goin on, it was quiet an everythin was still. I looked around tryin te get me senses. The light was comin through the yard winda an Mister Mullins was gone. I looked over te the armchair. I must a fallen asleep an slept in tha all night.

Suddenly a big noise hit the house an me heart crossed again then leapt, landin itself in me mouth. I dived under the table as the hall door smashed in against the wall, then I heard voices an loud gruntin. It's the robbers! Or might even be the policemen lookin te arrest me! Or worse then worser! It could be Father Flitters wit his cruelty people, it's like Mister Mullins said, he's come now te take his vengeance on me an Ceily, an tha's because we bested him! Or wha about the animal gang? Them's terrible killers! Everyone says no one's safe from them!

The shock took the legs from under me makin them shake like jelly, an I started te shiver all over. I held meself waitin te see who or wha was goin te come through the door, an I readied meself te run. I breathed down through me nose makin meself go still inside, then gave a quick look around te see where te run or hide. Me head flew thinkin, out the back door an down the lane, or stay here under this table? The cloth will hide me. I listened hearin the voices.

'Are ye right?'

'Yeah grand, now grab up your end.'

Tha's two men I nodded te meself, suckin on me thumb wit me ears open an me eyes starin. I was watchin the door, listenin. I'm wantin te be wide awake now, like I was told te do by Ceily.

'Wait! Let's see first where we go. Inta the parlour?'

'No! It would be more better if we get upstairs.'

'Wait! Where's himself? He's over there talkin te Birdie Brain.'

'Mister Mullins! Where do ye want this?'

'HERE, WAIT!' a woman shouted. 'Go back out an give us room, we'll sort out youse men.'

I stopped suckin an pulled me thumb out thinkin wit a sudden shock, it's them women again! They've come back te get us! They probably think we started the killins yesterday.

I breathed fast moanin out a long keen, 'Nooooo, don't let them get me!' Snots started teemin down me nose, gettin flushed wit me heavy breathin. I wiped them away wit the back a me hand, then saw it was all wet an sticky. I licked it fast te clean it, then went back te me keenin.

'Someone save me. Ohhhh I don't want te be kilt,' I moaned, makin it into a song wit me whole body rattlin an me head shakin up an down. 'Loads a peoples are at the door, we're not supposed te be lettin anyone see us. Mister Mullins said tha, he warned! Wha's happenin? Why they all here?'

I heard feet hammerin along the hall an suddenly the door pushed open. Me eyes shot te the pair a black boots then up te the long grey skirt, then came another pair a boots marchin in behind, wit the two wearin nearly matchin white aprons. An I could see the hem of a black shawl on the pair a them.

'Bring it in here! Come on!' they said, whippin open the door wide fer somebody.

'Where? This is heavy, missus!' a man moaned.

'Don't know, where do you think, Essie?'

'I don't know neither,' moaned Essie.

Then two pair a men's boots turned an staggered around the room at the same time, tryin te see where's best.

'Here, Banjo! Let's leave it down here easy while them women are makin their mind up.'

'We have te go, missus! Have youse decided yet?'

'No! Hold yer patience, you're too well fed, tha's wha's wrong wit you men today! There's nothin te be had outa ye's by way of heavy work!'

'Hang on, missus! Wha do ye think we are? Bleedin Samson?'

'None a tha disgustin talk here! An further, youse are gettin paid fer it, an good money at tha!'

'Wait! Grab the stuff offa tha table, Nellie. We'll put the Delft in the scullery.'

'No! Why don't we put tha in the scullery, then we can work in there?'

'But how are we goin—'

'Come on, Banjo, enough is enough, land it down there over in the corner.'

'Right you are, Mousey,' said Banjo, an landed a lovely shiny brown wooden box down wit brass handles, then they dived on their hunkers an started te work on it.

I pulled the cloth back but feet moved all around it, an now I could get te see nothin.

'Where are youse?' said Mister Mullins comin through the hall wit more people walkin behind.

'Here we are,' said the men wit the box.

I inched meself out pullin away the cloth an liftin me head from under the table.

'What are ye's doin? Take her upstairs!'

'Wha?' said Mousey lookin confused, holdin a screwdriver up to his head, scratchin it.

'Ah yeah,' said Nellie. 'Didn't I tell youse tha? Wouldn't listen te me, Mister Mullins. Wanted it all their own way!'

I stared, gettin the fright a me life seein the body in the box, it was a coffin!

'Get my Delia up offa this floor before one or ALL of youse will be needin a fuckin coffin!' shouted Mister Mullins. 'Her own room up them stairs is where she will be waked!'

'Too right fer ye, Mister Mullins! Isn't tha right, Nellie?'

'Yes! Proper order!' shouted Nellie. 'No respect an them gettin paid good money te bring her home from tha hospital! Didn't we just say tha, Essie?'

'We did, true fer ye!'

'Get outa me fuckin house the lot a ye's!' Mister Mullins suddenly shouted, grabbin his hat offa his head bunchin it up an flingin it across the room. Then he rushed around makin fists, an then came rushin back tearin at his hair.

'Shut the fuck up the lot a ye's an get outa me sight!' he roared, grabbin hold a the men an pushin them out the door.

I dived back under the table.

'Ah Jaysus, don't be like tha! Sure we meant no harm,' said Banjo.

'No! Not at all,' said Mousey, shakin his head an wavin his arms like he was surrenderin.

'Oh indeed not, sure God help us all an protect us in his holy name! NEVER! That's as sure as my name is Esther Bullcock.'

I crawled back out on me belly just enough te get me head out.

'No harm at all,' moaned Nellie, cryin wit the arms out, but only soundin it because no tears gushed out.

'Here! Let's get poor Delia waked, may God be good te her an may she now rest in peace,' another man said quietly, blessin himself an comin closer, bendin down, pointin the arm at Delia in her coffin. 'Wouldn't you agree wit me, Mister Mullins, when I say it's the right thing te be doin now, an that's wha poor Delia would want? After all, gettin yerself all worked up an upset is not goin te make anythin better!'

'Yeah, true fer ye,' whispered Nellie, tryin te give a smile an make the peace, lookin up at Mister Mullins.

Mister Mullins gave a little nod. 'I'm sorry, ma'am. Sorry to you too, missus. An all of you,' he said, givin a big bow te all the men.

They all nodded mutterin quietly. 'Indeed God bless you, sure we're terribly sorry for your trouble.'

'We'll take her up,' whispered Mousey.

'Do,' Nellie whispered back, all tryin te keep nice an easy wit gettin the sudden peace. 'We'll start boilin the water te lay her out. Have youse brought the habit?'

'We have indeed, missus. The Sodality of The Children Of Mary. She was in tha, you said, Mister Mullins?'

He nodded, lookin very white.

'Oh indeed she was,' said Essie, 'an many a long day tha was too. Years, she was in it. Did everythin fer them she did. No one's more entitled te wear tha habit than poor Delia, she will need tha when she gets te heaven an meets our blessed Lord an His Holy Mother.' Then she blessed herself.

Wit tha they all copied an blessed themself quickly then four men, one a little aul fella, jumped forward. Up te now he had been hidin outside the door, but every now an then he put his head in te see who was goin te get boxed, then whipped it back out again. He was like me, afraid a his life of all the fightin goin on.

They all bent down an lifted the coffin an started te back

away shufflin, headin towards me an me head. I ducked back under, watchin them step away an stagger out the door leavin the lid of the coffin behind.

The women rushed inta the kitchen, then turned and headed back out again, sayin, 'Best first we get Delia sorted, we'll get her outa the coffin an onta the bed. Then we'll get the water on te boil fer washin her, but first thing now, we get rid a the lot a these aul fellas. Then after tha we can sort the house. Maybe we should ask—'

'No! No more talkin, Essie! Bejaysus, if we don't get a move on, Delia Mullins will be startin te stink te high heaven! They will smell her before they see her! Let's go.'

I listened hearin the rumblin a voices an the ceilin shakin, yeah, it's all quiet down here, they're all up there now. I crawled out an stood on me feet gettin a look at Delia's coffin lid. Ah poor Delia's dead. It's like Mister Mullins said, she was me mammy's really ever bestest friend. They sat together in school an even made their first Holy Communion together. Ah poor Mister Mullins, he has nobody now, not even Snotty Delia, because tha's wha people called her. But they won't say tha now, because everyone says you can't never speak ill a the dead.

I'm hungry, it looks like nobody's goin te feed me. Wha will I do? Feed meself!

I looked over at the gas stove then wandered me eye lightin it on the press in the corner. Tha's where Ceily put the stuff when she cleaned up. Then me heart jerked an me happy thought went from me head. Is she dead too?

I turned an rushed out the door headin fer the hall an upstairs. Mister Mullins will know.

'Right you are, God bless ye,' said Banjo.

'Yeah, God bless you,' said Mousey, headin down the stairs bangin their big heavy boots makin the wood hop an the house shake.

I made it up the third step but changed me mind wit the whole gang of them comin teemin on top a me backin me down, makin me turn fast an rush fer me life. They didn't seem te be mindin me. They were too busy wit their necks in the air te look down an watch fer wha was in front a them!

'Fuckers!' I snorted, lovin the sound a tha, then hurryin te reach back te me hidey-out under the table. Tha probably was not a good idea after all, no, because Mister Mullins said we were te keep ourselves quiet an not draw attention. I wonder did Ceily make tha mistake when I was asleep? Or did the monsters take her?! Because she was callin me terrible names? Well maybe not at this time, but she does.

I'm not likin any a this, I'm goin te have te make me mind up good an proper because God knows everythin, he can see me mind! *So, are you listenin, God? Ye can stop makin me suffer now. I'm goin te be terribly really very good! So, is tha OK? Will ye bring everythin back te the way it was? Let me mammy come home an Ceily too of course! Just make everythin right again, an I'll make up me mind I'm goin te become a saint!*

I thought about tha, because I didn't want te make a fool of God if it turns out te be a pack a lies. *Yeah! Ah, yeah definitely, tha's fer definite I'm goin te become a saint an get meself canonized, just like 'The Little Flower, Saint Theresa of the Roses'. They even writ a song about her! So yeah, I'm goin te give up me sins!*

Now I'll have te wait until I'm dead before they can make me one. The nun at school told us all about it. She said ye can only become a saint when you've gone through terrible shockin sufferin. Well I'm grand there, because I've definitely suffered shockin! Now there was somethin else? Oh yeah, so when I get te heaven I have te do loads an heaps a miracles. Curin disease an the lame an cripples an all tha. Just like Saint Bernadette in Lourdes. Hundreds an loads a people all go there te pray te her to do them a miracle. So, tha's me sorted out. Now I can tell everyone when they ask me wha I'm goin te be. Workin te get meself canonized, I'll say, because I'm goin te be a saint! Gawd the nun at school is goin te love me! At the minute she hates me, but now she might even get the rest a them te pray fer me good intentions. I can't wait!

I stayed very quiet thinkin about tha, then gave a huge sigh of contentment. Yeah, the best marvellous idea I've had in all of me life!

I didn't hear their step until they were nearly in on top a me. I dived further under the table only wantin te be seen by Mister Mullins.

'I'll put on the water te boil, Essie, you strip an get Delia ready fer her wash.'

'Right, Nellie, oh but listen, we better get a hurry on ourselves, or the mourners will be in on top of us before we know where we are! An we still have te get this place ready. Here! Will we move this dresser, Nellie, an put tha table over be the winda? Make more room.'

'No! Leave well alone, we don't want aul Gunner Mullins down our throat again, you know how touchy he is at the minute. No! In here just cover all the mirrors, or turn them to face the wall, an black out all the windas in the house.'

'Oh yeah, he may have death-notice cards in the shop, you tell him we need tha te put up on the hall door, Nellie.'

'Who?! Me tell him? Not wit the state he's in! You ask him or let it go. Listen, we may end up yet gettin ourselves scuttered out tha door an poor Delia left lyin up there in her skin. Not te mention I need the few bob. Tha fuckin eegit of mine got hold an blew my last few shillins on a lame horse – I got tha money bringin Dozy Bonepick's babby home fer her! An tha wasn't easy I may tell you! On me, I mean, not her! The roars outa tha one an she not even halfway there wit her labour!

'I went off an told tha eegit clown of a man a hers, te come back an get me when she was ready te show me somethin. An how right I was. Do you know how long more before tha one dropped it?'

'No! Tell us, Nellie.'

'Two nights an a mornin! Three times she had me traipsin back an forth to tha tenement room a hers! Even her fella fecked off an left her. He was gone celebratin! An nothin even yet te be talked about! Sure it could a been borned dead, how was he te know? See they haven't had a live one yet. Five a them, an only one opened the eyes an gave a cry, few minutes it lasted, then snuff, gone!'

'Ah men!' snorted Essie. 'Should be all drownded at birth!'

'Wha?! But then wha would we do? We're handywomen! If there was no one borned, then we'd have no one te be waked. No,' sniffed Nellie, 'we bring them in, an we see them out. That's our job tha we were just born te do, an me mother an all before her God rest her soul,' she said, blessin herself. 'Right,' she went on. 'So we get on wit our job. We get himself Mister Mullins te get a loan of a long stool from Hop Along, the aul publican in the Shoot Out Saloon. He drinks there, tha will do nicely left in the hall fer people te sit an eat. He can sort tha out when he goes in te order the barrel a porter. He better see too about gettin the snuff an gettin someone te cook the pigs' cheeks. I'm not doin it, he should know by now wha needs te be got, sure doesn't he run a shop himself?'

'Right, an we won't worry about this place, we'll sort out here when we're finished an readied the other lot.'

Suddenly there was a bang on the door.

'Who would tha be? Maybe it's the linen cloths wit the silver cross an candles sent over on loan from the convent. We need tha an more fer the altar. Where's himself got to? There's nobody answerin!'

'Sure there's no one here to. He went off wit Squinty, the

coffin maker next door. He's probably in there now gettin a drop a hard stuff. You open it, unless ye want Delia te rise up an answer it herself!' moaned Essie, then the pair a them roared laughin, an I heard a big snort soundin like snots gettin sniffed out.

I looked out te see Essie lift her long skirt an give a blow te her nose an then wipe it, usin the leg of her navy-blue knickers. Then she sniffed again, sayin, 'I have te keep the rest a me clean. Sure, who's goin te see me drawers?' Then they opened their mouths an screamed, laughin their heads off again.

'Ah here! Fuck sake! The goins on a the pair of us! We're gettin nowhere doin nothin,' moaned Nellie.

'Speak fer yerself! I have the water on the go!'

'Answer it, then come on! Tha water should be near ready be now, where'd I put tha big enamel basin?'

I heard the door open an a voice said, 'Sister Mary Penance sent this parcel over for Mister Mullins. Is he here?'

'No, I'll take it, thanks, Brigid, we're here now, meself an Nellie Fry gettin poor Delia ready te be waked.'

'Right so. I will leave you to it! Oh did you hear? Poor Granny, Missus Kelly died too, this afternoon in the hospital. Her heart gave out. Mother Mary Bethlehem said someone will have te go around there an sort out the wake. The neighbours are in doin what they can. I've just come from there, it's torment! The doctor had to be called te quieten down Babby Kelly, he went outa his mind when Sister Mary Penance called to the house te tell him. I don't rightly know what's goin on, or what's happenin, but I believe listenin to them talk, I mean her and the doctor, an ambulance has been called to take Babby off te Grangegorman! He's not goin to manage by himself.'

'Noooo!' shouted Essie in a big whisper.

'NEVER!' breathed Nellie, rushin herself te the door wit an awful long hiss a breath comin outa her.

'Jesus, we better hurry! Thanks fer lettin us know, mind yerself now.'

'Right, good luck,' said the culchie woman, then I heard the door slam an the pair a them rush back in.

'Quick! If we're fast we'll get there ahead a the posse. Dirty Doris can smell money a mile away, she'll take tha from under our noses if we don't get there quick!'

'Right, Essie! Grab up the brown parcel there wit the stuff, you go on ahead an get started. I hear now the water boilin ready, I'll bring it up in the pink enamel basin, I have the washcloth, soap an towel ready, let's go. We'll clear outa here as fast as we can!'

'Yeah but wait, another thought just hit me!' breathed Nellie, openin her mouth wide sayin the words slowly. 'Did you hear the bit about Babby gettin himself locked up in the lunatic asylum?' she said, gettin outa breath now wit it catchin in her neck. 'Tha house will be up fer grabs! Just like the Carneys'!'

'Oh indeed yeah!' said Essie. 'She had no livin relatives except fer tha foolish son. He'll never get outa the mad house, they'll never let him free. Because as you know well, Nellie Fry, once in you never get out! An as I said, you know tha place is no holiday camp.'

'Here! Hang on a minute now, Essie Bullcock!' Nellie suddenly roared, leanin her head inta Essie wit her fist slammed against her hip, then lettin herself drop sideways restin on her right leg.

Me heart leapt. 'Oh ah. It looks like a big fight comin an me stuck just under the table,' I muttered te meself, then movin well back an grabbin me thumb, goin fer a really big suck while keepin me eye on them an meself well outa harm's way, as Mammy always warns me.

'I beg your pardon but I know no such thing! Sure how

would I know about the lunatic asylum when I never set foot inside one in all me borned days? Just who do ye think you're talkin to? Answer me!'

'Wha? What you talkin about?' said Essie, droppin her mouth open an blinkin like mad, lookin very confused. 'Oh ye mean . . . Well now God forgive you fer thinkin such a thing, tha I would think such a thing as to think somethin like tha about YOUUUU! An God forgive me fer givin you tha terrible idea in the first place! Believe me, Nellie Fry, I'm very chastised, tha would be an awful thing te think about anybody! Never mind the like a you an somebody a your calibres an pedigrees wit years a good breedin behind ye, an all tha came before you. Oh believe me, Nellie, oh be God by Jesus! I didn't mean tha by way of any insulutations . . . insultans, I mean . . . No! I was not meanin te be takin yer character at all. Sure don't ye know me well, Nellie? I mean how many babbies have we brought home? An further, how many corpses have we laid out together?' Essie said, gettin all hoarse, now lettin it come out in a squeak.

I watched seein her blink an wave her hand then look like she was washin it.

'I'll lay you out, Essie Bullcock, if you don't watch wha ye're sayin about me!' Nellie warned, leanin her face inta Essie an clampin her mouth shut. Then she shifted back an straightened herself, sayin, 'Now come on, ye aul fool. You nearly landed yerself there wit tha one. Only I'm a very forgivin soul, you mighta been gettin yerself planted along wit Delia Mullins! Now let's go, fer the love a Jaysus! There's no work te be had outa the pair of us this day. Tha poor unfortunate soul is up them stairs waitin on us. At least let's show somethin fer our day's efforts.'

12

I CRAWLED OUT FROM under the table just as the hall door opened an Mister Mullins appeared, he stopped an stared down at me lookin like he was wonderin where I came out of.

'Mister Mullins! Where's Ceily? She's not here,' I said, wavin me hand an swingin meself round te show him the empty room an pointin up the stairs. 'Nowhere,' I said, showin me empty hands again.

He stared sayin nothin, I stared back seein loads a more wrinkles an he looked like he got smaller, an very old all of a sudden.

He shook his head then said, 'Gone, is she? Tut tut! That's terrible,' then walked off inta the kitchen lookin like he lost somethin.

I followed behind hopin he would be the real Mister Mullins himself again. Maybe cook us somethin te eat an talk about Ceily, where she is an when we can go an get her. Do somethin! I don't care wha, anythin is better than hidin under tha table wearin out me belly.

He turned suddenly crashin inta me, then stared down lookin shocked an annoyed, mutterin, 'Child, will you stop trailin me an find who ever owns you!' Then he lifted his head lookin over at the door inta the shop, wit tha he rushed over an grabbed out his keys lockin it, then turned an rushed off out the front door again.

I stared after him, seein now only the empty place where he'd been a minute ago. I'm on me own again. An he didn't tell me wha te do or give me somethin te eat or even talk te me about nothin! Wha will I do? I have te eat, me belly is tippin the floor lookin like a bursted balloon from the hunger. An I have te find my Ceily. An I have te get me own stuff, I thought, lookin down at Delia Mullins' knickers hangin down te me feet an trailin along the floor. An Mister Mullins' socks is trippin me up, I look like Coco the Clown tryin te walk in them.

'Ehnnnn!' I started te keen, feelin a rage rise in me. I wanted te dance up an down an scream me head off, but there's no one te hear. 'An them aul ones upstairs will only ate the head offa me,' I sniffed, feelin a heat from me rage rush around me chest makin me snort down through me nose. I listened, hearin it sound like a monster gettin ready te grab someone.

Me eyes looked at the empty table wit nothin te show fer eatin, except the sugar bowl an butter dish. 'You can't eat tha on its own,' I muttered, lettin me lip turn up wit a snarl.

The food press! I grabbed the heavy chair pullin it over an stood up openin up the door. Me eyes slid along takin in the cans, no good, don't know wha's in them an can't open them anyway. Then onta the packet a Bisto, tin a Horlicks, red jelly! I grabbed hold a tha, wha else? Nothin worth lookin at, packets a flour tha's it. No biscuits, no cake, where's the bread?

I looked around seein the breadbin standin on the shelf close te the press, it was holdin all the jugs, the teapot an loads a Delft.

I leapt down an dragged across the chair then jumped up openin the bin. Nothin! I stared very annoyed lookin at the mouldy crumbs. Why's this? So how can it be like tha when we're in a shop? Well, the Mullins live in a shop.

Oh yeah! I stuffed me gob wit nearly the whole loaf a bread, Ceily gave out te me fer doin tha!

Me heart slid down te me belly an I felt the tears comin outa me eyes. I stood down an dragged across the chair, then sat meself an buried me head in me arms. 'Ceily! Where are ye? I miss you,' I whispered, startin te break me heart wantin te cry me eyes out. I shook me head. 'I don't understand why youse are all gone! Mammy's gone an left me, an now you're gone too. Me home is gone, an I'm not supposed te let anyone see me. Wha will I do? There's no one te ask. Oh, come back to me, Mammy, I promise I will be good. I won't torment ye any more. You too, Ceily! I'm lost without you. You're me big sister.'

I heard movement an a door bangin then footsteps on the stairs. Me head shot up an me body went stiff, wha will I do? Will I hide again? I didn't want te no more, I'm fed up, I don't care! But before I knew where I was I was clatterin offa the chair an divin meself under the table breathin heavy an waitin te see wha happens now. Suddenly I had a thought, no! I'm not goin te disappear like Ceily! She must a done somethin an let people see her. Well tha's not goin te happen te me! I'm not as stupid as I look. Tha's wha Mammy always says about herself.

The boots were bangin along the hall now makin te come in here, when suddenly there was loud knockin on the door soundin like someone was at it wit a hammer. I could hear childre shoutin, 'Are ye in there, Mister Mullins?'

'Who's tha?' said Nellie's voice. 'Open it, Essie. Might be someone important.'

Nellie then pushed in the door an made straight fer the table pullin a chair out from under it.

I held me breath wrappin me hand over me mouth tryin te hold it in. Suddenly I couldn't breathe, I shot out me tongue openin me mouth te let in air, an now I was pantin like Nero.

Tha's Janie Mulberry's dog. He does tha he does, when he does be gettin too hot.

I watched as she landed the chair over at the mantelpiece then dragged her skirt up an hauled herself onta it, puffin an pantin. So she didn't hear me, at doin the same thing. I stared as she lifted the mirror offa the nail an held it by the cord, then turned it around lettin the glass face the wall. Then she stared at a big cobweb wit a dead spider hangin out of it an she looked like she was wonderin. I watched as she looked down an lifted her skirt makin sure te keep the snow-white apron well outa the way, wantin te keep it clean. Then she had a go at wipin away the cobweb, but the skirt wouldn't reach. Her eyes shot wide open, just before she suddenly toppled an went skiddin sideways, then slowly her head leaned through the air an the next, she was flyin te land flat on her face an belly! I heard a grunt then a moan an watched, as her face went from turnin snow-white te bright-red, then went purple an looked like it was goin black. She opened her mouth an nothin came out but a wheezin an a hissin air, then a grunt, an suddenly a piercin scream. 'MERCY! HELP! I'M KILT!'

I watched as she tried te turn her head mutterin, 'Oh God te night, me end's come!'

Essie missed out hearin the screams as she opened the door an I heard a young fella say, 'Is Mister Mullins here?'

'No, he's not, wha do ye's want? You better not be wastin my time, I've more te be doin than runnin te answer the door fer the like a youse!'

'Oh no! We're not doin tha, sure we're not, gang? No we're not, missus. Honest te God, cross me heart an hope te die! We came because we want te say we're sorry fer poor Mister Mullins' trouble,' shouted a young fella.

'Right! Thanks very much. I'll tell him. Now goodbye, I'm busy!' said Essie, soundin like she was makin te shut the door.

'WAIT! WAIT!' a load a voices all shouted at the same time. 'Wha about the hooley, the wake? Is it startin yet?'

'NO! Ger away from this door, or I'll drown the lot a ye's wit a basin a cold water!'

'Well can we ask ye just? Is there goin te be lemonade an biscuits outa the shop fer the people, fer us? We knew poor Nosey, I mean Delia Mullins, all a her life!'

'Did youse know her all her life? Really? So youse lot must be a pack a midgets, an here was me thinkin ye's were childre. An ye're cheeky midgets at tha! Callin the respectable Miss Mullins "Nosey". Listen, I know your faces, youse are all from the tenements up the road. You've no business comin down this end. So get back where ye came from, an don't be comin down here botherin the likes a yer betters. We're the respectables down here, now get yer foot outa the door or I'll take it off fer ye!' Essie said, just as the almighty scream came outa Nellie.

'JESUS WHA WAS THA?' screamed Essie. 'WHAT'S HAPPENIN? WHA'S WRONG? I'm comin.'

'Oooaa ahhh! Oh Jesus, oh I'm fadin,' moaned Nellie givin a big sigh then lettin her eyes roll.

'I'm here! Hang on!' keened Essie, rushin in the door mutterin 'Where are ye?' wit her head spinnin around tryin te spot Nellie, she was lyin plastered the other side a the fireplace, behind the armchair.

Me eyes shifted from her te Essie. She stood starin bitin her fingers wonderin wha could a happened. Then she leapt, rushin herself te Nellie, sayin, 'Did you have a blackout? Wha happened? Is it the heart? Ye're lookin very blue, I think it may be the heart, it looks like it could a burst, Nellie! God you're lookin very bad!'

'Do something, I'm fadin fast, Essie! Me hour has come!' said Nellie, moanin barely a whisper wit her voice soundin like a little child's.

Essie leapt up rushin fer the door, shoutin, 'QUICK, SOMEONE! HELP! THERE'S A WOMAN IN HERE HURTED! She's dyin! Get the ambulance! Bring the priest!'

Suddenly noise erupted, feet came rushin in an a load a childre flew through the door shoutin, 'Are ye all right, missus?'

All I could see was filthy scruffy legs wit dirty pot-black bare feet, an I could get the smell a piss an shit. I lifted the cloth an poked me head out te get a look.

A sudden roar came at me. 'LOOKIT, EVERYONE! Tha's the young one tha's missin!'

Feet stopped rushin an heads turned, all lookin te see where the young fella wit the dirty face an the snotty nose was pointin. I pushed me way back further, not wantin them te see or get at me. Then I saw dirty black skinny legs rushin around the other side, then droppin down an lookin in at me.

'FUCK OFF!' I heard meself suddenly eruptin.

'Ohhh! Did ye hear tha? Did you hear wha tha young one just said, missus?' said Snotty, swingin his head te Nellie an pointin the arm at me, hopin she would be shocked.

'Ohhhh me back's broken, me neck's twisted,' keened Nellie, not carin about nothin.

'Wha's happenin? They're comin, Nellie, hang on!' puffed Essie, rushin herself back wit a load a feet hurryin in behind her. 'Come on, she's in here!'

'Where is she?' breathed a skinny woman outa breath from the shockin news, she had a turned eye an she was wearin a headscarf knotted at the chin. She stopped wit her hand on her chest te take in the sorry sight a Nellie, it was terrible, Nellie looked now like she was not goin te make it.

'Here I am, over here,' keened Nellie in a weak voice, strokin her forehead then leavin her hand coverin her eyes.

'LOOKIT WHO WE FOUND! It's tha Lily tha started all the

eruptions! The young ones from around the corner!' screamed a young fella wit the eyes jumpin outa his head.

'She's on the wanted list! The police an everyone is wantin te get their hands on tha young one!' a smelly young fella roared, pointin one hand at me an cockin his leg scratchin, pullin away his trousers stuck up his arse wit the other. 'We all know her! Don't we, gang?'

'Yeah we do!'

'Is there a reward fer catchin her?' a big young fella said wit the hair standin on his head lookin like his ma chopped it leavin him wit the bald patches.

'Who's tha ye're talkin about? Where?' said Essie, seein them all pullin the cloth tryin te get at me under the table. I heard her gruntin then saw her knees, she was tryin te bend herself an get down at me under the table. Hands suddenly started comin from everywhere tryin te reach in an grab hold a me.

Me heart flew an I twisted meself, slidin me legs an arse an all a me, tryin te stop someone grabbin a hold. 'NO!' I screamed. 'Let me be. I didn't do nothin! Don't touch me,' I keened, frightened fer me life slappin away a dirty paw grabbin out at me.

'Is tha the Lily Carney child?' said Essie, not able te get down an see me. 'Is tha you, Lily?'

I didn't answer, hopin she might tell them te leave me alone, leave me be where I was.

'Lily Carney, get out from under tha table! Where did you come out of? Where did she come outa?'

'We saw her!'

'No ye's didn't I did!' roared Snotty.

'Mammy! Ceily! Someone save me!' I keened, draggin up me knees an shovin me thumb inta me mouth, losin me mind wit fright.

Then me eyes lit on Mister Mullins' socks, I tore them offa

me feet an twisted me legs out from under the table jammin the socks under me arms, then I was on me feet runnin. Before anyone knew it, I grabbed up Delia's big knickers holdin onta them an ran fer me life. Out the door inta the hall headin straight inta the stretcher comin fer te cart Nellie outa the house an off te the hospidal.

'Easy, easy!' said the ambulance man.

I ducked down flyin meself under the stretcher an made straight up the stairs. I lashed inta the open room an slammed the door shut behind me, an dived under the bed. Me heart was hammerin in me ears an the snots was pourin outa me nose, an I was lickin an breathin an keepin me eyes on the door, watchin an waitin fer it te open. But nothin happened. They must a forgotten about me, or don't care because I can hear the commotion an the fussin wit everyone shoutin orders an all tryin te help the ambulance men.

'Here! Clear a path!' someone shouted.

'Yeah, let the ambulance men in,' some other fella barked.

'Give her air,' an aul one screamed.

'Exactly! Stop crowdin the door,' another one roared, not wantin te be left out wit the helpin.

I listened wit me ears buzzin an me eyes blinkin, feelin me nerves is gone.

'Ger outa here, youse young fellas!'

Tha's Essie Bullcock startin the roarin now, she sounds like her nerves is gone too!

'Look! Will someone shut tha front door. There's too many of youse wanderin in.'

I listened hearin the goins on, then someone gave a hoarse roar.

'Missus! Would you ever get yer hands offa me neck. I can't breathe!'

I leaned my ear onta the floor fer a better listen, then hearin tha, an nodded my head satisfied. Yeah, tha's Essie losin the head in her rushin an hurryin. Now she's tryin te strangle the ambulance man.

'Here! The place is crowdin wit the lot a ye's an the wake is not startin yet! Would youse all ever leave an—'

'WHAT NOW, IN THE NAME OF GOD, IS GOIN ON HERE?'

I stopped suckin. Mister Mullins! He's back!

'Out! Get out of my house fast, each and every one of you! Or by Jesus I promise you there will be even more bloodshed before this day is out!'

Everythin went quiet, it was like the quiet when ye hold yer breath not te make a sound. Then I heard a rumble, it was like the sound a bare feet slappin on wood. Then more noise as boots an shoes clattered after them.

People mumbled, 'Sorry fer yer trouble!'

'Yeah, oh yeah! Very sorry fer yer trouble!'

'Oh excuse me! Here, stop pushin you!'

I listened thinkin about wha he said, an me heart slid down inta me belly makin me terribly afraid. Mister Mullins might kill me as well!

I crawled out from under the bed an put me hands inside the socks pullin them all the way up me arms an onta me shoulders, they'll be easy te carry an keep me nice an warm. Then I tried te twist open the door handle wit me two hands but it wouldn't work, so I pulled off me new gloves now whippin the door open easy. I put me gloves back on then grabbed up me Delia's knickers an rushed meself down the stairs goin fast, I was doin tha by usin only the one leg an goin sideways, holdin onta the banisters. There was a heap a people all shufflin out through the hall, then I was on the ground an rushin inta them all hurryin now te get out an away from the house.

I turned left wit everyone goin in different directions, then flew up the road, lookin like I was goin home. But at the last minute as I got te the corner of my street, I skidded right, an shot onta the road, straight inta the path of a big black motor car. Me eyes flew te the driver an he stared back, lookin annoyed. Then his face changed an it went lookin ragin, wit the eyes leppin an the face turnin roarin red. I saw his mouth movin, then it turned up his nose in a snarl. It was FATHER FLITTERS!

'MAMMYEEEEEE!' I screamed, turnin into a statue wit the fright an me not able te move.

The motor car stopped dead an the door opened. He leaned over te pick up somethin, then heaved himself outa the seat in an awful hurry, an now I could see he was wavin a new black stick. It looked like a twisty thorn stick people use fer walkin.

'Stay there! Don't move, you little cur,' he growled, keepin his eyes on me while he made te stand straight an get himself goin.

I couldn't move! Me eyes stared an me mouth opened an closed but nothin came out. I was stuck fast!

'Ger offa the road, you stupid child! Are you tryin te get yerself kilt stone dead?' a man's voice suddenly roared, wakin me up. I looked around blinkin, seein a coalman, he was tryin te get his horse an cart around the motor car stood in the middle a the road. Wit tha I held up the Delia knickers an flew fer the footpath, rushin past a gang of kids playin outside a tenement house.

'Get back here! Stop that girl! Lily Carney, I will give you a fine good thrashing, when I get hands to you!' the priest roared.

I looked back te see how far he was. Me eyes lit te see he only got te the footpath an he was miles behind me, but he was ragin, spits was comin outa his mouth an he was wavin the new stick like mad.

'Eh you, young one, come back! Lily Carney! Stop! Wait it's me, Neddy!'

I looked back te see Sooty shoutin after me. He was standin wit Father Flitters' old stick in his hand an the hat spinnin on the top, while a gang a young fellas all stood around watchin an laughin, delighted at seein this.

I looked at him then looked te see Father Flitters standin an pointin, he was talkin to a policeman who was starin up the street lookin after me. I watched Father Flitters' allegations, not likin the way he was flappin his mouth wit his head hammerin up an down an the stick pointin te me, keepin in time te wha he was sayin. There was even a crowd now all gatherin around on the footpath te watch wha was goin on.

He's gone mad, he's out te kill me! 'Oh Mammy, I'm dead, they're goin te hang me!' Tha's wha Mammy always said when we drove her mad. 'They'll hang me! Or lock me up fer good in the mad house for takin your life,' she would say te me an Ceily.

Mammy never had the police after her, or the parish priest! But I have. I'm now a baddie on the run! I turned around an startin runnin fer me life, not carin where I went, so long as it got me far away from them.

13

I RAN WIT ME mouth open an the sweat pourin down me face, cryin me heart out. 'Ceily, I'm lookin fer you! Stop hidin on me, ye must hear me, I'm shoutin, where are you?' I cried, lookin from one side a the road te the other. I was gallopin down Killarney Street then came runnin past Buckingham Street an wondered if she was down there, around be the train station at Amiens Street.

I turned onto it an went rushin past all the tenement houses wit kids playin an runnin in me path, an I had te swerve outa the way an onta the road te stop meself gettin hit by a young fella swingin a stick. He was chasin two other eegit fellas tryin te give them a belt. They were duckin an laughin, an not carin about nearly knockin over a little babby. It was crawlin along the footpath, tryin te make its escape like me, an all while the big young ones were busy sortin themselves out. They were playin house wit cardboard boxes, settin them all up, fixin them an forgettin about the babby. I betcha they took tha babby outa his pram, I thought, throwin me eye te the empty pram while I was runnin an cryin me eyes out.

I roared me head wit me mouth wide open an lookin at young ones playin skippy rope, jumpin in an out without standin on the rope makin it stop twirlin. If ye did tha, then ye lost the game an ye were out. I love te play tha, I do, but now I just want te find me mammy an me sister.

I ran on roarin me head off. A big young one looked at me, she was sittin behind her counter, a stool wit her broken bits a Delft, playin shop.

'Oh lookit tha cry babby!' she moaned, throwin her head an pointin her finger at me, curlin her lip up.

I was ragin, I looked at the big sore on her mouth an chin an roared, 'Fuck off, ye scabby cow!' An kept on runnin, then went back te me roarin an cryin. Me heart was really breakin now, I was losin me rag because everyone was out te get me, an I'm goin te get them too. They're not robbin me of me sister! An me mammy! An me house an get away wit it! No! Mammy always said, 'Stand yer ground an let no one walk on you.' So I'm goin te do tha now, Mammy, fer you. An Ceily. They won't walk on me, I won't let them. Ceily says tha so she does, an I'm sayin it too.

I turned right an ran on, then stopped under the train-station arch wantin te cross the road. The traffic was tearin up an down wit no let-up, an I rocked meself backwards an forwards, ready te make a run fer it when I saw a gap.

I stopped me cryin fer a bit an just keened while I kept the watch out. Me head followed the traffic rushin past an the lot goin down the other side, but nothin yet. I'm fed up waitin an me head's gettin dizzy, they're movin tha fast. I can't run out an make them stop, because they're leavin me no room te do tha. Then me eyes lit on the Guinness float, it was comin behind the bus wit nothin up behind tha. I started rockin goin backwards an forwards like mad, shovin out me right foot. 'Get ready, on yer marks,' I muttered. 'GO!'

I lunged just as the two huge horses roared past wit their white big hoofs stampin the ground an their matchin white manes streelin out behind them.

'WATCH OUT!'

I reeled at the last minute wit me neck swingin on me shoulders, just before nearly crashin inta the fella on the bicycle gettin himself a free jaunt. He was flyin along hangin onta the long cart wit the barrels a porter rollin an rattlin, an he not able te tear his eyes away. It looked like te me, he had the longin te get his hands on one a them barrels.

'Don't cross, wait!' said a man comin outa the cake shop behind me. 'You'll get yerself kilt,' he said, wavin his finger at me, then lookin up an down at the traffic. 'Where you comin from?'

'Diamond Street, mister.'

'Off Portland Row, isn't it?'

'Yeah.'

'Does yer mammy know where you are?'

I shook me head. 'No! I'm goin te look fer her,' I said, seein him look annoyed an worried at the same time, because he thinks I'm runnin wild on me mammy an I'll get meself kilt.

'I won't get meself kilt,' I said lookin up at him, not wantin him te worry.

He took in a big breath an shook his head not believin me. 'Come on,' he said, grabbin hold a me hand covered be the sock, an I grabbed up me Delia knickers an rushed wit him gettin us te the middle a the road, then he slowed down te watch an put out his hand te stop the lorry makin head on, straight fer us.

'Now, here we are,' he said, lettin go a me hand an openin a brown paper bag. Me eyes lit up an I whipped the socks offa me hands watchin him open it, an I could get the smell a hot cakes straight away.

'Here, have one a these, an go easy on them roads, stay away from them,' he said, puttin a big jam doughnut in me hand an pattin me on the head. 'Now be good! he whispered, bendin down inta me face smilin, then he went off givin me a wave.

I stared after him then down at the cake, I could feel it soft an the sugar stickin te me fingers, an I lifted it te me nose gettin the smell of the jam. 'Oh Mammy, it's gorgeous!' I mumbled, takin a big bite. Wha a pity he's not me granda! Whoever has him is very lucky! I thought, lookin back down at me cake. Then suddenly it was whipped from me hand.

'GOT YE! Give us a bite!' said the big young one I just told te 'Fuck off' wit the scabby chin an mouth. 'Followed you here te box ye!' She crowed makin it a sing-song all delighted, an now lookin down admirin me cake gone te sit in her hand. 'Then I watched te see you might get yerself kilt tryin te get cross tha road, an more's the pity ye didn't! But sure never mind, this is even better! Thanks very much,' she laughed, then turned an rushed back across the road an disappeared around the corner.

I couldn't believe me eyes, I stared after her wit the bite I got hangin outa me mouth not even tasted yet, never mind chewed. 'Hnnn,' I moaned, givin a little keen, not able te do nothin else wit me gone inta shock. Me heart was breakin fer the want of it back, I chewed now, keened an stared over at the corner where me cake disappeared, not knowin wha te do next. I looked fer the granda te see if I could catch up wit him an tell him wha tha young one did te me, but I couldn't see him, he was gone. I wanted te scream, cry me rage an jump up an down doin a war dance, or scream murder fer someone te kill her an get it back. But I couldn't do nothin. Then it hit me, I should a watched behind me when I called her names. Then I could a run fer me life when I sawed her comin! Ceily is right, I am pure stupid!

I looked around me wonderin where I should go, then saw the young fellas hoppin around playin on the train station steps an watchin me. As soon as they saw me lookin they opened their mouth an laughed, pointin at me then roarin, 'Ahhaha! Serves ye right, eegit! Dozy Dozy Donah, lost her donah, dirty-lookin gobshite got no cake!' They sang it, makin it into a tormentin song.

I stood starin then shouted, 'Fuck off, smellies. Ye're eegits yerselves!'

I could feel a huge heave a big cryin comin up me chest, but I held me breath an turned away, makin te rush back across the road, not wantin te let them see me cryin.

I stopped beside two aul ones waitin te cross an they looked at each other, sayin, 'Lovely fresh crisp day fer January, isn't it, missus?'

'Oh indeed it is, an wit tha bit a sun comin in through the windas, it should a warmed up lovely the house fer when I get home.'

'Ah yeah, I'm the same, it's nice te have tha te look forward to. Still, we're out in it now, an at our age you need te wrap yerself up well!' she said, fixin the black shawl on her head pullin it tight around her.

'Oh ye're right there,' the other aul one said, doin the same an wrappin herself tight inside her shawl, leavin only a bit of her face te catch cold. 'Oh yes,' she repeated, lookin like she was mutterin to herself wit her mind miles away. 'Oh yeah, ye're right there, indeed you are. At our age you have te take all the bit a comfort you can get, no matter where it comes from.'

Then the traffic eased an we all left the footpath together wit me followin beside them. Fer these few minutes I didn't feel on me own any more, an I didn't even feel cold an lonely.

We walked up all along the street wit shops at every door. Me mammy comes here te do her shoppin on a Saturday, I think it's Talbot Street. Yeah, I know it is, I remember where we are now. But she never let me come this far on me own before. An tha road back there is very treacherous! If Mammy knew I tried te cross tha on me own she would kill me!

The two women walked together now chattin like they were old friends, but they only met. You can tell by the way they first talked, lookin, but not catchin the eye. You do tha in case someone doesn't want te talk to ye, then you can pretend te be talkin only te yerself an the fresh air! I know all this because Mammy would say it when someone wouldn't answer when she talked, 'Look a tha! Ignorant aul cow nose in the air thinks she's too good fer people, wouldn't talk te you, just as well I was makin company wit the fresh air an not dependin on her fer the time a day.'

'I'm headin in here te the Clothin Mill,' one woman said, slowin down.

The other one stopped an stared in, lookin like she was thinkin. 'Do ye know I think I will go in an have a look meself, there's a few things I need te get.'

'Come on then, let's see wha they're offerin,' said the first woman wit her face covered. Then she lifted the shawl off her face an lowered it down wrappin it around her shoulders. I could see now she had snow-white thin hair showin her scalp all bald, an it was pulled tight an tied in a brown hairnet at the back.

The two a them went in an I followed, it felt now like I too was a part of them. They just met each other an I just met them, so we're all pals, even though they don't know about me.

'Where's the tea towels?' said the hairnet woman. 'Must be in further,' she answered heself. 'Let's keep movin. I want te see wha they have.'

'Oh look, missus! Aren't they just beautiful now?'

'Wha?' said Hairnet, seein the woman pointin up at the white-wool blankets hangin down from the wall.

'Foxford!' said Hairnet, lettin it come out in a moan. 'Oh

wouldn't I just love a pair a them now on me bed? Oh but the price a them, God bless us! You would need a lifetime a savin te afford even one a them! An look a tha, beside it, the gold eiderdown wit the satin cover. The weight of it! Oh you could get tha te go wit the Foxford blankets.' Then she suddenly bent down an whispered inta the other woman's ear, I moved closer fer a listen. 'Then you'd never need a man te keep ye warm!'

There was quiet fer a minute then suddenly they threw up their heads together an roared laughin.

'Oh be God ye're right there, who needs them when ye have all the comfort wit tha lovely bed stuff.'

Then we wandered on.

I stopped te look at the wires an pulleys flyin across the ceilin wit the little box attached. It pinged an banged when it hit the woman waitin at the counter, an she grabbed hold an opened it. Then she took out the receipt an the change in money an handed it to the customer waitin wit her brown-paper parcels all tied up wit twine. I watched another shop assistant take a big green pound note from a customer an put it in the little box, wit a ticket. Then she pulled a knob an the box flew off singin an buzzin through the air makin its way across the ceilin, then up it went to a glass an wooden box where a woman sat waitin fer it. It flew in through the open winda straight to her waitin hand, an she grabbed hold an opened it.

Oh I would love te do her job, I thought, starin up at her sittin behind the dark-wood desk. She was wearin a uniform, it was a lovely black frock wit a white-lace collar. She looks very important so she does, up there wit her grey wavy hair tied back in a bun an the glasses sittin on her nose. I watched as she took out the docket an the money an wrote somethin in a big book, then put her hand in a big polished box, fixed in the money an took out the change. Then wrote somethin on a form, wrapped the change in it, put it in the box an flew the lot back te the shop assistant.

I turned then te watch an see wha she does. She was wearin a shop coat, it was a navy-blue smock, an right beside next te her she had huge rolls a brown paper wit big balls a twine waitin te be cut, tha was done by tuggin it at the brass edge of the counter. She had big long measurin tapes fer measurin stuff, an I even saw a woman gettin her waist measured.

I rushed up te get a look at tha, an the woman had her coat off an she was wearin a navy-wool jumper wit a heart over the chest. She looked young like she just got married an she was lovely lookin altogether. Her mammy was standin beside her wearin a fur coat an holdin loads a parcels from other shops. 'Oh yes, dear. I think we should. The Clothing Mill is best for that you know, dear,' she said, smilin at the shop assistant who looked like she was on her best manners because this was very important an respectable customers.

'Yes, Madam, I do agree,' she said, bowin her head an givin a smile without openin her mouth.

I gave a big sigh forgettin all about me troubles. Oh this is great, I thought, enjoyin meself no end watchin all the goins on. Then I looked te see me two old women, but they were gone! Me heart dropped wit the sudden fright. 'Where's the grannies got to?' I muttered, feelin meself startin te panic wit me head shootin around the shop not able te see them.

Then I heard them, but I couldn't see them in the crowd. I tried lookin down at feet, but I don't know wha theirs look like. I think they had black boots wit narrow heels, but then there's loads a black boots all sittin on feet wit different size legs an shapes, frocks, coats an lengths. Some are short, an some are coverin the ankles wit only the boot or shoe te be seen. Mammy said we have nearly gone out of the Dark Ages an now we might start te get a bit more modern, like wha the people write home about when they go te England, because we have nothin here, Mammy says. She calls Ireland the hothouse fer breedin workers an cattle te be shipped te England. They even go te America when they save up enough fer the passage after workin in England. Mammy says we would be all dead an planted, if it wasn't fer the few shillings sent home te the fambilies from all them workers. Yeah, I know all these things, because I love earwiggin when the big people are talkin. But ye get a box in the ear when they catch you! Mammy says I'll grow up wit cauliflower ears if I don't stop me earwiggin.

I came back te me senses an stood starin, wonderin wha I was supposed te be doin. Oh yeah, the grannies!

Me eyes flew takin in the people. Ah! There they are, the pair a them are near the front a the shop, they were makin their way out away from the counter an lookin like they were headin fer the door.

I pushed me way out fast catchin up, then stood, seein them havin a last word before goin in separate directions. I began te feel lost again watchin them part. One woman went right an crossed the road headin in the station direction, then turned left, goin back the way I came. The other one started te fix herself, she pulled the shawl back over her head coverin it, an only leavin out a bit of her face te be exposed.

Wha will I do? I felt meself wantin te cry, open me mouth an cry me heart out. I could feel the cold hittin me now, me stomach was empty an I felt tired, very tired, cold an hungry. But I don't know anyone te go an see. I have nowhere te go an no Mammy te mind me! I started te cry feelin meself heat up wit the hot tears splashin down me face, an I couldn't see wha was happenin, because the tears was blindin me.

The other granny was gone, but I could still see the one wit her head covered, she was far ahead in the distance headed up

Talbot Street. I'm goin wit her! The thought suddenly hit me makin me feel better.

I rushed off then started flyin me arms makin me go faster, me feet was hurtin me on the hard stone ground an I wanted te stop an put me socks back on, but they wouldn't let me walk in them, they're huge big men socks an I'm still a bit too little. Not tha little, because I'm seven now, but still a little! I thought te meself catchin up now, because I could see the granny nearly in front a me.

Just as I got up next te her I slowed down then to a walk an kept a little behind her. She can't know I'm trailin her, because I don't really belong te her an she's goin te get very annoyed, because she will think I'm watchin her business. I'm not, I just want te be wit someone an pretend they're mindin me.

We walked on an stopped at the lights waitin te cross Gardiner Street, I know this place too, because this is the way Mammy goes when she wants te get her shoppin. But we don't always come this way.

I stood waitin, hoppin me feet te keep out the cold, I never went in me bare feet before an I don't like havin te do it now. It kills you wit the painin cold an gets you all sore, from walkin on the cobblestones. Then it's havin te watch out fer broken glass or walkin on pebbles an hittin yer big toe against broken bricks. No I definitely don't like it, even though lots a childre run in their bare feet, but they don't care, because they're used te it! Then suddenly I heard me mammy's voice say, *Lily Carney, you're used te better, now get yer shoes on ye.*

I looked around just te make sure, but no, she was not around me or beside me; it was only my hearin her voice in me head.

14

THE LIGHTS CHANGED an we moved on, I kept very close behind her not wantin te lose her again. I don't know why, but the granny makes me feel like I know her, yet I know I never sawed her before. Very peculiar tha!

We stayed walkin on up towards the top a Talbot Street without stoppin. Now we did stop again, because we're now at the lights on O'Connell Street waitin te cross over te Nelson's Pillar. I know all these places, this is exactly where me an Mammy an Ceily go te do our shoppin on the Saturday.

We all watched the lights, they went green, then we were on the move again, marchin across the road an on te Nelson's Pillar.

'Ah it's yerself, Mona! How're ye keepin?' an old woman said, she was wearin a plaid shawl an a grey woolly hat wit a big pin pushed through it, tha was te keep it fastened onta her head. An I stood admirin her lovely mother o' pearl brooch, she had tha sittin on the shawl, pinnin it together. She looked very fancy compared te the granny.

'Ah Lizzie Dungan, well if it isn't yerself! An here we are an the dead appeared an arose to many!' the granny roared, laughin an gettin all delighted.

'Sure look, you wouldn't know me! I've been across the water an back! The big young one, Mary-Josephine, brought me over. She lost the husband, he died sudden, but he had a good job on the railway over there, an now she has the widow's pension, an not just tha! But she got a big insurance payout on the death policy, now she's in clover!'

'Go 'way! Amn't I just delighted for you, Lizzie!'

'Oh indeed yes! Now there's money plenty, she can send me the fare, she said she would! An I can go over again at Easter!'

'Oh isn't God good? You landed on yer feet wit tha bit a good fortune! An wha about childre? Has she many?'

'Oh indeed she has! But look, they're all done for, up reared an married all five a them!'

'God, Lizzie, but don't the years do fly! Wha age would she be now? Mary-Josephine wasn't it?'

'Yeah we called her after the two sisters a mine who died young. You remember?'

'Oh indeed I do, Lizzie, beauties the two a them, died a consumption they did, God be good te them an rest them. So, where were we?'

'Mary Josephine, she's fifty-two!' said Lizzie, rememberin.

'Ah will ye go on outa tha! Are we tha old?'

'Oh indeed we are, Mona, the years flew! Do you remember when we sat together tha first day in school? Gardiner Street, down the lane it was! An we wha? Only four year old! How long ago is tha may I ask?'

'Well come this March I will be seventy-six year old, Lizzie! Oh the years flew, we've had our time, now every day's a gift from heaven, Lizzie!' the granny said, soundin very sad, shakin her head an starin inta the face of Lizzie.

Lizzie clamped her mouth an smiled but looked very sad too, starin back at Mona. Now I know wha the granny is called.

They stayed quiet fer a minute then Lizzie said, 'I heard you lost poor Toby.'

'Ah God love him, he's gone now,' keened Mona, soundin

like she was cryin. 'Ah I miss him somethin terrible, he was great company! Even poor Sheila is gone, the cat! Nineteen year I had her, an fifteen year I had Toby. God bless us but by the time he went he was stone deaf, half blind an his poor hips was riddled wit arthritis! Ah but he was me constant companion. People used te say, you see me ye see him! Now I'm lost, Lizzie, I keep wantin te turn around an see if he's behind me. I can't get used te not havin him around. It's very quiet, too quiet without him.'

'Ah well. That's life,' said Lizzie. Then said, as she put her hand on Mona, 'You mind yerself, darlin, an we'll say a prayer fer each other. God has been good te us! There's better than me come an gone, it's been a hard aul life, some be times terrible! But here we are still around, pullin the devil be the tail, but we're still alive te tell the story.'

'Mind yerself, Lizzie, an God bless you! Bye now, I better hurry on an get me few messages, it looks like tha weather is goin te change fer the worse,' Mona said, now lookin up at the sky wit the sun gone, leavin nothin but black clouds, cold an the wind comin up.

I shivered sittin on me spot on Nelson's steps. I looked up seein him standin up there wit the missin arm an his one eye lookin down the length of O'Connell Street, he was keepin tha one eye peeled on the river, our River Liffey. Mammy used te say he was watchin out, just in case foreign ships came in wantin to invade the city! Just like the Vikings did. Mammy said they built Dublin, over in the old part, the Liberties where Christ Church Cathedral is.

I leapt up, after forgettin meself, when I sawed her rushin across the lights an now headin up Henry Street. I flew after her te catch up an stayed just behind, not wantin te lose her in the crowds. She turned down inta Moore Street an I followed feelin all happy. I looked from left te right at the dealers on every side a the street sellin their flowers, an another had vegebales, then another aul one was roarin, 'Four pence the dozen apples! Do ye want some, missus? Just offa the banana boat they is, collected them meself! Knew you were comin an lookit! Don't go, missus, wait!' she shouted, grabbin hold a my granny not lettin her move.

'I don't want any apples, sure lookit! I have no teeth te eat them, missus,' the granny said, openin the mouth te show her gums.

The dealer looked, then blinked thinkin. 'Never mind, here! I knew tha might happen, an just in case ye didn't want them I got these special! They're soft, come on! Here, where's yer bag?' she said, grabbin at the granny's string bag an shovin in a big bunch a rotten bananas.

'Ah no! They're too many!' the granny tried te say.

'Take them! They'll make yer teeth grow back!' the dealer shouted, then put her hand out, sayin, 'Now! I'm lettin you have them fer sixpence, it would be eight pence te anyone else or if I didn't like ye!'

The granny tried te give them back but the dealer said, 'No go on, ye're not robbin me, don't even thank me! Sure amn't I known up an down the length an breadth a Moore Street fer me generosity? Not te mention me honesty. Ye owe me sixpence!' she said, lowerin her voice an sayin it fast, then holdin out her hand waitin.

The granny slowly let down her shawl an rooted around inside lookin fer her purse. Then took out two pennies, two ha'pennies an a thruppeny bit.

'Lovely, God bless ye,' the dealer said, checkin it on her hand te make sure it was all there. 'FOURPENCE THE DOZEN ROSY APPLES!' she went back te shoutin an we moved off, te continue makin our way down the Moore Street.

I felt like sayin te the granny, 'Do ye want me te carry yer shoppin?' She had a little brown parcel tied up wit string from the Clothin Mill an now she had the bunch a bananas sittin in on top a tha. I counted, there was six. I'm good at countin I am. But I can't read yet, only a tiny bit.

We walked on then stopped outside Sheils's the pork shop an looked in the winda. Then the granny turned an hurried in te stand beside the counter an wait in the queue te get served. I slid along on the sawdust thrown on the floor, it was put there te stop people fallin an maybe breakin their necks on the tiles. Tha's just in case, because it can happen when it rains. Mammy told me tha, because we come in here too, it's te get our food fer the evenin tea an breakfast on the Sunday mornin, an loads a other stuff.

I looked te make sure the granny was still there, then bunched up the sawdust an tried te mash it between me toes. Then I heard a roar an looked around, it was comin from a young fella, he saw me lookin an leaned his head at me snarlin. 'Ger away from my sawdust, it's not there fer your enjoyment,' he snorted, givin me a dirty look before goin back te throwin more clean sawdust down on top a the dirty stuff. He had a bucket an he was grabbin out handfuls and shakin it on the floor.

I went over an stood beside him te watch. After a while I said, 'Eh! Can I have a bit te throw down too?'

He just ignored me an went on shakin it, makin sure not te let it go on people's shoes, because they were givin him dirty looks an grabbin a stare down at themself te make sure.

'Eh, young fella, do ye not hear me? I want te give you a hand. Give's a bit a yer sawdust an I'll help ye throw it down.'

'Go on then,' he said, shovin the bucket at me, lettin me dig in an grab two handfuls, but when I looked there was only a little bit, it all got spilt out before I could get much.

'See it's a knack,' he laughed, grabbin up a handful an shakin it all around him.

'Do you work here?'

'Yeah.'

'How old are ye?'

'Fourteen an two months! How old are you?'

'Eh, seven an eh . . .' I tried te work it out! 'Loads a days.'

'So, you just got yer birthday, I bet ye!' he said, lookin happy I was not nearly as big as him.

'Yeah! But still an all! Seven is big! Isn't it?'

'I suppose. But you still have years before ye get te be like me. A workin man wit a wage in me back pocket.'

'Yeah, but you have te give the wage packet up te yer mammy, don't ye?' I snorted, ragin because he was makin out like he was already a big person an he was now his own man.

He gave me a dirty look then said, lettin his head drop sideways, 'Would you ever go way now like a good little child an leave me te get on wit me job a work. Go on ye'll get me fired, I'm not supposed te be slackin.'

'All right then,' I said, movin away an lookin over at the counter te watch fer the granny. She was nearly there, just at the top a the queue wit one other waitin ahead.

'Now, ma'am, wha can I get you?' said the fella wit the white coat givin his hands a quick slap on the counter, thinkin he was playin the drums.

'Give me four streaky rashers, love,' she said, pointin down at the ones she wanted, sittin in the front a the winda.

He put them on white greaseproof paper an slapped the lot on the white scales lookin at the weight, then rolled up the paper sayin, 'Anythin else?'

'Oh yeah, wait now till I get started. Gimme a bit of tha back bacon ye have over be the wall, I want a nice bit fer me dinner on the Sunday. Then give me a quarter pound a Granby sausages, a nice bit of black an white puddin, an finish it off wit half a dozen nice big eggs. They'll do me the week.'

'Tha the lot?' he said, wrappin it all up an liftin the pencil sittin behind his ear, he was wantin now te work out how much she owes him.

'That's one shillin an eight pence,' he said, wrappin the lot in one big sheet a white paper an handin it to her.

She tried te lift it wit one hand an manage the string bag in the other, but the parcel was too heavy.

'Here, ma'am, let me help ye, give me up the bag an I'll put it in fer you.'

'God bless ye, son,' she said, handin up the bag then takin out her little brown purse an rootin fer the money. 'There's two shillins,' she said, givin him the money an takin the bag.

I could see it was gettin heavy now, an was dyin te ask her te let me carry it. Me an Ceily always did tha fer me mammy. Help her carry home the shoppin. I felt me chest an stomach tighten, an it took away me happy thoughts makin me want te cry again. I miss me mammy terrible, somethin terrible, it pains me heart so it does. *Oh God, send her back, I want me mammy, you can't keep her, God! She belongs te me an Ceily! An where's me Ceily? Why did she go?*

I held me breath waitin te hear, but nothin came te me, God's not talkin.

I watched the granny go more slowly now, makin her way out the door wit the bag lookin heavy. Then I trailed after her, wishin I was really belonged te her. She seems somehow like me, on her own an a bit lonely. Tha's because she lost her dog an her cat, they were her friends! So we're the same, because I lost me mammy an me sister, an me home! An me wellie boots, well the one. But tha's no good, I thought, starin down at me feet lookin black wit the dirt an blue from the cold.

The granny crossed the road an looked in the butcher's

winda. Then she went in an I followed, wantin te see wha she got.

'Yes, darlin, wha can I get you? We have a nice bit a steak today, special offer! Shillin a pound look! Best rump.'

'Ah will ye go on outa tha, you aul fool. Every bloody week ye say the same thing, knowin it's been a rare day, an a very rare one at tha, since I ever bought a lump a steak. Sure where would I get the money? Never mind the teeth te chew it! Sure don't ye know I haven't one left in me head.'

'Sure I haven't one meself,' he said, shovin in his tongue then suddenly liftin his teeth an grabbin out the top set.

'Oh holy Jesus! Willie Wilson! Don't let them drop on me meat, or ye may say goodnight te any money ye might a got from me!'

'Tut tut! There's no pockets in a shroud, Mona, ye can't take it wit you! Why don't ye take me out an we'll paint the town red?! Wha do you say? A couple a bottles a champagne, you get the glad rags on, drag out tha frock you've been savin since the Charleston first came out, an we dance the night away! Roses an candlelight, chandeliers, diamonds in yer hair, Mona, settin off the sparkle in your lovely blue Irish smilin eyes, my lovely Mona! Can you see it?' he said, leanin over the counter an talkin very softly te her, like she was the only woman on the earth.

Then he put his hands on her wrinkled hand sittin on the counter, an the shop was very quiet. Everyone wanted te hear him talkin lovely te Mona, the old wrinkled granny. Then a tear poured down her cheek an a man coughed an a woman standin next to him said, 'Tha was lovely. I never knew you had it in ye, William Wilson! But then you never know someone, do you?'

'God, it was like listenin to the pictures,' said another woman, smilin wit everyone lettin out their breath.

Then Willie shouted, 'RIGHT! What's it te be this week? Sheep's head, anyone? Only sixpence, boil the shite out of it an make yourself a lovely pot a brawn. Now I can't say better than tha!'

'Have ye a nice bit of neck a lamb?' the granny said, lookin along the winda an seein wha he had lined up on the shelf behind him.

'The very job te put hair on yer chest,' he said, whirlin himself around an grabbin up bits a meat hangin off a load a bones. 'Thruppence! Tha do you?' he said, rollin them up in white paper an handin them te her, without waitin fer an answer.

'Tha will do grand,' she said, takin out three pennies an puttin them in the palm of his hand, held straight out. She put tha in her bag leavin it hangin, not wantin te let it down in the sawdust coverin the dirty floor. The dirt was dragged in from the street, an blood splattered the floor as well, tha was comin from the meat hangin by the door, held up on big hooks. Then she made her way out an I followed. She eased her way down the street an stopped at a dealer, she was sellin cauliflowers an cabbages, an loads a different vegebales.

'Wha do ye want, granny? Here, how about a nice cauliflower, or wha about—'

'Give us a nice green head a cabbage, missus,' interrupted the granny, knowin wha she wanted.

'Oh ye're right, they're lovely today, came fresh in the market fer the weekend. Have you a bit a bacon te go wit tha, missus?'

'Yeah indeed I have. Got a lovely bit a streaky up in Sheils's.'

'Oh God, isn't tha lovely fer ye? Now wha else do ye want? Will ye be havin a stew? Wha about a nice few carrots an onions? I'll throw in the bit a parsley an thyme fer you. I won't charge ye, missus. Here, give me yer bag over an I'll stick them in fer you.'

'Ah ye know me well, Chrissie!'

'Well, if I don't know your ways after sixty years on the street, I must be dotin! Gone senile! Isn't tha how long ye're comin te us? It was me mammy then, God rest her soul, but sure I'm reared on these streets. Mammy, God be good te her, used te leave me sittin in the orange box there, shove a banana in me mouth te keep me quiet, an no one more contented than me, I can tell you! Twelve of us she reared on these streets, out in all weathers, she was, an us along wit her. She lived te seventy-two, God bless her. Used te sit on tha stool over there, givin orders from her throne she would.

'Yeah, Tessa Blackstock, my mammy! I'm goin te get a petition up te get the corporation te put a plaque up in her memory. I know down through all the days there was a lot a dealers here, but she was down here as well, right in the middle a them she was, when she only eleven days old. Tha's right! Her mother, my granny, used te keep her wrapped up inside her shawl an she all the contentment an comfort a babby could want. Oh, yes, wit her able te suck away on the diddy – sleep an suck, me granny said. Not a bother on her, an Mammy did the same wit all a us, kept us wrapped inside her shawl te suck on her milk an sleep away to our hearts' content. Sure wha more would a babby want?'

'Ah nature's a great thing,' said the granny, holdin open her purse waitin te hear how much.

'Sixpence, love!'

'Thanks, see ye again soon,' said the granny, smilin an movin off.

'Thanks, missus, you mind yerself now, an take it easy home wit tha bag. It looks heavy.'

'Ah, I'm used to it!' the granny said, walkin slowly towards the corner wit the bag draggin her down, makin her go very slowly.

I stayed behind really wantin now te rush up an ask te carry it fer her. She made her way goin really slow up Parnell Street wit the Rotunda hospital on the left. The path was crowded wit people hurryin te get the shops before they closed, or the good stuff was gone. It must be Friday, I thought, knowin people only make fer the shops then, because tha's when the men get paid or the workin women like my mammy. Then people start rushin te pay the shops tha they owe money to, an all the other people tha give them 'tick'.

We stopped at the lights on O'Connell Street and the granny leaned her shoppin bag on the ground but didn't let go of it, because then all the stuff would tumble out. Then we were movin again onta Parnell Street an I wondered where we were headin.

We came te Gardiner Street an stopped at the path waitin fer the traffic te ease, but she didn't turn up the hill headin fer Mountjoy Square or any of the laneways off the hill, nor did she go headin down stayin on Gardiner Street. So maybe she will do tha when we get te the other side.

We waited an waited wit no traffic lights te help us, an it looked now like we were goin te be stuck fer ever! It's Friday an everyone wants te get home wit their wages an give it up te the fambily. Nobody stayed on the path long, they all dashed out inta the traffic makin it stop, but me an the granny couldn't do tha. I was too small an she was too old. At last, the traffic eased an a coalman wit a black face an empty sacks wit his day's work over sawed the granny an me standin waitin patiently an pulled up his horse, sayin, 'Whoa, easy there now, girl,' an stopped te let us go past an get across. There was only me an the granny now walkin slowly, other people came runnin an flew past us, but you could see me an her was together.

'Missus! Do you want me te give ye a hand?' I suddenly said, puttin out me two hands showin her I wanted te help.

'So well ye might ask,' she said, lettin the heavy bag ease in her hand by droppin it down fer the ground te take the weight. 'Wha's wrong wit you? Are ye lost?' she said, lookin at me wit her head shakin, like she couldn't understand wha was happenin.

'Yeah,' I said. 'No! I'm not lost!'

'So tell me, chicken, why are you followin on my tail since early today? An tha's hours ago,' she said, lookin around seein it was startin te get dark now wit the lights comin on in the shops an the lamps on the front a the cars. 'Where do ye live?'

'Off Portland Row.'

'Do ye? I don't live far from there meself. Who is your mammy? Maybe I know her.'

'Missus Mary Carney,' I said, lookin up at her, wonderin wha she's goin te do te me. Maybe get Father Flitters after me!

'No! Haven't heard tell a her. Where's she now? Why you runnin wild? Where's your shoes an yer coat? You're half naked as I can see, here! Give tha foot up te me.'

'Wha, missus?' I said not understandin.

'I want te see the state a yer feet.'

I sat down on the ground an lifted me foot, lettin her have it. She rubbed her hand up an down then let it go, easin it back onta the ground. 'I thought so, soft as butter, them feet never walked on cement in all yer borned days! An where did ye get the women's knickers from? Wha's goin on?

'Here, we're goin the same direction, I don't live too far from there, I live beside Summer Street off the North Circular Road. You go down past the old maids' home then left, inta the row of nice houses there, don't you?'

'Yeah I do. But me house is gone!'

'Wha? Here, grab up the handle of the bag there an we'll carry it between us. We can walk at our ease an you can tell me wha ye're up to. Have we a deal? Are ye game fer tha?'

'Yeah, we have a deal,' I said happily, delighted she was talkin te me, an not even tellin me te ger away or wantin te shout at me.

I took hold a the handle an lifted up the weight, then grabbed hold a me Delia knickers pullin them up an holdin onta them wit me other hand. Then we started te walk slowly up Summerhill.

'So tell me, where's yer mammy? An wha do ye mean yer house is gone? Were youse evicted?'

'Wha does tha mean, missus?'

'Get thrown outa yer house an end up on the streets wit yer stuff all around ye. Very often happenin every day a the week,' she said, clampin her mouth shut an shakin her head.

'No tha didn't happen, missus. Our stuff is still in our house. But me sister an me mammy is gone missin.'

'How tha happen?' she said, lookin very confused wit her face leanin over te me, bendin her head.

'Mammy got buried, she got put in a hole in the ground, but it wasn't really me mammy, it was someone else! Because I sawed the corpse an it didn't look like my mammy at all, not at all like her,' I said, shakin me head makin tha very definite.

'I see,' she said, speakin very quiet now, an noddin her head like she knew wha I was talkin about.

'Then Father Flitters came te the house wit the cruelty peoples, a man an a woman an they tried te take us away.'

'Ah enough said, if tha evil man was involved! God forgive me an he a man of God. But I wonder. Oh God, he sure knows how te pick them! God forgive me, Lord, but I often wonder wha the method in the madness is. Makin aul Flitters a priest. Mind you, havin said tha, there's many more like him. Country men brought up hard, an comes up here te make life even harder, fer us city people. Worse than ever he, or they got it,' she said, talkin te herself not lookin at me.

I kept shakin me head agreein wit everythin she was sayin, but I didn't really understand any of it. But it did sound right.

'So go on, tell me. I'm listenin!'

'Yeah, but they didn't get me because Ceily told me te run an I did. An I brought back Mister Mullins, he owns the corner shop.'

'Oh yes, I think I may have met him, but I would only know him te see.'

'So him an Delia came up te help Ceily an stop Father Flitters an the cruelty peoples takin us away. But there was terrible fightin an people got hurt!'

'Wait a minute now! Are you the Carney childre they tried te put away into a convent? A terrible riot broke out an spread fer miles across the city! Right over te the south side it did, went on fer three long nights wit runnin battles between the animal gangs from the north an southside a the city an the police. Innocent people was caught up in it! Over forty people badly hurt an three people lost their life! It was in all the papers sure. Never mind tha I meself witnessed the killins an runnin battles wit ambulances comin from all over the city, not te mention the fire brigade! Homes went up in blazes when people left their tenement houses te come out onta the street te witness the ructions. Yes! The sparks from the fire hit the floorboards or anyway, must a lodged somewhere in the rotten wood. Sure two houses alone went up on Gardiner Street. Jesus mercy tonight, an you're tha child?

'I heard tell, but I didn't get the full story, or even the half of it. So wha happened to the other child ye say is missin? Your sister was it?'

'Yeah, Ceily me sister. I don't know I woke up an she was gone. Mister Mullins was takin care a us, but then Delia his daughter died, she got kilt in the fightin, Mister Mullins brought her home from the hospidal an now she's dead in the house. The handywomen are gettin her ready fer her wake.'

'Who? Who's layin her out?'

'Nellie Fry an Essie Bullcock.'

'Oh tha pair, say no more,' she said, throwin her eye at me an clampin her mouth shut then lookin away. 'Come on, we're just here,' she said, turnin right onta the North Circular Road, then left down the lane to a row a cottages.

'Where did you get them knickers? They're makin a holy show a ye, child. Sure you'd get two a me in them, never mind an infant like yerself!'

'They belong te Delia, she's dead now. Tha's Mister Mullins daughter.'

'Who put them on ye?'

'Ceily me sister. She had te wash me own because they was dirty, I fell down on them when I was hidin in the lane where me backyard is. An me coat got dirty too! So did me socks, an I lost me wellie somewhere, but I don't remember where.'

'Right, I'm here! Hold onta tha bag while I look fer me hall door key,' she said, pushin me back against the wall, lettin the bag rest against me belly an wrappin me hands around the handles.

'Here we go,' she said, pushin in the blue door into a little hallway. It was lovely an warm, wit stairs lookin ahead of us an two doors, one on the right an the other on the left. She opened the door te the right, an immediately I saw a lovely red-hot coal fire. It was just sittin there glowin bright red in the dark, because she had banked it up, doin just like Mammy does wit her wet slack from the coal. I knew this was right, because ours always looks like tha when we go out, the coal put on then packed high wit wet slack. Mammy always does tha, because she wants te keep the fire burnin without usin up all the coal. Otherwise, it would be usin the good fuel an havin the fire go out anyway.

The room looked lovely wit the roarin-red fire sittin in the fireplace, an around tha a wooden mantelpiece goin all the way up te the ceilin. It was glitterin shiny polished dark wood, an it had a big mirror in the middle an more at the top, an the sides had the same wit shelves as well. An they had lovely little ornaments sittin on them.

Beside tha under the winda, lookin out onta a backyard, was a little dinin table wit matchin chairs an a lovely cream frilly lace tablecloth. Then, as well as tha, she had another heavy plain green cloth sittin underneath. I looked over at the two comfy-lookin cushy fireside chairs wit cushions fer yer back, they were beside the fire one each side. Oh it would be great if I could sit down in one a them now an get a bit a heat fer meself, I thought, feelin very ill at ease standin close te the door. I was wonderin an feelin worried if she was goin te tell me te go. She might just say thanks fer helpin me, then open the door an let me out, wantin me te go. It was nice te talk te her an be a part of somethin fer a while, but then it ends an I think ye're worser off. Because then it hurts. Yeah, I'm thinkin tha now. I've had te be doin a lot of thinkin since I got te be seven an me mammy died, or just went away. No she didn't die! Not my mammy! She would never do tha!

'Did ye hear me?'

I came back te me senses an looked up at the granny seein she was sayin something.

'Wha?' I said, lookin up at her, seein she was starin at me lookin confused wit her now gettin annoyed.

'Are ye listenin te me, child? Ye're gone miles away, is your mind ramblin or wha?'

I said nothin, just waited fer her te finish.

'I need te put this stuff away before the heat from the fire gets at it,' she said, draggin up the heavy bag an makin fer the scullery. I could see tha straight ahead te the right, wit the door leadin out from the sittin room. I rushed te grab up the bag an carry it wit her.

'Put it down on this,' she said, landin it on a little kitchen table wit a shiny red top an two big grandfather kitchen chairs, they had brown cushions on the seats te keep yer arse in the height a comfort. I wouldn't say tha word out loud, you would get a box in the mouth fer tha, it's bad language. But it's great te be able te think things in yer own mind an keep it te yerself, then ye don't get inta trouble an you can wonder wha ye like.

'Will ye bend down there under tha sink an hand me up the big pot?' she said, holdin out the meat an takin the paper off.

'Tha one?' I said, handin her up a middle-size pot.

'Grand!' she said, takin it off me an runnin it under the tap. She rinsed it out then filled it half up wit water an put in the streaky bacon. 'Let tha steep, here! Put it back under the sink, it will keep cool there. I won't be wantin tha until I cook it on the Sunday fer me dinner. Now, tomorrow I'm goin te make a nice bit a stew, so this neck a lamb should keep grand till then,' she said, takin down a big white Delft bowl an puttin in the meat. Then she covered it wit a small plate.

'Here! Take out them vegetables fer me an put them over there, in tha box in the corner. Can you see wha ye're doin? I can't see a bloody thing in this dark. The light from the fire is not throwin much in here. Go in an get me the box a matches sittin on the windasill, I'm goin te light this lamp,' she said, takin down a brass lamp from the shelf over the sink, then liftin off the globe an pullin up the wick.

I rushed back inta the sittin room an grabbed up the matches, then stopped te look at the rest a the room. She had a china cabinet over against the far wall, tha's to the right when ye come in the door. I leaned across te get a look, seein all her china ornaments sittin on velvet-covered shelves. Then me head moved around seein wha else she had. Oh tha's lovely! I thought, wit me eyes lightin up takin in the big fancy brass lamp wit the coloured glass globe. I wonder will she light tha?

'Come on, child! I'm waitin, wha are ye doin, makin the matches?' she said, leanin her head out the scullery door te get a look at me.

'Oh sorry, missus!' I said rushin te her wit me hand out holdin the matches.

'Oh come on! The night will be gone if I don't get a move on,' she said, openin the box an takin out a match. Then she loosened the bottom of the lamp te check how much paraffin oil was left. I could smell it straight away, it was flyin up me nostrils makin me head give a shootin pain. I moved away not wantin te get any more fumes, an suddenly the tiredness hit me.

I feel sick now an me head is startin te pain me. I want te get somethin te drink an lie down an go te sleep, an I want te be all wrapped up lovely an warm, I don't care about eatin, I'm not hungry any more. I was too tired te do any more than just stand outside, starin in the scullery wit me eyes followin the granny.

She was busy moochin around gettin herself all sorted, now she was bendin down an liftin up the fryin pan, then havin a grand conversation wit herself. 'Where's me drippin? Where did I leave down tha fork? I'll do two rashers, tha young one must be hungry. Wonder when she got fed last? Where are you, child?' she said shoutin, an me standin lookin at her.

'I'm here, missus,' I said, wantin te be over on tha fireside chair an close me eyes.

'You must be starved wit the hunger, ye poor cratur, I'm goin te give you somethin warm in yer stomach, then we'll see about gettin you sorted. Wha did you say about tha Mister Mullins? Is he goin te mind youse? Can he do tha? Sure he's a widow man on his own now, them authorities wouldn't let a man on his own who's not a blood relative take care a two little girls,' she said, starin at me, waitin te see did I understand this. Then forgettin about me, because she was now starin at nothin.

I don't understand why Mister Mullins can't mind me an Ceily when she gets back. I can't understand nothin, an I don't want to, I just want te get warm an go te sleep, I feel sick!

I looked over at the fire wit the red-hot coals, the heat comin from it was lovely. It was because the coals were packed high, sittin up in the grate. I turned me head back te look an see wha the granny was up to. She was busy now doin her fryin an butterin bread, then heatin the teapot wit boilin water, ready te make a pot a tea.

I inched me way over te the fire keepin me eye on the granny. I was gettin desperate wit me tiredness, but I didn't want her te think I was makin meself at home in her house. She won't like tha an she might open the door an push me out, because you can't do nothin in someone else's house until they tell you. You have te wait te be asked before ye can sit down. Oh but I am so tired, me eyes won't stay open, it feels like there's a heavy weight pressin them down. I'll just sit here on the rug in front a the fire, because me legs won't hold me standin no more, an me head is splittin wit the pain.

I slid meself down onta the rug feelin the heat roar out on top a me, an I gave a big sigh an closed me eyes. Oh I'm in heaven.

15

'LITTLE ONE, WAKE UP, come on up ye get!'

I felt meself shakin an me eyes shot open. I stared into a wrinkled old face wit muddy grey eyes starin back at me.

'Do ye know where you are? Ye fell asleep. You've been like tha fer over three hours, look there's the clock,' she said, pointin at the big wooden carved clock on the mantelpiece.

I couldn't read the time yet, only a little, but not proper.

'It's nine o clock! I should get you movin, come on come inta the scullery an have yer bite te eat. Look! I kept yer tea warm sittin on the hob by the fire.'

I followed her finger seein it pointin at two plates. They were sittin, one on top of the other warmin on the hob, tha's wha you can use te cook on the fire. Lots a people do tha, it's when they don't have a gas cooker like my mammy an the granny has.

'Grab a tea towel,' she said, makin te stand herself up from the fireside chair.

I just sat meself up an yawned, scratchin me head an wantin te go back te sleep. I gave another yawn an left one eye open te follow the granny, watchin her headin fer the scullery then come back holdin the two hot plates. She was makin sure te carry them in the safety of the tea towel.

I felt a bit hungry now, an the pain in me head was eased.

'Here, get tha inta ye, you must be starved te death wit the hunger.'

I watched as she lifted the white plate leavin the big one sittin on the tea towel te stop it burnin the table, then she pulled out the big chair fer me, sayin, 'Sit down an eat this, come on!'

I sat up an looked te see wha I was gettin. A fried egg hard in the middle an a sausage an rasher! The smell went straight up me nose, makin me belly rumble an me mouth water.

'Here! Have tha cut a bread, it's fresh turnover, lovely an soft. Then we have te get you movin. I better go down an see tha Mister Mullins, find out what's happenin. If he doesn't take ye then you will have te go into a home, they'll put you away in a convent. Your mother's dead, Lily. She won't be back an you're goin to have te face it. You might not even have a sister, it looks te me like she got lifted as soon as she set foot outside the door, she's now a goner, put away an locked up in a convent somewhere. You may never find out fer years, or maybe not ever.

'You have te understand now what's gone an happened. Because of the terrible trouble, you've come to the attention of all the wrong people – the parish priest, the authorities. That's bad for you an hard fer anyone who wants te just take you in an rear ye wit their own. In your kinda situation it happens more times than not people, neighbours, they do tha quietly without any fuss or bother. It's understood an accepted by everyone. But once you get attention drawn down on ye, especially from the powers tha be, then you're done for! They come after you wit the full power a the law behind them. So, my suspicion is that's what's after happenin now, your sister has been pulled in an sent away.'

Then she stared at me an pointed the finger, sayin, 'You poor unfortunate cratur, but if I'm not very much mistaken, you are next. I would say they're on your tail even as we speak,' she said, wit her head noddin an her eyes lookin very worried.

I stopped wit the fork aimin fer me wide-open mouth an looked up at her. Me heart crashed inta me stomach fillin me up wit sick. I dropped the fork, not wantin te eat, an I didn't want te stay here wit her neither.

I stood up fast an held onta me Delia knickers an rushed meself through the sittin room, then stopped dead, lookin at the front door, it was shut an I can't reach up te open it. I know wha te do! I turned meself around an flew back an grabbed hold of a chair, then dragged it pullin it along the floor te open the door.

'Come back, where ye goin? Child, you can't go out now ramblin this time a the night, it's too dangerous!'

I didn't listen, I opened the lock then stood down an pulled away the chair. Then I whipped open the door an flew fer all I was worth. I shot across the road on Summerhill not lookin left or right an not even thinkin, I just wanted te run an get away from tha granny an make wha she said go away. My mammy is not dead, an Ceily is not caught an taken away, an tha won't happen te me neither!

I ran down Portland Row past the convent wit the old maids' home, I could see lights shinin in the windas. Then I turned off te the left, makin me way home te me own house. There might be a light in my winda too, an Ceily might be home an even Mammy!

I ran faster wit tha idea an me heart was shiverin in me chest wit tha great thought. I turned right onta my street seein lights in windas wit the lamps makin shadows flickerin on the curtains. 'My street, my house, my mammy, my Ceily, my fambily!' I muttered, singin it out wit every step of me foot hittin the hard cobble-stone ground. I was ragin an excited an wanted te make war wit the whole world if they tried te do wha the granny did. Everyone has wha belongs te them. Why is it an how then can the peoples in the world think they can take wha belongs te me an my fambily?

I stared ahead lookin te see my house, it was comin closer wit every step. Then it was close an I was right up to it, but now I could feel the heart goin outa me. 'It's dead, it's black, it's quiet,' I muttered, sayin all the things tha can happen te make somethin become nothin an turn inta somethin dead.

My house is dead, so Mammy didn't come home, an, no, not even Ceily made it back. I climbed up onta the windasill an looked in through the curtain. I couldn't see nothin, only shapes tha look like furniture. I'm now dead too, everyone's dead, all me fambily! We're all dead. I'm goin te make meself really dead too! I can . . . how can I do tha? Easy, wait fer a motor car te pass an run under! Find the canal an throw meself in! Yeah. Lots an lots a way te die.

'God! You up there? You're not my friend no more! I won't ever listen when people start te talk about you, I don't want you, God! You took away my mammy an ye kept her fer yerself. Ye're no good! You can strike me dead, go on I dare ye!' I said, feelin the rage at him makin me chest stick out an me body go all stiff. I wanted te fight him!

'YE'RE NO GOOD, GOD! Fuck you an fuck the powers tha be an fuck grannies an fuck?! An fuck . . . you, Ceily, fer runnin out an leavin me all on me own! An, Mammy! You did, you must a got died! Why did ye let God get away wit it? Did ye not think a me an Ceily? I HATE YOU, MA! I HATE YE! An I'm callin ye ma because you hate te be called tha, you always said it was common! So there!' I shouted, feelin me voice go all hoarse an me throat sore an me head start te pain me again.

'MAMMYEEEE! Come back! ' I screamed, hearin it come out in a terrible croak. I slid down the door onta the stone-cold ground an heard meself lettin out a terrible keen, it sounded so high it was like the Banshee. Then I opened me mouth wider an howled like a dog after gettin an unmerciful belt of an iron crowbar. I seen it happen an I heard the dog cry, a woman come up beside me an said, 'He was howlin from the pain.'

'Well, tha's wha I'm doin now, God! I hope ye're ashamed a yerself! An I'm not afraid a you because you can't do me harm no more so ye can't.'

I began te shiver like mad an suddenly the cold of the damp stone moved all the way through me. I could see the shiny frost on the ground. Me teeth keep knockin, if only I could get back inta me house, then find my Ceily. Then we could go an look fer Mammy! Because a new idea was comin te me about God. Sure wha would he want wit my mammy? She's no oil paintin she says, but I think she is, I think she's a very beautiful oil paintin. But if she thinks tha then maybe God thinks tha as well. Yeah, it's a mistake! People are always gettin everythin wrong, lookit the nuns! They thought they was goin te stop me makin me first Holy Communion.

Tha nun was definite. 'No!' she said. 'Over my dead body!' She hated me tha one did. She said I had too much te say fer meself fer someone so young, an further! I was beyond turnin into a civil human being because I was too wild an too cheeky te tame. Well! She changed her tune very fast when my mammy had words wit her! Tha's wha Mammy reported te the neighbours when they waited te hear the result. I was earwiggin, so I heard it all. So yeah, people say things but they get them wrong, an they're wrong now about my mammy bein dead.

Yeah, an I just had another good idea, me coat an stuff is hangin in Mister Mullins'. Ceily washed an cleaned them, then left the lot hangin on the clothesline strung high up the ceilin. An the key a my house is in me coat pocket. Oh this is a great idea! I'm goin te take meself around there this minute, an I'm just goin te go in sayin I'm gettin me stuff. Then I can come home te me own house, an nobody will be able te get me here. I can do wha I like an even go lookin, searchin the streets fer me mammy an Ceily.

I put me hand out te get meself up, but now I'm stuck, me legs is seized up like two iron bars, I want te cry wit me pain, I'm sore, I'm tired, I'm hungry an I'm so terribly freezin wit the cold an the damp an the frost. Mammy hates January, she always says it's a curse wit it bringin the dark an the terrible wet an cold. I wonder did she know wha it was really goin te do te her an all of us. Did she really meet her end? Tha's wha the big people call death. Because it broke us all apart an then took our home.

I put me hands on the ground an pushed meself up hearin meself creak. I wonder is this wha the old people mean when they say, 'Oh me poor bones. I'm kilt wit the painin.'

I rattled off feelin like a skeleton wit me bones knockin an creakin because I'm all very stiff an cold. An I must be gettin te be a skeleton now anyway, because I got nothin te eat since weeks. I wonder is tha goin te make me dead too. I shivered holdin in me shoulders tryin te get meself warm, an keep out the icy wind makin the hem a me frock blow back an me Delia knickers blow out like a balloon. Me head is painin an me eyes are all watery an hurtin. I'm so tired an I'm thirsty. It's pitch black an there's not a sign of a cat or dog, never mind catchin sight a someone out on the night.

The light from the street lamps was yella showin all the air was turned te white mist tha looked like the freezin icy cold. I stared at it wit me back hunched an me feet limpin from one foot te the other, wantin te give a hop an a skip te warm me. But I couldn't, me body had no strength te do tha. I stared inta the cold white mist seein it turnin a pale yella an glitter like diamonds when it got close te the light from the street lamps.

It looked lovely, but only if you didn't have te see it now, walkin in the dead a night dyin wit the cold an hunger freezin te death.

I turned right an walked on past the houses not seein a light in any a the windas. Everybody's in now home an safe, an they're all in their beds snuggled up fer the night, I thought, lookin back at my corner an across te the tenements. Not a one person te be seen. Never in me borned days did I see the night like this, never mind be out walkin in it! I wonder wha Mammy would say if she knew? I know her forehead would crease, an her eyes would jump outa her head, an she would box me ear an slap me legs an grab me arms shakin me, roarin, 'Lily Carney! You're goin te be the death a me wit yer carry-on! Wha would I do if you got yerself kilt stone dead? They'd have te bury me down on top a ye, because me heart wouldn't take the strain a losin you!' Then she would grab hold a me an squeeze the life outa me, sayin, 'You're my everythin! You're my breath, me life an my hope! But I swear te the livin Jesus! I'm goin te kill you stone dead one a these days, the way ye have my heart broke!'

Yeah I thought, shakin me head, me heart scaldin wit the pain of wantin her back, wantin te feel her arms around me an me head buried in her belly. I keened wit the pain of wantin te feel her rubbin me head an fixin me hair, then her sayin, 'Oh Jesus, Lily Carney, ye're a demon!' Then she would laugh I know she would, sayin, 'Come on! You've had nothin te eat, you must be starved wit the hunger. Wait until ye see wha I have, I have somethin lovely kept up for you! It's gorgeous, a lovely mince meat stew! Me an Ceily had our share, oh it was very tasty! Get it inta you now, eat up.'

The picture was so real I could feel her beside me, touch her warm body an smell an taste the stew. I could look inta her eyes an see them smilin, an the happy look on her face at seein me home, back wit her again an she wantin te mind me! An havin somethin good te give me. She is the best mammy in the whole world. Nobody is bester than my mammy!

I started te cry but the pain was not lettin out the tears. It was hurtin too much now, it felt like they're only wastin their time. Tears is not enough, I cried so much, too much, but it did no good. Nothin gets better, she doesn't come back te me, an even Ceily stays silent, from wherever she is. So I keened, it matched the throbbin hurt in me heart, the sound was like measurin the pain. Out here in the icy-cold dark night I can see it all an feel it all. It is like I have nowhere else fer me mind te go but see everythin around me an in me an before me an behind me. It's all comin at me te let me see the world is bigger an stranger than I ever knew or thought before. I'm seven, just become seven, I'm a child I know I am, yet suddenly I know I have lived for ever. It is like I know all the time ahead of me an the time long gone before me. But it is all the same, because I have lived it all.

I am old, very old, a voice whispered comin from far off, yet it was very close, so close I could hear it in my heart an in my mind an in my creakin bones. I felt strange listenin te them thoughts it was like I was someone else, yet someone I've always known, a very old part of meself.

Then I heard a buzzin noise of voices comin te me from up the road. I stretched me eyes, tryin te open them wider then squinted, tryin te see in the cold foggy white air. Is tha a light comin outa one a the houses up ahead a me? It might be Mister Mullins! Wha's happenin? Oh yeah Delia, he has te keep the wake, I forgot about tha!

16

I SHIFTED MESELF INTA goin faster, wantin te get there now hopin te see Ceily was back an Mister Mullins won't be wantin te kill everyone. I could hear me bare feet slappin along the ground an the pain thumpin up through me, it was like gettin hit wit a bamboo stick. Tha's wha the nun at school hits us wit!

I slowed down at the door seein it was left open a bit an I could hear people in the hall. It didn't sound like there was any trouble. I pushed it in easy, not wantin te be spotted straight away, an came face te face wit a gang a aul fellas wit wrinkled faces, one aul fella's cheeks was hangin off tha much it was drippin inta his glass a porter. He stopped guzzlin then wiped away the froth from around his mouth wit the sleeve a his coat makin it wet an more shiny against the rest a the dried, caked-in hard dirt. 'Lovely stuff,' he sniffed, shakin his head lookin very impressed an slappin the glass down on the chair pushed in the middle a the corner, just behind the door. They were usin tha chair, an keepin it fer themself te hold all their stuff. I could see they were not short wit their bottles a porter. They each had loads all full lined up in front a them, an loads more all empties, left standin underneath. Then they had a little saucer wit wha looked like about a teaspoonful a snuff, an one fella was chewin his gums on a ham bone, an the other was wolfin down two big cuts a loaf bread wit a lump a cheese stuck in the middle.

Then one aul fella wasn't bothered at all about the plate a pig's cheek still sittin in front a him. He grabbed up the bottle a porter then slopped it inta the empty glass an started pourin it down his neck.

They looked at me an nodded. 'Night, child!' one said.

'Mind yerself,' the other one said, nearly chokin tryin te manage the half loaf a bread he was shovin down his gullet.

'Grand bit a stuff tha,' the man drinkin said, smackin down the nearly half-empty glass back on the chair an noddin, pointin from me to it.

'Sure wha would I care?' I sniffed te meself, annoyed he thought I wanted te know about his drink!

I made me way through the hall seein a crowd of aul ones sittin at the other end an spreadin themself onta the stairs wit loads a grub, bottles a stout an more stuff all sittin beside them on chairs an inside up against the wall. They were all suckin an puffin on clay pipes stuffed wit tobacco, an they had more a tha left sittin in a heap on the chair next te their saucers a snuff. The smoke was blowin inta each other's faces, but they didn't care.

I came to a crawlin stop te take in an aul one, she had long grey hair an it was streelin down, hangin in bits a thread around her shoulders. She leaned in wit the pipe hangin outa her mouth, then gave a little cough, wit the pipe landin smack on the floor, after gettin a blast a smoke from another aul one. She was busy suckin an blowin like mad, lettin it billow inta the middle a the other aul ones, all leanin in te talk an be heard.

'Ah oh well the curse a Jaysus!' screamed the aul one, bendin down heavin an puffin then lettin a roar, when she picked up the two pieces tha was left of the pipe.

'Never mind, Lolly! Here! Take this, I grabbed a couple

when the goin was easy. Good aul Mullins didn't stinge on the pipes!'

'Oh the blessins a God on ye, Biddy O'Toole, may ye be rewarded in the next life,' Lolly said, wit her eyes lightin up at the sight a the new pipe.

'Never mind the next life, let's enjoy this one first! Now go on. Tell us the story before we are all next te be planted.'

'Ah Jesus, Nanny Nagle! Don't take all night finishin wit the bloody story!'

'Ah well fuck off then! If that's yer attitudes, I'll keep me own counsel!'

'Ah no. Ah no! I was only jokin. Go on tell us!'

'Are youse sure?' said the story woman, lookin suspicious an hurt an ragin all at the same time.

'Oh Jesus yes! Isn't tha right?'

'Oh God yes!' they all agreed, noddin an lookin very serious an tryin te look as if they were cryin because the story woman was nearly cryin, ye could see tha, be the way she was now sniffin.

'No word of a lie! Bent he was, stiff as a poker, so they tied him up.'

Cough splutter, went another aul one, spittin out gobs a tobacco, because she wasn't just smokin it, she had the stuff tha ye can chew as well as her pipe.

'Wait! Don't interrupt!' said an aul granny wit lumps a brown snots hangin down her nose from all the snuff she shoved up. She was tryin te listen te the next story teller. 'Go on, Queenie! Tell us, now it better be good! Because youse all keep interruptin me when I try te tell me own story!'

'Oh this one is good! Right!'

'But now before ye go on, tell us. Was this "Grab yer knickers Dirty Macker" ye're tellin about?'

'The very one, Biddy! Wait till ye hear—'

'ACHOO!' The granny suddenly exploded, sendin snotty snuff, lumps a bread an bits a bacon inta people's open mouth, then their flyin hands knocked bottles a porter, an a glass a stout got thrun in the air wit the sudden fright everyone got.

'Ah fer the luv a Jaysus, Jinny Coalman!' Biddy roared, clampin her mouth shut chewin her gums, then lettin the lot sit under her nose snufflin like mad.

'Me nostrils blew! I couldn't help meself! Sure wha do ye's expect? This is the very good stuff. Works grand,' the granny moaned, shakin her head slowly, lookin pained, tryin te get them te understand. Then leanin over te pinch up more snuff wit her thumb an finger, then easin it onta the knuckle of her left hand.

I watched as she stared, keepin her eye on them while she sniffed an shoved, first the left then the right nostril, heavin it all up. Everyone watched wit their own noses brown, covered in snuff an their mouth gapin open, wantin te eat the head offa her, but they were too annoyed wit watchin her doin it all over again.

I didn't want te get hit in case someone takes a fit an starts throwin somethin, ye don't know. So I eased meself past them, mutterin, 'Excuse me, missus,' then made me way inta the sittin room full te the brim wit people. They were sittin on the floor an chairs, an anywhere they could find a free spot. A load a mammies wrapped in black shawls an smokin their pipes was sittin on the floor over be the winda, they got tha corner fer themselves. I shuffled over te see wha was happenin.

'No, no, he wasn't dead at all, he woke up in the dead house!' said a lovely-lookin mammy wit jet-black hair, it was fallin in waves te her shoulder, an she had huge blue eyes wit rosy-red lips. She's very young an she only has five childre. Her eldest child is in my class at school. She was sittin wit her back te the wall an her legs stretched out covered wit a long brown skirt an a wraparound blue an white bib. But she had a big belly, because she was married an was a mammy. Tha's how ye know a mammy a mile away. They always have a big belly or a new babby hidden inside the shawl suckin on her diddy. I'm not supposed te even think tha word, never mind say it, because people would say I'm usin shockin bad language. Or them's terrible thoughts I'm thinkin, an then I would have te go te Confession an tell me sins te the priest.

I looked down at her bit a style, seein she had laced-up brown shoes tha looked nearly new, an you could see her legs was wearin thick brown stockins. Not many mammies get te wear them, they have te wear bare legs because stockins cost too much money.

I leaned meself against the winda an listened.

'Sure I wouldn't tell youse a word of a lie! May I be struck stone dead this minute, if there's not a scrap a truth in wha I'm tellin youse,' she said, lettin her nose narrow an her head drop back, lyin it on her shoulder. Then she lifted her eyes te the ceilin starin te the heavens.

They all took in a sharp breath, so she slowly brought her face back lettin her now sorrowful pious-lookin mother-of-all-sorrows eyes rest on everyone, one be one.

'Oh go on, Emily, sure don't we believe every word,' breathed another mammy whisperin wit the fear a God on her, then lookin around te see if everyone else agreed.

'Yeah!' they breathed, lettin the eyes fall outa their heads an the mouths hang gaped open.

'Sat up he did, threw back the sheet coverin him an stared around wit the eyes comin outa his head. This is all true as I'm sittin here tellin youse! Sure I was there! In the other room wit me own dead babby! I had her on me lap cradlin her an fixin her hair. All on me own, just me an the dead in the dead house I was. Or I thought I was, till I heard the groans an looked around wonderin where it was comin from,' Emily gasped, wit everyone startin moanin an keenin now, ready te cry. But she stopped them wit her starin eyes an a wave of her hand, then leaned her head in heavin up her breath. 'Wasn't I there completely desolate,' she whispered, wit the breath comin in gasps. 'Wit nothin an nobody in there te protect an save me but meself an me own dead babby!'

Everyone held their breath.

'Dead she was, died only two year old, died in the hospital on me she did. A beauty if ever there was one.'

'Yeah, tut, yeah shockin! Tha was very unfortunate!' everyone moaned, lettin out the breath in terrible banshee keens.

'Oh God rest the poor mite. So go on! Wha happened next? Was he dead?'

'No indeed he was not! Anyways, as I was gettin on wit me story tellin ye's—'

Then a mammy wit a head a roarin-red hair said, 'Now before ye start again, just so we have it straight. Was tha "Fuck The Weather" Johnjo Dolan ye're tellin us about?'

'The very same!' snapped the missus, givin the mammy full marks fer gettin tha right. 'Anyways, one minute the body is lyin there dead as a corpse, covered by a white sheet, then the next, up he shoots wit the sheet still coverin his head. Down go the hands under the sheet flingin it outa the way—'

'An tell us! Did you see, witness all this?' said another mammy, lookin terribly shocked an interruptin the story.

'Oh indeed I did! Seen the lot I did, seen everythin there was te be seen. Sure aren't I tellin youse? I was only feet away, standin in the little part tha holds only the one stone slab. You just have te lean yer head in an ye can see the whole stretch from corner te corner, the whole a the dead house.'

'Oh my Jesus sweet mercy tonight! An here's you still here te tell the tale. If tha was me now, I would be dead an buried, dead an buried I would be from the outright shock of it!' snorted a mammy clampin her mouth shut an takin in a huge breath not able te get over it.

'There ye go now!' said the lovely-lookin mammy, lowerin her eyes te take in her skirt an flick an invisible bit a dirt away.

'So wha happened then?' said the red-haired mammy.

'Well! So ye may ask! To this day I am still not the better of it!'

'Tha bad?' snorted another mammy, ragin somethin like tha could happen ye.

'Worse!' snorted Lovely-lookin Mammy.

'Did he attack you?' said a mammy wit the eyes goin cross-ways because they kept turnin in the back a her head, an she couldn't get them back proper, it was all the shock comin at hearin the terrible story.

'Attacked was it? Wait till you hear this! He sat up straight as a poker wit the head slowly turnin on his shoulders, lookin from one dead corpse te the other. All covered by sheets they were, an lyin stretched out cold on a stone-cold slab just like himself. Then he pulled up the sheet te get a look down at himself, then felt the cold on his back an arse. It was takin him a bit a time but slowly he was gettin there. Yes, he was in the dead house an they were gettin him ready. An it could happen any time – they will cart him off an bury him. Then his head lifted an he looked straight at me wit the eyes bulged outa his head, an I stared back wit the colour drained outa me, the strength leavin me legs an the power a speech gone from me. I wanted te scream but me mouth kept openin an closin wit nothin comin, nothin! Not a sound. Then I looked down at me dead babby, Elizabeth Emily, wit the most gorgeous mop a curly light-brown hair an the pale-blue eyes starin up at me but seein nothin now. She died wit her eyes open an nobody bothered te keep them shut. Wouldn't waste the two coppers, may they all die roarin God forgive me,' she blessed herself.

'May God forgive them,' they repeated and blessed themselves then waited, goin back te very quiet.

'Then I looked up again, seein the corpse open his mouth an whip off the sheet, throw down the legs landin them danglin over the side, then lettin go an almighty howl outa himself. It went on fer a full five minutes, then slowly died down an stopped altogether. Then he just stared inta nothin wit the face turnin white an gettin whiter be the minute. Tha went on until he was the colour a the sheet, an ye couldn't tell the difference. Then wha do ye think happened?' said the mammy, lookin around at all the faces starin back at her the colour of a white sheet. She stared goin from one face to another.

'No, tell us,' one mammy breathed.

Then she looked to another mammy, she couldn't get the words out, so she just slowly moved her head side te side gone inta terrible shock altogether, an mouthed the words, sayin, 'No, tell us.'

The lovely-lookin mammy, satisfied they all wanted te know wha happened next, took in a deep breath an fixed her hands holdin them together restin in her lap an said, 'He opened the mouth an slowly, very slowly,' she said, openin her mouth wide flappin the tongue wit the words snappin, givin them a very evil-lookin stare. 'Then he let himself fall back until he was hangin down dead, collapsed stone-cold dead all over again. Stretchered the width a the bed he was, legs an feet danglin one side, head, neck an arms the other. An wha was worse?' she said, askin the question but ready te give the answer.

'No, wha?' they all whispered together, tryin te take in wha she already told them.

She waited until they woke up an said again, 'Wha? No,

wha?' Then she looked around te see who else may be listenin, but didn't see me wit the curtain wrapped around me. I was hidin meself not te be easily picked out an get in trouble.

'The only thing standin straight as a poker now, was the thing between his . . .'

But I didn't get te hear the rest, because she dropped her voice too low fer me te catch it. Then she lifted herself straightenin, takin in a huge deep breath wit the mouth clamped, an said, 'Huge it was!' She breathed, starin wit the remembrance not able te get over it. 'Huge!' she repeated. 'You never saw the like, an I doubt I ever will again! Imagine wha tha would do te ye,' she asked, takin in a slow snort lookin ragin at the idea.

There was a terrible silence then, an they all stared at each other shakin their heads an lookin very shocked.

Then without warnin they erupted inta screams a laughin, roarin their heads slappin an pullin each other until they ran outa strength an just fell wit their heads in their laps. Then the red-haired woman lifted her skirt an started wipin her drippin nose wit the inside a the hem, sayin, 'I don't know, but it sounds te me like tha could a been the cure fer all women's ills. Dip a tha now would do me good. All I'm offered is brewer's droop!'

Then they erupted again, this time spittin out huge sprays a porter an spillin their glasses a stuff all over themself an each other.

'Me pipe, me smoke! Is it broke? Where is it?'

'Mind it's burnin the feckin skirt a me!'

They shouted an shifted, liftin up an laughin. Shakin themselves te dry out the wet, then spillin more wit bottles a porter. I would a lovin te know wha was great gas te make them laugh like tha. I moved away wit a ready smile on me face.

I would like te be able te laugh like them again, I thought, puttin me hands out an gently pushin me way through the packs, tryin te ease me way makin fer the scullery. 'But now I'm tryin te get me stuff,' I muttered, gettin suffomacated wit people's smelly arses shiftin an turnin, then settlin pressed inta me face. I stopped pushin an whisperin 'excuse me's', an suddenly roared wit pain, 'GER OFFA ME, ALL A YOUSE! YE'RE STANDIN ON ME TOES! Let me get pass, move out the way! Gimme room!' I shouted, puttin out me hands pushin an shovin a gang of aul fellas. They were standin wit drink in their hands talkin te other aul fellas wit big roarin red faces from sittin be the fire. They had managed te grab tha spot by gettin there first.

I got stood on again, an screamed as pain squeezed the life outa me. Some aul fella was just after stampin his cobnail boot straight down, on me bare foot.

'Me foot! Me foot! You broke me foot!' I shouted pushin an aul fella, then grabbin up me foot holdin onta the tail a his coat te keep me standin.

'Wha? Wha's goin on?' he muttered, whirlin himself an me around, spillin stout down me neck sayin, 'Wha the fuck? Who's under me way?'

People moved an I let go, hoppin meself through the gap makin fer the scullery.

The place was crowded wit aul ones, grannies. They were all gathered in a heap standin the width an length a the scullery, drinkin smokin an lookin like they were tellin each other terrible happenins. Tha's wha ye do at wakes. Tell stories about things tha happened te you, or yer granny told ye, or ye heard other people talk. An it's mostly about dead people, corpses an things an happenins at other wakes.

I pushed me way through, wit no one lookin down gettin bothered at me. I managed te squeeze me way inta the wash trough, wantin te maybe climb up there on the drainin board, then I could get a clear look at the ceilin an grab hold a me things.

Me eyes peeled along the wooden drainin board seein it heavin wit empty an half-filled porter bottles, glasses a black stout an wrinkled old hands. They were holdin an strokin the glasses an bottles a stout like they were babbies, all givin an gettin great comfort. Ah it's covered wit stuff, an even the wash trough is choked wit dirty Delft waitin te be washed. Then I heard a voice in the crowd I recognized. I lifted me head an squeezed through, tryin te push in te get a look.

'Collapsed on the job he did, out cold he went, after six goes an me stripped naked, in me skin I was!' moaned Nellie, lookin large as life an ugly as sin me mammy calls it. She says tha when someone appears back, an they after supposed te be at death's door.

I stared, she looked grand, she was sittin in the corner the only one wit a chair an everyone else leanin themself against the wall, or the rest, leanin in holdin each other up.

'An wha about him? Was he, ye know?' an aul one whispered, noddin her head in the direction a Nellie's belly, then chewin like mad wit her gums knockin. It was all the excitement of hearin a terrible story.

'Ohhh now, wha do you think?' she complained, givin them all a dirty look. 'Buck naked te the skin the day he was borned, only now the length a him covered in hair, it grew everywhere! An the first sight wit we in the bed, all I could see was a black hairy ape. It was like strokin a blanket! Oh Jesus, got an awful let-down I did, thought I'd gone an landed meself wit a bleedin gorilla! But to get back te me sorry story—'

'Yeah go on, we're dyin te hear!' said the gummy aul one, leavin down her pipe wit it still lettin out the smoke an liftin up a sambidge, takin a huge bite, then a sup a porter.

'Ye see, it was all the excitement a the weddin night! Not te mention the barrel a porter he poured down his gullet. Too much ye know! It was all too much fer him, he had wore himself out,' moaned Nellie, shakin her head rememberin back te tha terrible time. 'So it ended wit me gettin buried, an why?' she asked everyone, lookin from one te the other.

They all shook their head not knowin.

'I'll tell you why,' she said, as if warnin them never te make the same mistake. 'When it was over, ye know! The other thing.' Then she mouthed something, wit her eyes dancin te the words. 'Well it must a been! I got nothin out of it! He collapsed paralytic on top a me! An when I tried te move I discovered we were stuck together,' she mouthed, sayin it in a loud whisper, not seein me earwiggin wit me mouth open as everyone leaned in te catch wha she said.

'Me predicamentation was now somethin shockin. Sure we had only a sheet thrown across the middle a the room te give us the privatezy. An wha happens? I'm now lyin there plastered te the mattress wit his wick like a red-hot poker still stuck up me, me diddies stretched an ripped when I try te move, our bare skins sweaty an dryin inta each other. I was in shockin order! Oh somethin cruel it was, an knowin me whole family, me ma an da was in the next bed thinkin I was enjoyin meself no end. Pantin an cryin I was, oh great excitement I must be gettin they thinkin. No such thing!' she said, lookin at them wit terrible regret. 'Wha was I te do? The thing between his you know wha, "How's yer father!" never let the air out, never went down! He didin't care. Out cold he was splattered on top a me, an me not able te breathe!' she roared, lookin at the aul ones like it was their fault.

'For fuck sake I was cursed. By the time he dragged himself loose I was screamin the roof down! Couldn't walk fer months!' she keened, lettin her eyes hang outa her head.

They stared wit the mouths hangin down te their belly buttons an the eyeballs restin on their cheeks.

'Crushed te near death, thought me end had come!' she whispered, droppin her head lookin very sad.

I stared, wonderin wha could a happened? Why were they showin their skins together? I think tha's one a the sins the nun at school told us about. Tha was when we was gettin learned our prayers an all the sins ye have te save up an remember te tell the priest in Confession. So mammies an daddies must be terrible sinners if they get in their skin an look at each other! Oh ye go te hell fer tha!

I moved away fast knowin the aul ones would kill me if they saw I'd been earwiggin all them sins. Where's me coat an all me stuff? I need te get them. I leaned me neck back tryin te see up te where me clothes is. But I couldn't see anythin, the line was empty. Someone must a taken them down.

'Oh Mammy! I hope they wasn't robbed!' No! People don't do tha, they never rob stuff Mammy said. The people tha live around here are very honest she says, shakin her head makin tha definite an thinkin how good everyone is. They must be put somewhere, but where? An where is everyone gettin their food te eat? Tha's all made-up stuff, someone got tha ready.

I pushed outa the scullery an wriggled me way through the crowds a bodies, tryin te find where they got the big feeds a grub. The table tha sits in the middle a the sittin room is gone. I wonder where tha is? I thought, just as I came right up to it.

'Here! Do you want a sandwich, love?' a little fat woman said, lookin at me wit a big smile on her face.

'Yeah,' I said noddin me head, lookin at wha she had on her chest. She was wearin a grey apron wrapped around her waist an a brown jumper wit a pile a miraculous medals hangin down, they were danglin like mad. I watched them swingin when she moved, they flew, gettin battered when they hit her big chest then took off swingin again. I could watch them doin tha all day, but the starvation hunger got the better a me.

'Here! Is tha too much, or have you a hunger on ye fer more?' she said, handin me two thick cuts a loaf bread, wit a lump a cheese stuck in the middle.

'No! I've a big hunger on me. I'll have more if ye don't mind thanks please, missus!' I said, puttin out me hand an grabbin the plate, just in case she changed her mind an handed it te the aul one come up beside me.

'Here I'll take tha one!' said the aul biddy, puttin out her hand te take my cheese sambidge, then lettin her black shawl fall loose an open, showin the bottles a porter, bread an a lump a meat hidden inside the shawl.

'No this is mine!' I said, holdin it away from her. Then I turned back to the little fat woman, sayin, 'An can I have maybe four more sambidges, missus, please? An do ye have any biscuits, or maybe a bit a cake?' I said lookin up at her then along the table, hopin I'd get lucky.

'Well now, me little chicken. I think your eyes are bigger than yer belly! How about if I give you a bacon sandwich, wit two more cuts a bread? Would tha do ye?'

'Listen! Never mind tha young one. She's just chancin her arm wit wantin te clean the place out!' snorted the aul biddy, pushin her arms up te stop the stuff from fallin down, all the lovely things she'd hidden under the shawl.

'Ah now, Maryanne, I don't think you'll do much starvin, not judgin be the big bulk on ye there stickin outa yer chest! God, you put on an awful lot a weight since ye came through tha door. An tha's, wha? Only about four hour ago!'

'Is tha right now?' snapped the aul biddy, givin a big sniff lookin disgusted wit the insult. 'Well you shouldn't be worryin yerself about me, or fer tha matter wha's been handed out here in this place, it's not comin outa your pocket, is it?' the biddy snorted, narrowin her nose an lookin up an down the table, then landin it back on the fat woman, sniffin like she was gettin a bad smell.

'Some people were let loose wit a shop an it's gone te their head. Power mad they've gone, thinkin they're now moneyed! Listen, Deena Maypole, I've known you since you ran around them streets wit not even a pair a knickers te call yer own! So don't be talkin about me like I'm a beggar, or worse! A robber! Now, I will take it you're sorry fer yer big misunderstandin a me, an you want te now make it up te me. So, you can give me a share of whatever ye have hidden away there fer yerself an yer cronies. Now, would ye mind givin us a few a them biscuits you have hidden there on the chair, under the table?'

'No, they're not fer givin out,' the little fat woman said shakin her head, then givin it another long shake when the biddy stared, wit her mouth open.

'Wha? So you are plannin on keepin them fer yerself? Now why wouldn't I be surprised tha you are not standin behind tha counter fer the good a yer health. An doin wha? Te make yerself look important! Stand there the whole a the afternoon slappin a bit a butter on the bread. Now ye think you own the whole kaboodle, shop, house, the lot! Is him next door the coffin maker not enough fer ye?'

'Oh, so ye saw me help out the poor man? Oh, you may sneer all you like, Maryanne Morrissey, but wha goes around comes around an fer your badness you may yet get your—'

'Excuse me!' I said, interruptin the fat woman in the middle a havin her row. 'But can I have me four sambidges an me cake an biscuits, please? An can ye give me a hot mug a tea te go wit tha?'

The fat woman stared at me, then threw her eye at the biddy an turned away lookin like she was too good te talk te the like a tha aul biddy then smiled at me. 'Sure why not? Are you the poor orphan tha lost her mammy not even two weeks gone, an you not a livin soul left te mind you?' she said, lookin back at the biddy like she now knew somethin the biddy didn't.

'Yeah I am,' I said, noddin me head an lookin te see wha else she could give me.

'So where are you livin now?' said the aul biddy, wantin te know me business.

The fat woman gave her another dirty look then stopped butterin me bread, waitin wit the knife in the air wantin te hear anyway.

I said nothin, just stared ahead takin a huge big bite outa me sambidge, but I couldn't get me mouth around it. I whipped it out an had a look, then lit inta nearly a whole slice an bit inta the bacon. I started tryin te chew, but it was too big, I took too much an had te stop an pull it out again.

The pair watched me lookin like they were waitin fer me answer, then their face curled up turnin away, not likin the sight a me spittin the food inta me hand. But then they turned back te look, followin me every move wit their eyes never leavin me. I didn't care, I was too busy tryin te make short work a me bread an bacon.

'Tha's lovely,' I said, finishin it off while the aul biddy got her share an I wondered if there was anythin still left fer me. I looked the length a the table seein the bread was all gone. Me mouth dropped open wit shock an me belly still rumbled.

'Tha was not enough, missus!' I said, shakin me head in terrible sorrow at the loss. Then I whipped me head te the aul biddy, lookin at her wrappin her arms under her pile a stuff, it was all heaped on the mound she already had hidden.

I felt like cryin an I was afraid te ask her fer some in case, she took the head offa me. But the food is supposed te be fer everyone! She must be a bleedin cronie! Because how come she got tha much?

'I'm starved, missus,' I complained, wantin te let her know I think she's very mean. But then instead all I said was, 'Am I too late? Is the food all gone?' I said whisperin, knowin it was.

'Aren't you the hungry little devil,' said the aul biddy, narrowin her eyes like I had done somethin wrong.

I felt me belly go hot wit an annoyance creepin up me chest. The cheek a her! If I was big I would love te say, 'Ah, go fuck yerself, missus, ye're only an aul robber!' But I'm not big, an I don't think I ever will get te be big, because I'm goin te starve te death. There's no one te feed me!

I sniffed lookin up at them, feelin it's shockin a child should have tha happen te them. I wanted te cry fer meself.

'God almighty!' said the fat little woman. 'You've turned on such a sad-lookin face it would be enough now te make a turnip cry! Jaysus ye might even squeeze a tear outa her,' she laughed, pointin her finger at the aul biddy.

'Come on "Saint Do Good", you say ye're here fer te be helpin the bothered an the bewildered, so would ye mind gettin on wit the job? Where have youse hidden the snuff?' said the biddy, lookin around seein nothin.

'Gone! Take a look in yer apron pockets,' snapped the fat woman, lookin at the huge bulges weighin down the biddy.

'I've had enough a you! Ye may keep wha's left,' snorted the aul biddy, then turned an beat her way out, pushin from side te side wit her elbows.

'Outa me way! Come on move!' she ordered, pushin all ahead an behind makin people shift outa her way.

'Here, you stay there, I've got somethin fer you,' said the fat little woman, noddin at me.

Me heart lifted as I leaned meself up on the table an watched her move over an bend down, takin up a big loaf a fresh bread from a long stool. Then she lifted up a pot sittin on the floor, when she took the lid off, it was stuffed wit bacon. 'Pig's cheek, do ye want some?'

'Yeah, oh yes please, missus, I'm starved wit the hunger!' Me heart leapt at the sight a the bread an meat, an me mouth started chewin, gettin ready te taste and eat the good food. 'I'm never goin te stop eatin fer the rest a me life,' I muttered, watchin her saw the loaf a black-crust bread in chunks, then plaster on lovely golden butter, not sparin any of it! We always have te spare everythin, an Mammy makes sure te cut an butter our bread in case we go mad an take too much, or use too much butter. But then she doesn't mind when she manages te bring home a big lump of butter wrapped up in wax paper, an wit enough bread if she can get some, then we're grand fer a while.

'Tha do ye?' said the little fat woman, handin me two big thick cuts a bread an a big lump a bacon.

'Tha's grand thanks, missus! Can I have more? An wha about the biscuits an the cake?'

'Are you really tha hungry?' she said, not able te believe me.

'Oh yeah I haven't eaten fer . . . loads an loads a time,' I said, puttin out me arms tryin te let her know it was a long time since me belly got food.

'OK, you stand there an while you eat away I'll cut up more fer you, ye poor unfortunate, oh we can't be leavin you in tha state now, can we?' she laughed, bendin down an lookin inta me face.

'No, missus, ye can't starve childre, sure you can't,' I said, thinkin she was a great mammy altogether.

'Oh indeed not. We wouldn't let tha happen te you. Now, put tha under yer arm an don't let anyone take it from you,' she said, seein more people wander over an throw the eye at my stuff.

I had half a sambidge left in one hand an nearly half a loaf wit lumps a meat in the other held under me arm. An she gave me four Marietta biscuits wit a thick slice a apple tart an a big mug a lemonade.

'That's homemade by meself tha apple tart is, an the lemonade, I made tha special fer you childre. So, go on off an find some corner an enjoy yerself. Why don't you take yerself upstairs? It may be a bit quieter up there, an say a prayer fer poor Delia.'

'Yeah, thanks very much, missus,' I said, noddin me head at everythin she said, an smilin all delighted wit meself, an her, fer lookin after me an givin me so much good food.

'Go on, mind yerself,' she said, comin around the table an gettin ahead a me te push people an make them let me pass.

'Thank you very much, missus!'

'Go on ye're grand now,' she said, then made her way back in, heavin an shovin te get people te move.

I shifted slowly, makin sure not te get me drink spilt, or the sambidges knocked down an walked on. People were busy talkin an eatin an movin around, tryin te get room an shift into a place fer more comfort. It was gettin very crowded wit more an more people turnin up fer all the free drink an food. Not te mention the entertainment a meetin each other.

I made me way slowly up the stairs past people sittin wit their back te the wall an talkin in whispers tryin te keep themself easy, because you can't talk loud when ye're near te the corpse. I could smell the burnin candles an see the shadow of people dancin on the wall a the dark landin, they looked like matchstick people wit their hair drawed in usin a black pencil, maybe done by a child. Then someone was danglin an invisible string makin them inta puppets. It was lovely, wit the tongues a fire flickerin, then lightin up an dyin down. It was comin next te the black an yella white of the walls, they were turnin tha colour wit the dark night an the light of the flames.

17

I MADE EASY TOWARDS the room an stopped outside, hearin the quiet hummin comin through the open door. They're sayin prayers fer the dead Delia, gettin the rosary. I could hear an old woman's voice givin it out, sayin, 'Hail Mary, full of grace, the Lord is with thee. Blessed art Thou amongst women, and blessed is the fruit of thy womb, Jesus.'

She sounded like she was tortured but so tired an weary she just kept goin, because that's all she could do now, an she was a martyr te the cause a livin, sufferin the constant fear an the constant worry. Now havin te pray all these prayers, but it had te be done so just keep goin.

As soon as she finished the last word a the prayer, people were in wit their answer, 'Holy Mary, Mother of God, pray fer us sinners now and at the hour of our death. Amen.' They answered wit a long keenin moan soundin like it was a warnin, somethin terrible is comin along the road, so be ready.

I looked down at me half-eaten sambidge sittin in me hand, an the rest a me grub held tight under me other arm. I didn't want te go in lookin an eegit wit this stuff. Anyway, they would tut tut at me, sayin, 'Get out, young one, don't be comin in here te show disrespect.'

No I better keep easy an do nothin. I moved meself away keepin very quiet an stood in the dark at the next door wit no light showin. Oh, this is the room where I slept, but only the once in here, then after tha everythin got bad an people disappeared, my Ceily did. She went missin an Delia got kilt, an Mister Mullins shrunk into an old man tha doesn't look at you no more, an now he sees nothin an no one. I wanted somethin of tha time back, when I slept here an Ceily was still alive, or not gone missin. I want te be warm an te sleep an not be hungry or afraid all the time. I'm at the mercy now of everythin an everyone. The monsters can get me now, I thought, givin a look around seein all the corners wit the dark hidin them. No it's OK, everyone is in the house, so all I have te do is shout.

Oh Mammy, I want te sleep. I'm so tired, I thought, lookin at the door then down at the handle. I slept here, I told meself again. I could feel me chest buzzin, gettin somethin good comin te me. Then it hit me. I know wha I will do!

I put me mug a drink on the floor an shoved the sambidge grippin it inta me mouth, an held me other stuff tight under me arm. Then I got me two hands an turned the handle, lettin the door push in.

I listened te see if someone was comin. No! I grabbed up me drink an made me way inta the dark room seein the bed starin straight ahead a me. It was lyin just the way I left it, wit the blankets an sheets still tossed not made up tidy again. Me heart was flyin wit my darin, tha's wha Mammy would call it. You're very bold, makin yerself at home in someone else's house without even waitin fer an invitation! Well I don't care no more, *God helps those who help themselves!* I laughed, hearin a little voice suddenly comin from nowhere, sayin tha in me head.

I put me drink on the chair beside the bed an the grub next te it, then climbed up an crawled onta the mattress. I could feel the lovely soft warm eiderdown under me an the springs ease up an down, lettin me feel all the lovely warm an softness. I felt meself meltin inta the heat, an suddenly me eyes was closin gettin very heavy. No ye better not! You have to . . .

'Wha?' I moaned, wantin te sleep but knowin there was somethin I should do first.

I was sprawled on me belly an lifted me head lookin over at the door, yeah, it's shut.

Wha about Delia, goin in te say a prayer?

No! Then ye might get throwed out, you never know!

Don't care, I'm stayin.

OK, I hauled meself up an lifted me head takin off me frock an throwin it on the end a the bed. Then sat in me Delia knickers an me own vest an dived meself under the sheets an blankets. Bits felt warm from where I was lyin an other spots was stone cold. I gave a little shiver all delighted wit meself, then put me two pillas behind me an sat up against the mahogany back rest an reached over te lift up me mug a lemonade an me half-eaten sambidge.

The room was dark, but not too dark wit the light thrown in from the street lamps, they were able te shine in the winda because the curtains was left open. I wonder why the handy-women didn't black out this winda. Oh yeah, Nellie got carted off te hospidal first. Tha's lucky fer me, I can see wha I'm doin.

I took a huge bite an a sip a me drink, an munched away, lookin down at me bed an all around me wit great comfort. 'Oh Mammy! This is heaven. Peace an quiet, food an heat an a bed, an sleep in a minute. Oh wha more could a body want?'

Me heart was poundin an I was kickin wit me mouth wide open not able te get out the scream! I couldn't breathe! Me arms was wavin an I was starin back at Mammy, I could see her gettin dragged, pulled through the air, caught between two horrible-lookin women, witches they were. They had long black nails grippin Mammy's wrists, an yella eyes, an black lips wit big teeth, an they were laughin an swingin Mammy around an through the air like she was a skippin rope. She was lookin back at me twistin her head tryin te see me an cryin, wantin te get back te me.

I was screamin inside meself, gettin dragged along by a big black monster, it was like a giant animal outa the devil's hell. It had red-hot eyes an huge fangs an it had a hold a me. I was caught by the leg between its teeth, an it was draggin me down the lane. Ceily was tryin te help me. She was runnin from far away tryin te get te me, but then suddenly she was gone, turned back an was very fast fadin inta the distance. Now I couldn't see her no more!

No, no! Save me! Me head flew swingin around fer someone te run an give me mercy. There's no one, it's dark an quiet, the world is empty. It's just me an the monster left!

Me heart roared an thumped drummin a hole in me head wit the pain an the noise, then suddenly it stopped! I lifted me head feelin the lovely air rush inta me lungs an cool me face. I was awake.

Oh I was only dreamin. I was havin a nightmare! Me hair was soaked, plastered te me forehead an the back a me neck. Now I felt meself gettin all cold an chilly. I shivered an lay back down in the bed coverin meself up wit the blankets.

I stared around, seein it was comin mornin time, the dark of the night was turned te blue in the room, an tha was now givin way to the grey of the early mornin. I could hear noises comin from the death room next door. Tha's the people keepin the wake. Then I heard a door bang an someone shout. It was a man's voice an it was out on the street. I could hear other voices joinin in arguin, an some were talkin easy like they were tryin te placate the rowdy fellas. They sounded like they were all drunk an in the middle of a row.

'HERE! HOLD THA COAT! LET ME AT HIM! HOLD ME BACK, I'LL ONLY KILL HIM!'

'Hold him back, Jembo! Don't let him loose!' a woman roared, soundin worried.

'HERE, SOMEONE! HOLD MY COAT! NO DON'T STOP ME! WAIT! HOLD ME BACK OR I'LL ONLY BE HANGED FER HIM! NO LET ME AT HIM, I'LL DO TIME FER HIM!

'Ah will ye's all stop it outa tha, youse load a dirty-lookin shites! Will youse cut it out an go home an sleep it off! Now come on wit ye's, let's go!' said an aul fella soundin really fed up like he had enough a them an now only wantin te go home.

'FUCK OFF OUTA THA, YOU! THA WINDBAG IS NOT CALLIN ME AN AUL WOMAN AN LIVIN TE TELL THE TALE!'

'YE ARE A WINDBAG! NOW COME ON, FIGHT! I'M READY TE TAKE YOU ON!'

'YEAH RIGHT! AN SO AM I! READY, WILLIN AN WAITIN!'

'FUCK YOU! SO WHA ARE YE WAITIN FOR, YE WIND BAG? YE'RE ONLY HOT AIR!'

'MURDER! Stop them!' screamed a woman's voice. Then I heard a police whistle.

'Ah Holy Jaysus! Make yerselves scarce!'

'COPPERS! BLUE BOTTLES! SCATTER, EVERYONE!'

Huh, tha ruggy-up didn't last long, I thought, listenin wit me head sideways, lookin up at the ceilin. But yeah, tha was all hot air as someone kept complainin. They usual do box each other then go back inta the pub wit their arms wrapped around each other, all best friends again! Everyone enjoys watchin a good row when the pub closes, or at a wake or a weddin. It's a sign of a good wake, a great send-off fer the dead person. For tha you have te have plenty a everythin, especially the drink. Then you get the good fights an people will talk fer years about the great send-off the dead person got. When they talk about it, it will become a story fer the next wake an go on fer years wit it gettin compared wit the best. Some a the good ones go fer ever, cos the happenins get bigger an longer wit the storyteller addin their own bit on.

I need te go te the tilet. I'm not goin out te the backyard. Anyway, it's probably crowded around wit people. I can hear the buzzin wit their talk, it's carryin all the way te the front here.

I wonder if they have a piss pot in here. I leaned meself hangin outa the bed an looked under it, me eyes lit up. Ah lovely, I won't have te fight me way out there.

I hopped outa the bed an pulled it from underneath. Oh it's a nice flowery one, an it looks lovely an clean. Pity I have te piss in it, if they see tha they will eat the head offa me. Pissin in their pot, as well as makin meself at home, an all comfortable in their house! Fer this I'll be hanged. Still! It won't stop me!

I pissed away wonderin wha te do wit the pot. I know! I lifted it up an walked around the bed an over te the winda. It's a bit high up. I need te stand on somethin.

'Right!' I puffed, draggin an liftin the heavy chair over te the winda. I was stranglin meself wit the weight, tryin not te make noise, so they won't hear me next door an come in. I climbed up on the big windasill an grabbed hold a the two handles fer liftin, then pulled, fer all I was worth, draggin the heart outa meself. Finally it gave an slid up, lettin in a sudden draught of icy-cold wind. 'Oh Mammy!' I wriggled, givin a sudden shiver.

Then I got down an lifted up the pot. It was heavy an me hand was shakin, because I had only the one, the other hand was gripped onta the windasill, tryin te haul meself up onta the chair. I stood up now balancin meself an grabbed the pot wit two hands, then held it out the winda upside down. I was pourin away, lettin the piss teem down now onta the footpath, but it was just as the door opened an two aul biddies came staggerin out.

'Oh we'll be drownded, Molly. It's pourin wit the rain!'

'Gawd ye're right there, Maisie, but it's warm rain!' said the other one, puttin her hand on her head, feelin it lashin her skull but not botherin te look up.

I got such a fright I nearly dropped the pot. I flew me head in left down the pot an grabbed hold a the handles slammin the winda shut. I could hear meself breathin heavy an me heart thump like a sledgehammer, makin me chest fly in an out. Tha's lucky! Luckier still it wasn't a policeman slowly steppin past, then I would a been on the run again. Oh it's just hittin me now, tha was a terrible idea! It looks like Ceily was right, I'm goin te become a baddie an get meself locked up! Because I'm always gettin inta trouble, no wonder tha school nun hates me, she says I'm a crucifixion. Yeah, an Mammy says I'm a shocker.

I started smackin me lips, I'm thirsty, I was very hot because I got meself buried underneath all the blankets, it was when I was havin me nightmare. Then I got into an awful sweat tryin te beat me way out an I didn't know where I was, because I was still asleep.

I had a look on the floor at wha's left a me grub. Nothin! Just one biscuit an nothin te drink. I looked at me bed, wantin te get back in, but instead reached fer me frock an pulled it on over me head. I'm goin te get meself somethin more te eat an drink, because I'm starvin again.

I opened the door an went out, wanderin off in me Delia's knickers an bare feet. Oh, where's me Mister Mullins' socks? I lost them somewhere, must a left them in the granny's house.

I stopped outside the death room gettin the smell a death, it's comin from the candles an the snuff an the porter an the cookin a pig's cheek, an tha's all the kind a smell ye get wit death. Everyone knows tha. Yeah, it's easy, you can smell death a mile away.

I heard a rumble comin from the room an took a step in, lookin te see wha's goin on. Mister Mullins was sittin over in the far corner wit his head down an his hands restin in his lap, he was lookin very bad now from when I sawed him before. His skin was turned all grey an his cheeks was sinkin inta his face, but his eyes was terrible, he was starin like he was an old dark stone statue wit dead muddy-grey marble eyes. The life was all gone outa him.

'Are you the relation?' said an aul fella staggerin in an pointin at people.

He was lookin fer the corpse relations, an he was very shifty altogether, wit the eyes takin in the faces, hopin te see wha else is goin fer free.

'Sorry about dash,' he said, pointin at the bottle a porter spinnin across the floor spillin stout an leavin a trail on the varnished floorboards.

'Tut tut, drunken aul fool destroyin the man's house,' an old woman muttered, lettin it come out in a low moan an shakin her head wit disgust. He had just woken her up wit all his noise, an she'd slowly lifted her head lookin around wit the red eyes exhausted. Then she let them rest, takin in the drunken aul fella wit the bottle rollin an spillin, an him staggerin around, not knowin where he was.

'I knew him well! Lovely man,' he gasped, tryin te get his breath out all in one go. 'Shush! Say no more!' he said, spinnin around lookin at the room wit his eyes crossin an the finger te his mouth. 'Shockin young, only me own age! Went te school wit him!' he hiccupped, then put his hand holdin a drink he thought he had te his open mouth discoverin nothin there. His eyes flew open wit his head spinnin lookin fer the drink tha was now lyin empty, under the dead Delia's bed.

'Where's me drink?' he asked, twistin his head an body around, balancin himself on wobbly legs, lettin his feet stand still. 'Me drink is all gone,' he said, shakin his head lettin his eyes cross thinkin about it. He was lookin very sad now, gone all mournful wit the mouth clamped shut.

'There ye are, I'm lookin for you!' said a woman in a plaid shawl hangin onta her pipe, it was empty now wit no smoke comin out. 'Come on, we have te get home to the childre, you have te get up early an go down to them quays, you might get a day's work if ye smarten yerself an sober up!'

'Fuck off, go down yerself, ye lazy aul hag, if you want a day's work!' he snorted, flyin his arm at her, wantin her te clear off.

Suddenly Mister Mullins lifted his head an came alive, he gave a big snort takin in a huge lungful a air an got up then walked quick across the room an out the door. People were still sleepin not bothered about the drunk, an the old woman had dozed off again, leanin her head on her chest. People were all wantin te keep the wake wit Mister Mullins for his Delia. So they were all content te sit around the room wit their backs te the wall, an easin themself wit droppin off te sleep. But I wonder wha happened te Mister Mullins. He woke up an changed very suddenly, gone all stiff wit his head in the air an his back straight. He looks years an suddenly loads a years younger!

I wanted te see Delia, but the man was gettin noisy an the woman was tormented tryin te get him te leave.

'No! Go home. Your place is there, missus, wit the childre, an ye may wait fer me te get back, an tha will be when I'm good an ready!'

'You're a black-hearted no-good waste a space,' she moaned, lettin it come out in a terrible keen, like she was goin te start breakin her heart wit the cryin.

Mister Mullins came walkin fast back inta the room wearin his top coat an hat.

'He's leaving now, missus, don't worry,' he said, marchin up te the drunk then takin him by the neck a his coat. 'I don't know who you are, I never met ye in me life. And over there lying in tha bed is my dead daughter, she's not a he. Now! I don't know if you know anything about me, but if you care to enquire ye might be told I was handy in me time, very handy! And I haven't lost it yet.' Then he bent down wit his hand in his coat pocket an pressed it up against the drunk man's back, an whispered somethin inta his ear.

I watched the drunk man's face go from the eyebrows lifted an the eyes darin like he was lookin an ready fer a fight, then they suddenly changed as his face fell flat wit his mouth open an his eyes starin, lookin like he had the fear a God in them. He was listenin very carefully wit his head not movin an his ear cocked, then suddenly he was on the move.

'Ah, no harm done, sure it was only the drink talkin!' he rushed, lettin his voice talk it all out in a hurry. 'Ah yeah, tha was very wrong a me te be bringin disrespect te yer home an your blessed lovely daughter, God bless her may she rest in peace an God bless yerself, an I'm sorry fer yer trouble an I won't bother ye again!'

Then he was off, walkin himself fast wit only a bit of a stagger when he hit the door an sayin, 'Where's me missus? Where are ye, Mindy? Where's me Mo? Ah there you are, come on, love! Let's get home.'

I moved meself outa the way lettin him get past, an Mister Mullins followed up behind him. Then they were makin their way down the stairs an I could hear him still talkin, all real fast without hiccuppin now or losin his breath. The only thing is, he's now talkin in a high voice soundin like a woman wit her nerves gone bad.

I stood wonderin wha Mister Mullins said when he whispered inta his ear. Because I never sawed before in me life somebody change inta bein good tha fast.

The room was quiet now wit only the sound a heavy snorin. I looked over at the bed seein a body lyin stiff, but I couldn't get te see much from here. So I made me way slowly over an stopped beside the little table, it was covered wit the white-linen lace cloth, an it had the holy cross embroidered inta it.

The convent nuns must a lent tha! Because the Mullins or Delia was very good at helpin them. If the nuns asked Delia te look after a mother tha was ailin, or needed somethin, then Delia would do it. Mammy said very few people knew the real Delia Mullins. She hid it behind a very gruff manner, Mammy always said, but nobody yet born was ever kinder. It is true! She didn't want te come out inta the wet an windy cold night all over again, because she was already soaked te the skin. But she did, te help me an Ceily. Now her an her friend my mammy is gone, maybe they is dead together. I hope not! Because I want my mammy te come home an we'll all be happy again.

I looked down at the table wit the silver cross standin in the middle an two big white lighted candles. I wonder who's keepin an eye on them an puttin in new ones when these burn out. There was a bowl a holy water an a feather sittin next to it wit a bowl of snuff, tha's fer people te help themself an take a pinch. Then they can sit down here in the death room an talk about the corpse. Everyone will say how good she was an remember funny things she did, an the devilment she got up to when she was a girl. Tha's wha ye do at wakes, you can't speak ill a the dead.

I picked up the feather an dipped it inta the holy water an shook it at Delia's face. I could see now from down here she was already soaked te the white embroidered pillacase, an tha was soppin too. I went in close te the bed an leaned on it te hike meself up an get a good look at her. Because all I could see at the minute was her body lyin in the blue habit, wit the writin on the front an the big cross. I wonder wha tha says.

I looked around seein the old woman who was givin out about the drunk, she was now watchin me wit her eyes half open. She looked very suspicious, givin me the eye by raisin the left side a her eyebrow an givin a little shake, tha was te show she was watchin me an I better not do anythin. I turned around an dropped me hands lettin them sit where she could see them, then stared at her, wonderin wha te do.

'Missus,' I suddenly breathed, gettin a good idea te let her see I meant no harm. 'Wha does it say on the middle a Delia's death habit?'

'Wha?' she said, chewin her gums, movin her mouth up and down, wakin up an gettin interested.

'Wha does it say?' I whispered, goin over an talkin inta her face.

'Oh right, chicken. You want te know tha? Well, it says, "I Have Suffered".'

'Oh,' I said, openin me mouth an starin, thinkin about this. 'So did she suffer then?'

'No! Mary the mother of God did. Tha habit is for her. The Sodality of the Children a Mary, they pay their devotion te her, to "Our Lady".'

'Oh,' I said, tryin te work out wha she told me.

'Yes. So now you know,' she said, fixin herself an pullin the black shawl around her, gettin her comfortable. Then she put her hands together and leaned back stretchin in her chair, sayin, 'Go on over an say a little prayer to Our Lady fer poor Delia. Ask her te intercede wit our blessed Lord, to take our poor Delia straight inta heaven without havin te be hangin around waitin at them pearly gates. Delia never had much patience, but tha's neither here nor there, I'm not speakin ill a her. Not at all, there's no one more deservin of a high place in heaven than her, she was very obligin, very decent may God rest her. Now go on, get yer prayers an leave me in the peace. I want te get a bit a rest before the day crowd turn up.'

I went back te Delia an lifted up the feather again, then stared te see where I should bless her. Me eyes rested at her hands lookin very white, it was like you could see through them, an she had a big pair a black rosary beads, they were knitted through her fingers wit the cross standin up.

I wonder wha it's like te be all dead. Really deaded like her, she is, but not my mammy! I dipped the feather in the holy water again an gave a splash to her hands te bless them, then decided te give another go at her chest, because tha's where her heart is, an you need te bless tha too. Then I got a picture of Father Flitters when he's blessin anyone, like wit a babby at a christenin, or when someone is in their sick bed or dyin. He keeps on blessin them wit the holy water, lashin away wit all a the blessins. I can do tha!

I kept dippin an blessin an prayin an lashin until me hand was grabbed an someone said, 'That's enough now, you've enough water thrown over poor Delia to empty the River Liffey.'

I blinked, tryin te get me eyesight back because I was so busy I forgot where I was. Mister Mullins! He closed his eyes givin a nod, then turned me fer the door sayin, 'You go on, you should be asleep in yer bed.'

'Yeah but, Mister Mullins, do ye know wha? Ceily is—'

'Go on!' he said, throwin his head at the door not wantin te listen te me. He turned an stared at Delia wit his face gettin an awful pained look, then turned away lookin very confused now like he didn't understand wha happened. Then he looked over at his chair in the corner an dropped his head lettin his shoulders sink. He was suddenly lookin very old again.

I watched as he slowly made his way te the chair an sat, easin himself down like his poor bones pained all over. Then he closed his eyes an let his hands drop in his lap, lookin now like the last a his strength was all used up, he was now a very old man wit all the life left him.

I stood there starin takin it all in watchin him. Me heart was gettin very heavy, I could feel it droppin, goin all the way te fall outa me an leave me too, without any life. Then I heard a little voice whisper in me head, *Mister Mullins is all gone now, an so are you!*

A terrible fright was hittin me. I whipped me head around wantin te scream an find me Ceily. She can get Mammy back fer me! Then a sudden noise made me scream. 'Ma! Mammy!' I went all red an hot in me face an looked te see wha made the noise.

A man gave a sudden snort, it was comin from his big loud snorin!

'Jesus Christ wahwastha?' an old woman said wit her eyes flyin open an her body leapt in the chair.

'Oh mercy!' said the old woman who keeps watch an gives out. 'It's tha bloody young one moochin around an causin devilment! Get her outa here!' she roared, wavin her two fists at me, lookin like she wanted te kill me.

'Yeah,' moaned the other one, 'an tha roar a hers is after shakin the guts outa me wit the fright. If this keeps up youse may lay me out next, then bury me down on top a Delia. I'm not a well woman ye know!' she complained, lookin around the room, then lettin her eyes burn a hole in me. 'It's not good on the aul heart at my age!' she snorted.

'No! Nor mine neither,' complained the busybody, fixin herself wit the shawl an givin me a dirty look.

Then the aul fella snortin who started it all, he suddenly shifted an opened his eyes stretchin them wide. He was wantin te wake himself up an look around te see where he was. Then he remembered it all, an looked te see where his drink was sittin waitin fer him. He sprang his hand down an grabbed up the bottle, sayin, 'Lovely stuff!' an guzzled the lot lettin it make a big noise gluggin down his neck, an we could hear it sloppin inta his belly. 'Lovely! Anyone got a bit a tobacco?' he whispered, lookin around at all the women starin at him then seein them makin terrible faces at me.

I dropped me head an made me way out the door fast. I went te go fer the stairs but turned left fer me room, then changed me mind an headed fer the stairs again. People were nodded off te sleep wit their heads in their lap an their backs against the wall, stretched out on the stair. 'Excuse me,' I said, tryin te haul meself up be the banisters an lift me legs swingin them, but I didn't get far enough an landed on the legs of an aul biddy. She was fast asleep wit the mouth wide lettin huge snorts blow outa her nose.

'Oh Jesus mighty!' she screamed, lashin out wit her arms, givin me an unmerciful belt in the side a me head.

I screamed wit the pain, an people stirred wit mumblins comin from all directions, sayin, 'Wha's tha! Someone hurt?'

'I knew it would happen! It's tha trouble-makin young one at it again!' shouted the busybody aul one from up in the death room. 'This time she's gone an kilt someone!'

'Help, I'm hurted! Ceily!' I screamed, gettin rolled down the stairs, then comin to a stop in the lap a the fat mammy, the one who gave me the big feed.

'Easy wit you, where's yer hurry?' she said, then laughed seein me lookin up at her all hot an bothered. 'Wha ails ye, love?' she said, not knowin wha happened, because she was busy havin a smoke of her pipe an talkin te an old man.

I started rubbin me head, sayin, 'I'm after gettin an awful dig, an then comin on top a tha I got the fright a me life. Tha woman hit me cause I hurted her,' I cried, throwin me hand pointin me finger at the aul one roarin at me.

'Me leg, me bad leg! Bloody kids, some a them should be drownded at birth.'

I grabbed hold a me thumb an sucked like mad watchin te see if the aul one was goin te get up an kill me.

'Are ye all right there, Maggie? Can you move it? Ah she didn't mean it, she's only a child. Aren't you, ye little demon?' the fat mammy roared, givin me a squeeze in me belly pretendin she was annoyed.

'No!' I said, shakin me head like mad wantin the trouble te be all over.

'It's all killins an more killins an I seem te be always around fer it happenin. Nothin like this came te me before! Me nerves is gone! No! I can't move it! I'm crippled,' roared the aul one stretchin an rubbin her leg, wit the sudden smell a pissy knickers. I know tha smell, because tha's wha happens te me when I wet me knickers be accident an I don't like tha! Because then everyone calls ye 'Pissy knickers'! An they have te stay on me if it's not Sunday, tha's when I get clean ones put on me fer the week.

'Why you not asleep?' she said, foldin me inta her chest, lettin me lie back an suck me thumb. I snuggled in fer more comfort feelin meself gettin lovely an warm, lyin on a big cushion.

'Wha happened te your feet? Why have you no shoes?' she said, pickin up me foot an strokin me toes. 'They're black as the ace a spades! Jesus, you're gone wild, completely neglected, an look a tha hair, it's all matted an tangled. Child! You look like somethin . . . a dog tha got deliberately strayed,' she said, shakin her head around at other people seein them look at me, then nod at her an turn away.

'Shame,' muttered the old man, talkin te her again.

'Yeah, no one te claim her, looks like they may have to . . . you know what!' she said, mouthin words an noddin down at me, then over at the old man.

He chewed on his tobacco an nodded, givin his head a long slow bow then lookin te stare at a spot on the ceilin.

'Yes, Frankie is goin te have to sort this out, an make it quick!' she said, soundin really sad an fed up.

'I think tha has happened already,' the old man said, still lookin at the ceilin. 'Be the look a things, it won't be long before he's joinin his beloved Delia, this has broken his heart. Oh! Comes to us all, comes to us all,' he keened, shakin his head lookin up at the ceilin.

'Oh indeed it does, life is a cruel taskmaster,' she muttered, shakin her head too, starin inta nothin.

'Shush is nomb!' I said, sloppin me tongue lettin me thumb hang in me mouth.

'Wha? Wha ye say, love? Here! Take yer thumb out an tell me tha again,' she said, grabbin me hand an holdin it, starin inta me mouth.

'Ceily's gone!' I said, lookin up at her lettin her know the terrible news.

'Wha? Oh yeah,' she said, slowly openin her eyes wide an starin at me. 'Now tha you come te mention it, I hadn't thought about her, the big young one! Yer sister, how old is she?'

'Ceily's twelve an I'm seven. She's gone!' I said, shakin me head, soundin like it's all over, the end a the world has come.

'When did tha happen? Where did she go?'

'I dunno! I went asleep an when I waked up she was gone.'

'Ohhh my gawd!' she said, lookin around at everyone then restin her eyes on the old man.

He clamped his mouth an shook his head, sayin, 'Must a been lifted! Tha parish priest, you cross him at your peril!

You'd be brave to take him on! He's a cantankerous aul git, he's got a lot a power an no one more vicious wit it, if you get on the wrong side a him. It would take the likes a Frankie Mullins, a real fightin man, a rebel an a hero, he took on the Black an Tans an ran rings around them! He then fought, brother against brother in the civil war.

'His own brother, Christy. He was shot dead after comin back from France, fightin in the Great War he had been. He survived that he did, only te be shot dead by Irish Rebels as a traitor. He fought for the wrong side they said. So, te stand up against someone like tha priest, only he could do it! Flitters has no control over him, he's a man of great independence. Better men than Flitters have tried an failed. God knows I know him well enough, I've known him all his life. He was a great boxer, could a turned professional an gone to America an had his turn on the world stage. But not fer him, as I said, the civil war came along an claimed his time, so here we are. That's the only reason tha child there sittin in your arms is still here.'

'Do ye think Father Flitters knows she's here?' asked the woman.

I stopped suckin lettin me thumb dangle te listen.

'Say no more, little piggies have big ears,' he said, pointin at me.

'Come on, you. Let's get you down somewhere fer a few hours' sleep. It's still early. Wha time would ye say it is, Johnny?'

'Well, knowin as I can't see out te the sky from here, but it could be anywhere between five an six, or least thereabouts anyway.'

'Where are you sleepin, me little fairy?'

'Ump ghkr.'

'Tut, I can't understand you, take tha outa yer mouth! Where's yer shoes?'

'I don't know. I only have one wellie. The other one left me.'

'Is your house locked up?'
'Yeah,' I nodded.
'Have you the key by any chance?'
'No! Yeah!'
'Which is it?'
'Dunno!'
'Right did you sleep upstairs?'
'Yeah.'
'Where?'
'Next te the death room! Beside Delia! An lookit, I'm wearin her knickers!'
'I know, I wondered where you got them. Poor Delia, she'd be charmed te see them gone to good use! Now come on, let's get you up them stairs an inta tha bed. You look terrible, your face is all pale an pinched, you can't be left like this, somethin needs to be done! You need takin care of,' she said, starin at me lookin very worried.
'Yeah, there's no one te mind me. Me fambily's missin,' I said, seein her eyes water lookin at me now all sad, like I should be pitied.
Suddenly I could feel meself gettin all sad too. It's terrible, I thought, wantin te feel shockin pity fer meself, an I began te feel a big heave a sad comin all over me. I started te sniff an gave a moan, tryin te get the tears comin an looked up at her, wantin te see if she was goin te cry too.
But she just stared, watchin me mouth start te shiver, then she suddenly started roarin laughin. 'Oh you're such a cod, Lily Carney! Would ye look at tha "Abbey Acting",' she roared, turnin me around te face the old man.
I stopped shiverin me mouth te stare at him, wonderin why they was laughin at me.
He gave me a good look then shook his head, sayin, 'Oh tha's a face fer ye all right, mustard an mortal sin. Rightly

enough, she will indeed surely go far in the Abbey one day. Up on the stage you'll be, my girlie, entertainin us all, an we'll be able te say, "Sure we knew her, Lily Carney, when she didn't even have a pair a knickers te call her own."' Then he threw back his head an laughed, an everyone else started too, roarin their heads laughin at wha he said.

I stared wonderin wha he said tha was funny.

'Come on,' the fat mammy said, takin me hand an pullin me up the stairs. 'Wha room? In here, was it?' she said openin the door te me bed, seein the piss pot sittin on the windasill.

'Wha were you up to? Did you leave tha pot sittin there?'

'No! I didn't never see tha in me life!' I said, afraid fer meself in case she'd take the skin offa me arse.

'Oh now!' she said, liftin it up an puttin it under the bed. 'Now get under them clothes an get some sleep, you're far too young te be ramblin around the night wide awake, then havin been passin the days goin in hunger.

'OK now, Lily, I got your stuff from the scullery, so you can leave them aul knickers behind. Just use them fer sleepin, then put your own stuff back on, an here! Where's your other boot?'

'I don't know, it got lost!'

'Tut, right here's yer coat an the rest of your stuff,' she said, openin the wardrobe then somethin fell onta the bed.

'What's this?' she said, pickin up a key fallin outa me pocket.

I looked te see an me eyes lit up. 'Tha's my hall door key! I forgot it was there!'

'Right! That's grand an handy havin tha,' she said happily, puttin it inta her apron pocket. 'I'll mind tha fer when it's needed.'

'Do you mean fer when Ceily comes back an we can go an find me mammy?' I said, lookin up at her ready te be gettin very happy.

'Oh all good things come te little girls who do wha they're told.'

'Oh I'm goin te be very good, an do ye know wha?' I said, just rememberin wha I want te be. 'Do ye know wha, missus?' I said, not waitin fer her te answer. 'I'm goin te become a saint an do loads a miracles an get everyone te pray te me, fer me te do me miracles! Just like the little flower an the child a Prague! Mammy has a statue of him hangin over the front door. Wha do ye think a tha?' I said, now waitin fer her answer.

She looked like she was goin te laugh, but then changed her mind an shook her head lookin at me, sayin, 'I knew it! I knew you had tha look of a saint about you! Oh indeed you will make a great little saint, you should tell tha te the nun at school, I'm sure she'll be delighted!'

'I THOUGHT A THA MESELF TOO!' I roared, gettin all excited.

But then suddenly she let a big snort outa her nose an turned her head away makin noises an then coughin. I watched seein her face go all red an her eyes started te water, an even her nose turned red.

'Are ye ailin now?' I said, gettin worried because she was coughin an chokin like mad.

'Oh don't say another word, chicken! Jesus you're a tonic an ye don't even know it! God bless your innocence,' she said, pattin me on me head. 'OK enough, get inta the bed an get some sleep, come on,' she said, liftin the blankets an shovin me legs under, then coverin me up an rubbin me face an hair, sayin, 'Ah sure you're a grand little thing, a lovely little girl, tut tut, it's a bloody cryin shame this has te be happenin.' Then she walked over an pulled the curtains together pushin out the light pokin itself in through the winda, now it's all dark again. Then she was gone, closin the door quiet behind her leavin me feelin lovely an warm, all snug as a bug in a rug.

I gave a big yawn an turned meself over onta me side, then scratched me nose gettin an itch an let out a huge sigh, feelin the height a comfort. 'Oh yeah, this is lovely,' I sighed again, lettin a big smile on me face then eased off, sinkin down into a deep sleep.

18

'EXCUSE ME! CAN I have me breakfast, please?' I said, tryin te mill me way in an hang onta me spot around the kitchen table, but the aul ones an aul fellas were pushin an diggin me out wit their elbows an gettin there first.

'Mara! Give us another bit a tha bread, an have ye any more a tha lovely hard cheese?'

'Wha do ye think I'm runnin, a bleedin cafe?'

'Ah go on, you know I'll look after ye! Didn't I mind tha dog a yours when you went off gallivantin on yer travels to Bray? A whole week ye went missin, mindin tha old invalid on a paid holiday you called work. Jesus, work? I think it was man huntin you were. Hangin around them slot machines an rushin around in them bumper cars. An me left wit yer feckin bowzie of a dog! Tha thing's wild, I had te pay tha butcher nine pence fer tha pork chop when it lunged up an grabbed it offa the counter! Which reminds me, you never paid me back tha money yet!'

'Ah listen. Why don't ye tell them wha you told me about tha aul invalid,' said Essie, pourin out the tea from a big kettle they borrowed from the convent. She was standin beside the skinny woman wit the dyed blonde hair wearin the red blouse an black pencil skirt. It had a slit up the back an she was wearin nylon stockins. The women don't like her. I do hear them givin out mad about her. They said she was a man-eater an she was very fast! Whatever tha means. Because I think she's very slow, she can't walk on them high heels, an she can't move much in tha tight skirt. But the men's eyes always light up at the sight a her.

'Will I tell them tha?' said the skinny woman Mara, smilin, showin a row of lovely white teeth an red-rosy lips covered wit lipstick.

'Ah go on it's priceless,' said Nellie, pushin her way in wit clean mugs an plates, she was lookin grand again back te her old self.

'Well!' said Mara, leanin her head inta the crowd an them pushin forward wit their head, leavin me out in the cold. All I can see now is arses an legs packed tight together. I walked te one end then turned an walked te the other lookin fer a way te squeeze in, I couldn't see me breakfast an I couldn't earwig on the story, but I could hear the laughin an the pauses wit, 'Yeah! Go on go on!' Tut! I hate big people!

Suddenly the door pushed in an a voice shouted, 'Come on! Come on! They're gettin ready te move, if you don't get goin now Delia Mullins will not just stink te high heaven as she is now, but we'll need a shovel te get her inta the box! Never mind te dig the hole!'

All heads turned te look at Squinty the coffin maker from next door, he was all agitated chompin his gums up an down an starin from one te the next wit his eyes crossin.

'We're ready te take her now. Tha Father Flitters is walkin up an down the church grounds sayin she won't get a Christian burial if youse don't bring her over fer the burial Mass now! This is the fourth day you've had her lyin up there!' he said, curlin up his nose an clampin his mouth givin a sniff like he got a bad smell.

'Right! We're off, are they here?' someone said, wantin te be in control an take charge.

'No! There's murder up there!' someone else said. 'People's bein usin her coffin as a nest place te hide their bottles a booze from each other, an on top a tha they was usin it as a bench an a table fer holdin their grub. Frankie Mullins, he's gone mad up there tryin te clean it!'

'Will youse move! Shift yerselves fer fuck's sake!' Squinty roared. Then he turned, wavin the arm at everyone te follow.

'Let's go!' people shouted, startin te clear away from the table leavin me wit the whole place te meself.

'Can I have me breakfast now, please, missus?' I said, starin up at an old woman starin down at a lump a cheese in one hand, an the big bread knife in the other.

'Do ye want some?' she said, lettin her big black tooth take a bite outa the lump without cuttin it.

I stared at the dirty tooth mark not likin the look of it an shook me head, sayin, 'No. Just give us a bit a bread, please, an a sup a tea. Or have ye any biscuits or cake or jam or nothin like tha?'

She shook her head munchin on the cheese eatin the rest of it now, wit her cheeks bulgin out, makin short work of it wit her gums. Because tha's all she had, tha an the one tooth.

'Easy now easy, mind the walls. Here! Don't hold it over the banisters, we'll lose her!'

I munched on me bread an supped me hot tea, me an the old woman made a hot pot, an we guzzled the rest a the fresh bread an found three eggs hidden in a pot under the sink an we boiled them. She got two an I got one, an we're enjoyin ourselves wit all the grub an the sudden peace an quiet. Except fer the stairs, they're makin their way down now, an everyone has an opinion on how te get Delia down the stairs in her coffin, because the landin an stairs is very narrow, an there's too many a them all squashed there tryin te own the coffin. Some a them are still drunk, like the granny here. I can smell the porter offa her, it's like the Guinness brewery!

I could hear grunts an moans, then a scream, 'Pull back! Youse have me kilt against the wall!'

'Ger out the way then! Ye're not helpin!'

'Wha do you know about it?'

'Here no fightin! Let's get her down wit her coffin in one piece before ye's start!'

Meself an the drunk granny munched an listened te the killins, the bangin an shouts, then a squeal, 'Mind me hand!'

Then panic, 'Watch the coffin!'

Then footsteps staggerin, landin in the hall.

'Here we are, are we right now? Open the door wide, are youse ready?'

'How many carriers have we got?'

'One, two . . . eh, ten!'

'Ah fer fuck's sake, there's no room fer tha many hands an feet under the box!'

'Who's got the flag?'

'Wha flag?'

'The fuckin Irish flag! The one we fought for!'

'Who fought? You?! Sure you couldn't fight yer way out of a paper bag, Sloppy Pooley!'

'Who can't? I'll show you in a minute, ye flat-nosed fucker!'

I rushed out te get a look seein two aul fellas the age of Mister Mullins buryin their noses in each other's face.

The granny flew up behind me. 'Oh should a known! It's only them two eegits,' she muttered, lookin disappointed. 'They've been scrappin since the day they were borned, right from the cradle now te the grave, the aul fools.'

'HAVE RESPECT!' a man snorted, lettin it come up in a growl from his big chest, he had the chest stuck out an his arms swingin, lookin like a gorilla ye see in the jungle.

I blinked an cleared me eyes te get a good look. He was wearin a cap sittin on top of a mop of curly blond hair, an he came struttin himself up wit Mara rushin behind him on her high heels.

'Oh lookit, all smiles an outa breath pushin out the diddies!' muttered the granny, givin her a dirty look.

We watched wit our mouths open listenin.

'Rocky! Haven't seen you in an age!' Mara breathed, soundin like a kitten gettin itself strangled.

'Not now, not now,' he said, wavin her away like she was a tormentin dog turned up wit the mange.

'Oh all right then,' she said, stickin out her pointy chest gettin it jammed up the nose of Sloppy Pooley. He opened his mouth gettin suffomacated an started breathin hard suckin in an out.

Then an aul one roared, 'Lookit him, tha dirty aul fella suckin on the diddies a Mara Maple! I'm tellin your wife so I am!'

'Ah shurrup, you! I'm tryin te talk,' complained Mara, then said, 'So if you're too busy te escort me to May Flower's weddin, I'll take up Smiley Rich's offer te take me in his new cream motor car.'

'Wha?! Not on yer nelly! Tha mammy's boy is takin you nowhere, my little sugar plum juicy drop!' Rocky said winkin at her, givin her a slap on the arse.

'Ohhh! Wha a man!' the aul fellas roared.

'Disgustin little trollop!' muttered the aul ones.

Then Rocky turned on the two aul fellas arguin. 'Cut the feckin language,' he ordered. 'Stop the shapin up, or I'll . . . But sure that's only fer rebels!' he said, lookin down at the flag now appearin on top a the coffin all folded up lovely, wit nice sharp creases.

'Don't let himself hear ye say tha!' moaned Sloppy turnin

away, leavin only the one eye in the head te be seen, wit the fear a God showin in it.

'Come on open it up an spread it out,' said Squinty, grabbin it up an shakin it.

'No! Ye can't!' roared Rocky, snatchin it from his hands.

'Put tha back on my Delia's coffin,' said Mister Mullins, who was watchin quietly from the hall door.

Then he walked over an Rocky dropped it down an moved away, sayin, 'No harm done! Meant no harm, sorry about tha, Mister Mullins.'

'So ye should be,' said Mister Mullins quietly. 'My daughter died saving the life of a child . . . two childre! She's a hero! She got crushed under the feet of them animal-gang bastards an the fuckin police causin an even bigger riot. An you're one a them, Rocky Rice. If you're not outa my home by the count a three, Squinty Reilly will be busy measuring you for a box te plant you! NOW GET THE FUCK OUT!' he exploded, makin a run at Rocky wit his two arms held rigid up against his sides.

'I'M GONE! Keep yer hair on. I want no trouble!' screamed Rocky, soundin like the Banshee keenin in our ear. He was gone, flyin out the door like his arse was on fire, then it was all quiet, nobody said anythin an we just waited fer Mister Mullins te stop starin at the ground wit his hands coverin his face makin a shield.

'OK, I'll take the top, right shoulder, Squinty,' said Mister Mullins. 'You take the other side an can two more of you just take the back?'

'Lovely grand,' said Squinty, movin over quietly to ready himself te lift.

'You go ahead,' the men said quietly, movin out an others movin in te grab up an lift the back onta their shoulders.

'Are we ready?' Mister Mullins said.

'Ready!' they said, an started te lift Delia inta the air an carry her in the coffin on their shoulders.

We all stood back as they marched out slowly matchin their steps an lettin their feet settle goin from left te right. Then they were on the road an everyone got in line an slowly marched behind. Now we were on the road wit aul ones mutterin prayers, an the lot of us marchin our way, all followin the coffin carryin Delia te the church fer her funeral Mass.

The young priest was scatterin holy water over Delia's coffin while Father Flitters swung the incense box mutterin, singin an moanin, I think they was hymns. People sang up but then everyone started singin in the wrong tune, because Father Flitters was makin them go too low, so they ended strangled. I gave a big sigh lettin people know I was fed up.

'Go easy there,' Nellie said, givin me a dig te shut me up.

I looked up at her an yawned, then forgot meself an let it out in a roar.

'You bold lump!' Essie beside me moaned, grittin her gums sayin, 'If you draw the attention of tha Father Flitters down on us! By Jesus, I'll give you such a kick up yer arse, Lily Carney, you won't be able te sit down fer a week.'

'Yeah too right!' sniffed Nellie, an the two a them gave me another dig, because I was squashed in between them.

They didn't hurt me, so I wasn't bothered an lifted me legs stickin out me knees an examined me wellies. 'Lookit!' I whispered, showin her me missin boot. 'I got me wellie back, it was sittin on the floor at the end a me bed when I woke up this mornin!'

She looked down then clucked her tongue an shifted her eyes lookin them up te heaven. 'Put them feet down, tha priest is watchin you,' she warned, now grittin her gums makin a big noise suckin in her spit.

I shrrup real fast, because now she's goin te kill me!

*

'The Mass is over, it's ended. Come on, get up!' Nellie said, draggin me te me feet, then watchin an waitin fer the coffin te march past. Tha was followed by the altar boys, we could see one shakin the incense box while the other held onta the chain, he did tha in case the young fella tha got te swing it maybe ended droppin it, because it was heavy, very heavy the young fellas tell people. Then quick behind them came the priests shakin the holy water, one lashed it over the coffin an the other priest threw it over us, drownin us in blessins.

Then we were outa the benches an everyone goin slowly but ye could see they wanted te rush. It was very stuffy in the church an full a smoke from the incense. As soon as we hit the air it was gone very dark an cold.

'Oh I don't like the look a tha sky,' said the drunk granny, lookin up wit one eye closed, like it was blindin her. 'Who are youse goin wit?' she said, easin her way up te stand in the middle a everyone. 'Is there any room fer me?' she asked, lookin at the women all lookin at the horses lined up ready te take people te the graveyard.

'Here we go,' muttered the fat mammy, makin her way te stand beside Nellie an Essie an all the other people. 'Well we're not short a hackneys an cabs. They all must a heard an come rushin down, hopin te turn over a few bob,' she said.

'Well, I don't know if there's many a halfpenny, never mind a penny, te be made among these paupers!' sniffed Nellie, givin a dirty look around at all the kids standin in their bare feet, an the mammies wit babbies under their shawls, suckin fer the milk in their diddies. I'm always sayin diddies in me own mind. We're not supposed te say tha word, but all us childre do! Mammies think we're foolish we don't know nothin, but we know tha!

Everyone was out te watch Delia gettin put inta her hearse an say goodbye te her before she left fer ever. We all stood around while Mister Mullins spoke wit the priest, I inched me way over then stood up close te get an earwig.

'You'll get yer money, your ten pieces a silver, when you finish the job.'

'The job! How dare you?! I am a man of God!' barked Father Flitters.

'YES THE JOB! Man of God you are not! Judas you are! You betrayed Christ by turnin on his people. You are a bloody Pharisee, squawkin fer yer money on the steps of the house of God! BE CAREFUL YE'RE NOT STRUCK DEAD!' roared Mister Mullins, gettin snow-white wit the rage on him.

'WHEN,' then he lowered his voice, 'you have buried my Delia will you get your money, an only then! Now let's go before I have you up in front a the bishop,' he said, then nodded at the funeral men te close the carriage door on Delia, an then rushed te climb inta the cab an two horses waitin behind.

Father Flitters rushed after him, nearly trippin up in his purple robes, an grabbed up his holy water an shook it like mad through the open winda, drownin Mister Mullins. 'You! You imbecile! You pagan! Take that!' An he threw wha was left of the holy water in the silver holy bowl wit the long silver chain right inta the face a Mister Mullins.

We all took in a sharp breath, lettin it out in a heavy moan.

'You are possessed by Satan!' warned Father Flitters, fixin his face in a laugh wit the eyes hoppin. 'But you will pay for this outrage!' he screamed, goin mad all over again wit his face turnin purple.

'Fuck off, ye aul redneck bog-trotter!' snarled Mister Mullins, flyin up the winda, then lookin away.

The hearse wit the two midnight-black horses an big black plumes on their head took off slowly, an Mister Mullins' carriage took off wit it.

Suddenly there was an almighty rumble on the footpath, an

people stopped gawkin wit their mouths open an made a stampede fer the cab an horses, the pony an traps, an whatever else they could grab an haul themself inta as they filled up one be one, makin an awful commotion, wit the jarvey roarin an givin out.

'In here, come on move up make room. We'll save money wit the one cab.'

'Ah come on now, missus! Six a youse won't fit in me cab, wit only enough room fer two normal-sizes people. One a youse is enough te make three! Wha's more, ye're damagin me! If youse look down now, ye's will see, youse have flattened the rubber on me wheels leavin them standin in their rims!'

'Right!' they said, then there was another rumble an a lot a rushin up an down wit people choppin an changin, then finally they took off te follow behind.

I watched them all trot off one be one, an stood wavin an gawkin, listenin an smilin, takin it all in enjoyin meself.

I was standin there still wavin, watchin the last a them take off, the only one left behind from the wake, me an the drunk granny standin beside me wit a sour look on her face, then she sniffs wit a bad smell, 'Lookit them go! Misery loves company, an tha shower a shites is all in good company. Oh miserable load a gits, aren't they, love? Wouldn't spend a penny te take us wit them. Wouldn't mind, but there's no pockets in a shroud an some a them wit the look a death on them won't be fuckin comin back! Wouldn't ye think they'd spend it on us, the old an the young? Fuck them! I hope they fall inta the grave hole,' she snorted, leanin over te spit on the ground then fixed her shawl, wrappin it around her head tight an said, 'I'm goin home te me own place. Sure there's no fire like yer own fire. Fuck them!' Then she bent her head inta the wind an made her way off.

I watched her go then turned te see everyone scatterin now,

all goin home an about their own business. 'I'm on me own,' I muttered. 'How come tha happened again?'

Then I saw the hearse wit the big black horses an their plumes bouncin up an down, they came trottin around the corner an past the house again, you do tha three times, it's fer the corpse te get a good last look an say goodbye, an fer the neighbours te do the same. They all cover their windas an come an stand on the edge a the footpath an wait, then bow their heads as the funeral procession goes past, then the third time they come, it's goodbye fer ever!

I watched, takin it all in, feelin very scalded in me heart. It was just like me mammy's time all over again. Except me an Ceily an Delia, an Mister Mullins, sat in the first cab wit the two horses. It's bigger than all the rest. Ceily was cryin, but I was just lookin out the winda at all the people standin on the footpath. I waved at me friends from school an Delia gave me a box. 'Will ye cut tha out! You're not royalty an we're not goin on holiday!' she snapped, holdin me hands in her lap te keep them quiet. Now it's her turn an we didn't even know tha. Wha's worse, there's only two of us left – me an Mister Mullins. Delia is gone an Ceily is missin.

I watched the hearse comin around fer the third an last time, then it hit me. 'HEY WAIT FER ME! Wha about me?' I shouted, runnin like mad wit me hand up gettin outraged, like Father Flitters calls it, it's at bein left behind. Yeah I'm outraged, I thought, the cheek a them all leavin without me when we let all them come when we had a funeral!

I like the priest's words, I'm goin te learn them fer when I'm becomin a saint. Then I can say them te the sinners when I'm outraged wit their sinnin!

I shot across the road, right under the hoofs of the big black horses, makin the driver flash his whip, pullin them up.

'Whoa, whoa! Easy, boys! Wha the fuck?! Are you blind?' he

shouted at me, standin up on the footrest wit the cloak on the shoulder of his long black coat catchin the wind an flyin out behind him.

I stared up at the lovely red-silk linin, then takin in the big tall hat standin on his head. 'Wha? Oh sorry, mister, but youse are goin without me!' I complained, then rushed around te the cab seein Mister Mullins stick his head out the winda, shoutin, 'Come on, you little feckin demon, your mother always said ye had no nerves in yer body, an one day yer darin would get you kilt! Get in here,' he said, steppin down an haulin me up be me knickers an the collar a me coat, then sendin me flyin te land in the lap a Squinty's wife, the fat mammy!

'Here we go again, doin a flyin leap te get inta me arms,' she laughed, grabbin hold a me an squashin me in between the pair a them. Then we took off, around the corner onta Portland Row, then across Summerhill an onta the North Circular Road.

'We goin te Glasnevin, where we left Mammy?' I said, gettin the idea this is where we went before, an knowin the name a the graveyard where we was supposed te have buried me mammy.

Nobody answered. Mister Mullins stared at the brown-leather walls like he was lost in himself, an Squinty an the fat mammy just sighed an stared out the winda, lookin like they was sleepin wit their eyes open. It was the rockin mad of the cab, the springs was very bouncy an we were all like babbies in a rocker, gettin sent off te sleep or lost in our own world. I gor a picture in me head of the men slowly lowerin me mammy in her coffin down inta the big black dark hole. I never left me eyes off it, down it went bit by bit wit the men holdin it back on the rope so as not te topple it. I looked up at their faces seein the heavy rain pour down their caps an land on their nose, then hang an drip wit their eyelashes catchin the water an lettin it hang like sparklin white jewels. Their faces were shiny wit the wet an it trickled down their necks an onta the collar of their long mackintosh oil coats. Their big black wellington boots were thick wit the grey dark mud, an they kept draggin their feet together – it was te stop them slidin an landin Mammy an her coffin crashin te the bottom of the great big black hole. We was soaked te the skin. I looked up te Ceily standin beside me an her face was torn asunder wit the terrible pain an loss a our mammy.

Tha was the only way ye knew she was tearin herself in two wit the cryin, because tha sound was taken away an lost on the wind. Nor even did her face show the tears, it was too busy gettin drownded wit heavy buckets a rain comin down, because the heavens had opened up lettin out all the water te wash away the tears.

But I didn't cry no, I didn't. I just stood there without movin. The rain poured down my face too, it soaked me curly hair flattenin it te me scalp turnin me head te ice, but I didn't move. I wanted te miss nothin, I had te know wha was happenin to my mammy. Me wool coat tha Mammy bought me fer my first Holy Communion last year soaked an sopped inta me, but I didn't move, no, an I didn't cry.

'Because it's not true,' I muttered te meself, shakin me head then lookin out the winda. My mammy never died. Big people are always makin mistakes an they'll see I'm right when she comes home an she'll be all smilin, laughin because they're eegits believin she was died.

Now we're flyin along the big open road of the North Circular, it goes fer a long way, an it's the road you take when for the graveyard. Behind us I could hear the gallopin hooves of the other horses comin up behind, an I could hear the horsemen shout an give a lash of the whip. 'Go on! On ye go!' Wantin te keep up wit our two black horses tha were tearin along wit their necks strained te keep up wit the two big black stallions pullin the shiny black hearse carryin Delia inside her coffin.

All the horses were tearin along, an the hooves were now makin flyin sparks crashin out from under the steel shoes ridin on the hoof of the dashin horses. Poor Delia, I wonder when she sat next te Ceily an me in our funeral carriage if we could have warned her by sayin, 'Delia, be careful! Because next time we come along this road you will be lyin in a coffin inside a hearse bein pulled along by two great big black stallions, an they will have plumes dancin on their head. Just like Mammy is now.' Or . . . no, not my mammy!

We got te the top a the road an now turned right onta Dorset Street, then left, up the Whitworth Road wit the canal on our left. The horses trotted now slowin down te take in the sights an enjoy it at our ease. But the carriage rocked so much people were nearly asleep wit their necks shakin an their heads wobblin, but their eyes were closin like they was enjoyin it.

Now we turned right wit the Brian Boru pub on the left an kept goin. I was starin out lookin at the shop windas wit their cardboard pictures showin the Bisto Kids – they were followin the smell a gravy sittin on roast meat an potatoes, wit it takin them all the way home! They'll have a mammy waitin fer them when they get back there, an brothers an sisters an even a home te go to. No one will have robbed tha, I shook me head thinkin. Then another thought came, how can ye lose your fambily? I wondered, how did it come te happen to me? I don't understand tha, I just don't!

Suddenly we heard the horseman drivin the hearse up ahead let out a roar. 'GO ON, BERTIE! GO ON, SAMSON! SHIFT, ME LOVELY BOYS!' Then a lash a the whip.

Wit tha our carriage suddenly rocked an heaved, endin balancin on its two back wheels as our driver did the same – let out a roar wit the lash of a whip. 'COME ON, ROSIE! GET GOIN, DAISY!' Then the cab rocked back onta four wheels an we took off into an all-out gallop.

'KEEP THEM OUT, WALLY! DON'T LET THE FUCKERS IN!' roared the horseman drivin the hearse, wit him shoutin back at our fella.

'Wha's happenin?' breathed Fat Mammy, leppin up in the seat wit the eyeballs burstin outa her head.

'Dunno!' said Squinty, leanin te take a look out the winda wit one eye closed blockin the blindin light, but sure the sky is pitch black.

'Ah it's a race,' said Mister Mullins, the first te see the black hearse flyin up beside us wit two horses frothin at the mouth, an the driver, he was standin wit the reins gathered in one hand an lashin away wit a long whip in the other. He gave a quick look over at us at our driver, then I leaned me head out, seein our driver do the same.

He stood up an lashed the two horses wit them flyin, they were gallopin all out now, keepin neck te neck. I looked back seein the cab behind wit the driver standin shoutin himself hoarse, he was tryin te get his horse te fly. It was a tinchy tiny grey thing an its little legs was flyin like pistons, but the carriage was takin its time, barely movin.

'GO ON, ME LITTLE BEAUTY!'

So he did, he flew the little legs wit the head hammerin up an down stretchin the neck, he was desperate wantin te keep up.

'THA'S IT! Show them big overfed mutants how te do it!' screamed the jarvey, all delighted he was doin grand, but his shout came out in a croak because his voice was gone.

I looked seein he was a tiny little aul fella an I wondered if he was a midget, because he's very small an the two a them match, him an the horse. Yeah, I think he might be a midget!

I could see the rest of our funeral procession was comin up fast behind him, nearly wantin te pass him out! An right beside us was the other procession flyin up behind their hearse.

'There's an awful load a horse traffic an they're all comin up behind us in an awful hurry,' warned Mister Mullins, not lookin too happy.

'Fuck me!' Squinty suddenly said, gettin ragin. 'Them lot will get us kilt wit their racin, an all because they want te get ahead of each other in the queue fer the gravediggers!'

'Oh, now, not such a bad thing, less time for drinking if we spend it sitting behind each other in a bloody queue,' said Mister Mullins wit a half-smile on his face lookin from Fat Mammy te Squinty, then they laughed.

Squinty leapt up an stuck his head out the winda, shoutin, 'Go on, show them!' Roarin at the driver te get the horses te go faster.

I leapt fer the other winda wantin tha fer meself, but Fat Mammy hauled hersef onta her feet, sayin, 'Give us a look.' She laughed, then put her arms around me an leaned the pair of us out far, holdin onta me tight.

'LOOK, MORE!' I shouted, seein more hearses an funerals flyin towards us from the other direction.

Suddenly I felt like I was in the middle of one big terrible sensation. Tha's wha Mammy calls it when ye're stuck in the middle a the road ready te get kilt. The speed wit things flyin past an the jerkin of me insides, the roars a people all shoutin an laughin an cursin an spittin when the other side got close enough. The sound of horses' hooves clashin an crashin on the sett stones, an the clinkin a harness an the tumblin wheels a the carriages rumblin over the black stone road. An the smell a sweat from the backs of the horses, you can see the white foam of it turnin the black coats on their skin a shiny wet.

'Jesus it's like the devil on horseback flyin te hell,' muttered

Mister Mullins, leanin out te take in the great race we were havin.

'Whose winnin?' I shouted, pushin me voice out in a whisper. I was afraid te breathe, because somethin was tellin me we could all be kilt stone dead.

'They're mad. They're all mad, these horsemen drivers! They won't give an inch,' muttered Fat Mammy, half-laughin but lookin worried wit the eyes pained.

I watched us comin closer, gettin very close te the big entrance gates of Glasnevin Cemetery, wit all of us tearin towards each other.

'Who is goin to make it through the gates first?' muttered Fat Mammy, keepin her head movin first one way, lookin quick beside us at the hearse still tryin te get past us.

I could hear the heavy snorts of the two horses tearin their hearts out runnin beside us so close, I could reach out an stroke their necks if it wasn't a dizzy speed. I could see the spray of white misty water blowin outa their nostrils, it was makin a white hood around their brown heads, an the white creamy foam hangin out, caught between the steel bit in their mouth. I could hear the springs an see the carriage rockin fast, very fast, goin from side te side. The carriage door was so close I could see the dents on the silver handle, an I could, if I had a mind, reach out an open it now because we were at matchin speed.

Then it suddenly rocked swingin smack at us, nearly takin the nose offa me face. I screamed an bucked back, hittin me head against the side a Fat Mammy's head as she pulled the pair of us back. It was so sudden, we crashed against Mister Mullins an Squinty, nearly topplin them outa their winda wit the weight an speed of us.

'Ah ohh, me back,' she moaned.

'Me head,' I squealed.

'Me legs is broke!' screamed Squinty.

'OH, HOLY SHITE!' shouted Mister Mullins, gettin squashed up against the corner wit his nose pressed inta the leather wall.

'Get us up!' shouted Fat Mammy.

'Get yerself up offa me, I can't move, ye fat cow,' whined Squinty, moanin an keenin soundin like he was painin te death wit his stuffin knocked out.

I twisted meself out from under the right hip a Fat Mammy an pressed me hand on her belly, throwin me right leg over her. Then I shoved me left knee on her chest an hauled meself up, givin her a clout a me hand on her nose an face.

'Ger offa me! Ye're killin me, Lily Carney!' she shouted, givin me a push tha sent me flyin te land on me arse beside the door.

I threw me big mop a curls back offa me face an looked over givin a big blow te get rid a the hair stuck te me nose ticklin it. I could see they was all still tangled.

'We're still alive,' I puffed, gettin ripples runnin through me, feelin the wheels tumblin like mad under me arse an flyin sparks wantin te set it on fire.

'Stay down,' Mister Mullins said te me, then leaned down grabbin the shoulder a Fat Mammy, sayin, 'Move over, I don't know where the fuck is best to be safest. What's these fuckers up to?'

'Can I get up an see, Mister Mullins?'

'No, stay there, ye're safer, it looks like that hearse got ahead an now we're definitely ridin wit death, racin him all the way te hell! If this carriage crashes or turns over, Squinty, our best bet is lyin flat out, take the seats an the floor. It gives us a fightin chance te roll away runnin when we hit the ground,' he said, then he looked out seein somethin just ahead, an suddenly, without warnin he was takin a flyin dive an grabbed me up onta the seat, then he threw himself down lyin flat out on his belly wit me buried under him.

Then everythin slowed down an things was burstin apart, the carriage rocked an swayed on its side, then it turned an rolled an I could hear the squeak an creak of wheels bucklin an wood breakin, I could hear the complainin snortin of horses gettin a fright, then their hooves slippin an the thud of heavy bodies hittin an slidin across the wet shiny black hard stones cut inta the road. Then the screams of these horses, an suddenly it was now all mixed wit the piercin screams of people gettin terrible tortured pain, then the quiet moans of others wit not the strength te scream or roar or shout. Then mercy, the rushin merry-go-round of things spinnin an us flyin an the dust an dirt of it, an all mixed wit the sound of screamin an snortin an people's agonized moans seemed te die, then we were come to a stop.

19

I WAS LYIN ON somethin hard wit my ears roarin an a stillness in me mind watchin an waitin, it was fer a sensation flyin through me an all around me body te start doin somethin, start painin me. The world stood still an I waited wonderin why it was so dark, there was somethin pressin down on me. Then it came, not wit pain but a terrible tightness, I couldn't get a breath! I was gaggin, tryin te get me wind. Someone came scrabblin on their knees, pullin stuff offa me, it was bits a the roof an the winda wrapped around me chest.

'There's a child under here! She's blue, she's not breathin!' a man said, lookin straight inta me eyes.

I stared back wantin te tell him the terrible fright I'm in, an all about me terrible worries. But I could only talk wit me eyes borin inta him. *Help me, mister, please help me get a breath! Oh don't let me go an die like Delia! Just get me up an let me walk.*

He pulled me out an lifted me sittin up restin in his arms. My body jerked wit me head goin up an down tryin te find a breath, but nothin came. Then he started te rub me back whisperin inta me face very soft. 'Easy, shush,' he says, lettin it out in a long easy breath, the air makin its way comin inta me open mouth. 'Easy there easy, little one, shush come on, you're safe in my arms now, just let it come.'

But it wouldn't come, my face was burstin an me chest was

stranglin me. Oh the pain has me gripped in a too-tight bear's hug. I lifted me head an stared straight inta his eyes feelin death was waitin te snatch me, but God was here mindin me in his arms an talkin softly, an he was holdin death back, keepin him well away from me.

'Go on!' he whispered, shakin his head givin it a slow nod. 'You're OK! You will be fine. Come on, breathe.'

Then I heard the sounds fightin outa me. 'Hhhhhah,' then a scream erupted but caught.

'Easy, easy, let it come,' he whispered, strokin my back an starin inta me eyes, smilin.

I let go an dropped me head an eased through the fright an the pain an then it came, a lungful of air heaved in an I let it out. Suddenly I was breathin an screamin an holdin onta the arm of God, not wantin te let him go. The shock an the fear had me openin me mouth an throwin me head back an screamin up at his house in the heavens. I didn't want te go there! An I certainly didn't want te ride wit the devil on horse-back an go all the way te hell as Mister Mullins had warned. I threw me head back even more an screamed wit the rage. Then I heard another ragin scream.

'Get me the fuck up outa this! Who is tha? Is tha you, Frankie? Get me up fer fuck's sake! I'm wrapped under this green stuff!'

I stopped screamin an looked around seein flowers in the middle a the road move an the Fat Mammy lift her head wearin a lovely bunch a them, an spittin out more. They was all packed tight around her mouth an face. Then she lifted up an a big wreath was crownin her head, but ye couldn't see the rest a her because tha was buried underneath.

'THE CURSE A JAYSUS ON THE FUCKIN LUNATICS AN THEIR MAD DASH FUCKIN RACIN!' shouted a voice.

'TOO FUCKIN RIGHT YOU ARE THERE, SQUINTY!'

roared Mister Mullins beside me, crawlin out from under the seat lyin on top a wha's left a the carriage. 'They won't get a penny outa me for this! I can tell you that!' he spat, sendin somethin white flyin outa his mouth. 'There go the last a me fuckin teeth,' he spat, bringin out another one wit threads a blood hangin from his mouth.

'Can you stand up?' said the lovely man te me, easin me offa his arm an liftin me onta me feet.

I looked down, seein me wellie was gone an me foot was cut.

'Wriggle your toes for me.'

'Like this?' I said, liftin up me foot, nearly shovin it under his nose an inta his mouth wit a big wriggle.

'Ah not a bother on ye! You're a grand little thing, I think you'll live! Now, where is yer mammy?'

'Wha? In there, they put her in a grave in a big black hole but it's not really her! They were mistaken,' I said, leanin in te tell him tha, just so he would know tha childre can tell these things, we're not all fools like they try te think.

'Oh,' he said, clampin his mouth lookin very sad but agreein wit me. 'You could be right,' he said, shakin his head thinkin about it. 'Where is yer wellington boot?' he said, lettin me go an liftin things outa the way, lookin fer it.

'There it is!' I shouted, rushin over te see it was thrun over the railings an sittin on a grave inside the dead yard.

'I'll get it,' I said, hoppin an hobblin wit me foot startin te drip blood. Then I saw the hearse lyin on its side all battered, an the flowers thrun around wit some lyin in a heap. Then on the side a the road close te where me boot landed was a coffin, it was smashed wide open against the footpath. There was nothin in it! The white-satin linin was all torn an muddy an tha was sprawled on the footpath.

'OH SWEET JESUS! LOOKIT THA! OH MERCY!' voices started te scream.

I looked around seein faces starin an pointin at me. No! I looked again, they was lookin behind me up at somethin. I looked around then me eyes lifted an went foggy. I blinked an rubbed them then stared hard. It was the corpse starin down at us! It was caught hangin up on the spikes a the railings, an it was held there be the strings at the back of the shroud, an now all ye could see was the bare white skinny legs of an old man wit his eyes wide open starin back at us.

I stared wonderin, did they leave the pennies on his eyes te keep them shut when they put him inta his coffin? Me eyes peeled around lookin te see if I could spot the two pennies. No, I'm not goin te be tha lucky, I thought, now beginnin te take in the roarin an shoutin, then the ringin bells of ambulances an the police whistles blowin in the mouths a coppers, they've all come flyin in, hangin outa the Black Maria.

'Fuck! Wha a consterdenation!' snorted a horseman standin on the road just beside me wit his neck shiftin from left te right, an his eyes not knowin where te look next.

'Murder mayhem! Youse are all killers!' shouted a skinny little granny, tryin te hurry herself gettin helped by three other old grannies, they were all wantin te get their hands on a horseman, tha'd be Wally the driver. He was busy examinin the bits wha was left of his carriage.

'Eh you! Mister!' they shouted, wantin his attention from starin down, he was lookin very sad at all his loss. 'We're gettin our death a cold out here,' they complained, noddin an agreein te each other.

I could see they were wrapped in shawls, but yeah, they were all lookin blue an white wit shock an the blue bits looked very frostbitten.

'Tha's her husband!' they shouted, pointin up at the corpse lookin like he was ready te give a wave, because his arm was stuck in the air. 'Youse load a no-good, not-worth-rearin-never-mind-feedin lumps a thick shite!'

'Yes!' croaked the granny, agreein wit her friends.

'May youse die roarin,' they said.

'An I curse youse all to hell, the lot a ye's!' cried the granny, openin her shawl an makin a run now losin her rag at the driver, then she whipped it at him, tryin te blind him. You can do tha wit a shawl, lots a mammies do it when they is fightin each other, it's mostly over childre gettin hit be one a them. The mammies fight by pullin hair an flyin out the shawl tryin te catch the eye an blind you.

'How will I get me boot?' I asked, lookin around at the crowds all millin their way now te get a look up at the corpse. I don't know why everyone is gettin into a big state. Sure I see corpses all a the time, an they're stone dead! People are always dyin. You get fed up after a while goin te wakes, because the biscuits an lemonade an cake does be gone as soon as it hits the plate, word spreads very fast then the childre do be queuin before the door even opens. Then they get the best pickins. The only ones tha really like the wakes are the mammies an grannies, they think it's like a holiday, wit all the free food, snuff an tobacca an of course the drink! Tha's wha the men come for . . . an the grannies! Except if the wakes fer a child, then people don't say or do much.

I stood lookin at them now, they were pushin an shovin then standin an gapin, grabbin each other an goin mad wit them all moanin. I watched them hold their mouth then slowly drop their heads an quickly bring it back up again, lookin te see were they mistaken. No! They shook their heads not believin it.

I was lookin an listenin te them, they were more interestin te me now than the corpse they were moanin at.

'Oh Jesus, missus! Oh, me nerves is gone after seein this. I'll never be the same again.'

'No nor me!' whined two women wearin headscarves, an one had a hat over hers te keep out the cold.

'Poor Arty Mildew, he couldn't even have a funeral in peace! It's a cryin shame.'

'No, indeed, missus, true for you! An he never did a bit a harm te neither fish nor fowl, never lifted a hand in anger te no one he did! No, not in all his borned an livin days. Now look at him! This is how he's ended! Up there hangin, like he's been sentenced fer commitin murder!'

'Oh it's a cryin shame, shockin it is, scandalous altogether. Wha should happen now is them bowzies should be hanged. Hang them I say. Hang the lot a them!'

'An I'll second tha, missus! Yes! Hang them, but draw an quarter the bowzies first!'

'Where are they, them cursed murderin horsemen?' the hat woman said, wit the two a them lookin in different directions. The hat looked around, seein Wally gettin smothered by a gang a women, they were all shoutin an roarin, tryin te tear lumps outa him.

'Lookit! Looka tha! Quick, Nora! Biddy's managed te get her hands on one a them, now she has him be the hair an is swingin fer him! Go over an give her a hand!'

'Who? Me?' said the skinny woman wit the red sore eyes. 'I can't be gettin inta fights, I'm ailin! I'm under the doctor's orders, he wouldn't let me!' she puffed, lookin like she was goin te collapse from even the idea.

I whipped me head te get a look just in time te see Wally squealin wit his head bent an the hands workin, he was dancin around like mad havin a tug o' war, tryin te peel the aul ones' hands from the grip on the hair of his head. They were reefin the hair outa him.

'LEMME GO, YOUSE AUL HAGS!' he was screamin.

Me eyes lit up, the fight looked good, I rushed over, shoutin,

'RUGGY-UP!' Then suddenly there was a blast, an people looked around.

'Tha was a gunshot!' said a man mutterin te people, wit everyone lookin, tryin te see where it was comin from.

I lifted me eyes an looked inta the crowd. They was millin everywhere, an it was terrible upset no matter where me eye landed. People were slumped against railins gettin helped wit hankies pressed against their face, all covered in blood. An some were sittin on the edge a the footpath lookin shocked, wit holdin their head in their hands.

I rushed inta the crowd headin fer the direction I heard the shot, then saw it all happenin. Over here was the ambulances, all lined up behind each other on the middle a the road. They were loadin people on stretchers an the police was everywhere, doin everythin an stoppin fights an arguments. Then I saw the horsemen gettin talked to be the police, an they were lined up, five a them, against the railings beside the big entrance gates te the graveyard.

I heard cryin an looked over, people were bein moved apart an pushed back. Then I saw it. A horse lyin on the ground an a man kneelin beside it. He was wearin a long trenchcoat an brown horsey boots wit ridin trousers an a dark-green hat on his head. I was wantin te move but didn't get goin an just stared.

He had his arm stretched out dead straight, an a gun in his hand pointed right at, just inches, from the head a the horse.

I rushed over wit somethin makin me move fast. Ah no! It's the little flyin horse wit the tinchy small legs. Ah how could they do tha te him? Let tha poor little horse come te harm like this? They're bad! People are bad! Me face creased up lookin the length a him. He had a fat little body an tiny legs, but he had a gorgeous mane a blond red hair te match his colour, he was so little, tweeny weenie inchy small. His big brown eyes stared straight inta the face of the man wit the gun, like he knew full well wha was comin.

Then I heard the cry again. I looked around seein the little midget man gettin carried off in a stretcher te the waitin ambulances. 'No! No ah don't ah God, Jesus no, not you, Flasher,' he cried.

His arm was out wantin te stop the killin an his face was flooded wit tears an covered in blood, an the gushin tears was turnin it to a watery red flood. It was all now drippin down on his torn white shirt, an his black overcoat was in ribbons. The ambulance men covered him wit a blue-wool blanket, then lifted him up inta the ambulance.

I turned away an looked back at the horse, just, as a blast from the gun went straight through his skull. He jerked then slumped, an his eyes closed instantly. I could smell the gun, the blue-grey powder hangin around his head, an it burnt me nostrils. I started te keen hummin out me pain. 'Ah the little horse, the little man,' I muttered, feelin me own heart startin te scald. Where's his cab?

I looked around movin off slowly, the police was pushin everybody back, them tha wasn't hurted, or just passin an stopped te get a look. Here an there an everywhere, no matter where I looked I could see everythin, people an things, was lyin in smithereens. There was another dead horse wit blood dripped from its head onta the black cobblestones, it was lyin just a bit away. Now tha I open me eyes an take it all in, there seemed te be an awful lot a broken bits of everythin. There's bits of harness an bits a carriage, an a door from one tha flew a distance an landed against a wall up the road. There's blood on the road an more on the footpath, tha came from people tha made it, lived te walk away an drip their blood where they now stood an sat. Everywhere people were cryin, or tryin te talk but in terrible shock, the voices was only comin out in a whisper.

I started te cry, wantin things te go back. The little horse te be whole again, an the little man te be standin straight, happy wit his little pal the horse! I just know they was great friends, you can tell these things by lookin at the way he loved tha little fella. He could fly, or his legs did. An all the people! I cried lookin around me. Everyone is in tatters, everythin is wrecked! Men are so stupid. All because they didn't want te wait their turn on the queue, so they could fill their belly wit drink. They wanted te get te the pub fast, or it would be less drinkin time Mister Mullins said.

Where is he? Where's the fat mammy? I could feel a panic suddenly rise in me! Have they gone without me? Can they walk?

'MISTER MULLINS!' I took off in an awful hurry pushin me way through people, then suddenly I went flyin, head first over an old woman sittin on the footpath. She was gettin fixed up by the St John's Ambulance Brigade.

'Ahhhh! Me head! The pain!' I held me forehead feelin a lump rise, then erupted wit the screams an started te roar me lungs, cryin fer all I was worth.

'What's wrong? Are ye all right?' people said, rushin te bend down an take a look at me forehead an examine me skull. They did tha by rubbin their hands around me head. 'I don't feel no cracks, do you?' a man said, talkin te an old woman rubbin one side, while he felt the other side.

'Hang on! We need ice for that,' said the St John's Ambulance man.

'Yeah, where is it?' said a mammy-lookin woman.

'We haven't got any,' he said.

'Jaysus you're a great help,' she snorted.

'Anyone here see what happened? Better still, was involved in the funeral carnage? I'm looking to speak to the mourners,' an aul fella said wit a hat sittin on the back of his head an a card stickin out tha spells 'PRESS'.

I don't know wha tha means, because I only know me letters, an I can't read yet.

He whipped his eyes fast te everyone, takin us in one by one.

'Any one of you the mourners? Or are you just angels of mercy givin assistance? More like gettin under foot,' he muttered, turnin his head lookin around, then he spotted someone. 'Over here, Paddy!' he roared, liftin himself up te be seen over the crowd an wavin his arm at a fella. He was wanderin around wit a big camera strapped te his neck an bangin against his stickin-out belly. Then he whipped the head te us again an pushed the hat, lettin it tip back until it was barely hangin.

'Now, what about you?' the hat man said, bendin down an lookin at me.

'No! I'm not a moaner,' I said, shakin me head not wantin te be called tha.

'Are you hurt? Were you in one of the cabs?' he said, droppin te his knees an swingin on his hunkers, givin me a good look over te see was I gushin blood.

'Yeah I was! Kilt stone dead I was, nearly!' I then said, feelin a bit disappointed I had te tell him tha. 'An I'm hurted, me foot is gushin blood,' I said, liftin me bare foot te show him.

We all stared at the long streak a dried blood. It had stopped.

'Will I get a bandage fer tha?' I said lookin at him, then pushin him outa the way te talk te the St John's man, he was busy now, lookin after an old man tha came over wit his nose all drippin blood.

'MISTER!' I shouted, shiftin meself up te pull the leg a his trouser.

'What?' he snapped, lookin down an gettin annoyed at the crease I pulled, it was now gone outa his lovely uniform.

'Can I have a bandage . . . a big one?! Like he got!' I said, lookin over at the man sittin on the path wit the big bandage wrapped around his hand. 'I want one like tha an tied wit a big plaster,' I said, liftin me foot an givin the cut a squeeze te get it goin again, I didn't want it te stop bleedin until I got me big bandage.

'Yeah ask him,' he said, pointin te another St John's man givin an aul fella water from his flask.

'Right, give us a few details,' said the man wit the hat hangin on the back a his head.

'Wha paper you from?' asked the mammy-lookin woman wit the big red cheeks, an she had a lovely big cushy chest fer restin yer head on, or fer a babby te sink its gums in an get a grand suck a milk. She was keepin her big blue eyes fastened on him, while all the time tightenin her fancy red shawl wit the tassels on the end. But I think she was really only wantin te show it off.

'The *Morning Press*,' he said, lookin her up an down givin her a big smile.

'Hmm, is tha right now?' she said, givin him the eye.

I could see they like each other, you can tell these things. But I don't think her husband would like it! When ye see a woman do tha, the other women all turn up their noses an they won't talk te her no more.

'It was a massa me cation,' I said, wantin te interrupt an get them back te lookin an talkin te me.

'A what?' he said.

'It's a big word, it means everyone's goin te be dead!' I said, seein him lift the eyes te stare at the sky, tryin te understand wha tha word meant. I took in a deep sigh feelin very satisfied wit meself.

'Do you mean a massacre?' he said, lookin at me waitin te see wha I thought.

'Tha's it, tha's the very word,' I said, noddin me head doin an sayin exactly wha Mammy says, an the way she says it.

'Oh right!' he nodded copyin me, then looked around givin everyone the laughin eye. I could see it! You get te know all these things when ye earwig on the big people. If ye're very quiet when they start te talk, then sometime they can forget you're there. Tha's the best way, because then you don't have te strain yerself listenin.

'So first tell me, what's your name?' he said, grabbin a notebook an pencil outa the big pocket of his long heavy overcoat.

'Me name is Lily Carney.'

'How old are you, Lily?'

'I'm seven, sir. I'm goin te be eight next!' Then I sucked me mouth an started clickin me tongue. I love answerin hard questions, an this is a bit like school.

'Where do you live?'

'Off Portland Row, sir.'

'Is that off Summerhill?'

'Yeah! Tha's it,' I nodded, givin a big bow wit me head, just like Mammy does when ye talk te her about somethin important.

'Now, who died? Were you with the funeral?'

'I was, sir! I was right in the very importanted carriage. The one at the very front goin behind the hearse.'

'Oh very good,' he said, gettin all happy wit his eyes lightin up. 'So then you saw the crash. You had a first-hand view of the impact . . . the, eh . . . collision?'

I stared, waitin fer him te tell me wha he was wantin te know.

He shook his head. 'You don't know what that word means, do you?'

'Wha?' I said.

He sighed an sat back on his arse lettin go one leg te grab hold an stretch, then whippin it back an stretchin the other. 'Move up!' he said, sittin himself down beside me an pushin in beside the mammy woman.

'Oh, you're a fast worker,' she muttered, all laugh, teeth, eyes an lips! She blowin kisses wit the lips, flappin the eyelashes an showin her white teeth.

He loved it an pushed out his own lips forgettin himself wit watchin her.

'Talk to you later,' he whispered outa the corner of his mouth an inta her ear. I caught it all, because I'm very good at watchin fer people passin secrets. Big people always do tha when childre are earwiggin. They use their head an their eyes te talk te each other. They think we's are stupid but we know wha they're up te.

'So what happened?' he said, givin me all his time wit the eyes starin only inta me.

I took in a deep breath. 'Well,' I said, takin a cough an stickin out me tongue te get meself ready te tell me story . . .

'. . . An Mammy's dead in a big hole, but me mammy's not . . .(drone!) . . . An then Delia got kilt stone dead an I didn't know it . . . (drone!) . . . An the coffin . . . An they was usin it te hold their sambidges an . . . Father Flitters got very annoyed wit Mister Mullins! An me sister never camed back so she never didn't! An I lost me wellie again so I did, an after me findin it, I just did found it only this mornin! Now it's left me, all gone an lost again! An . . .'

'Yeah, yes! OK, kid, enough of that. Now! What about the collision?' he snapped, gettin very annoyed all of sudden fer some reason.

'Wha's tha mean?' I asked.

'Ah, for fu . . .' he snorted, clampin the mouth, now lookin like he was losin the rag.

Me face dropped. 'What I do?'

'OK,' he sighed, lettin out a breath an givin the top of his legs a slap, then shuttin his note book an leppin up te take a stretch.

'Do you want to walk with me? I can take down your particulars and we can have social intercourse,' he said, throwin his head at the mammy woman givin her a little smile wit a wink. Then he fixed his face, watchin her wit the eyebrow up, waitin fer her answer.

'Wha's tha mean?' she said, lookin suspicious but laughin anyway.

'Follow me and find out. I'll educate you,' he said, turnin te move an head off.

'Right, OK, but will I like it?' she said, rushin after him makin their way around an across people lyin an sittin wit some waitin fer help.

'You will love it!' he said, leanin in an laughin inta her face. Then he was lookin around wit his head swingin on his shoulders takin in people, then clickin his fingers at the man wit the camera. He would rush over an stand back bendin himself, then – Bang! – a big flash outa the camera an move on again. She was tryin te talk te the press man but he was distracted wit his head spinnin an his eyeballs swingin, intent te miss nothin. Then he looked at her an smiled like he heard wha she said, but then forgot her again, movin on an goin about his business.

Tha's very peculiar, I thought, starin after them an lookin at her wit me mouth open. Why is she followin him when he doesn't really mean wha he says? 'Let's go and talk,' he said. Sure he's not bothered about her never mind talk te her! I snorted te meself in disgust. I wouldn't waste me time if I was her. No! People can be very igorant, Mammy does say, when people act like tha.

Right! I told meself, wonderin wha I should do now. I know! I'll go an look fer me boot an find Fat Mammy an Mister Mullin, an Squinty. Yeah, I better hurry, or I might end gettin left behind then lost.

I leapt up suddenly, gettin an awful fright wit tha thought. 'Mammy!' I keened, lookin inta the graveyard, then gettin a sudden cold feelin of knowin tha I'm all alone an took off, rushin te look fer them.

Oh me boot! Now I know where it is! I turned me head te go back, feelin all delighted I just remembered. But then turned me head an kept goin. It's in the graveyard lyin beside the railins, I'll rush inside an go an get it. I might even find everyone there, maybe they're all lookin fer me. But they shouldn't be losin me in the first place, it's not proper, I thought, beginnin te feel me annoyance stirrin up. Mammy says te Ceily you have te keep yer eye on me, or I can wander off an get meself lost. 'Yeah, I could be lost for ever an it would be all theirs's fault,' I snorted te meself, rushin like mad now, not likin the feelin I'm lost an on me own.

I hobbled me way in through the gates seein the police everywhere, swarmin like bluebottles. Tha's wha the big people say. They was standin men an women, everyone! Up against the walls, an they had their notebooks out an was takin down information, I could see tha.

'Smack head-on!' a fella wit a peaked cap pulled down makin it hard te see his eyes said, he was keepin his head well lowered, starin at the footpath. He was lookin at it like it was a fillum, or somethin so interestin he just couldn't pull himself away. An he had the neck buried in a heavy overcoat wit the collar turned up, an his hands lost inside deep pockets.

There was a woman standin beside him an she too was findin the ground very interestin. 'Too fast is all I'm sayin, too fast is wha I could feel. Course, I saw nothin, I was doin me lipstick when it happened.'

I moved in fer a closer look when she said tha. Her face was covered in red lipstick it looked like it got strewled the length from her mouth, right up te the eyebrow! I felt sorry fer her, because nobody told her she looked a holy show.

Then I heard the bangin an looked around, just beside me was a Black Maria standin wit people locked in the back bangin an shoutin. I stopped te get a look. They were goin mad, the doors were hoppin wit their hammerin, batterin an kickin, an they were screamin blue murder.

'Let me out, ye's dirty, thick culchie bastards! Youse overfed, red-necked fuckers! Youse flat-foot no-good whore's melt! The fuckin cheek a ye's! Comin up here after climbin outa the bog an takin over our Dublin! Youse have no right te be doin this!'

I took in me breath lettin it out quick wit me mouth left open. Oh tha's shockin terrible bad language, they will go straight te hell if they die without gettin quick fast te the priest in Confession.

Right! I think it's a sin te be listenin, I better go, or I will have te get me confession too. Ah there's me boot. It's lyin waitin fer me! I thrun meself onta the grave wit the grass all wet, I was forgettin about me coat tha Ceily had te scrub clean from last time. Then I hiked me boot on an stood up, givin it a slam down te feel me foot warm again, an better still, no more walkin an gettin the bare feet cut offa meself. Then I stood still lettin me eyes move easy, I was takin in the sight a nothin but graves an trees an huge statues, all goin farther than me eyes could see. Where's me Mister Mullins an me fat mammy? I can't see sign of any a them here.

I started te wander away from the railins an go straight across, I was headin now fer the old dark parts, wit all the big trees an overgrown graves. I walked slowly, keepin me head down an me eyes peeled, because you can get kilt by fallin into a hole where the grave has collapsed. Many a one has done tha! Even the drunk granny knew tha. She put a curse on the lot a them! Maybe tha's why we had the terrible crashes.

'Fuck her!' I muttered, beginnin te lose me rag at the

thought it was all tha aul granny's fault tha I'm lost now an can't find me Mister Mullins. I'm never goin te find them, I must a been lookin fer hours, now I'm definitely lost.

I lifted me head an looked around takin in the time tha's passed. It's gettin late, I thought, beginnin te see the wintry day was lettin in the grey light, an the cold was throwin up a white mist of damp frost. 'Oh where am I?'

I spun me head around twistin meself lookin te see which is the way back. There's nothin here but graves an trees blowin their bony arms at me, because the winter stripped them a coats. I don't like the sounds comin at me from somewhere. It sounds like a ghost rattlin its rosary beads an comin te get me! 'I'm cursed, the old granny put a curse onta me! Oh an I'm goin te be lost here all night wit the dead in the pitch black!' I muttered, then I held me breath wit me eyes hangin out thinkin about tha. Then suddenly I erupted. 'MAMMY! CEILY! SAVE ME!' I flew chargin over graves wit chains around them an ones heaped wit flowers, I'm now leppin an runnin fer me life!

'SOMEONE COME AN GET ME! Oh no, don't leave me here,' I begged, runnin wit me hands joined prayin while I ran.

I heard a voice sayin, 'It's goin to be OK', repeatin it over an over again. It was me, but it sounded just like Mammy's voice. I'm sayin it but it's her voice. 'OK, Mammy, yes, Mammy. I'm goin te be OK, because I'm a good girl I am, aren't I, Mammy? Yeah I am!'

Then I heard somethin, I stopped te listen but me heart was flyin makin too much noise in me ears. I watched an waited, listenin, then the sound came closer an I could hear voices. Suddenly I saw men comin around the corner way down in the distance. They were gravediggers pushin a handcart tha they use fer carryin the coffins te the graveside. Me heart leapt. 'Oh Mammy, ye're right, I'm goin te find me way out!'

I started te run, then saw more people comin after them around the corner, I slowed down tryin te make out who it was. It looks like . . . YEAH! It's my Mister Mullins wit wha looks like Fat Mammy shakin from side te side, gettin herself movin in a hurry, an other people all followin wit them.

I leapt inta the air hoppin up an down, then got straight on me feet an flew. 'MISTER MULLINS! WAIT IT'S ME, LILY!' I roared, shoutin before they could even hear me. 'Wait it's me,' I muttered to a whisper now, me breath was all gone from runnin an shoutin.

'Mister Mullins! Where was youse all? Youse lost me!' I said, tryin te talk an get me breath at the same time. I rushed in front a him an he stepped outa me way barely givin me a look, then walked on lookin inta the distance like I hadn't appeared at all. I stopped an watched him go, then let me eyes fall on Fat Mammy, she gave me a look wit half a smile, then let her eyes look straight ahead starin like she was lost in her thinkin. I stood still lettin people get past, they were all goin about their business not lookin left nor right. Nobody wanted te know me, everyone was talkin quiet an lookin like they had their own thoughts te be thinkin, an didn't want te talk much. It's just everyone seems now very downhearted.

I wanted te ask them did they bury Delia. I know they must have, but still. I wanted te know wha happened. I'm sorry I missed tha. I'm sure she would a likin me there. Because she was always givin out te me but she didn't mean any of it. She used te say I make her laugh, I was a very comical child God bless me, an, 'Mary, you would be lost without tha child. She keeps you on yer feet, but God, she's very funny be times the things she comes out wit.' Tha's wha I heard her say te Mammy, tha an many a time lots a things like tha, so she did like me. She was me godmother. Now I have no mammy an no sister an no home an no Delia, an no dog . . . We didn't have a dog! But we could a had, then I would a had no dog neither, because he would a ended up in the cats' an dogs' home! It's easy te know tha, because if they want te lock up childre in a home, then they would a taken our dog too. He would a been called Spot, because I would a got one wit a white coat an a black spot. Or a black one wit a white spot. So yeah, Spot me dog would a been robbed too!

I sat down on the edge a the footpath, not wantin te think about all me loss, because somethin in me mind is tellin me it's like the bogeyman, he's waitin in the dark corners te come out an eat me up! I can't think of all me loss. No! I got te keep tellin meself Mammy will come home an Ceily will come home, an until then I belong wit Mister Mullins an I can talk te Fat Mammy. Right! Tha's settled so, tha's wha I'm goin te do.

I looked around, seein they was gone miles ahead, an soon they would be disappeared outa sight if I don't get meself movin. I leapt up an flew, chargin fer all I'm worth seein them still miles ahead, an now they're crossin over the road, headin away from me. I can do tha here – cross over before the heavy traffic, it's bad down there comin from the Mobhi Road.

'Wait! Wait fer me,' I keened, runnin fer me life te catch up. I don't want te lose them fer good. But I can't see them now! 'Oh wait!' I moaned, gettin tired now wit me legs seizin up.

Suddenly me heart lifted. Ah there's some a the funeral people headin in the door of tha place.

'Come on!' a woman shouted to a crowd of people makin their way somewhere else. 'They're gone in here te The Dead Man's Hangout. Let's go in after them, the world an his wife is here! It's the waterin hole fer after the graveyard,' she said, tryin te get them to stop.

The crowd hesitated not lookin too sure.

'I don't know about tha place, Lila. There does be killins

goin on in tha dump,' a very pale-face man said, lookin very worried.

He's not a well man I thought, he looks starved an bony wit his cheeks all sunk.

'Ah come on. The laugh will be mighty!' she coaxed, droppin her head onta her shoulder lookin at him then wavin her arm, sayin, 'Come on, we'll only stop for one if we don't like it.'

He stood starin chewin his gums wit the jaws workin up an down, then dropped his head makin his mind up, an took off in after her. The rest of everyone then followed, wit them not lookin too sure neither. When everyone had gone inside, I looked, seein tha was the last a the people. I could hear the shouts an the laugh comin from inside but there was no one out here, it was all quiet except fer the traffic, wit carts an horses, bicycles an delivery vans, all rushin up and down.

20

I STOOD AN KEPT me place just inside the door, an now the rain is startin te come down. I only hope nobody comes out an tells me te move away an stand outside the door. They do tha because childre are not allowed te stand inside pubs, it's against the law. So childre always have te stand outside no matter wha the weather. The worst is when they have te stand in their lovely white frocks an coats an veils on their first Holy Communion day! Tha's when pubs all over the city does be crowded wit peoples, an their childre get left te stand on the street outside, tha happens until the pubs close an everyone gets thrun onta the streets. Yeah! But they get loads a sweets if the mammies an daddies don't get too drunk an then forget about them. But my mammy never drank a drop a stout in her life. No, my mammy is a good mammy!

The cold was gone right through me from sittin on the icy damp ground. I pulled the feet tight against me an grabbed me coat, twistin the ends behind me legs, tryin te keep out the rain an cold blowin in the door. The tiles was all wet an slippy from people comin in an out all the day long, an now I don't know wha te do. It's gettin dark an Mister Mullins or no one has come out all day te see was I here. I tried te sneak in fer a look earlier, but the place is packed te burstin an everyone was gettin drunk. Ye couldn't see nothin because the air is thick wit smoke from cigarettes. An I didn't see nobody, not any people tha I know.

Oh I just want te go te sleep an get warm, I'm so cold, an I'm tired an hungry. I just want te go home, but where is tha? I wonder wha I should do. I don't know me way back, it's too far! An even if I got there, Mister Mullins won't be back.

The door opened an a man came out wearin a long grey apron, it was saturated wit wet an covered in brown stains. 'Wha you doin down there? You'll catch yer death a cold! Get up outa tha an move around. If Mister Hillman comes out, he'll run you away from this door altogether!' he snorted, grabbin me arm an puttin me out the door.

'Sorry, mister,' I whispered, gettin afraid a me life because he was very annoyed.

I stood meself against the wall wit me hands behind me, afraid now te move. I don't like it when men give out te me, because they're not like mammies. Men can hit ye an hurt you.

'Eh! Come over here!' a voice shouted.

I looked around wonderin who was shoutin. Then I saw a man get off a bicycle an come on the footpath, he was lookin an headin straight fer me.

'Lily Carney! Wha are you doin hangin around here?' he said, comin an standin right up te me, wit his bike pushed at me face, leavin me no escape.

I looked up at him, seein his eyes dance in his head, all delighted he'd come across me. It's Mister Lawrence the caretaker at my school. Nobody likes him an the big young ones whisper te keep away because he'll try te do bad things te you, he does tha to childre! I don't know wha they mean, but it doesn't sound like somethin I want te find out.

My mammy hates him because he pulled my frock up when it got all wetted by the kids throwin water in the playground tilets – tha's when we was all havin a water fight. He said I should take me frock off an he would dry it fer me. I said no an ran te me class because I was hidin from the teacher when she was killin everyone fer sloppin the water everywhere, an then everyone endin gettin soaked te the skin. I told me mammy wha he said, an she went an waited until he came outa the school gate an boxed him in the face. He gor a black eye an his nose pumped blood! I heard it all when she was tellin Delia, they always had their nights sittin together be the fire wit a nice cake, or whatever she brought home from the mad house. Tha was their enjoyment, especially on the Saturday night, when me an Ceily was in bed after us gettin our bath.

'Well, well, well! Look at the state of you! You look now like a pauper wit no rearin, in threadbare order. Well isn't tha interestin now,' he laughed, leanin himself comfortable restin his chin on his arms spread on the saddle of his bike. His eyes was starin inta me face an I didn't like it, so I dropped me head an looked down at the ground.

'Here you are, the young one of tha hag Mary Carney! Thought she was too good fer everyone, tha one. Now look wha happened te her spawn. She's now gone, dead an buried planted, pushin up daisies an offerin her rotten carcass as food fer the worms! What's her young one doin? It's now left standin outside a pub – no better, no different from any other dirty paupers walkin the streets a this city,' he said, liftin his head te give a big spit. 'The ones tha sit outside waitin fer their da's te come out so they can whine, until they take the last few pence sittin in the man's pocket, then run back te their rats' nest of a home, an hand it over to the lazy whore sittin on her arse by the fire.'

I didn't like the angry way he was talkin an sayin terrible things about my mammy. An as well as tha, it wasn't nice wha he was sayin about other childre's mammies. It's true the childre, they always look dirty an have disease an no shoes on their feet. Mammy would often make a sambidge or keep somethin over an give it te the childre sittin outside the pubs where we live, because she knew them. They was from the tenements. But then she would say, 'Don't let me catch you playin around wit them tenement childre, Lily Carney, or I will take the skin off yer arse! You'll catch disease!' So I don't understand tha bit. Anyway, I haven't got me feet bare an me head is not shaved an all covered in sores, so I'm not really like them, just a bit! I know I haven't had a wash fer a long while now, but still an all, I'm not filthy dirty. Me hair is just matted a bit, I thought, then I lifted me hand from behind me back an suddenly gave a push sendin him flyin an rushed meself inta the pub standin just inside the door. He went flyin backwards because he wasn't expectin tha. I just lost me rag without me even knowin it! I was shiverin an shakin wit the fright, an people came rushin over te pick him up an shout at me.

'You little animal!' a woman roared at me. 'Wha did ye go an do tha for? I saw you! I was a witness,' she said wit her eyes narrowin, lookin at me like I was a vicious dog.

'Are you OK?' a man said, helpin Mister Lawrence offa the ground an steadyin him, then bendin down te pick up his bicycle.

'Here, there's your hat, put it on yer head,' a woman said, pickin it up from where it blew on the side a the road.

'No! Get tha young one over here. I'm takin her home! She refused te come when I tried te take her!' he said, rubbin the back of his head wit the face gone snow-white an his eyes waterin up all shiny, they had a glassy look in them an he was starin at me. I don't like the look a them eyes, he's goin te hurt me!

'Here! Come on, you, behave yerself! Go wit yer father an stop yer carryin on!' the aul one said, grabbin hold a me an pushin me inta him, waitin wit his hand out te grab hold a me arm.

'Lemme go! MISTER MULLINS! Help me! No don't send me wit him!' I shouted, as he tried te pull me after him.

'Go on go! You cheeky little cur!' the aul one shouted after me as her scarf slipped off lettin her fluffy grey hair escape, it blew inta the air an waved around her head freezin the bare skin wit all the bald patches.

I let meself go an landed on me back lettin him pull me along wit me arse skiddin, tearin inta the ground. 'No, no! He's not me da! I don't have a da!'

'Hey, mister! Wha's happenin?' shouted a load a kids rushin along pushin a babby's big pram without the babby.

'Oh lookit! Just guess who it is, everyone? It's dirty Larry from our school, the one wit the rushin hands an roamin fingers! Hey, Mister Lawrence, wha you doin wit tha young one?'

'Help, he's tryin te take me away!' I shouted.

'Oh lookit! He's doin a kidnap! Tha's not his young one! He's not married,' they shouted, all runnin over an pointin the finger at me.

'NO I'm not I don't belong te him! Oh yeah ye're right! Please save me! He's wantin te take me off, he's goin te hurten me!'

'Wha? What's tha you just said?' the woman tha picked up his hat said, liftin back the shawl tha covered her ear so she could hear better.

'Is tha right?' said the man who helped him, now lookin shocked an movin over closer te hear better, wha's happenin.

'Liars! You bloody shower a pig-ignorant paupers the lot a youse!' screamed Mister Lawrence, gettin in a rage.

'I know who tha is! Tha's Lily Carney,' said a young one. 'My little sister Lola is in her class at school.'

Me heart leapt wit the excitement.

'Oh yeah, I know her too te see. They live in Summerhill!'

'LET HER GO!'

'YEAH, LET HER GO!' the childre shouted.

'Get the police!' shouted the granny.

'Get help! Get someone te help the child, he had me fooled!' shouted the woman.

'Poxy bastards!' Mister Lawrence snorted, givin me a kick in the arse when I'm still lyin on the ground, then throwin his fist at the childre swearin. 'I'll see youse in hell first fer this!' he shouted, turnin green then blue wit shock, an leppin his leg over the bike pedallin off like mad.

'Wha happened? How did all this come te happen?' the childre asked wit their eyes bulgin, an outa breath, then swarmin around me wit excitement.

'Yeah, wha was tha about, love?' the woman tha picked up his hat said, bendin inta me.

But before I could open me mouth, the grey-haired woman wearin the scarf said, lookin like she was nearly cryin, 'Sorry, I'm so very sorry! I come along when you were just tryin te save yerself. An wha do I do? I nearly end up handin you over as his Christmas dinner! Oh Jesus, the thought of it!' she said, puttin her hand on her face an droppin her head, goin all shocked. 'You poor little infant, havin te be matched against a big monster of a terror like tha animal! Come here te me!' she said, grabbin hold an squashin me inta her bony chest, strokin me head.

I could get the smell a cabbage an onions, an stale tobacco an porter, it was pourin up me nostrils an smotherin me. 'He tried te take me!' I sobbed, tryin te cry but I couldn't get it out now. I was feelin too happy wit everyone savin me from gettin a terrible hurtin from Mister Lawrence. He never liked me since me mammy hurted him. He always gave me a dirty look outa the corner of his eye, like he was a dog afraid a me, but at the same time he wanted te get his teeth in an do me damage.

'Where's he now?' a man said just after stoppin te listen.

'There he goes! Headin fer the Phisborough Road,' shouted the woman, fixin the scarf on her head an tightenin it.

We all turned an watched him flyin his way in an outa the traffic, he was tryin te make distance an lookin in a shockin hurry.

'Yeah, the coward, the dirty animal, a danger to all little innocents,' she said. 'He should a been drownded at birth!'

'Well, the only answer fer the like a him!' the granny said, stretchin herself up an tightenin the shawl under her chin, the eyes narrowin wit a rage. 'Someone should do a job on him wit a razor blade! That's the cure we have fer the likes a him!'

'The very thing!' said the man who stopped te listen. 'Let the animal gang play wit him, they'll sort tha fucker out good an proper,' he snorted, then he laughed.

'Anyone know where he lives?' the man who helped him suddenly said, turnin around an lookin at me an the rest a the childre.

'No, but we know where he works!' the young fella pushin the pram said, pullin it over an takin a big breath heavin his chest out before shoutin up givin all the information.

'Lovely, thanks, son!' the man said, then he nodded at the woman givin her a smile an did the same wit everyone else, noddin his head an closin his eyes then openin them, sayin, 'Tut tut tha child was very lucky!' Then he shook his head an gave a wave goodbye.

'I better move too, I left the dog sittin be the fire on his own. He's goin te be wonderin where I got to!' said the granny starin an thinkin about it, gettin very worried.

'Yeah, funny you should say tha, but I've been out all day an I went early, up te Mary Street te get a few things, an look at me! The night pitch-black an I still not home, an now I'm kilt worryin about me husband's dinner an me—'

'I know! Where does the time get to?' interrupted the granny, wantin te get her say in fast. 'It's the older you get, I think we're gettin short changed be the clock. It's goin like the clappers, gettin sick of lookin at the same faces an wants rid of us!' she complained.

'Ah no but wait!' said the scarf woman, puttin her hand on the granny's arm wantin te tell her story. 'Wha I was goin te say was me poor budgie, Bluey he's called. I put him out this early mornin te catch the bit a sun. Sure I went out leavin him sittin on the windasill, an Holy Jesus te night! He's still out there, missus! By now he should be frozen solid into a block of ice! I better run!'

'Yeah goodbye!' they said, givin a quick wave, then took off hurryin in different directions. We watched them go, then turned te look at each other.

'Where you goin, Lily Carney?' said the big young one who knows me wit the little sister.

'I'm waitin fer Mister Mullins an his friends te come outa the pub. They was at a funeral.'

'Yeah, so was my ma, an they came te this place. A neighbour turned home an came up to our door te warn us te bring the pram, because our ma needs it. She's mouldy drunk an this is the only way we can get her home.'

'Yeah, an we all came te give Bisto a hand. Didn't we, Bisto?'

'Yeah! Youse are me best pals!'

'Don't mind them. They're only hopin te get a few coppers outa the drunks when they come reelin outa the pub,' snorted the big young one, throwin back her head te lift the big mass of orange hair tumblin down, coverin her eyes.

'Let's wait! It should be throwin-out time any minute now!' Bisto said, bringin the pram over an pressin it against the wall fer us all te lean an wait.

'Let's hope she doesn't break the springs again!' said a young fella wit a half-laugh on his face but then lookin worried.

'Nah! If she does, we'll have te carry her.'

'Jaysus, not me! Your ma's not light like a feather!' said a young fella wit dirty blond hair an a black snotty nose.

We watched the door wit us risin up alert every time it opened te let someone out, but then dropped when it was only a stranger tha staggered out, not one a ours. Then we heard the big brass bell bongin like mad just as the doors blew open, we watched as the man wit the apron shot his head out givin us a look, then flew it around, shoutin.

'TIME'S UP, EVERYONE! Men, get yer spurs an ride tha horse right outa here, get yer womenfolk an start te roll them wagons!' he shouted, clappin his arse an roarin it out then givin a hop like he was ridin a horse.

'Tha aul fella fancies himself, he thinks he's a bleedin cowboy in the fillums,' muttered Bisto.

'Move back, you scavengers!' the cowboy aul fella roared, throwin his head wit the thumb pointed then movin towards us, makin us grab the pram an shift ourselves.

We moved back even further when the drunks piled out all hangin tight together so they wouldn't fall down.

'Oh me darlins! Oh me darlins,' croaked two aul fellas havin a sing-song as they flew fer the wall landin together in a heap.

'Where we are?' one said, liftin his head te get a look around just as a pile more came out an a voice shouted, 'Neddy Knowles! Get up, ye dirty sod, you never kiss me like tha!'

Then three bodies all linked together an laughin their heads off tripped an poured down on top a them.

'Oh this is lovely!' someone said.

'Oh mind where ye're puttin tha hand!' someone complained.

'Oh give us a push up quick, I need te do me piss!' moaned a fat woman lyin on top a the heap.

'Rosie Parson, don't even think a lettin a piss drown down on me!' roared a voice buried underneath.

Then suddenly the cowboy grabbed hold, shoutin, 'Come on, youse have beds fer tha carry-on! This is not Biddy Bangers knockin shop youse are in!'

'Hey let's go! Tha's my ma, she's here!' shouted Bisto, grabbin up the pram an givin it a shake wit the brake comin off, then flyin it over te stop beside the heap.

'Ma, ma! Come on ger up! I brought the transport lookit! We have the pram fixed! Can ye ger up? Come on, gang, give us a hand wit me ma!'

'Which one's your ma?' said the cowboy, wit two aul ones wrapped around his neck.

'Tha's my ma there,' Bisto said, grabbin hold of a huge mammy wit the hair swingin an the arse in the air, tryin te haul herself up.

'Grab her legs, Ammo. I'll hold under her arms, an we'll all haul her inta the pram,' sniffed Bisto, tryin te catch an lick a snot swingin outa his nose. 'Mona, you hang onta me ma's middle an we'll ease her in!'

'No just swing her in,' shouted Ammo.

'Fuck off! Youse will only break her doin tha!'

'Ah hold it! Give us a hand, Lily! The weight's killin!' shouted Mona, lookin like an English sheepdog wit the hair buryin her face.

The huge mammy opened one eye seein the childre grippin hold, tryin te cart her. 'Ah, me lovely treasures! Not a word of a lie! I'd die fer you! I swear te the livin Jesus an all above! Oh fuck, wait!' she said, lowerin her voice, then we heard a grunt an a splashin hit the ground. 'I need te do me piss,' she said, lettin it out on a long breath.

Then I got a smell just as I felt somethin hot hittin me boot. 'Ahhh!' We all screamed. 'SHE'S PISSIN!'

'YEAH! RIGHT ON FUCKIN TOP A ME!' bawled Mona, lettin go an droppin her right te the ground hittin her arse.

'Now look wha youse done,' moaned Bisto, lettin his end down gently, sloppin right inta the pool a piss.

'Oh the smell!' we all said, holdin our nose gettin ourselves away.

Bisto stared down at his ma lookin like he wanted te cry. 'Ah fuck it, why did ye have te go an do tha for, Ma?' he said mutterin te himself, because his ma closed her eyes goin off te sleep wit a contented smile on her face.

'Come on, we have te get her home,' he cried, creasin his face but there was no tears.

'No, Bisto. Ye can go an get yerself stuffed, I'm not comin next or near your ma. She stinks,' complained Ammo.

'Yeah, an my ma is goin te kill me when she gets the smell a me an sees me coat an frock all destroyed!' complained Mona, shakin her head lookin an smellin the sleeve a her coat, then cryin at the state she's in.

I looked down seein the mammy only got me in the one boot, because I wasn't really near her. No, I was only pretendin te lift wit me hands out.

'Do youse want a hand, childre, te get yer mother up?' said a man wit a red face an only half drunk, wit his wife standin next te him holdin onta his arm, linkin it.

'Yeah oh yeah, will you please, mister?' Bisto said, wipin his snots wit the dirty sleeve of his man's jacket. It was greasy as hell an miles too big fer him.

'Hey, give us a hand, fellas!' the man said, lettin go of his wife then throwin the arm at a crowd a men staggerin outa the pub all singin their hearts out.

They didn't hear a word an held tight linkin arms, dancin to a song. 'I'M A RAMBLER, I'M A GAMBLER, I'M A LONG WAY FROM HOME! AN IF YOU—'

'Eh, misters! Give us a few coppers! Will youse?' shouted Ammo, rushin over te dance in front a them, tryin te get them te stop.

But they just laughed an kept goin, makin him dance backwards. 'NOW MOLLY FLYNN SHE HAD A TWIN—'

'Fuck youse!' shouted the half-drunk man an bent te pick up the huge mammy himself. 'Heave!' he shouted, draggin her be the feet, then tryin te get her standin up straight, te land her in the pram.

The man wit the apron turned his head away from tryin te push everyone out the door an keep them movin, then turned te the man, sayin, 'Hang on! I'll give you a hand.'

Wit tha, he hurried over an grabbed her legs givin her a big swing, sendin her sittin smack inside the pram.

'Grand!' the apron man grunted, slappin his hands together then sayin, 'I think she's wedged in there, ye might have a bit of a job tryin te get her out. But my advice is, when you get her home leave her there te sleep it off. Then bejaysus, be the time she wakes up in tha state, she'll get herself out in a fine hurry, never you fear, son! Now go on, all of you, get home an inta bed the lot a ye's, it's too late te be walkin the streets at this hour. You'll only get picked up by the peelers.'

'Thanks, misters, youse are very good!' Bisto said all happy.

Then everyone got behind the pram an they heaved an pushed, gettin it movin, then they were on their way.

'Mister, I'm waitin on Mister Mullins an his friends. Can ye tell me, please, when they're comin out? I'm waitin here the day long, will ye go an see fer me?' I said, lookin up at the apron man, not afraid now, because I was desperate.

'Hang on, I'll go in an see.'

I waited watchin the door seein more an more people

comin, but no sign of the apron man or Mister Mullins. Me nerves was goin an I was hoppin up an down tryin te keep the cold out, an stop the nerves worryin me.

'No! Not here, you must a missed them. There's no Mullins in this place now, nor anyone knowin him. Ye better go home fast!' he said, lookin after the other childre all pushin the mammy tryin te get her across the road without all gettin kilt stone dead. They were pushin fer all their worth, but only gettin across slowly, it was the heavy weight a the pram. I could see their heads all lookin up an down, they were watchin out fer traffic tha might come in the dark appearin outa nowhere, an they still stuck in the middle a the road.

I stood still watchin them, goin inta fright wit hearin tha Mister Mullins is nowhere te be seen. I watched the childre make it, then head around the corner an down the Whitworth Road. They live in Summerhill, tha's near where I live! I took off flyin meself across the road an down the hill rushin te catch up wit them. They can bring me home! The bangin pain in me chest eased, makin me feel better wit the thought, they know the way, so I'm not goin te be lost.

21

I STOOD OUTSIDE MISTER Mullins' house lookin up at all the windas wit no lamplight showin out, not even the sign of a candle burnin. Where is he?

I started te cry. I'm bangin an even kickin the door but it's just all quiet comin back at me. Wha am I goin te do? I'm locked out on the streets in the pitch-black night an the monsters can come an get me!

I looked around at the empty streets an all the houses gettin dark wit no lights showin. Everyone's gone te bed te sleep, an I'm the only one left in the world wit no bed te go to, an no mammy or sister te look after me! I could feel a terrible fright risin in me, an started te run up an down whingin, wit the fright gettin bigger in me.

'What's goin on here? What are you doing out this hour of the night?' said a man's voice comin at me very close.

I looked up inta the red face of a big huge policeman standin lookin down at me.

'What's your name?'

I stared sayin nothin, me nerves was now all gone an I couldn't move wit the fright. A policeman! He's goin te arrest me! I'm goin te jail fer breakin the law, I shouldn't be on the streets this hour a the night. Ye're not supposed te be, unless ye're makin yer way home! I started te shiver an me teeth started te rattle, makin a knockin noise in me head.

'You're freezing with cold, how long have you been out here?' he said, lookin around te see was someone comin te claim me. 'Do you live around here? Are you going to answer me? OK, let's sort this out, come with me. I better get you in somewhere warm. Have you eaten?'

I still stared not able te take in wha was after happenin. There's nobody here te claim me, an now I'm gettin taken away fer bein a baddie! Ceily was right! Oh Mammy! Where are you? Ceily, I want you te come back!

I then erupted. 'I want me mammy. Where's me mammy? Where's me sister? I want te go home! I want me own fambily back!' I shouted, turnin te run an took off flyin, headin fer me own house wantin te get home an find everythin OK again. Mammy will be waitin an we'll have chips an sausages fer dinner, an me sister will laugh at me fer sayin or doin somethin stupid. An I won't fight wit her. I will just kiss her an tell her I missed her. An I won't ever leave the house again without kissin Mammy goodbye, an then, makin sure te get a long good look at her.

I shook me head from side te side breakin me heart wit the thought! I never said goodbye, an I didn't even get te see her the last time I left. Tha was when we was all together. Now I'm all on me own wit no one te say I belong. Mister Mullins or Fat Mammy doesn't want me, they went off an left me.

'Ohhhh!' I rushed te the wall an slid down breakin me heart wit the cryin. 'Mammy oh Mammy, ye went an left me! Why did you do tha?'

A pair of black boots appeared an stood in front of me. I just stared, not carin no more. Mammy's gone. Ceily's gone. I want te go too. I want te go wit them! I looked up at the big policeman lookin down at me, he didn't look angry, just worried.

'Will you take me te where me mammy's gone? Do you have te die te get up to heaven? Because I thinks tha's maybe where she's gone after all. They lowered her down inta her grave, an I was there today when they went te put her friend Delia into a big hole as well. An I got afraid because I was lost, an Mammy came whisperin in the trees te talk to me! She told me te be easy, I would get me way out an I did!' I said all this then went quiet, lookin down at his boots again.

He said nothin an we just stayed tha way fer a few minutes. Then he bent down an put out his hand, sayin, 'Come on, little girl. Let me take you out of the cold and see if we can get you something to eat.' Then he lifted me up an carried me in his arms sayin nothin.

Then I let meself go an just rested wit me head on his shoulder not thinkin no more, or even carin. I only want te be wit my mammy an sister, I don't want nothin else.

I woke up hearin the clatterin of a machine spillin out white paper, an people talkin, an bodies movin in an out. I looked around squintin me eyes because the bright lights was hurtin me.

'Eat this,' the policeman said, liftin me down off the two chairs pushed together an made soft wit blankets. I gave a big yawn an grabbed me head fer a scratch, I could feel it in a pile all standin up.

'Come on, have that,' he said, puttin down a white plate wit two ham sambidges an a cup of milky-lookin tea. 'That's for after your breakfast,' he said, puttin down a big bar of Cadbury's chocolate wrapped up in silver an purple paper. I could nearly smell the lovely taste from here, without even openin it.

Me eyes lit up! I took a huge bite of the sambidge tastin the ham an the butter, it was gorgeous, an the tea was lovely an hot an sweet. Me eyes stayed glued on the chocolate, knowin I have tha fer afters.

'Now, when you finish that in a little while we are going to take you for a jaunt in a motor car! Won't that be nice?' he said, smilin an rubbin the top of me head tossin the standin-up mop of hair, then tryin te run his fingers through the curls te flatten it down. He just stared when he finished, then shook his head givin up.

'Needs a wash and a good comb,' he muttered. 'Wouldn't my mother just love to get her hands on a head of hair like that! It would keep her occupied for hours,' he laughed. 'I better get out to the desk, the Superintendent will be putting me on boot-polishing duty if I'm caught slacking.' Then he went off out the door about his business.

'Ready?' he said, fastenin the big silver buttons up te the neck of the long, heavy wool police coat, wit the silver bars an numbers on the shoulders. He was wearin a peaked hat as well, an I wouldn't a known him! He looked all spit an polished me mammy calls it, wit his shiny black boots.

'Ready?' a big man said wearin an even more important-lookin coat, wit stripes on the shoulders.

'Ready, Superintendent,' said my policeman then off we went. We walked out a back door an into a yard wit bicycles an a motor car sittin in the middle, it was waitin in front a the big gates, te take off out.

'In you get, sit in the back,' the policeman said openin the door an flyin me in te land on the soft cushiony back seat.

I got all excited an stood up te look out the back winda.

'Sit down,' he said, sittin in beside me an the Superintendent sat in the front wit another policeman ready te drive us away.

'I never was in a motor motor car before!' I said, hoppin me legs an bangin them against the back of the seat, wantin te climb up an ger a look out.

He gave a little nod flyin his eyes te the Superintendent, then winked at me lettin me know it was OK.

I leapt up an looked around, seein the Superintendent then whip his head back, he was turnin te look at the policeman knowin he let me. The policeman was busy lookin out the other side, an nobody said nothin.

'Oh lookit! There's young ones from my school!' I laughed gettin all excited. 'EH, YOUSE! LOOKIT ME!' I suddenly shouted, givin the winda an almighty bang an screamin the voice off meself.

'JESUS CHRIST!' roared the Superintendent whippin his head around, gettin the fright of his life.

'Holy Moses!' muttered my policeman givin me a shocked look. 'Sit down!' he said grabbin hold a me.

'SIT DOWN, YOU MENACE! You put the heart crossways in me!' shouted the Superintendent.

I flipped meself around wit the policeman draggin me down, then stretched out me legs fixin me coat coverin them. I sat wit me hands on me lap now, afraid te move, not enjoyin meself no more.

'Here we go,' said the driver, flyin over cobblestones then slowin down goin in through an arch wit big gates.

'Dublin Castle,' said the Superintendent. 'Driver, head around to the right and we are for the Children's Court. Get through this and we are done! It's up to the rest what they want to do. We will have done our job,' said the Superintendent, lookin at my policeman. He suddenly started playin wit his hat strokin an movin it around then givin me a look starin like he was thinkin an gettin very sad.

I started te feel me heart shift, goin from a tick-tock into a fast run. Me belly was gettin cold, an I could feel me body stiffen, gettin me ready fer a quick an fast run. Somethin bad is goin te happen! I just know it! *Mammy! Help me!* I muttered inside me head.

22

THE MOTOR CAR stopped outside a big black door an childre walked in trailin their mammies. They look sick, they're all lookin white as ghosts, an they even gor a wash wit their hairs flattened down wit water. Tha's wha some a the paupers do when they want te look polished. I need tha now! Mammy used te always give me a bath on Saturday night sittin in the tin bath in front a the roarin blazin fire. It was lovely! The curtains would be drawn keepin out the cold dark winter, an Ceily would sit readin me bits outa the *Bunty* comic. An even Mammy would laugh when we heard about the fat Bessie Bunter, she was gettin inta trouble over eatin too much at her lovely grand boardin school. Then after, we got cocoa an biscuits or whatever Mammy brought home from her work in the mad house. Then we went te bed, an before she sat down te enjoy her night by the fire eatin an talkin wit Delia, she would lay out our clean best clothes fer Mass on Sunday, an then our day out in the city. No, I was most definitely most NOT a pauper!

We walked into a dark hall wit an old narrow wooden stairs in front, te the left was a huge big area wit long wooden benches tha wrapped around the whole room. I could see in, an worried-lookin white faces lifted their head te look out at me. They took in the police ganged around me, then a woman gave her head a little shake, much as te say, *Aren't them the bastards!* Then she dropped her eyes again, thinkin an starin at the floor. Childre wit no shoes sat beside their mammies, wit their bodies jerkin an their legs shakin an wavin, they looked very afraid, just like I'm feelin now.

'You can come straight up, they're waiting on you, everyone is ready,' said a man rushin down the stairs wearin a long black gown wit important-lookin forms under his arm.

'Let's go,' said the Superintendent, an my policeman put out his hand and gently pushed me ahead, up the stairs in front of him.

I walked into a huge room wit a stage in front, an a man was up there sittin behind a big bench. He was wearin a white wig an a black gown wit a snow-white hard collar. When everyone walked in, he lifted his head lookin down his nose from one te the next, takin us all in through a pair of eyeglasses. He looked at me an nodded at the man wit the papers under his arm te come an get me. The policemen went in an bowed down te the judge then sat down in the front row on the other side a the room.

'You stand there,' said the paper man, puttin me standin in front of a fireplace wit an empty grate.

'I am representing the National Society for the Prevention of Cruelty to Children,' I heard a voice say. Then it hit me! It's the cruelty people, the pair a them are over there sittin on the other side a the bench next te the big winda!

Me heart leapt an me stomach twisted then shot up me breakfast, it was all lumps a bread wit bits a chewed ham an all covered in brown from the chocolate. I could smell the chocolate an it made me heave even bigger an it kept shootin out until now it's only dribbles. I lifted me head wit the dribbles of brown sick hangin in threads from me mouth an me coat was destroyed. I moved away drippin sick wit me an started te cry.

'Take her out! Can someone get her cleaned up?'

Then the paper man rushed over an whispered somethin inta the judge's ear.

'OK, yes, I see that now! Put her sitting down then send for the cleaners when I have dealt with this matter,' he said, givin me a look from under his glasses like you would look at a dirty dog eatin its own shit. Then he said, 'Let us continue. The child must remain during these proceedings; meanwhile, I believe it is necessary we expediate this as a matter of extreme urgency. It is a possible difficulty with transport, if transport may prove to be necessary. Would that be correct, you people of the NSPCC?'

'Yes it would, your honour,' the skinny man said, standin up quickly an bowin te the judge, then sittin down again.

'OK, what are the facts of this case?' the judge said, lookin down at his papers then lookin around, landin his eyes on the police superintendent.

He stood up, lookin down at his papers, sayin, 'The initial charge is a case of common vagrancy, your honour. We are charging this person, Lillian Carney, having reached the age of reason, that being seven years old, she now being of age, seven years with eleven days, thereby the age whereby she can now be charged with a crime under English common law sixteen hundred and . . . Further, the National Society for the Prevention of Cruelty to Children, represented here today by Mr Ernest Willows and Miss Mabel Wallis, will give evidence that the child has neither a place of abode nor the protection of a guardian, the mother, Mary Carney, being now deceased this two weeks. This matter has been taken in hand by Father Joseph Mary Miles Flitters, parish priest of the defendant's parish in the north city of Dublin. It was he who expressed concern some almost two weeks ago for the welfare, security and fate of this girl. Affidavits signed by him and witnessed have been put forward here as evidence, your honour.'

Wit tha, the paper man whipped out papers from under his arm an handed them te the judge. Then the Superintendent bowed. 'I will now rest my charge and allow the NSPCC society to present their case.'

'Yes, but before we proceed further,' the judge said, lookin down at the policeman then along te everyone else all sittin waitin for te hear wha he says.

'I intend to strike out the charge of vagrancy. That law does not apply in this case, the child still being under the legal age where she can be held responsible for her actions.

'What I shall do is consider the matter for the concerns of the child, Lillian Carney, being in need of care and protection. Very well, we may begin,' he said, noddin te the lot a them.

I sat rockin meself backwards an forwards wit me leg flyin an me stomach wantin te heave again. It was the sickenin smell a vomit blockin me nose an pourin outa me clothes. I don't understand wha anythin they're sayin about me! Wha did I do? How did I get te be a baddie? I don't understand nothin! I'm worser off now than the paupers, they might be dirty, well, so am I now. But they have a mammy an sisters an brothers, an I don't have tha no more. So, I'm now a baddie, it's a sin te be poor, to be a pauper, no one wants te be next or near you. So I'm worse now, I'm a baddie! It's all God's fault, he was very selfish wantin te take her all fer himself, an it was all so of a sudden she went. The bleedin cheek a him, I will never have anythin te do wit him again. The devil can have me! *GO FUCK YERSELF, GOD! Tha's the best thing I can think te say to you.*

'So, it is agreed as everything is in hand. I understand now – it becomes clear your wish to have this matter dealt with in all possible haste. You have a long tiresome journey ahead of you. Father Flitters the parish priest has already made arrangements for the girl to be taken in by the Order of the Holy

Crucifixion. These nuns lead a very simple and austere way of life. It is the furthest point west and lies almost in the western isle. They live off the land and I believe it is very isolated, primitive and barren, with only the pounding noise of the sea roaring ferociously when the storms come thundering in across the Atlantic Ocean. Yes, I have been close to that area, it has a wonderful cove, my wife and I discovered it when we were first married. It was during our honeymoon. We brought a picnic lunch I remember,' the judge said smilin te himself, gettin the picture back of tha time.

'Hm, yes, very beautiful,' he said, lookin all lost in a happy dream. Then he said, 'To live in a convent there, what a wonderful way of life, far from the dangerous world with all its bright lights, temptation and horrid evil ways,' he sniffed, lookin now like he had a bad smell under his nose.

'So, I will sign the order incarcerating the girl until her sixteenth birthday. Then she will be released if the good nuns think fit, it may be appropriate. But I shall make it an order that the girl, Lillian Carney, may, and can, be held under their authority after this date, until they decide otherwise. That will be it!' he said, givin his hammer a bang on the bench, then stood up makin his way outa the court.

'Thank you, your honour,' everyone said, all sayin it at the same time.

He nodded at them then said, 'Court usher, a word! I won't come back to hear any more cases this morning until that mess has been cleaned up and that disgusting stench has been removed,' he said. 'And before you do anything else, open the windows,' he demanded, barkin his annoyance.

'Yes, your honour,' bowed the paper man.

Then I was grabbed by the policeman, sayin, 'Come on downstairs with me, we have to get you cleaned up first.'

'Where am I goin?' I asked, wantin te get sick wit the terrible pain comin in me head. 'I'm thirsty, can I ger a drink a water, please?'

'Hurry,' he said grabbin hold a me, an half liftin half pullin, I was dragged down the stairs wit him holdin me arm under me shoulder. When we got te the ground floor he turned right, headin down more stairs into a dark dungeon. Then he knocked on a door an twisted the handle. 'In here,' he said, goin into a stuffy little room wit no air an a heavy musty smell of thick dust. It had a big enamel trough wit one tap fer washin, an underneath an in open cupboards was cleanin stuff wit everythin ye need – tin buckets, mops, cloths an sweepin brushes. The shelves over the sink was lined wit bars a carbolic washin soap an other stuff all fer the cleanin.

'Come on, take off that coat,' he said, makin me open it, because it was covered in wet sick.

'Jesus,' he said, takin it from me wit two fingers then holdin it, not knowin wha te do wit it.

'I can clean it, Mister Policeman,' I said, lookin up at him in case he wanted te get rid a me one an only good coat. It was the only one I had. Me Communion one Mammy bought me!

He turned on the tap an lifted me up, sayin, 'OK, blow your nose and throw water onto your face and wash it.'

'Wha, will I put me two hands together?'

'Yes of course, now hurry! They're waiting outside, we have no time!'

I put me hands together an threw water on me face an blew me nose but it was all stuck. 'Mister Policeman, me nose is blocked it won't come out,' I said, wit him hangin me over the sink danglin on me belly.

'Keep blowing and putting the water on, and will you hurry?!'

I blew and put more water on me face but nothin happened.

'Come on,' he said, turnin me around te see how I looked, then wantin te put me on me feet.

But just as we looked at each other, I gor a tickle in me nose an suddenly shot out wit a big spray a snots an a thick lump a sick.

'Oh sorry,' I said, seein him close his eyes an slowly open them, then lookin at me wit his eyelashes coverin in bits, an even more, drippin offa his face an chin. He went very still not movin fer a few minutes, then dropped me te the floor lettin me land wit a bump on me arse. Then he was all action.

I watched as he rushed te drown his face in water blubberin his mouth an shakin his head, makin all sorts a noises te give himself a good wash. I picked meself up an then the pair of us stared again.

'Wha do we dry ourselves on?' I said, lookin up at him then around wit me face wet, an now me wet snots. It was drippin down me frock makin me all dirty an wet. 'I think I'm worser now,' I muttered, lookin down at meself gettin all dirty filthy scruffy.

'I'm never havin kids,' he muttered, then whipped himself around te look an grabbed up a dust cloth. He wiped his face then grabbed at mine givin it a hard rub, before throwin it inta the trough, sayin, 'Out! Come on,' an rushin me out an inta the open air lettin me breathe again. Then we stood on the footpath wit him lookin up an down seein wha we do next.

I watched his head movin then when he turned te look down at me I said, 'Ye have a black face, but around yer eyes it's all white! Is mine black too?' I said, liftin me chin te look straight up at him.

'Ohhh fuckin Jesus!' he said, givin his big boot a stamp on the footpath. 'Did anyone ever tell you . . . Oh never mind! Where's these bloody people?' he said, cryin wit the want on him te now get rid a me. I can tell these things. But sure the cloth must a been dirty, I thought, it certainly was smelly!

Then we spotted the little black motor car drivin along slowly wit the two cruelty people lookin out at us.

'Oh here we are!' the policeman suddenly squealed, soundin like he was half cryin half laughin when the motor car pulled up. 'In you get,' he said, whippin open the door an flyin me te land on the back seat. 'Now, is that it? Are you all prepared to start off on the travel, oh and the business at hand. Do you have all the necessary court papers for the child to be taken in to the convent?'

'Oh indeed we do. Thank you so much. It all went very well according to plan. And we have you to thank for playing your part in this whole affair,' the woman smiled, lookin at him but me too I think, because she has two crossed eyes, an they can look in different directions at the same time.

The skinny man drove off slowly, starin straight ahead an liftin his neck up te make sure, he could see over the windashield.

'Goodbye now, little girl! It was nice knowing you,' said the policeman happily, givin me a little wave, then turned and moved off. I watched him comin up behind us, he was makin his way outa the castle, then we drove through the arch and the big entrance gates headin te make out inta the traffic. We had te sit waitin in the castle yard entry fer all the bicycles, horses an carts te pass, an even a big cattle lorry. It was probably comin from Smithfield, tha's where you have the market te buy an sell all the animals.

The lorry was now makin its way through the city and down te the North Wall, headin fer the cattle boat. They bring the cows an even horses te be slaughtered over in England, then they get sold fer the English people's dinner. But they don't eat the horses, Mammy said, they go te the French, because they love horse meat. But we wouldn't eat tha, because we like our horses.

We turned left then right makin our way slowly through the traffic.

'Oh dearie me! Let us hope, Miss Wallis, we are not unduly delayed,' said the skinny man starin wit one eye ahead lettin the other one fly te the gunner-eyed woman. Tha's wha we say – 'gunner-eyed' – when people's eyes are crossed.

'Oh I think we ought to offer a little prayer, Mister Willows,' she said, flyin open her handbag an whippin out her rosary beads.

I dozed off in the back seat listenin te them singin their prayers in a low keen. Then me eyes shot open when it changed.

'Oh this fifth decade of the Rosary should be for a safe journey. Oh yes! We will offer this to Saint Christopher, the patron saint of all travellers.'

'Most excellent idea,' said Skinny, givin his neck a jerk wit his agreein.

They finished tha long list a prayers an now Skinny said, wit the two a them takin it in turns te pick someone or somethin in need of a prayer, 'I think this ought to be for our wonderful patron Father Flitters, for without him we would not today be doing such a wonderful job and with such ease. His engineering of this case, right to the smallest detail has been faultless, impeccable,' he said, not able te get over Father Flitters bein so good. 'Oh, his handling was masterful,' said Skinny gettin all carried away not able te get over it.

'Oh but sure of course, the man is my hero! A saint,' she breathed.

'A holy man,' Skinny interrupted, flyin his head at her without takin his eyes off the road.

'Oh such a power of a man, they are only born once in a lifetime, they are so few and far between,' she whispered, nearly cryin then lettin it out in a sigh. Then she turned te Skinny givin I think a smile, but instead looked like she was snarlin wit her nose an mouth gone twisted.

'Well now! Was that not marvellously timed? Here we are arrived and we just finished saying ten whole decades of the Rosary,' sang Skinny, gettin all delighted wit himself an pullin up the motor car te stop.

I looked seein we were stopped right outside a hotel an a row of shops.

'Oh it is true, Mister Willows, you are a marvel indeed,' gushed the aul one restin her arms stretched on her handbag. For some reason she was gettin all excited, wit her eyes turnin starry she was tha delighted.

'I better go and check on himself,' she said, pushin out her chest and fixin her hair. 'Would you mind?' she asked, pointin te his mirror tha tells you when somethin's comin behind.

'Oh but of course, Miss Wallis. Let me help,' he said, twirlin the mirror fussin an fixin until she said, 'Lovely! I can see now what my face looks like. A bit of lipstick would not go amiss. What do you think, Mister Willows?' she said, pushin out her lips, makin a kiss te show him!

He went dead still like a statue an stared, wit his own lips makin a kiss, then he coughed, sayin, 'Ahem! I think your, em, is absolutely divine if you, Miss Wallis, don't mind me passing remarks?'

'Oh my goodness noooo! I think you are, em, a very interesting man, Mister Willows!'

'Really?' he said, soundin shocked an delighted all at the same time.

'Oh yes! For a widower you have kept yourself in fine trim. I have often said this to my sister Maud, what a fine man you are, Mister Willows!'

'And you for a spinster . . . oh my goodness! That was an unfortunate turn of phrase! I did not mean—'

'No of course you didn't, Mister Willows! Now I really must hurry, thank you indeed I am very much obliged. So! I shall be back at my post come Monday morning, wide eyed and bushy tailed!' she laughed, lettin it out in a terrible cat's scream. Then she turned on me, givin me an annoyed look like I was goin te interfere wit the idea she had painted fer herself, tha thinkin she's a picture of beauty. But she's not, wit her cross-eyed look an her fat body an hairy chin. She's as good-lookin as any gorilla tha you'd find hangin out in the zoo. No! Changed me mind, they're better-lookin!

'Come along, child, don't dawdle, we do not have time to waste,' she said, grabbin hold a me by the arm an pullin me out an tossin me on the footpath, tha made me stagger an nearly trip. Then she reached in again an pulled out a little brown suitcase left sittin on the back seat, then she slammed the door shut.

He took off wavin his arm slowly without lookin back, then he was gone an so was the aul one. Me eyes stared an I had the idea fer a split second there was somethin I should work out. It hit me just as she came flyin back out of a sweet shop givin an unmerciful screech.

'How dare you not stick close to my heels?' she roared, givin a slap te her hip makin me come te her like a dog, one tha's learnin te do wha it's told! Me idea tha came was 'RUN'. But tha went an I woke meself up an quickly moved over seein she was intendin makin fer the sweet shop again.

'Don't take one step behind or away from me, stay close to my heel! Do you understand?' she said, pointin her finger, flingin it up an down at me.

I stared fer a minute an she waited so then I nodded.

'No manners, badly brought up!' she snorted, then turned

on her black laced-up ankle boots an marched inta the dark sweet shop.

I blinked when we came down the step, then lit me eyes on the cat, it was next te the sweet jars sittin up on the big wooden counter.

'Give me a packet of sailor's chew! An erm . . .' she said, lookin around, 'give me a bar of Cadbury's chocolate! Oh, and a quarter of those nice-looking boiled sweets.'

Then she gave her snarlin smile an the shop woman said, 'Getting to be dark out there, looks like we might have rain before night falls.'

'Yes oh you could be right,' said the aul one, lookin around then back at the sweets gettin measured.

'Four ounces did you say?' said the woman, throwin on the scales two more sweets tha was left sittin on the shovel. 'Are you travelling, going across to the Kingsbridge train station?' said the shop woman.

'Yes,' the aul one said, noddin an openin her handbag takin out a big fat purse an leavin tha open waitin.

'That will be two shillings an five pence ha'penny.'

The aul one took out a silver half crown an handed it over then put the stuff in her handbag. Then she put the halfpenny change into a charity box sittin on the counter. 'For the NSPCC,' she snarled, givin one a her smiles te the shop woman.

'Very kind I must say,' said the shop woman, not lookin too impressed wit the ha'penny goin in.

We were outa the shop an crossin the road headin fer the train station, I was hungry now an wantin somethin te eat. But she didn't open or touch the sweets, they stayed fastened in the bag.

Just as we got te the entrance a the train station a big black motor car pulled to a stop an Father Flitters heaved himself out, then grabbed hold of a shiny brown-leather suitcase, roarin, 'Goodbye, Doctor O'Connor, thank you for that lunch! Excellent fare, wonderful place and the port! Did we get the year? We did! OK I'm off.' Then he slammed the door shut and turned himself around lookin te see where he was goin, then he banged his stick on the ground and took off walkin, then into a march makin himself in a hurry.

'Oh my goodness there he is,' waved the aul one gettin all excited. 'Father Flitters!' she croaked, flappin her fingers an wavin the hand lookin a bit mental.

He ignored her, marchin himself straight past.

'Reverend Father!' she screeched, losin the run a herself now, gettin worried he wouldn't stop fer her. She chased him inta the station forgettin about me trailin behind, an I suddenly decided te make me move. She wasn't goin te give me nothin te eat anyway, never even mind! The stupid idea I had, she'd give me a taste of her chocolate.

I turned meself back fer the entrance an headed straight inta the hard belly of a man in uniform, the silver buttons put a dent in me forehead.

'Easy! What's yer hurry?' he said, grabbin hold te stop me fallin. 'Come on, I see your mother's waitin,' he said, lookin up at the aul one now managin te get hold a the Father Flitters. He was lookin around, then said somethin te her. She whipped her head seein me gettin brought along held be the arm.

'Is this yours?' the uniform man said, handin me over.

The aul one shifted lettin her nose curl makin a face, then held herself away, gettin a bad smell.

'Don't let that pup escape, do not take your eyes off that brat for one second!' Father Flitters barked, lookin at me like he wanted te kill me.

'Oh yes. Oh my goodness!' she moaned, puttin her fist te her mouth wit the eyes starin gettin a fright. 'STAY!' she roared, ventin her disappointment at me wit him givin out te her. I could see tha was really her annoyance, because she said he was her hero.

'Do you have the court documents sending this child to the reformatory?' Father Flitters snapped at the aul one, wit him all red-faced an annoyed.

'I do, Reverend Father,' she whispered, bendin down an openin her suitcase takin out a big brown envelope.

He snatched if off her an whipped out the papers. Then he read them an his face shifted into a half-smile lookin satisfied. 'Good! Everything as I instructed! They have the authority to keep her in saecula saeculorum. My job now is to ensure my will survives even beyond the grave. We, I, will be travelling down there to speak to the Mother Superior in person. Yes by God! I will use all the power at my disposal. No Carney will ever set eyes on the setting sun again, or wake to a new morning, or look up at a sky, never again no, not as a free person anyway. What's more, I will ensure no Carney will follow after this one, she will be the last of her line. I tell you, Miss Wallis!' he said, hammerin his fist inta his open hand. 'This is only the beginning, the first of a long list who will live to rue the day they crossed Holy Mother Church by crossing me! Yes, I will drive them to hell! All of them, one by one they will march to their doom!'

'Amen to that! And all the devil's children,' the aul one said, givin a sniff an blessin herself like it was a prayer.

I heard it all an didn't understand a word. But somehow it didn't sound good at all. Certainly not fer me, he kept mentionin Carney, tha's me. Wha did I do wrong? Why does he hate me? An why does God hate me this much fer it all te sudden happen? I don't understand nothin, no I don't know nothin. I just wanted te sit down somewhere an be left alone. If people don't like me or don't want te know me, then the best

I can have is tha they leave me alone. I'm tired, cold an hungry, an I'm so very lonely without me fambily. So the world can just leave me alone, stop botherin me.

'Follow me!' he commanded, an the aul one took off hoppin her foot te march in line, managin te get up beside him.

I trailed behind until she remembered me an turned around lettin out a roar. 'How dare you stray behind when I deliberately made myself clear you should keep up with me!'

I stopped te listen an stared, wantin te hear wha wrong I was after doin.

'Come along, you foolish-looking creature! MOVE!' she shouted when I still stood gapin.

I then woke meself up an flew, wantin te stop an tell her she's not much better-lookin herself. Anyway, I'm tired an I'm hungry, an the hairy-chin aul cow won't feed me.

All the peoples was hurryin, but gettin weighed down carryin bags an suitcases. Yet they was killin themselves rushin te get on the train. It was standin on the station blowin an puffin screamin an moanin, wit smoke fartin out, coverin everyone an everythin.

'Tickets, please!' the man in the uniform sang, waitin at the little box te stop ye gettin on the train until you show yer ticket.

'First class. For one,' snorted Father Flitters snappin over the ticket, then handin another one showin second class fer the woman.

'Oh you are not travellin together?' said the ticket man lookin from the priest te the hairy aul one, then down at me.

'What business is it of yours with whom and how I'm travelling? Mind your own business,' Father Flitters said quickly, lettin his voice drop a little.

'Fair enough,' said the ticket man, not lettin him get the better of him. 'But what about the child? Is she travellin wit youse?'

'HOW DARE YOU QUESTION ME?!' screamed the priest, gettin himself all red in the face then turnin purple.

'OK I apologise so. The child has her own ticket then! Can I ask tha?'

'No, mister, I haven't,' I said wantin te be helpful, because I felt sorry fer the poor man gettin eatin alive be the Father Flitters.

'How dare you speak?!' snorted Father Flitters, spittin rage down at me, then he turned te the ticket man, sayin, 'Put her in the mail car, she can travel with the cargo.'

'What?! Aw here! I'm gettin the station master, this is too much fer the like a me!'

'Fine!' snapped Father Flitters. 'If you want me I will be in my first-class compartment. Now, if I was you, I would keep quiet and just make the arrangements to have that matter seen to post-haste!' Then he cocked his head listenin te wha he just said, sayin, 'Post-haste! Is that not a witty repartee, Miss Wallis?'

'Oh, Father, you are marvellous, you remind me just now of the great Noel Coward!'

Then the pair a them moved off an I followed, forgettin I wanted te make me escape, because I wanted now te travel wit the cargo an find out wha tha was.

'Hey, Dickie!' the ticket man shouted, roarin to an aul fella pullin a trolley wit wheels an stacked high wit big sacks a mail. 'Take this young one an put her in the mail carriage.'

'Wha?'

'Yes, go on go on! Ask no questions.' Then he said, lowerin his voice whisperin, 'Come here, come over te me an I'll tell you! She's wit tha priest gone ahead there, an the woman standin wit the child. Him, the priest, is headin fer first class an yer woman is stoppin in second class. But they won't buy the child a ticket! He's said I'm te stick her in cargo. So go on, do tha.'

'Follow me,' said the mail man comin up an takin me arm, then he walked me back te his trolley an pushed it off, sayin, 'Stay wit me!'

The first part a the train was wide open an they were throwin up sacks a mail from the trolleys an loadin up wooden boxes an all sorts a stuff.

'Hey! Oxo, this young one here is goin te be travellin wit youse in cargo. Tha all right?' Dickie said, makin te throw up his sacks a mail.

'Wha? Don't be stupid. Why would ye do tha? Sure why is the child not travellin in the passenger carriage?'

'I don't know, I'm under orders from Monto. He's takin his orders from a priest an a woman. He's travellin first class an the woman's travellin second class an the young one is goin no class at all!'

'Ah will ye go on outa tha! Sure it's months away yet until we get te April Fool's Day!' laughed Oxo, who started te grab up the sacks landin just inside the door from Dickie.

'Tha's the lot. See ye!' said Dickie, makin himself off in a hurry.

'Hey get back here! Wha about tha young one?'

'Wha about her? Lookit, it's nothin te do wit me, just do as ye're asked, it's simpler when you're dealin wit the clergy,' said Dickie, slappin the dirt offa his hands then grabbed up his trolley pushin it back the way it came.

'Shite! A child! That's all I need te complete the fuckin picture, now we have Noah's bloody Ark!' Oxo snorted, takin heavy breaths an lettin it down his nose.

'Come on get up!' he said, seein the hairy woman watchin makin sure I was gettin onta the train. 'Hurry, we haven't all day te babysit you!' he said, wavin me te climb up onta the wagon an get in wit all the stuff.

The noise hit me as soon as I climbed inside. The place was

chopper-blocked wit boxes an sacks an bicycles. They was all stacked high against the walls an more piled in the middle. I looked te see where the cryin was comin from. It sounded like a babby!

I looked down seein two greyhounds standin in the corner, they stood still, starin back at me. Then me head flew the other end lookin, seein a white nanny goat starin back at me, it went all quiet fer a minute wantin te take me in. Then it lowered its head scrapin its back feet an made a charge, but instead a gettin me wit the horns, it ended wit its legs in the air an the neck gettin choked. It forgot it was tied to a rope.

I watched as it ended splattered fer a minute on the floor. It stayed down thinkin about this, then got up an went really mad, roarin its lungs out wantin te get at me.

Then they all started – the greyhounds lifted their heads howlin like mad, cryin like the Banshee. Then they really let rip enjoyin themselves no end wit their heads thrown back. They were soundin like a huge pack a hounds, them's the ones ye see on the fillums, they go dashin out wit the gentry fer a hunt. Then the nanny goat joined in cryin even louder, it got terrible, wit them all wantin te best each other, see who's makin the biggest noise. It sounded like they were singin, but it was an animal choir!

'Oh fuck! Wha the Jaysus hell did I do te get this? I'm gettin outa here! Don't move, stay there. I'm goin fer a Woodbine, a smoke,' Oxo said, tearin out a little blue box tha gives you five Woodbines. I know tha because all the men smoke them so they do.

I looked around seein there was no seat fer meself te sit on, an worser! No winda fer me te look out.

'Hey, mister! Where can I sit? Do I have te stand?' I said, gettin ready te burst meself inta tears, because I'm not havin this, I'm very tired so I am an I'm goin te start doin me war dance! Yeah, tha's wha Mammy calls it when I lose the rag. An I will too if there's nowhere te sit.

He said nothin, just sucked on his Woodbine pretendin he didn't hear me.

I had enough. 'Mister! I'm goin te roar me head off an do me war dance if ye don't let me sit!'

'Here!' he said, losin the rag an makin a run back at me. 'Sit, lie, sleep – do wha ever you want!' he said, grabbin sacks wit every word an landin them in the corner, makin a nest fer me, an away from the nanny goat. 'Now! Get in there,' he said, slappin down the sacks, makin it comfy fer me.

I climbed in an collapsed on top, gettin a big smile on me face. 'Thanks, mister, tha's lovely,' I said, feelin them all soft as I wriggled around gettin the best spot.

23

'HEY, OXO!' SHOUTED Dickie appearin at the door, he was holdin out a package wrapped in greaseproof paper. 'Listen take this, it's the sandwiches me missus made. I worked me dinner hour, so I'm knockin off earlier. You're on the late shift, so get them inta ye. The bit of extra grub will do you no harm, ye look like one a them greyhounds there, only they're better-lookin!'

'Man alive!' groaned Oxo, wit the eyes standin up in his head. 'Just wha the doctor ordered! You have your missus well trained, mine has me starved on fuckin bread an drippin!'

'Ah go on outa tha! You're just a covetous aul fucker! So go on, have them while the goin is good, I'll catch up wit you again on the Friday shift.'

'Thanks fer tha, good luck now, Dickie.'

'Yeah, good luck, see ye, Oxo,' said Dickie, walkin off wit a swagger like he was the Lone Ranger.

I was standin lookin out the door wit me mouth open gapin, then I spotted Hairy Chin makin her way down te me. I leapt back fer me new nest an rolled meself up, not wantin te hear her start again.

'Porter!' she said, takin in a sharp breath gettin ready te fly another annoyance. 'Now, you are being instructed—'

'I'm not the porter,' Oxo interrupted.

'What?' she said, gettin all confused.

'I'm the mail man. I sort out the mail. I also be times look after nanny goats, dogs . . . greyhounds an—'

'I don't care what you are! Will you please listen while I give you your instructions.'

'Are they from the Railway, the station master?' he said, interruptin her again.

'REALLY! You are an obstinate, obnoxious, horrible little man—'

'Missus! Get outa me way,' he said, puttin his arms out an flappin her away.

She stood back an he grabbed the doors an rolled them together slammin them shut leavin us all starin in the dark. Then there was complete silence. Even the goat shut up!

'YOU ARE TO KEEP YOUR EYES FIRMLY LOCKED ON THAT GIRL IN THERE! SHE IS A WARD OF THE COURT!' Then she went silent waitin, but we all stayed quiet.

'SHE IS IN THE CONTROL OF THE STATE!'

We still stayed quiet. Then we heard the heave of huge breath an we all held our own breath, because I heard no one breathin.

'IF YOU LET HER LOOSE YOU WILL GO TO PRISON. THESE ARE THE ORDERS COME DIRECTLY FROM THE REVEREND FATHER THE PARISH PRIEST!'

I watched Oxo standin starin at the doors, just listenin, then he whipped them open again, sayin, 'Missus, go home! But first would ye ever listen?! When God was makin the human race, the fact tha you look like his experiment gone badly wrong is no excuse for givin me nightmares for the rest a me borned days! Now fuck off!' Then he slammed the doors shut again.

'I'm getting a policeman for you!' she croaked, because the voice was now all gone.

'Go ahead, missus! But hurry before I let the goat loose!'

Then we heard the whistle blow an screechin te 'Hold the train!', wit runnin feet.

'That's the aul biddy lunatic,' muttered Oxo, tellin us all without lookin around.

We listened as the noise went through the roof, then the train started rattlin inta life, an I looked over seein the goat was gettin the life shook outa him, along wit the rest of us.

Then Oxo whipped open the doors stickin his head out, shoutin, 'We ready for the off?' Is tha the lot?' he said lookin up an down, givin a last check.

Then the whistle blew again givin a long blast this time, an we shook an shuddered wit the goat lettin it rattle his voice enjoyin the noise it was makin. Then we heaved an took off goin completely blind when the steam blew in, wettin an warmin our faces givin us all a wash. Oxo went over an took down a storm lamp hangin up inside a closed press. Then he lit it an went over an shut the doors.

'Now, shut up the lot of youse, an no more guff outa you,' he said te the goat, givin him fresh water in his tin bowl. Then he rummaged in a sack left sittin beside the goat, an gave him a handful of vegebales an rotten fruit gone soft.

The greyhounds went mad, barkin their head, wantin their grub too.

'Yes, yes, hold ye's are patience,' he muttered, makin his way down te give them the same, wit pourin them water. Then he opened a big butcher's parcel left sittin beside them.

'Now! Any more cheek outa youse two an I'll take this home an cook it fer meself,' he said, takin out two big bones wit raw meat hangin off.

They took one look an nearly lost their mind wit the want fer it. One fella did a twirl an the other fella lifted his head an howled at the roof.

'Shake paws, give us yours,' said Oxo, puttin out his hand.

The twirlin fella gave a big slap of his arse sittin himself down heavy, then stood up givin another twirl when he didn't get the bone, then looked te see, was tha wha was wanted?

'No youse are thick eegits,' said Oxo, wavin the bone. 'OK, sit down an start millin!' he said, givin them one each in their mouth. Then he slapped his hands gettin rid a the bits an bent down wipin them on the mail sacks.

I listened te them all slurpin their drinks an lorryin inta their grub. But he wasn't comin my way!

'Eh, mister. Wha about me? Wha do I get te eat?'

'Wha? Wha do ye mean? Since when was I in the business a feedin little banditos?'

'Wha?' I said. 'Wha's bandies?'

'Oh tut tut, Jesus te night! There's no gettin away from this life! Hold on just be easy, give us a few minutes te sort meself out an I'll see wha we can come up wit,' he said, goin over te lift sacks an look at the label, then throw them in different piles.

I lay down watchin an listenin te him hummin a lovely tune, then every now an then he would sing the words. Me eyes was gettin heavy wit all the comfort, it was the heat from the lamp an its lovely soft rosy glow, an even the goat an dogs was in their comfort. They all just lay curled in a ball after savagin their grub, now they're lettin their eyes get heavy, just like me own. 'Oh this is mighty marvellous,' I heard meself moan, just as I was dozin off wit the train rockin, fallin me into a lovely sleep.

'Eh! Little one, hang on! Don't fall asleep yet, you need somethin inside you,' said Oxo, rushin over to a press an takin out a big flask wit two parcels. 'Come on sit up! Have this hot drink, it's Oxo,' he said, pourin it out into a mug wit the lovely smell goin up me nose.

I grabbed hold wit me two hands an took a mouthful. 'Oh

it's hot!' I said, wipin me burnt tongue tryin te brush away the pain.

'Drink it slowly, I can believe ye're starved, but don't go chokin yerself on tha,' he said, openin the parcel an takin out two big chunks a loaf bread. They was stuck together wit brawn meat in the middle.

'This is the stuff my missus made, but the best is yet te come, we'll surprise ourselves wit Dickie's offerin. His missus is a born cook! Jaysus tha woman can perform the miracle of the five loaves an fishes. Oh you should see wha he comes in wit! Do ye know, I'm goin to tell you this now. Him an me get the same wages, we have the same number a kids – nine! We pay the same rent fer the corporation house. Well, he pays sixpence more te the Corpo. He's got a better place, bigger! Down there along the Liffey it is.

'Anyway, my missus complains she can't feed us on wha the wages I bring home, yet his missus feeds him like a lord. An she keeps him lookin lovely, you should see the style of him when he steps out fer Mass on a Sunday! Holy Jaysus, he looks like "Gentleman Jim"! Ye see, his wife was a dressmaker,' Oxo said, lookin at his sambidge, then takin half inta his mouth still tryin te talk wit burstin his cheeks.

'Nneh nah net a gaa!' he said, shakin his head lookin te see did I agree.

I did. 'Yeah, these sambidges are lovely,' I said, lookin te see how many more was left.

I sat back wit me belly stickin out ready te burst.

'Tha was lovely, I enjoyed tha so I did,' said Oxo, foldin up his greaseproof paper an fixin his flask, puttin it away back in the press.

'See I told you his missus would feed ye fit fer a king!' he said, bowin his head lookin happy he was right, then after tha gettin somethin gorgeous te eat. 'Them tomatoes, cheese an egg sandwiches was really nice,' he said, shakin his head an feelin his belly, givin a belch.

'You better get some sleep, did you come straight from the court?'

'Yeah.'

'Wha are they sendin you away for?'

'I don't know, because I suppose I'm a baddie!'

'Don't be silly, wha did you do? Did you rob?'

'No!'

'So wha then? Why you bein sent away? Is your mother dead?'

'Yeah, I think so, they put her in a grave, so I suppose she's dead now. But she's not comin back,' I said, shakin me head feelin me heart fall, now wantin te cry.

'So where are they sendin you?' he said after we kept quiet fer a few minutes.

'I don't know.'

'How old are you?'

'Seven, I got me birthday so now I'm big. They said tha in the court. I think they said I was enough years te be brought inta the court an made a baddie. So now I'm goin te prison!'

'PRISON? Don't be silly . . .' Then he clamped his mouth shut, sayin, 'Outa the mouths a babes. You could be right, be Jesus if it's where I think you're headed. Then may God have mercy on your soul!'

I woke up hearin noise everywhere. The doors flew open an people started draggin stuff out. Then I heard a man's voice say, 'END OF THE LINE! BALLINA!'

'Come along! No time to waste,' said the hairy woman, appearin outa the dark givin me a fright.

It was very late night-time, I could see the gas lights burnin an people rushin everywhere. The freezin cold hit me as soon as I jumped meself down outa the mail box an hit the damp ground. Me eyes an head hurt an I feel sick in me stomach. I just wanted now te go back te sleep an get warm again.

'Come along, you stupid girl!' Hairy said, grabbin me by the arm an rushin me beside her.

'Me arm hurts, ye're hurtin me, missus!' I said, tryin te pull me arm free.

'The Reverend Father has gone on ahead, if we don't move quickly he will leave us, or at least me, stranded behind!' she said, after stoppin te think about tha one.

We walked through the station then got outside seein donkeys, horses an carts, all waitin te pick people up, they were all the relations I suppose, comin te take home their fambilies. I wish I had me mammy an sister back. Oh why is God so mean? I hate him I do, I wish he would strike me dead so I can go an stay wit Mammy in heaven.

Then it hit me, I won't get te heaven fer sayin bad things, an especially not now! Not after just sayin I hate God. Well he can fuck off then. Mammy won't let him stop me. Nothin gets the better a my mammy!

'WAKE UP, YOU DOZY CRETIN!'

I heard the roar, then came back te me senses when she yanked me offa me feet an dragged me over to a big black motor car.

'Is there room in the boot for this?' the priest said, pointin at me an lookin at the man wit the fair hair, he was wearin a lovely wool country jacket wit brown corduroy trousers. An his brown shoes was so shiny you could see yer face in them. He stopped te look at me wit his forehead creasin, he was tryin te work out wha the priest was talkin about. Then he rushed te open the front-seat door an whipped open the two at the back.

'Father, you may travel in the front seat if you wish, the lady and child in the back.'

'What?' said the priest, seein himself gettin helped then nudged te sit in the front.

Then the lovely man waved his hand at us, sayin, 'Sit in the back quickly and shut the doors, the night is very cold!'

Hairy threw herself in shiftin her arse fer comfort, then dragged in her legs givin the door a bang shut.

I climbed in the other door gettin plenty a room fer meself, because Hairy was restin herself well away, wit her eyes already closin. I closed me eyes hearin the lovely man an the priest talkin quietly.

'So, you are not following in your uncle's footsteps, going into medicine, you are for the law, Tom tells me.'

'Yes, how long have you known my uncle?'

'Oh! Since I arrived in Dublin over forty years ago, was it? Yes, I think it could easily be that. So let me see now, I have known him for half of that . . .'

Me mind wandered an I missed wha he was sayin because I'm tired. Then I heard his voice still talkin.

'He's been . . .'

I felt me eyes gettin very heavy an settled meself stretched out on the seat, keepin me legs under me, then gave a long sigh of lovely comfort wit the heat pourin all round me, then felt meself fallin down, goin into a deep sleep.

The motor-car wheels pounded along, rollin over hard slabs of stone wit grass growin over them, then the uneven bokety road tried te lift the motor car, rockin an threatenin te knock it over. But the motor car held, rocked back an steadied, an then just kept on goin. On an on we went, past fields wit big hills behind them an huge rocks sittin around the fields. There was few houses, because most a them was now only half standin wit the walls collapsed an the stones scattered, left lyin around where they fell.

'Lazy Beds,' said Oisin the driver, pointin up te another hill sittin behind a big field. 'Planted with potatoes before the famine by tenant farmers,' he said. 'They had the cottage which was really a mud-hut hovel and an acre of land in return for working the estate owned by the aristocracy. The absentee landlord, he lived the high life in London, while his tenants lived less well than the aristocracy dogs. The poor tenant farmer, he had to divide and subdivide up the acre of land when a son married. So the only thing that would grow in such a small area and be sufficient enough to keep body and soul together was the potato. The Irish lived on that, hence they're called the "Lazy Beds". Overplanting caused disease and the potato crop to fail, rotting while still in the ground. All hail, commence the great famine,' laughed Oisin, but then gave a snort. He wasn't really laughin at all.

We came bouncin over a hill an ended wit us all lookin at the first sign of life we seen fer hours. I suddenly blinked an lifted me head te get a look out, feelin all delighted.

'This is the last post before civilization ends for the western world!' warned Oisin.

I looked out, seein a line of about five or six houses wit a shop an pub on each side a the road. People came rushin out te get a look, an stood gapin wit their mouths open. We had te slow down because a cow came wanderin onta the road an joined a donkey tha was already sleepin there. Then chickens came flyin down from the straw roof of a house an landed on the top of the motor car.

Father Flitters opened his winda, shoutin. 'YOU PEOPLE! Get these beasts out of my path and get this bird off this motor car AT ONCE!' He roared, liftin his walkin stick up an out the winda, givin a hammerin te the roof of the motor car.

The chickens squawked an flew down, landin in front a the winda. Then they sat themself on the bonnet givin a good shit, tha came scutterin down wit the fright they got.

The people ignored him an just crowded around, wit even more flyin out fer a look. Then a very old nun came rushin through a big door wit a cross over it, an stood starin wit a feather duster in her hand. Then she gave a shiver, shakin herself inta action, an came rushin over wavin her duster, sayin, 'Bless all travelling in this motor contraption!'

Then people nodded an shook their heads, blessin themself agreein.

'Oh, indeed so, Holy Sister! Bless all dem travellers dat have put body an limb in the power a dis contraption, trustings and hopings and prayings to get dem safe in der wanderin!' an old man wit a greasy black top hat said, then gave a jerk te his trousers tied up wit a rope an looked around at everyone, waitin te see wha they thought a tha.

'Ohh, the poet Milch O Muile-lihaun has spoken,' they all muttered, lookin very satisfied they owned a marvellous poet man.

Then he pointed te his black hat, sayin, 'Dere's a lot a wisdom passed through dis hat. Me father got it from the gentry durin the famine. It blew offa the gentleman's head when he runnin to save his neck from the Fenians. An upon my soul, no word of a lie! Dat Fenian was my father!'

'No word of a lie!' they muttered again, blessin themself an bowin in a holy prayer.

'Ohh be all the saints!' moaned an old woman givin a roar, not able te take in the sight a us strangers, an we all sittin in a motor car. 'An may God's mercy be on them if they don't live to tell the tale!' she snapped, clampin her mouth an lookin around te see wha they thought a tha.

Nobody thought nothin, an all the ones in the motor car just stared ahead lookin in shock. Oisin stared at the shit bakin on the bonnet, it was comin from the heat a the engine. Hairy looked out her side a the winda squintin, then openin her eyes wide, tryin te make out was we in the middle of a fillum. Father Flitters kept breathin hard down through his nose, tryin te work out wha te say first. I just took it all in enjoyin meself, wonderin if we was goin te stop fer somethin te eat.

Then we heard a big sigh an a voice gasp. 'Oh it's a Reverend Father!' moaned the nun in a whisper, goin inta shock wit her eyes takin in the white collar an the rest a him. He was all covered from head te toe in black.

'How are you at all, at all?' she said, pointin wit the fingers spread near the priest's arm, but not darin te touch him. 'Have you come far? Where are you heading? Is it here you are stopping? Is it me you want? I'm the Reverend Mother of the local convent school. But we don't have that no more,' she complained, lookin around at the old wrinkled faces starin back at her.

'The children are long grown up,' panted the nun, bendin down an breathin in the winda. 'There's a lot of emigration – America, England, Australia! They have us taken everywhere!' she whispered, mouthin the words like everyone was committin a sin.

There was silence fer a minute after tha, while everyone waited fer somethin else te happen. Then Oisin came te his senses an woke up shoutin. 'My father's motor car! It is wrecked for God sake,' he squealed, pointin at the hardenin shit pilin on the front. There was now a gang a chickens all crowdin on the bonnet, includin a big fella wit a huge crown of feathers stickin up on his head.

'What am I going to tell him?' Then he whipped open the door an lashed out te get a look up at the roof.

'Oh my God! It's ruined, dented! He will be very angry. I will have to pay for the damage,' puffed Oisin, givin a ragin look at Father Flitters, then divin back in an slammin the door shut.

'YES INDEED YES!' screamed Father Flitters. 'These damn fools! It is all their fault! Don't worry! I will find out who the parish priest is and make them pay for this!' he snorted, bangin his stick on the lovely wood panel inside the motor car.

'Father, please stop with the stick, you are damaging the rosewood dashboard,' gasped Oisin, losin his breath now lettin it out in a squeal. He was talkin through his fingers wit his hand coverin his mouth in shock, an his head was movin up and down wit the every bang the priest was givin.

'Tut, you young men have no regard for age or status!' Father Flitters moaned, liftin the stick an throwin it behind him, landin the flyin stick a belt te Hairy.

She got it on her funny bone, because lucky the stick missed me an landed her side a the back seat. 'Owww!' she screamed, givin a piercin squeal an grabbin hold a her arm rubbin an swingin it. Then she grunted a moan, turnin te look out the winda tryin te forget the pain.

'Incorrigible,' muttered Oisin under his breath then turned on the engine an made te drive off.

People kept leanin and sittin themself on the motor car an moved wit us still restin an leanin, even wit the motor car makin te go faster. So Oisin banged his fist on the horn an roared the engine, then went faster an finally people cleared outa the way. We drove off an I looked back seein them rush onta the middle a the road te watch us goin outa sight.

'The local natives don't see much activity coming through this place,' laughed Oisin, lettin out a big sigh. 'Any visitors or business would be from the last village we passed, and that was several hours ago. So one thing is guaranteed, certainly few would have business going beyond this point. From here now on, we will traverse the wild beauty of the land. It has little or nothing but the unforgiving and ferocious Atlantic Ocean roaring in to lash and tear at the cliffs below. On a bad day, the poor unfortunate fishermen, both they and their boat can get caught in a storm while out at sea. Oh it can happen suddenly, all too quickly when the wind changes. Then oh! It can be fierce. The great Atlantic will plunge into one of its mighty rages, wreaking the hell of all terrors and damnation on all and everything in its wake. On the next tide, it will then come thundering in to spit out the drowned bodies of the local fishermen. It is their way of life, fishing would be the local means of support here,' he said, wit everyone goin quiet now, thinkin about this.

24

WE HAD BEEN drivin fer hours more when Oisin suddenly said, 'Land ahoy! Finally we are here. We have arrived after two days of travelling, well, for me! It has taken three days for your good selves and the child.'

Then he looked around at me an stared, givin his head a little nod like he was sad fer me, then turned back sayin nothin. Big gates started te appear wit high stone walls an huge stone buildins sittin right under the dark heavy sky. I looked te see where we were goin te turn in.

'I take it these are the farm entrance gates,' said Oisin, lookin up at a long dark entrance wit the road made a hard granite stone. We drove on hearin the angry roar of the ocean an lookin down at it, seein it bashin inta the rocks just below the cliffs. They were very steep, wit them hangin down on the right side of the road. Me heart was startin te fly wit the nerves, an I wanted te run an bury me head in someone's arms te protect me, but there's no one te run to. I have no Mammy no more, an I just have te pray she will look down an protect me from heaven. I just have te know tha, because I want to believe it very truly.

We came te big gates wit nothin after it but high stone walls, an the ocean wrapped itself around it, just up above, because there was no more land.

'They're locked,' said Oisin, pullin the motor car to a stop an leanin over the steerin wheel as we all stared in at the big chains, they were wrapped around the gates, lockin them. There wasn't a sound te be heard, nothin but the roarin of the ocean an the quiet over this side. It looked so still wit all the big stone buildins an dark hidden places wit not a sign of another livin body.

'There's a bell there,' said Oisin. 'See!' he said, pointin at the big bell buried in the wall, then got out, leavin the motor car door open.

I watched as he pulled the bell, makin a big bongin sound. It was comin from the little stone house just inside the gates.

Nothin happened, so he leaned forward givin it another pull, then one more, just te be sure.

We still waited an I looked, seein further back a dark-brown heavy wooden door built inta the wall, it looked like a church door wit a stone arch over it. I bet tha's fer gettin inta the house tha's just inside, close te the gates there, I thought. It would make it easier than openin them big gates. But I would bet as well tha door's locked too.

'WE ARE *NOT* SITTING OUT HERE ALL NIGHT!' Father Flitters suddenly erupted, whippin his head around te find his stick.

'Give me my stick, woman!' he ordered, roarin his rage at Hairy.

'Ohh,' she started squealin, flyin her eyes lookin around.

'Someone's comin!' I shouted, gettin all excited when I saw an aul fella makin his way out slowly, he was takin his ease wit his hand rattlin a bunch of big keys.

'State your business,' he demanded, barkin his voice at Oisin.

'Em,' said Oisin, lookin around now not knowin wha te say.

'OPEN THESE GATES, MAN! YOU STUPID IGNORAMUS!' Father Flitters screamed, wavin his arm an goin purple in the face, then whippin around te look fer the stick.

Before he could open his mouth, I had it grabbed down offa the back winda an handed it to him. But Hairy was not quick enough, an she gor another bang when he reached te snatch it, takin it from me an wavin it in the air.

'My eye, my eye!' she roared, grabbin her face an holdin her eye.

'Stupid woman!' he snorted, bouncin te get himself outa the seat an get goin te sort the aul fella.

'How dare you?! Open this gate without further question, or I will bring this stick down on your humped back, you doddering old fool!' screamed Father Flitters, wavin the stick over his head.

'Now, now! Please, let us all keep calm, Father Flitters! Don't excite yourself,' said Oisin. 'It is bad for your heart in a man of your age! Open the gates, please, we have business with the Reverend Mother,' Oisin said, talkin quietly but demandin at the same time.

The aul fella chewed like mad on his gums, rattlin them up an down not knowin wha te do. I could see his eyes flyin one minute wit rage, then the next blinkin, lookin nervous. I could tell be tha way wha he was thinkin – would it be all right fer himself te let fly? Is he entitled?

'Open the gates or I will have you flung out on the side of the road, you will lose that fine house along with your keep, you old fool!' roared Father Flitters, gettin ready fer battle number two. Because he was losin number one – the aul fella wouldn't open the gate. He walked off rattlin his keys mutterin under his breath.

'Jesus! What do we do now?' whistled Oisin, lettin it out in a

piercin sound through his teeth, then he started grinnin.
I laughed te meself too, watchin Father Flitters stare after the aul fella, he was standin wit the fist under the clamped jaw an the eyes bulged, not able te believe the aul fella was even worse than himself. Because he was now makin his way back inta the house, bangin the door shut after him.

Father Flitters couldn't get over it. He turned himself lookin around, goin all colours wit the shock! Pink, then blue, turnin purple an now gone black.

'THIS IS . . .' he roared, holdin the stick in the air wit one hand an the other held up in a fist. 'HOWWW DAAARE . . .' he tore outa himself, holdin the breath, his face now burstin. Then he bent down givin the ground an almighty bang wit the stick, then lifted himself, makin a go at hammerin the big iron gates.

Suddenly the door blew open an a huge curly-haired terrier came tearin out an leapt fer the gate, makin te take a lump outa Father Flitters.

'Ahhh! It's the beast from hell! This man has now set his dog on me! CLIMB OVER THE DAMN THING, MAN, AND DEMAND THE KEYS TO THESE GATES!' screamed Father Flitters, ragin at Oisin an really losin the mind now, lookin like a babby not gettin his way.

Oisin looked at the dog, then looked up at the gates measurin the size, then down at himself then back up again, sayin, 'Oh now, I think, Father, you should have a go yourself at climbing over, you see, if there's any trouble . . . Well, you have legitimate business being in there. Me? I have no business at all,' he said, pointin a fist at himself. Then he rushed back te sit in the motor car, sayin, 'My goodness! It's getting very chilly!'

Father Flitters stared at the spot now empty where Oisin had just stood, then turned around lookin very confused, not knowin wha was happenin or where he was now. Then we heard a voice an looked up seein an old woman come out through the door of the house.

'Cuchullan!' she shouted, callin the dog away.

He looked back starin fer a minute, then gave one last bark an flew the tail waggin, slinkin over te crash his arse on the ground, sittin wit the paws on the woman's foot.

'Get up get in!' she shouted, wavin her hand ready te clout the dog if it didn't get goin pronto. 'Arrr bad cess to dem dat makes the trouble! Him an dat dog was sent to try me! A scourge dey is if ever one was born! Reverend Holy Father, gentleman an lady! A thousand welcomes! May the wind always be at your back an the sun in front to warm your face! Come in, come in!' she sang, bowin te everyone in turn, while all the time wrappin a red shawl around her head, coverin the snow-white hair, leavin only a bit of the face te be seen.

Father Flitters looked, turned te her then us, not knowin wha te be doin first, then rushed wit the stick in the air tryin te keep his balance an heaved himself back inta the seat.

'It is a miracle, God found someone with sense to open the gate and let us in,' he said, givin Oisin a dirty look, then one at the gate, snortin out his disgust at the whole wide world. It was as if him, next te God, were the only ones wit sense.

We turned in the gates then stopped when the woman said, 'You will need direction. I take it your business here is the delivery of an inmate? The child,' she said, throwin her head at me. 'Would dat be so?'

'Yes,' Oisin nodded an Father Flitters barked, gettin impatient givin his stick a slap.

'Tis the Cloister you will be wantin so! Ignore all the buildins come in sight on your path. Keep go firin ahead until you arrive at the biggest buildin, you won't mistake it yonder in the distance. God speed an bless all who travel these holy grounds,' she said, bowin an givin us a blessin.

'A thousand thanks for your courtesy and kind will, good woman. May you never be in want,' said Oisin, then we drove off headin inta the dark windin road.

Me nerves started te get bad again, worryin me heart inta painin me. For a short while back there, somehow I thought we were not goin te be able te get in. Then they would have te take me back te Dublin wit them, an maybe I could go home. I still can't stop believin somehow, somewhere, some way, everythin will turn right again. Then a miracle will happen, an I will be able te get me mammy an sister back. Yeah, I just can't help it, because me world is too dark without Mammy an me sister in it. If I had te stay in tha dark world fer long, then I would have te think of a way te get to heaven. Because the matter of the trouble is, I want te get te heaven but I don't want te die!

'Ah here we are. This looks like it,' Oisin said, finally turnin in off a long dark road wit nothin but high stone walls an buildins behind big yards wit gates in front a them. 'We reach the end of the road,' he said, comin to a stop in the middle of a big yard wit the ground all covered in slabs a grey stones.

'What a handsome courtyard, an enclosed cloistered walk built by the ancient monks,' he said. 'This place certainly has history, must be at least seven or eight hundred years old,' said Oisin, leanin down te look up at another arch just in front goin deeper inta the buildins.

'We'll park here and get out and stretch our legs. This looks as good as any a place to stop,' he said, lookin around again at the passages wit the stone carved pillars.

'It is the place!' commanded Father Flitters, talkin like there was no contradictin. 'I have been twice before in my priestly lifetime, come with business to these nuns. In this place is to be found the finest monastic way of life that has survived here for centuries. Miss Wallis, take yourself abroad out of that motor car and bring the creature Carney! I'm anxious now after a long journey to get this settled. Come, woman!' he said, hobblin off makin straight fer the arch tryin te hurry.

I sat lookin after him feelin me chest tighten an my stomach turn, wantin te get sick.

'Come along, wake up, you cretin!' shouted Hairy, grabbin me by the arm an yankin me outa the motor car after her.

Oisin took in a big breath then gave a huge sigh not likin wha she was doin, but he just shook his head in disgust an wandered over te get a look along the passages.

We followed Father Flitters under the arch, an came into another yard, wit a huge grey-stone buildin built all the way around. I looked up seein long narrow windas an carved stone over the tops. It looked like a castle or somethin, but I don't know, I never sawed a real castle before.

Father Flitters made his way up grey steps an stood under a stone arch wit a heavy black door an a big iron knocker. Me head flew an me eyes took everythin in around me. It felt like I would never see the world just like this again. Everythin was so quiet I could hear Father Flitters breathin, givin little pants as his eyes shifted an his hands lifted, gettin ready te bang the huge black iron knocker. Hairy stood at the end a the steps lookin nervous, she stared up, afraid te go there, because it would take her standin too close te the priest an she would get the head eaten.

I stood dead still, me eyes lookin up at the dark sky watchin the black heavy clouds chasin across the heavens. I could smell the salt air blowin in on the wind comin from the sea just behind an around us. I could see and hear an feel it all. If I stayed quiet like this I could hear the clockin of time tickin away my life. Somehow, some way, I have a sense again of bein very old, as if I have done this all before, a very long time ago.

I know things, I sense them now. This is a bad place, bad things happen here.

A sudden cry broke the silence soundin very lonely in the terrible dead quiet wit all the stillness. I cocked me head te listen, then I saw it pass over.

A big bird suddenly appeared flappin its wings an slowly makin its way across the sky. I watched it go, lookin like it was searchin, then it gave another cry like its heart was breakin, an looked around.

It must be lost, I thought, got separated from its fambily. It sounded lost an so lonely, him an me is the same. I wanted it te come down an we could be together. I felt meself reachin up te him. *Come down,* I said. *You can take me on your back, let me fly away on your wings an I'll be yer friend, because we two is lost now an left on our own. But this way we can be fambily an take care of each other.*

Then I shook wit the fright, as the big iron knocker boomed around the courtyard makin me think the hangman is comin te get me.

The door opened slowly givin a creak an a black figure suddenly appeared standin behind it.

'Mother Mary Augustus Martyr, I take it?' Father Flitters said, lettin his loud voice roar around the courtyard.

'Yes,' a voice whispered, because I couldn't see any part of her. Not even the hands, they were lost inside a big wide-sleeved black habit tha covered her feet. Her head was hidden under a black veil tha came down over her eyes, an the face was buried inside a white cap tha came over her eyebrows and covered the face leavin only the nose, mouth an a bit of face around it.

Me nerves went at the sight, an I wanted te turn an run fer me life screamin for help. But I knew I wouldn't get far, they would catch me, an it would only get me kilt wit more trouble.

She stood back an said quietly, 'Enter.'

Then Father Flitters looked te Hairy, sayin, 'Bring the creature, Miss Wallis,' an she grabbed hold a me shoulders an pushed me up the steps nearly smackin inta Father Flitters wit the hurry on her.

He was tryin te make his way inta the hall an bangin his stick on the shiny black wooden floorboards. I saw the nun's head drop followin the stick then she pointed her finger, sayin, 'Father! The stick, please, there is no need for it here, you may take your time to our parlour.'

'What?' he barked, lookin down at his stick then sayin, 'Oh yes, fair enough,' then staggered to a big dark door wit a shiny brass handle an put out his hand wantin te get in but then hesitated.

The nun's head nodded, then she moved te open the door an let everyone in. 'Please be seated, I won't take long.'

I was about te follow the priest when she grabbed hold a me, sayin in a whisper, 'Not you! Come with me!'

I was brought down grey stone steps an along a stone passage wit thick heavy whitewashed walls, then she took out a huge bunch a keys an opened a heavy door.

'Wait here,' she said, takin a candle left on a table in the passage an lightin it wit a box of matches left sittin beside, then led me over to a stone ledge hangin on the wall an put the candle restin on it, then said, 'Wait here, someone will come to you in due course.' Then she went out an locked the very heavy door wit no handle. There was nothin but a keyhole that you couldn't even see through. Except fer the top part, tha had an iron little winda te look in from the outside.

I looked around seein the thick whitewashed walls an the worn-away heavy stones on the ground, lookin like they were put there hundreds a years ago. A little voice was sayin, *Ye're locked up an you can't get no air.* I could smell the wax from the candle an see an get the smell of the smoke curlin inta the air. Only the one corner of the room had the light, the rest was completely pitch black.

Mammy, are you here? Where are ye, Mammy? Come an mind me! I don't feel good. I'm very afraid! I stared at the candle throwin out the only bit of light tha would stop the monsters comin this end te get me.

'They won't get me, I have the light,' I whispered, twistin me hands like I was washin them, then strokin me arms holdin meself an rockin. I don't want te be alone! I don't want te be wit these nuns! I don't want te be in this place. Then I started te hum it. The hummin was stoppin me from screamin.

The hours passed an no one came. 'They buried me here, no one's comin te get me,' I muttered, sayin it over an over again, walkin up an creepin back, leanin down, rockin meself te the ground.

The time is movin on, makin more hours takin away the minutes. I must a got seven hours stayed here all on me own, then it was minutes got turned to another hour an it got te be eight hours. Or nine hours or a hundred! I don't know, I only know I have te keep walkin an creepin an rubbin me skin an talkin te meself or . . . 'I don't know wha else te do. Mammy, I'm hoarse callin te you! Will you not answer me? Wha about you, God? Do you not hear me callin ye? Because I called you too I did, yes I did! But I only hear me own footsteps an me own voice cryin out me pain, then I only go quiet an listen te me own breathin, because then I know, no one is listenin. No one is goin te come.'

Ceily was right, an so was I. They sent me te prison, only there's nobody else here in the prison but me! I must be a special case, tha I need a special prison all fer meself. Wha did I do bad? Maybe I could think about tha, an it would take me mind offa all this, wha's happenin te me now. 'OK, wha's the first thing?'

But nothin came te me. *Come on, Lily! You have te work it out fer yerself!* I heard Ceily say, but it was only in me mind, not her voice in me head. But it made me ease.

'Oh yeah I remembers it now. I cursed God!'

I took in a sharp breath hearin meself say tha. Then I nodded me head up an down givin a sorta smile like Mammy does when she knows she got it wrong, an things went bad. Tha's why I'm here! Tha's why I'm gone te hell! But I thought you had te be dead first? No! You get there anyway without ye knowin ye're gone dead. I must be dead so, an I didn't even know it! Right! So then why do I want te do me piss?

I wrapped me legs around each other, holdin on like mad. *Oh Mammy, I'm dyin te do me piss! Wha'll I do?*

I swung me way over te the door an started bashin wit me fists. 'Open the door! Will youse let me out? I need te go te the tilet!'

I listened wit me ear leaned in but nothin happened. No rushin feet, no nothin! Then suddenly the light flickered an blazed up, then went out, leavin me standin in pitch-black dark. Me heart bounced then kicked against me chest, an me eyes stared through the black, hopin light would come. Then me mind went mad an I screamed wit every bone an muscle inside me, shakin me body like a lump a jelly. They must a put the lid on me coffin because I can hardly breathe an I can't see nothin no more! I want te tell them I'm not dead, because I want te do me piss! Or do ye piss when ye're dead? Why am I able to . . . To wha? Eh! Oh yeah, te think if I'm gone all dead, stone dead like a corpse! Shurrup, shurrup, I'm not dead!

I rushed te the door bangin an hammerin, shoutin, 'I'm alive! I'm alive! I'm not fuckin dead! Open the fuckin door an let me out, youse fuckers!' I screamed, ragin in me heart wit the ones who did this te me.

Nothin! No sound, no nothin. The rage eased away into a

pain burnin me chest, an I slid down the door lettin me nails scratch an scrape then sat where I fell. The touch of the wood against my face made me feel I have somethin te hang on to! I have the wood, the door is here wit me! Tha was put there te keep you in an keep ye out! But it's here now keepin me locked in an . . . An it don't matter, it's still somethin te hang on to! So I stayed next to it wit me face buried an me body restin against it, then fell asleep.

25

I OPENED ME EYES feelin the pain, I was knocked te the floor an me head hurt now I was gettin torn along the ground.

'Wake!' a voice said, comin out of the dark.

I was heaved all along the ground more, not knowin where I was or wha's happenin. The dark an the sudden gettin dragged, drove me te terrible fright!

'MAMMY!' I screamed, crawlin fast on me hands an knees, wantin te get away from whatever monster was tryin te take me.

I made it to a corner an squeezed meself in, pullin meself tight like a ball, so it couldn't grab a hold a me. Then a light slowly came in an around the door. One after another people came in, an I watched a black figure of a nun carryin a candle makin over fer the stone shelf. She left it down, then turned an nodded at two big young ones comin in wit buckets a water, it was steamin wit the hot. They carried scrubbin brushes an washcloths wit big bars a red scrubbin soap. She nodded at them te start cleanin. Then another two appeared in behind, an she lowered her head at them, te come te me. They bent down together an lifted me inta the air, then carried me off between them, danglin me feet an holdin me under me arms. It hurt, an I couldn't stretch me legs or straighten me back or hold me head up, I hurt everywhere. Me whole body pained me, an me head was hot an I was gone dry as a bone. Tha's wha me mammy would say when I was hot an sick, especially after I would vomit an get me guts thrun up.

They carried me down a long passage tha looked like a tunnel, it had whitewashed walls an a heavy stone ceilin tha came down low. All along the passage was lighted candles, they were sittin up on iron holders tha got pushed down through an inta the spikes stickin up. Then we turned, an I was carried into a bath house wit stone wash troughs along one wall, an three iron baths along the other wall. It had light comin in through a small winda high up in the wall, under the low ceilin.

They let me down te stand on me feet an me knees buckled, lettin me fall te the floor. I was stiff like a board an all in painin – it was from the top of me head down te me toes. Then they bent down without a word an started te peel the clothes offa me.

'Am I gettin a bath?' I said, sittin on the hard stone ground lookin up at the size a the bath. I never did see nothin like tha in me whole life! It looks like a ship tha comes bringin in the bananas.

Mammy took me when I was little, me an Ceily, down te the quays te see the big ship bringin in the bananas after the war. It was because we had nothin, no fruit nor nothin else up te then, she said. She managed te get the sailors te throw us down loads a bunches. We went te grab them, but a load a scruffy childre beat us to it!

'Ger a fuckin away from them bananas!' my mammy screamed, rushin te grab them back an clout one young fella runnin wit black bare feet an the rags hangin offa his back. 'You little bastards,' she shouted. 'I'll blind youse fuckin all if you don't hand them back!' she roared, givin terrible warnins then rushin an grabbin, slappin an wallopin.

Me an Ceily was shocked listenin te all her cursin! Because she would kill us if she heard us sayin anythin like tha! But we gor our bananas an she gave the scruffy kids one each, then told them te now fuck off! She was ragin she was! Yeah! An the ship was tha big, this iron wash thing looks nearly the same size so it does!

'Here! Young ones! I'm not gettin in tha te get meself drownded, so I'm not!' I suddenly shouted whippin meself inta action just like me mammy an Ceily does, when they do get ragin wit ye.

They just ignored me an whipped the last a the clothes over me head, leavin me sittin in me skin. Then, before I next had a chance te complain, I was carted inta the air an plunged into a bath a stone-cold icy water.

'Ahhhupo!' I screamed, before losin me breath an the water got inta me mouth nostrils an ears, then stopped me heart as I went under, wit me head held down. I opened me eyes fer a second seein the bubbles from me nose an mouth, then shut them tight again, feelin me heart about te burst from the pressure an the pain. Then my head was lifted wit water tumblin down an me mouth wide open, I gasped but no air came, then I gasped again an got a mouthful te open me lungs an scream, 'No, no don't do this no more! I'll be . . . glug . . . glug!'

They was plasterin me wit a soppin washcloth caked in Sunlight soap, smotherin me te death!

I tried te shake me head, but one held me wit me head lyin back, while the other smothered an scrubbed the skin offa me. Me last hour had now come an I don't want te die! *Oh God, please don't let me be kilt! I promise, I really promise I will never curse ye again!*

No never! I'm a woman of me word, I heard a voice say. It was Mammy! She's tellin me wha te say!

I'm a child a me word, God! I promise you, make them stop an I'll be good fer the rest a me life!

Suddenly I was let dropped an ended under the water again. Then I was grabbed an lifted wit me breath gone, an the water pourin outa me! Then I was lifted an stood down standin on me clothes makin them all wet.

'Is it over? Am I finished?' I squealed, lettin it out as a half-laugh wit me voice shakin an me body rattlin. Then a towel feelin like sandpaper was wrapped over me face and head, an I was rubbed an shook like mad, wit them goin at me, rubbin without mercy! Then me skin was red-raw an sore but I was now bone dry, an not even thirsty no more. Because I never want te see the sight a water again! When I get te be big I will never have te wash meself an I won't. Because I now hate water an it should never have been invented.

Then a big pair a grey knickers was put on me, they was made from flour bags! Then a long brown frock lookin like it was made outa sacks, ones tha get thrun over the horse's back when they is out workin, wit cartin around the coal. It's te keep the rain off an help keep the horse warm. Now they put me in one, it's got a hole fer me head te get through an two more fer me arms. Then a grey-wool jumper wit loads a patches from all the holes it got, tha was put over me head an was miles too big fer me, I was lookin fer me hands! Then next after tha they stood me still again an shoved another frock on me, this time it was a flour bag, like the knickers, an tha too had a hole fer me head an two more fer me arms. Then I was turned around an marched out, back down the tunnel passage again, walkin in me bare feet on the freezin-cold stone passage.

'Wha about me own clothes? Me good Communion coat an me frock?' I said, tryin te get them te look at me marchin one each side a me. But they didn't even look at me, they just kept their eyes lookin somewhere ahead, like they didn't even hear me.

Then I was taken into another room just like the first one,

but this had a bag on the ground, an I could see it was stuffed wit straw. Beside it sittin on the ground was a jug made of tin, filled wit water, an a tin plate wit a chunk a white bread. Then me eye got caught be somethin sittin in the corner covered wit a lid. It was a small fat piss pot made of tin an it had a cover an a handle. It was right in the corner down be the door. Oh tha's marvellous as Mammy would say when she got somethin handy, now I won't have te wet me knickers an destroy me clothes.

As soon as I made fer the straw bed an the grub, the big heavy door was slammed shut behind me an I was left on me own again. I listened an waited, hopin they would change their mind an let me out. But no, I heard a bunch a keys rattlin an the door gettin locked, then I knew they was goin te leave me left here by meself.

I looked over at the candle burnin on the stone shelf an felt glad I had the light again, but it won't last! I have te think wha I can do. Blow it out? I can't get up there, anyway, I don't have no matches te light it again. Pity! Then I lowered me head an looked down at me water an me chunk a bread. Tha's good! They gave me somethin te eat an a jug a water. Well, it's better than a kick up the arse me mammy always says. 'Don't ye, Mammy?' I said, hopin she was near an would talk te me.

I sat down on me new bed feelin the heat from the straw, it was snugglin around me when I sunk down into it. 'Oh nice,' I muttered, wrigglin te get the best spot an laughin te meself. The cold wash was enough te stop the livin an bring the dead back te life me mammy would say, but still an all, I feel lovely an warm again, because I was soppin after pissin meself an now this jumper an frock has me clean again.

I shivered wit me bit a comfort an picked up the jug an poured out some of the water, not too much! Because I got te spare it, I don't intend meself havin te go dyin fer the want of a drink again. Then I picked up me chunk a thick bread an examined it. Me face dropped when I saw some of it had turned blue. Ah fuck, they gave me mouldy bread! An it was hard! It was like a brick, I could use this te make me escape, hit them over the head wit it when they open the door, then run fer me life. Oh! An ye have te not forget to stop an grab the keys! Yeah, just like the baddies do in the fillums. Fuck! I forgot I wasn't supposed te say tha! I promised God I would curse no more. Still, he didn't do nothin fer me neither, he didn't make them let me out. So, no exchange is no robbery! Tha's wha Mammy says.

I picked at the bits a blue throwin them away, then took a little mouthful so as not te ate it all at the same time, I need te spare tha too! Because the hunger drives ye mad, an it will give me somethin te be contented about when I start te lose me mind again.

I chewed an chewed makin it last, rememberin how me an Ceily used te do tha. We would have a competition te see who could make their sweets last the longest, so we would sit an suck watchin each other's mouths makin sure not te be the first te swallow. She always won! Because she said I was too greedy! Well I'm not now!

I put the rest a the bread, it was still half left, lyin on the plate then had a look at me bed. It was lovely an soft, but then it hit me somethin was missin. I got no pilla an no blankets! I leapt up an lifted the bag, no, nothin under there. Then lifted the flaps of the bag an wriggled meself inside wit the bag over me, an then the straw wrapped around an under me. Lovely! Then me eyes closed an I was sinkin down inta lovely sleep.

26

I OPENED ME EYES seein it was pitch black an I wondered where I was. Then me heart started te make its way down te sit in me belly. No! Fer a minute I thought everythin tha happened was a terrible bad nightmare, but no! It's all here still happenin, the bad dream won't stop.

I know where I am, I can smell it! It comes from the musty smell a the room wit no air an the heavy thick walls wit the stone-cold ground. I can smell it from the soap tha washed me an the scratchy knickers an the sack frock tha rubs me skin an makes me all red an sore. I can even smell it from the straw, it's plastered to me, an the fuckin stuff keeps goin up me nose makin me sneeze, then wakin me up out of a lovely sleep.

I stared inta the dark seein it was different shades a the colour black. Me eyes is gettin used to it now, I can see through a nearly grey an pick up shapes tha look like the door. I can even walk now an nearly not bump into a wall, because I can feel it in me senses. Anyway! I put out me hand like a blind man an feel me way around the room. Now, I'm started te practise to run. Well, I discovered tha when I didn't want te get up an stagger about in me bare cold feet! Not on yer Nelly!

So now I have a new game, I see how many steps I can run goin from wall te wall without gettin smacked inta one! I have te be able te stop an reach wit me hand, keepin it near me belly, fer me te win. If I hit meself then I get hurt an I lose as well! So, I'm goin te get good at this, an then I won't need eyes any more. I'll be able te see in the dark! Maybe tha might come in handy! I could rob the nun an take her keys, because she won't be able te see in the dark!

Oh God, Lily Carney, you're a fuckin marvel! I heard me mammy say. But she wouldn't curse! Yeah she would an now she just did! Because I know she talks te me! Of course she does! I heard her voice fer long enough – seven years! Tha's me whole lifetime.

I let me eyes wander around lookin through the different shades an pickin out the different shapes. Me head moved an my eyes landed where I knew the piss pot should be. I stared until the shape came through, showin up in the dark, dark grey. Then me belly moved givin a nudge. I want te do me piss, but I'm not wantin te get up yet, it's too bleedin cold! I wonder how many days or weeks I'm here. You can't even tell if it's day or night, because there's just no way fer the light te get in. Except once I did see a light! It was comin in under the door an restin just inside on the ground, then it went so fast I thought I was dreamin it. But it must a been the nun floatin past, because they do tha – float! Ye can't hear them comin, you can't hear them at all! You don't hear nobody down here, because nobody but me an the spiders live here. I only see them rarely, an tha's after an awful long time!

Now I know how te spare me bread, I only take two tiny bites an make it last fer as long as I can. I have a new game now! It's te see how long I last wit me bread an water, before the nun comes, bringin the young ones wit me bread an drink. Or first, take me fer one a them killer fuckin washes!

I'm gettin very tired now, I feel a bit like an old woman, it must be because I don't get enough bread an food te keep me goin. The bread didn't last this time, it was gone for an awful long while before they brought me in me next entitlement. They must be makin the time stretch more, because I know I'm not mistaken in the longer length they took, fer this time round. I had nothin fer ever an ever, an I even stopped bein hungry. All I wanted was me drink a water, but there was nothin te drink, not even the wet left in the mug or jug. I know, because I stuck me tongue in an licked an even tried wit me finger an me hand – nothin! Dry as a bone like meself, as Mammy would say.

I haven't heard from her in an awful long time, she doesn't speak te me no more. So I try te sleep an not move too much, because movin makes me crawl back te me straw bag feelin terrible dizzy an tired, an tha's after only a few steps. I think now I know how I am goin te get along when I am seventy. It will be just like this, slow, bent an crawlin along. God help all the old people, now I know wha it's like te be them.

'God! Are you up there? Well if ye are . . . oh by the way! You know now I'm not afraid a you! I called ye names. I cursed you! An so you did this te me! You did all them terrible things, like even takin away me fambily an leavin me te end like this! So I'm givin meself the luxury a sayin wha I think te you! I'm entitled to tell you te fuck off! Yes, oh I very am! Because you get yer own back,' I snorted, gettin ragin wit his cheek. 'But look at me! I'm still alive an kickin an ye haven't managed te kill me yet! So you can . . . No! I'm not goin to tell you te fuck off! Wha I want us te do is, let's you an me do a deal! Tha OK, God? Are you listenin? OK, how about this. If I become a nurse an look after all the old people tha's sufferin somethin terrible. Because I knows now wha it's like! Or no, wait! Wha if I become a nun an teach all the little childre? I could teach them not te be cursin an makin you get ragin! So will you let me outa here, an I can go home an go back te school? I promise I'll be very good even fer tha school nun, an I won't scourge her no more, like she says I do! So! Ah go on, ah do, God! Let me go home. An I'll be so good you won't recognize me! Is tha a deal? Yeah!

I shook me head satisfied wit tha idea, an pulled the bag over me wantin me ease, wrigglin down inta the straw fer more comfort. Right! I'll wait now te see wha happens, let's hope me an God has a deal.

I gave a big sigh lettin out me breath, then eased meself off, fallin down inta sleep.

I woke up hearin somethin, me eyes shot open wit the shock. I haven't seen anyone for a very long time, so I got no bread an no water, an I'm hardly able te move.

Someone's comin in!

I followed the light from the candle showin them the way in. I watched as a nun appeared an walked over, puttin the lighted candle up on the stone shelf, then she came an stood in the middle a the room, watchin the two girls. One carried a tray an the other one carried a blanket all folded up. Me eyes lit up, followin it, then watched as she gently laid it on the bed, bendin down, then thrun it up in the air, givin it a shake te spread over me.

I didn't know wha te look at first! Me eyes flew offa her an up te the nun, she was standin watchin wit her face hidden under the veil an her hands lost, wrapped up inside the front a her habit. Then me head shot down takin in the stuff comin off the tray. Me jug a water wit two lumps a bread now, fer the very first time, an not just tha but a bowl a somethin hot tha smells like . . . I don't know. It's very watery-lookin an brown! But I can't wait te get goin on it.

Then the girls moved off together without even lookin at me, never mind talkin te me, an the nun did the same. I watched her go, turnin herself away an floatin out the door without makin a sound. All you could hear was the rustle of her habit an the huge brown rosary beads, they was belted around her waist wit a big brass cross left dropped hangin down. You could hear them, they were makin a clickin sound, knockin off her bunch a keys. She had them latched on to a white thick rope tied around her waist.

Then the room was empty again, but it didn't feel empty! I had the light an the lovely grub, now I have somethin te get happy about, an wha's more! Even somethin te look forward to.

They're not forgettin te feed me no more, an now I think all the time about wha I might get te eat. The last stuff I got was a bowl a soup wit somethin floatin in it. It looked like a bit of fat, an the coloured water was greasy, but it was lovely an hot an it tasted grand. But I still don't know wha it was.

I'm back te me runnin up an down in the pitch-black dark. It doesn't even feel dark any more, because I can see me way easy. Well, it's like I'm seein wit me senses, not me eyes! Anyway, me latest idea is te see how many times I can run without stoppin. I'm up te ten, because tha's all I can count to! So wha I do is count how many tens I run, an I get the answer! Two tens an a four!

I heard somethin an stopped dead te listen. It's keys rattlin an they're in the keyhole! Someone's on the move, comin in!

I dived over te me bed an made meself look like I was sleepin. Because them nuns are very threatenin-lookin! They don't say nothin, but I don't want te find out by gettin meself caught doin somethin bad!

The candle came in bringin the light, an the nun paid her usual visit over te the stone shelf an left it there. It reminded me of an offerin. People do tha wit petitions in the church. They pay a visit te God's house to put a penny in the shiny brass money box, then lift out a little candle an light it. Then they go off te their favourite saint, or maybe our Blessed Lord, or just go straight te his mammy, the Blessed Virgin Mary. Then they kneel down in front a the saint's statue an pray like mad, pleadin tha their petition may be answered. Mammy always does tha – light a penny candle an storm heaven te answer her prayers. Tha's wha she calls it. She does say, 'Come on, childre, let's go an storm heaven. I want te light a penny candle an say a few prayers fer me special intention. You two can do the same, our Blessed Holy Lady loves te see childre gettin their prayers.'

I hid meself under the flour bag wrapped inside the hay, then leavin only me eyes an a bit a me face te be seen. Somehow I know now it's best not te look at the nun. They don't talk an tha frightens the life outa me! It feels somehow like a monster tha doesn't make a noise because it just wants te watch you, then get you, spring on ye an eat you before you even knew it was there.

I watched as the nun stood in the middle of the room an stared over at me. She never does tha, just gives me a look then goes on about her business. She pointed her finger at the two girls waitin inside the door for her wants, then whipped the finger at me, an the pair flew over.

They grabbed me by the two arms an slid me out an up, tearin me straight from the bed. Then they dropped me standin, leavin me on me feet facin her.

'Has the Divine Lord spoken to you?' she whispered down at me, wit her arms folded inside the top part a the habit, restin them against her chest.

'Wha?' I whispered back, not makin out wha she was sayin.

'You came to us reeking, filled with the putrid pus of evil leaking out of your every pore, as it rushed, pumping through your every vein. You are the spawn of the devil, you are his instrument intended to carry his work into these hallowed grounds and corrupt those within these walls with his evil. But this you have been prevented from doing.

'We are under the protection of the most high! Our Lord Jesus Christ himself, Saviour of the world, it is our good and mighty Lord who has won this battle. It was very fortunate you lost your mother, this enabled you to come here and be rescued. You are now in a refuge for sinners, safe from the world and all its evil ways. Now you will live a life of simplicity and goodness. Your life will be one of penance and daily obedience to the will of God, through his servant on earth, our mother superior, Mother Mary Augustus Martyr. It is she who lays down her life daily to lead us. She does this in order that we may follow Christ's journey carrying his heavy cross on the road to Calvary. We will do the same, it is penance for our sins and the sins of the whole world. Here, the objective aim of our order is to raise saints for our Holy Mother Church! To this end we strive hard daily, very hard! No precious moment must be lost in order to make sacrifice and give glory to our Divine Lord.

'You have spent forty days down here in Penance Hall, now you will pray and hail the rising sun and with the lowering of your head, you will salute the closing of God's holy day. You are now ready to come into our sanctum and move among us. Now you must prepare for this, you will learn the rules.'

I stood gapin wit me mouth open wonderin wha, she was talkin about. Then I heard a word I know. Rules! Oh I don't like them, I thought, lookin at her. I always get inta trouble over them! It's things ye're not supposed te do. But then, ye see, when someone says tha te me – don't do tha because tha's a rule an you can't break it – then I do break it just te see wha happens! I knows I'm goin te get meself inta terrible trouble, but I can't help meself. I just have te do it. So tha's how I get inta shockin terrible troubles wit the nun an everyone else at school.

I listened tryin te take in wha she was tellin me about them, an wha not te do.

'The first rule,' she said, takin out her hand and liftin her finger. 'One! You must never speak. It is waste, you have nothing to say unless it is to inspire others to the further glory of God. This is impossible for someone like you,' she said, pointin her finger at me. 'You are nothing. All your thoughts, your actions, your whole being must be lived through our Divine Lord. Therefore there must be no distractions, you will keep your eyes to the ground at all times. We of the order call this keeping custody of the eyes. You must never raise your eyes to look another in the face. You must not be aware of your surroundings. You will work from dawn of first light to the closing of day with the setting of the sun. To disobey these rules is sinful behaviour, retribution will be swift and severe. The punishment is fitted according to the venal or cardinal sin committed. That will be all,' she said, then dropped her head and floated off.

I watched her go, wonderin wha was after happenin. I didn't understand nothin a wha she said. Nothin at all except the bit about not talkin. Sure! You have te talk! Wha about when you want te say, 'Sister, I want te go te the tilet! Can I go an do me piss?' An wha about me movin? Am I goin somewhere else, gettin te leave here?

Me teeth were knockin an I was standin shiverin in me bare feet wit the thin sack on me tha gave no heat at all. I'm always dyin wit the cold an I just want te get back inta me bed. This was all a waste a time. She was right about tha bit! I think she just wanted te hear herself talk because she hadn't talked fer probably ages! I wonder was she in the mad house where me mammy works. Because wha she said doesn't sound right te me.

Not te talk nor look at anybody! Sure tha's mental, I heard

Mammy's voice just say, whisperin it in me ear. Me head spun lookin around the room, she must be here!

I looked around wantin te know if I could maybe get te talk to her now. I miss her, she's been gone fer an awful long time an she never comes te talk te me no more. I looked back, seein the nun disappear out the door, an I thought, right! I'm gettin back inta me bed an I'll keep meself warm an eat me entitlement a grub I'm due. But then it dawned when I realized somethin had been missin! They was not holdin a tray bringin me grub. Their hands was all empty this time!

Oh no! Does tha mean I'm back te stayin in the dark again, goin wit no food or drink fer an awful long time?

Me heart was just about te start droppin when the door stayed open as the nun vanished, I watched as in rushed two more girls bangin buckets a soapy water an wash clothes. Then I was grabbed by the first two an pushed out the door an up the passage. They must be goin te start scrubbin an wallopin out any dirt caught in the place. Ah! They're goin te get Henry me pal, he's the little spider tha spends all his time spittin an weavin. Yeah, day after day he does be doin it, makin himself a long web tryin te stretch it from one corner a the room te the other, then all around the ceilin. I do watch him, an even talk te him, it's great havin him there because he keeps me company. I don't like bein all on me own! I think I would go mental just havin meself te talk to! No, definitely it's not very nice bein all on yer own!

Ah no he'll be grand, I'm not goin te worry meself, Henry is too cute fer them. He'll hide himself in a little hole somewhere. Wish I could do tha too, I thought, feelin me heart start te hammer in me chest wit fright, because I knew wha was comin as they walked me along the stone-cold passage in me bare feet. Yeah, I know now where we're headin – straight fer the bleedin icy bath house!

The roars hit me as we opened the door an walked into an almighty killins! Kids were flyin everywhere roarin the heads offa themselves!

'No! Get yer hands offa my little sister or I'll be fuckin hung fer ye's!' shouted a skinny young one holdin onta a little babby girl about two year old. There were three more little ones gettin walloped in a bath.

'Give her over to me or I will send for Sister!' said a big young one I never sawed before. She was wearin a long grey frock wit a brown-sack apron an it all reached down nearly coverin a pair of black heavy cobnailed boots laced up wit strong twine.

'You may send fer the fuckin army, but ye're not gettin yer hands on my Patsy!' the skinny little young one sniffed wit her nose curlin, an she sayin out the words slowly, so she wouldn't be mistaken fer havin said somethin else. Then she hopped the babby on her hip wit her leg held up, restin it on her thigh.

'Right!' said the big young one who looked in charge. 'Get down to the Hall of Discipline and see if you can find Sister Mary Saint Joan of Arc!' she snapped, turnin to a convent young one hangin onta me fer protection, she was lookin shell-shocked wit the big blue eyes bulgin outa her head, never havin seen the like a such cheek in all her borned days.

I thought this was great!

'Wha's your name?' I said te the new young one. 'Mine's Lily, Lily Carney! I'm from Dublin city! Where you from? Tell us yer name!'

She stared at me wit her rockin the babby an takin in the room, keepin her eyes pinned on all the big young ones. She was watchin fer any sudden moves.

'It's an awful fuckin kip this place!' I said, feelin all delighted te meet someone from me own kind. 'Did youse just get te this place?'

She nodded her head keepin the eyes on them. Then she looked over seein the rest a her little babby sisters gettin poured outa the bath, then only te be landed standin on their clothes drippin wit the wet an soakin them.

'Eh! Young ones! Them's me little sisters' clothes youse fuckers are wettin! Are youse fuckin mental or wha? Why don't ye say somethin?' she roared, seein the two girls lookin after the little ones completely ignorin her, like she wasn't there.

The three little sisters stood wit their jaws rattlin an their teeth gnashin, while they got the guts shook outa themself gettin dried an the skin rubbed raw wit a sandpaper towel.

'Yeah,' I said, 'they did the very same thing te my clothes, they got no respect fer other people's property!' I snorted, lookin down at the childre's dirty rags now gettin soaked in a filthy puddle. But still an all, it was them people's . . . childre's clothes, I thought, gettin ragin at the loss a my good Communion stuff.

Next thing I was yanked wit the shift gettin pulled over me head.

'No! Ye're not gettin yer hands on me!' I shouted, seein the young one was on her own wit me, an the new young one was gettin her way. If she can so can I.

'Let's stand an fight together,' I suddenly shouted, escapin an rushin over standin meself next te the new young one.

The two rubbin the skin offa the little ones suddenly stopped wit their mouths dropped open starin around at the young one after she losin the fight wit me. She looked around confused not knowin wha te do.

'See! They can't touch us when we stick together,' I said, nudgin her wit me fist hittin her on the shoulder.

Wit tha the two skin-rubbers suddenly made a move fer me an the other one followed. I leapt behind the new young one an she ducked away an over te her little sisters. One grabbed me from behind, while two a them grabbed hold a me legs an carted me over te the big bath an flung me in, still wearin frock an all. Then the door was thrun open an the new young one wit her gang a little sisters flew out.

'Jesus!' I heard the one in charge mutter, then they dropped me leavin me te drown an shot after them.

I gasped an thrashed, flingin me head, flyin me arms an flappin me legs, all wit the water teemin up an down an all round, drownin me even more.

'MA . . . MEE . . . gasp . . . splutter!' Me breath was gone but I was up in the air, now down again seein bubbles an me last hour comin. The back a me nose is gettin torn te shreads wit the pain, an me lungs is gettin a wash tha's not supposed te happen. An I knew now me last hour had come!

Then I was standin wit me arms held wide an the water pourin offa me like a statue in a fountain. 'I'm . . . gasp . . . alive . . . gasp . . . lemme out! Where's the floor? Gasp!'

Then I was grabbin fer the edge haulin meself up an throwin me leg over, runnin fer me life. Out the door I went hearin them all runnin screamin an keenin, up the passage everyone flew, wit all the childre runnin fer their life.

Suddenly I had the idea not te fly wit tha lot. I looked ahead seein they're all in their skin an goin nowhere. I have a frock plastered te me, but I'm wearin somethin. So if I hide I might manage te make me escape an get home te Dublin!

'You never know,' I muttered, turnin meself around an whippin in the opposite direction. I kept runnin hearin them an their roarin fadin away an the quiet comin all around me. All I could hear now, was me own bare feet slappin on the shiny black worn-out stones as I flew, on an on, goin further an deeper inta the dark. I could see me way easy, because I got used now te havin te live wit all tha dark.

Suddenly I heard somethin an pulled meself up fast. I came

to a skidded halt, wit me heart stopped dead, stone dead it's gone wit fright. I shook me head slowly, no, I don't want te get caught.

'Wha's tha?' I muttered, lookin around wit me mouth left hangin an me eyes an ears gettin wide open, ready te see the slightest move or pick up even the barest whispered sound.

I heard it again – a rumblin sound, maybe a voice. It was comin from far ahead, way along in the distance somewhere.

I wonder how far these passages go? I thought, makin te head off in tha direction but not runnin too fast, no. I want te be ready, just in case someone or somethin – it could even be a monster – suddenly appears outa nowhere an grabs me.

I kept goin hearin the noise gettin louder now, not turnin left nor right but only followin where the noise is comin from.

Then I rounded onta a passage tha was lit up wit candles an heard it very clearly now. A woman's voice was comin from down near the end, before the passage turns. I crept down seein stairs goin up te me right. I stopped te stare wonderin about tha. Would tha be a way outa here?

Then I heard the voice gettin louder. I turned me head te look, then I was on the move again without even thinkin, headin right down fer where tha voice was comin.

Go back! Why ye comin down here? You'll get caught! a voice was cryin in me mind, gettin ragin an afraid, me chest was poundin hard wit the pain of it. But I can't stop meself. I want te see wha's happenin.

I could see now it was just up ahead, the noise was comin from inside a thick heavy door an it was closed shut. I stopped before reachin it an cocked me head te listen.

'What is your name?' a woman's voice barked. It was low, yet ye knew she was stranglin herself wit rage, tryin not te lose her temper.

'My name is Ceily Carney, I was born Ceily Carney, an I will be Ceily Carney when I take it to me grave!' a voice said, soundin like a young girl.

Me heart stopped. I couldn't take it in! *CEILY!* I screamed in me mind, just barely managin te slap me hand over me mouth an hold me heart in, stop it from leppin outa me mouth along wit the screams.

'You are Mary Saint Jude! You will stay here for as long as it takes to indoctrinate you in our holy ways,' the voice of the nun ordered, speakin very slowly, soundin like it had even MORE than the power of God Almighty himself.

I could feel a rage comin up me. Who the fuck do they think they is takin away my sister's name?

I was movin in tha direction without even knowin, when I suddenly found meself starin at the door. I couldn't believe me eyes. The keys! The nun in her hurry must a rushed in leavin the huge bunch a them sittin in the lock! 'Oh Mammy! Wha will I do?' I breathed, barely whisperin wit only movin me mouth. 'Will I take them, lock them in? But how will I get Ceily?'

Me arm was reachin up very slowly, an wit one hand grabbin hold te keep them steady, me other hand was liftin out the key very, very slowly an gently, then stoppin te wait until she started her tormentin again. Wit tha I eased it out an held the mighty bunch a keys in both me hands an backed meself away.

Me heart was slammin in me chest an I could feel my face goin stone cold. Then I was turnin meself an runnin, makin back down the passage headin away from the light te hide down in the dark. I want now te wait fer them an see wha they'll do.

'They can't do much without the keys,' I panted, starin down feelin them bite inta me two hands tha held them squeezed tight inta me stomach. All I have te do now is hide meself watch an wait. I better pray not te get caught an hope they leave Ceily on her own while they go on their search.

Me mind was flyin, sure nothin could stop us then, we have the keys, we could lock them all in! 'Oh Mammy! Wherever you are, will you look after us? We need you now, Mammy, please come te us! Oh Holy God, don't let us down, we need you now more than we ever did before. Amen!' I prayed, blessin meself quickly, then slid into a dark hole wit a little door in front sittin close te the ground.

I shut the door behind me an crawled through the dark seein nothin. But I could feel damp air around me an lifted me head slowly, gettin up off me knees. I stretched me hands out wantin te feel somethin an hit only air. The stone ground was cold under me but not freezin an the air was the same.

I kept movin slowly wit me back hunched an me arms out wonderin how far this goes. Then I moved meself te the left an after more steps I felt the wall. It was bricks, an they felt warm an a bit crumbly. I put me hands over me head an felt nothin, the ceilin is gettin higher the farther I go in!

I kept goin, on an on I went, goin wit me hands trailin the brick wall an suddenly I was outa the dark an into a light. It wasn't much, because it was very grey, if you weren't used te the dark like me, then ye wouldn't be able te see in it. But I can! I can see very well in this dark-grey light.

I let me eyes open wide seein I was now standin in front of a stone stairs wit a small landin an a very heavy-lookin door. It was black an low, wit a steel cover around the lock. Beside tha was a slit just above the ground lettin in a slant of light. It had two heavy bars across an it was only a slit of a winda, but it was enough, it let in the light te show me where I was.

I looked seein where I was standin, takin it all in, then back at wha was behind me. It's a tunnel! I'm in a hidden passage an tha door up there looks like it could be the way out!

I felt the heavy bunch a keys weighin down me two arms an looked down at them. 'God, ye must be helpin me! Is this the way out? Oh Mammy! Do I have the key?' There must be a hundred, I thought, lookin at the old black huge iron keys.

Me hands was shakin as I slipped a key inta the lock. I pushed an twisted, but nothin happened. Wrong one!

I kept goin one after another, until me hands was hangin off an me fingers nearly broke. Then it happened! My eyes stared an I stopped breathin te hold meself dead still. The key was turnin an suddenly the door started te ease open! I heard the creak an watched it comin towards me. I moved me feet an suddenly I was on the outside wit the light blindin me shuttin me eyes fast. I was feelin the cold air an the wind on me face. I stepped out further, feelin grass under me feet an hearin the roar of the Atlantic Ocean in me ears. 'The ferocious Atlantic Ocean!' Tha's wha Oisin called it. Then me head cleared an me eyes opened te see where I was an wha was all around me. I was on the outside wit nothin behind me but the sea, an in front the massive stone buildin. It was so high me neck strained lookin up, an it's makin me feel very small, standin up offa the ground.

Me head spun around, seein a path leadin down an away from here, goin back te meet the road tha leads te Dublin an outa here! Wha will I do? Will I start runnin while I'm ahead as Mammy would say? Or will I go back now an try te get Ceily? If I got back te Dublin I could tell people wha happened! Tell Mister Mullins an the Fat Mammy wha Father Flitters did.

'Oh wha will I do?' I keened, feelin me heart racin an I'm goin all hot an cold now, it must be comin wit the sudden shock. Me teeth started te rattle an I could feel the soppin wet frock goin very cold as it started te flap an lift, wantin te dry out wit all the wind. I looked back at the ocean seein it ragin up against the rocks of the cliffs, then steam out again, goin all white an foamy. Me frock lifted at the back then slapped down again, smackin the legs offa me.

Lily! a voice whispered.

I held me breath te listen.

Keep your head, do one thing at a time. Listen carefully, the main thing is to stay hidden, use this advantage an work fast. Now ease your way back an get Ceily out. But listen, Lily! I mean move very carefully, especially when you get there, and whatever you do, stay hidden! Don't mess this up, Lily! It may be the only chance you will ever get! Now go! the voice whispered, wantin me te move, because I was tryin te work out who it was. It didn't sound like Mammy, it sounded like Delia!

I nodded me head an started te move back in, whisperin te meself. 'OK, Ceily! I'm goin te get you out! But whatever happens, they will never get me again, because I am goin te be like the spider. I will be here watchin an waitin, but they will never see me. I *knew* learnin te live an move in the dark would come in handy! Them nuns an young ones are used te the light from their candles. Fuck them. They're no match for me! I can be as bold now as I want!'

Martha Long was born in Dublin in the early 1950s and still lives there today. She has written seven critically acclaimed volumes of autobiography, including the bestselling *Ma, He Sold Me for a Few Cigarettes*. *Run, Lily, Run* is her fiction debut.